BURNING DESIRE

I stumbled through the dark house until I came to Janie's room. I slid inside and felt at once as if I had walked into something solid. The air was thick, almost tangible. It pressed on my skin like sexual static.

Suddenly every cell in my body demanded sex.

Janie was moaning in her sleep. I reached out a trembling hand and touched her breast. It was full and warm, and smooth as satin. My hand explored its pillowy softness and the nipple enlarged beneath my palm as I caressed the yielding flesh.

I couldn't help myself. I bent over the sleeping woman and sucked the hard point of her breast into my hungry mouth . . .

Also available from Headline Delta

Burning Desire
A Warning

Nadia Adamant

First published in 1994
by HEADLINE BOOK PUBLISHING

A HEADLINE DELTA paperback

10 9 8 7 6 5 4 3 2

ISBN 0 7472 4433 2

Phototypeset by Intype, London
Printed and bound in Great Britain by
Cox & Wyman Ltd, Reading, Berkshire

HEADLINE BOOK PUBLISHING
A division of Hodder Headline PLC
338 Euston Road
London NW1 3BH

Burning Desire

FILE ONE

The Theatre of Dreams

There were four women in the room. One lay on her back with her legs wide apart, up in the air. The watching man saw her long red-tipped fingers pull and pluck ceaselessly at what lay between her legs. She wore no clothes. Open for his eyes to see was her softly pulsing, vulnerable, sticky, sexual flesh. She pulled its soft parts, now this way, now that.

His own sex was exposed. It hung down, soft and damp from use.

Another of the four women was on her knees, her face to one side, down on the carpet, her cheek resting on its thin pile. She wore stockings and a garter belt in some shiny satin-like material, but nothing else. The black lacy lines of the belt still attached to her stockings, strained against the pale smooth skin of her thighs, digging into it and making red marks.

Her nipples pressed into the carpet. Her arms strained back. She reached for her projecting buttocks and pulled them apart. Her displayed sex pouted provocatively at the man. It was glistening. Small bubbles of sex-foam were exuding visibly from her swollen pussy. The snail-trail of love juice led downwards, a small slick of pleasure past.

The man's glance moved on. The other two women were on the bed. They were naked, quite naked, and apparently asleep, curled together with their long limbs

1

interwoven, their breasts pressed against each other's. The fair hair of one was tangled with the dark hair of the other. Their faces were closed and secret, softly smiling. They too had damp sexual parts.

The smell of sex hung in the air.

The man seemed to be satisfied. His fleshy body was relaxed. He turned for the door, his heavy sex swinging as he did so. He passed through the door and gently closed it. It made a soft click. Then there was the faint grating sound as a key turned in the lock.

Left to themselves, at first the women didn't stir. The two on the bed slept on, lovingly intertwined. The one on her knees swayed slightly from side to side, her anus projected rhythmically as she pushed it out and sucked it in. The one on her back sighed and continued to pluck.

After several minutes the two on the floor came insensibly together. The woman on her back got to her knees and came over behind the other woman. She lowered her face, pushing her hair dreamily out of the way. Her long pink tongue came out. It flickered like a snake. Then its extreme tip touched the pouting bottom in front of her. She dabbed gently with her tongue-tip several times. Then she ran her tongue lightly down to the warm pulpy flesh below. She tasted sperm.

She edged forward slightly. She put her hands on the pointed buttocks and held them open. She began to suck in earnest.

FILE TWO

The thing began this way, with Red Marsden. That is to say, this story begins with Red but of course her experience is only a chapter in a long tale, a tale about which neither the beginning nor the ending can be known. It's easiest to begin it with Red because her curiosity is what first revealed the affair for what it really was. She is sharp, bright, persistent and unafraid. She was unafraid, I mean. Like us all, she's running scared now.

My involvement in all this is simply as a friend of Red's. I occupy a minor post in the security services. Red thought I might be able to get the authorities interested enough to investigate the phenomenon officially, but she overestimated both my importance and the intelligence of the organisation that employs me. It didn't want to know. The police didn't want to know. Those whom we approached with what we discovered regarded us as slightly unsavoury freaks.

We were told to abandon our researches. We did not feel we could do that. Instead we compiled the dossier that follows, changing names and places to conceal the identity of individuals, including our own.

Much of the testimony that follows was initially recorded on tape. I transposed it to print and edited it where necessary. Red checked the whole thing for accuracy.

Make of it what you will. But consider yourself warned.

Testimony of Red Marsden

I'd better introduce myself. It helps to explain why I acted the way I did, and how I got into this mess in the first place. You see, they call me Red. I guess I have some stupid name like Gloria or Alice or Mary or something, but since I was ten years old they called me Red.

It really was red then, bright red and frizzy. Since I grew bumps on my front it got darker and wavy rather than frizzy. You could call it chestnut, pretty-spoken guys do, but it's red, my hair. And my name.

Roger was my old, old friend and he came to see me. I was pleased to see him, I admit. Roger was the first guy to check out that my pussy fleece was the same colour as the stuff sprouting on the top of my head. I was really very young and Rog wasn't a hell of a lot older, but he knew what was what and he taught me all he knew.

We fixed it this way. I wanted a pair of Peruvian gold earrings and a cross-over bra that hadn't belonged to my elder sister. He wanted new lamps for his bike. He opened a book on whether I was the same colour down below as I was on top. I wasn't supposed to know anything about it and I laid a false trail to keep the boys guessing.

We split the profit and cleaned up financially. Rog had to provide documentary evidence which he clipped off me using a boy scout's knife. I discovered I really liked having a boy look at my secret bits, and I enjoyed it even more when he started to play with them.

Since we both liked it and since we shared a secret, Rog and I kept pretty close. We'd go to the park on Saturday afternoons and, in the wild bit, we'd make a hide. We'd lie in it talking about this and that, what we planned to do with our lives, and Rog would take my pants off and play with my little closed tight secret pussy.

He let me play with his interesting bits, too. Were they interesting! I could make him stand up and say hello. With a little practice I could make him spit. So Rog would tickle me and I would tickle him and for the time being he was definitely the more interested of the pair of us.

We got a little older. Rog got a little bigger. I got better at making him come. We both got very interested in the whole thing. Then the day came when Rog very seriously tried to open my gates. He played with his fingers till my saucy red curls were sticky wet. We'd found somewhere more private than the local park now. Rog liked to stroke my bumpy bits and he liked to put his fingers in my tootsie and have me wriggle all over them. He could make me wet and sticky and I could make him wet and sticky.

So the day came when he plugged it in me. I thought it was great. I thought it was fantastic.

I still do.

Rog went away to college and we just saw each other in the holidays. In between I found out that other boys were made just the same way as Rog, with small exciting differences, and I really liked them plugged in.

Our ways separated, Rog led quite a wild life, I believe, and then the day came when he settled down and got married. I went to the wedding and I kissed the bride and, although I was as fond of Rog as I'd ever been, and I think he was as fond of me, we didn't keep in touch so much. This was hardly unexpected. Old girlfriends have no place in a newly-married man's life.

But now Rog had looked me up.

He called me on the telephone and arranged to meet me in a wine bar. We sat in a booth and downed a bottle of El Plonko while we relived some of the spicier bits of our past. I reckoned the marriage had gone stale and Rog was looking for safe available pussy. That makes him sound cold but he had my sympathy. Some females treat a man as though he was a bank account. They want to control what goes in and what comes out and they demand strict accounting. With me, a man isn't a financial structure, he's pure undiluted self-indulgence. I'd indulged myself with Rog quite a bit over the years and I was perfectly happy to start doing so again. The interval in our fun and games only made the whole thing spicier. I asked Rog if he wanted to come back to my place.

He asked if he should rummage in the freezer and stick something in the microwave. He felt he owed me a meal even if it was at my place.

I said what I was offering hadn't been kept on ice and was nicely warmed up already. The taxi journey was tense and when we got inside my front door I put his hand on my thigh and found out if his mouth still worked.

My pussy met his fingers like an old friend.

We got stuck in the hallway, me with my back up against the wall, Rog with his mouth doing the business over mine and my skirt somewhere up around waist level. That guy used his hands like a music conductor. He was inside my panties fingering, teasing, tweaking and finally entering the Jade Gate. I squirmed like I had ants in my pants but the truth was Rog had me impaled in a fistful of digits and I liked it very much.

That crazy man fell down on his knees and used both hands to get my clothes out of the way. His face met my pussy. He licked and bit what he could reach and we still hadn't moved out of the hallway.

Before I actually orgasmed into his face I forced him to take enough of a break to get us through to where the couch was. Rog undid my blouse and, with the freedom of an old friend, hooked each of my boobs out of their flimsy support and let them hang loose.

'Red,' he said simply, looking at them. My name is Red but my boobs are very white with bright chestnut-pink nipples, great big things, and they were projecting like two gun barrels pointing straight at Rog.

'I didn't mean to do this,' he added.

'Do what?' I said sweetly. I jiggled slightly to impart some movement to the mammaries. I liked Rog looking at them.

'You're gorgeous, Red. But I'm a married man.'

'You wear a chastity belt?'

'Do I hell.'

'You came to see me for my intellectual development,' I said brightly.

'You've got brains all right, though it isn't the first thing I think of when you come to mind.'

'What is?'

'That gorgeous red fleece. Your pink pussy with the bright red curls all round it. Age doesn't dim it, Red, nor has custom staled my infinite lust for you.'

'The moral dimension is new,' I said tartly.

'Sweetheart, I'm in trouble and I've come as an old pal to ask for help. But seeing you so luscious, so friendly . . . I can't resist.'

His lips began to trail about my pouting white flesh.

'How about,' I said cunningly, 'you get to work on them with some of this very attractive perfumed oil I have. Then I'll get to work on you where you are firm and bulging with the same oil and give you a good rub down. Meanwhile, while we're getting into all this aromasexuality, you can tell me what the troubles are that burden you so.'

He made a low moan of capitulation in his throat. Seconds later I was flat on my back with very little on below and nothing on above, and Rog was massaging my boobs with the oil.

The man had lost none of the class he used to have. He took one of my breasts between his two hands and he began to pull and knead and work the plastic flesh. I lay making small adulatory cries of pleasure. A great tingling began, little sparks building and building to the hot sexual flames threatening to burn in my pussy.

He did the two of them really thoroughly. Then he made me go on my hands and knees. Somewhere in all this he had shed significant items of his own clothing. Now I knelt, my aroused and tingling boobs hanging down with a great sensuous weight, my knees apart, my hair all over my face, and a sensation, fully justified, of almost total nudity in my lower parts.

Rog knelt over me. I felt his big firm naked dongo heavy and soft, brushing the backs of my thighs, grazing my buttocks. Instead of penetrating me he kept the agony going. He began to knead my down-hanging breasts as if he was milking me. He pulled and pummeled and drew on them till I was groaning with pleasure. All the time he rubbed against me, against my out-thrust buttocks, against my backwards-pointing pussy, against my thighs.

He stopped, having teased my nipples into long erectile worms of sexual excitement. I fell onto my side and took the little bottle of oil.

He was sitting back on his heels by now. His cock stuck up so that he could have modelled for one of those classical statues, one of the dirty ones depicting a satyr or a lecherous faun or something. I got myself up onto my knees and bent forward. I took his cock between my two hands and let the golden oil run down it. Then I caught it and began to massage him. I began to give his cock the full treatment, turning it from a man's sex into a quivering pulsing erect missile of desire.

'Let's do it,' he said, after some of this treatment. I hadn't been forgetting his balls and they lay like golden pleasure globes in their crisp bed of curly hair.

He was keen.

'Fire down below,' I murmured.

'I'll put out the flames,' he said.

And he did. I went over backwards on the carpet like a greedy teenager. Rog slid his greased pole all the way and then some. He began to swing it and himself and me backwards and forwards like a great pendulum. His cock got bigger, my pussy got steamier, we generated a volcanic heat and then he let me have it, great fountains of joy, sunbursts, starbursts of liquid pleasure.

We lay afterwards drinking wine and licking the greasy

bits of each other. He licked my shining boobs. I licked his shining cock.

'What's the problem?' I asked lazily.

'Being with old friends is good, very good.'

He was hesitant at first. I put this down to shame because his marriage must be getting draggy and that made him look a fool. But I was wrong. It was just that what he had to say was weird.

'You do private detective work, don't you?' he said.

This was true. When I was at school I never felt I was in the larval stage of becoming a hairdresser or a secretary or a lady librarian. The kind of butterfly I became is best called a freelance which isn't a very exact description but then, I don't exactly do the same kind of thing all the time. I do a little of this, a little of that, and the money comes in in trickles or surges and I get by.

'This is too screwy to ask a private detective,' Rog said sadly. 'He'd think I was crazy.'

'Perhaps you are.'

'If I am, you'll tell me. You never dressed it up, Red.'

It's true I'm not afraid of the truth. I'm a tall red-head addicted to sexual pleasure. That's the truth.

'My work takes me away from home a lot,' he began.

Yeah, yeah, I thought. Rog, you poor mutt. Your little wife is cheating and you have to make it fancy when all it is is plain.

'Janie's pretty straight. I don't think she strays. I just about never do myself.'

I spared a memory cell. This non-straying male had definitely just fucked me.

'You're different, of course. We go back so far.'

I didn't think Janie would see it that way but Rog was welcome to his convenient delusions, especially if I gained by them.

'Something's going on, though. I can't put my finger on it. Janie won't admit anything's wrong.'

He looked at me, all big soulful eyes. 'I'm frightened, Red. I'm more than worried, I'm scared.'

I took his cock reassuringly in my hand and tried to soothe him. 'Tell me about it,' I invited. I patted his sex organ encouragingly.

'She's started to look as though she has a lover,' he said bluntly. 'She hasn't got extra nice to me or extra nasty or anything dumb like that, but she's got this smoky look in her eyes and she'll smile into the distance and be startled when I speak to her.'

'The signs don't augur well,' I admitted.

'She's just as happy to fuck with me as before. She isn't more eager or less. She hasn't gone temperamental, she doesn't disappear for unexplained amounts of time, she hasn't suddenly joined a health club or knitting bee and started going out every week to something new.'

'Hmm,' I said. Rog knew all the excuses. I wondered how.

'She's just dreamy. Sensuous. Abstracted.' He wiped his brow. 'She's sensational. I mean, sex drips off her. It's just that I don't think I'm the one inspiring it.'

I stroked his cock which was getting quite inspired itself during all this. If Janie had bought herself a new toy, something in a plain brown wrapper from a catalogue, maybe she was getting it so good from the artificial stimulus that Rog was becoming little more than a pleasant housemate. I adored his cock in me and was hoping to plug it in again in a very short while, but to be limited to the same cock for months, even years, at a time, is the definition of dullsville. Even the tastiest cock palls. Sex is a pleasure that thrives on variety.

Marriage is unnatural. Janie seemed to have found herself a way out of the dilemma. Rog's ego was going to take some damage.

He arranged himself comfortably on his back, leaving me plenty of room to continue handling his equipment. 'One night I came home when she was expecting me to be out. The last day of a sales conference had been cancelled, I'd got my business done and was able to get back in the late evening. I admit I didn't warn Janie as soon as I knew. She would be expecting me to be away till the following evening. I'd never come home early before. She'd know she was safe.'

'Safe?'

'From interruption. So I came home with champagne and a bunch of flowers to pretend I was going to shout, surprise! Let's celebrate! I freely admit that if she had have had some bozo between the sheets with her, I would have wanted to make her feel as bad as possible.'

He stopped dead. I'm not surprised. He was telling me how he had planned to catch his wife in flagrante. It wasn't a pretty picture.

'I parked down the lane and clutching my bloody flowers and champagne I crept along the road to my house feeling like an idiot. I felt pretty lousy, too. I don't know if you know where we live, but it used to be a terrace of workmen's cottages. Most of them were pulled down long ago, tiny dark insanitary things that they were. Ours has survived and been knocked through so we have an old house, a long old house that used to provide the accommodation for several families. It's at least a hundred and fifty years old.'

I wished he'd get to the point.

'I let myself in. It was all dark. It was quite late and Janie said she usually went to bed early when I was away. Certainly the house lights were off. I slunk through it like a burglar. I dumped the flowers and booze in the kitchen. Then I went along the corridor until I reached our bedroom.' He stopped and sighed.

'I could hear her. I could hear she was rolling and crying out. She sounded exactly like she sounds in lovemaking. I became very angry and opened the door. I felt like hitting someone.'

This was strange considering he was naked with his

cock in a woman's hand and that woman was not his wife. I have often noticed that men have an attitude problem where adultery is concerned, though. Like that old Italian, Janus, they look two ways at once.

'The room was dark. Light spilled in faintly through one window. She was rolling about in the bed. As best I could see she was alone.'

His voice became very gentle. 'I put on the bedside light. She stayed asleep, dreaming I guess, her lips parted. She was moving about, obviously excited.'

'Hot dreams?' I asked, disbelievingly.

'That's the simple answer. Maybe it's the only answer. It's just that . . .' He stopped.

'Mmmm?' I asked politely. I fondled a little more. The man was remembering things, happy things. I could tell by the emotional barometer I was holding in my hand.

'A kind of wall of sex hit me,' he said flatly.

'Sure it wasn't Janie's lover coming out from under the bed?'

'A web of sex,' he amended poetically. 'I was enmeshed.'

I stayed silent and let this balderdash hang in the air between us. Gradually I became aware he was looking at me. I looked back provocatively.

'It was like it is with you, Red,' he said, all mousy soft. 'When you want a man, you come on like a train. You're birdlime, baby, and the man you're after is cock sparrow. I've seen you tie a man so tight he'd stand on his head to lick your pussy. It's scorched earth policy with you. You take a man for everything he's got, sexually speaking, and you leave nothing for anyone else.'

I bent down and kissed his cock. 'I don't know what you're talking about,' I said innocently.

'She was in the bed asleep. The atmosphere of sex was so thick you could spread it on bread. I tore my clothes off and fell on her. She didn't even wake up. She just gobbled me down, Red. She sucked my cock into her like her pussy was the vacuum cleaner and I was the dirt. I was in climax in about ten seconds. I started to apologise when I could get my breath back. I'd pounced on her and I'd come too fast. But she was still asleep. She was sucking her thumb and grinning. Suddenly I was hot again. I slid it in and gave it to her again. I could hang on properly this time, but it was still absolutely terrific. Her cunt was dynamite.'

I stared at him. This was certainly a man who didn't mind spilling intimate details. I hoped Janie would never find out. 'It turns you on, to go with them passive?' I asked acidly. 'You used to like ladies with a little life to them. Are you in training for necrophilia here?'

My whole approach at this stage was very flip. Roger had too many pleasurable associations for me to realise fully what trouble he was in. I was inclined to make jokes and use his body. I just didn't take him seriously at all.

That was to come later.

Now he went on; 'Janie could have driven steam turbines with the activity going on inside her,' he said. 'Sure she was asleep but she was writhing on the bed like a python. Any livelier and I couldn't have held her down to stuff it up.'

'You're certain she was asleep?'

'No doubt about it. But then I did it again.'

'Bragging?'

'The hell I am. I couldn't stop. I was like a rabbit. The poor woman lay there conked out and I shafted her five times.'

'She normally sleeps through it?' I tried hard not to sound as though I was condemning the wench, but I've never slept through sex in my life.

'She normally likes it once, maybe twice and she likes to feel involved. She never sleeps through it.'

'How was she the next day?'

'Pleased and surprised to see me. Dreamy. Sensuous. Abstracted.'

'And what happened that night?'

'We had it twice, we were both a bit boozed, and then we fell asleep. It was very nice but it was perfectly normal. I wasn't crazy to keep having it like I had been the previous night.'

'Did you inspect the bed afterwards?'

'What for?'

'Anything. Objects. Anything at all.'

'If by objects you mean sex toys, I didn't search the bed and I didn't find any, despite considerable rolling around in it,' he said coldly.

'Sweetheart, that leaves drugs. The lady is taking some powerful aphrodisiac. It makes her sleep and it makes her sexy.'

He looked dissatisfied, as well he might. He wanted to believe it was his own fair body that roused his wife, not something out of a bottle. 'There's no such thing,' he said. 'I wish there was.'

He had me there. Something that guaranteed sleep but gave you a gorgeous sexy time while you were clocking away the hours, that was the stuff of the dream makers and paradise mongers.

'I told her some of what happened,' he said abruptly. 'I told her she seemed to be having an erotic dream. I told her I made love to her in her sleep and she was astonished. She knew something had happened because she was wet when she woke up in the morning. She wasn't too pleased.'

'Ah,' I said.

'Not because I'd made love to her in her sleep. What annoyed her was that she didn't wake up. She said it must have been like making love to a hard-boiled egg.'

'So you told her she was the hottest lay she'd ever been and you'd ravaged her again and again?'

'I'm not that stupid. But the fact remains she was the hottest I've ever known her and I performed sexual feats I didn't think myself capable of. If she was affected, so was I. We were both odd.'

'Only you were awake,' I pointed out.

'I was awake,' he agreed.

'Did you ask her if she'd taken anything?'

'In a roundabout way. She said no. She hates sleeping tablets and won't have them in the house. She'll hardly take aspirin.'

'I hear you with my ears,' I said. 'But what can I do?'

'Suck me off,' he said. 'No, I didn't mean to say that. Red, you have a fantastic mouth. Forgive me. I was watching your lips move as you spoke and remembering all the dirty things we used to do together.'

'So long ago,' I murmured, 'when we were young and innocent.'

'We might have been young once but we were never innocent,' he said.

I kissed his pretty cock. He had a really nice one. He said nothing. I began to mouth him in earnest. I rolled my tongue round his fat tube. I licked the sensitive tip. I sucked so he jumped almost in pain. I nibbled down the sides so he groaned. All the time I fondled those plummy nuts of his.

'Kneel over me,' he whispered, 'so I can kiss you while you do it to me.'

I obliged. I knelt astride his face and he began to lick up at me, stabbing me with his tongue, penetrating me with it and teasing all the ridges and valleys of my sex. Meanwhile, my changed position enabled me to caress his hard pole with my big hanging boobs. I stroked him, I squeezed him, I let the contours of his hard promise fit into my soft yielding oily breasts.

Then I sucked him hard. I squeezed his balls, I pressed my breasts into his groin and I fluttered the muscles of my cunt on and around his tongue.

He came jerking up into my mouth so I bubbled with his spunk, my fingers playing his cock as if it was a trumpet. I came wet down into his face groaning with pleasure at the dirty feel of his nose and mouth and chin all rammed into my throbbing pussy. We both lay down side by side for a while and I licked idly at his salty cock and he licked idly at my wet pussy and it sure as hell was nice.

'I want you to hide in the house and watch her,' he said.

I couldn't believe my ears. 'You want what?'

He bit my curls and licked my thighs on the inside, where it feels nice. 'I want you to hide in the house when I'm gone. I'll show you how it can be done. Watch her for me, Red. If she's doping or getting a man in, I want to know. I want to understand what's happening.'

'You want me to hide and spy on your wife?' Jeeze, what a pervert the man was.

'Sure. I can't get a private detective to do it. She'll have to get undressed. Go to the bathroom. She might be having a man in after all and be totally naked rolling about the place with him. Whatever, I need someone I can trust. Someone broad-minded. Someone unshockable. Someone who'll tell me the truth. I don't mind hiring you, Red, if you make your business this way. But I've come to you as a friend. I couldn't go to someone I didn't know. Someone I didn't trust.'

I said I was a freelance. I never could afford a husband so I guess I'm a freelance in that department too. I admit to being fond of the male of the species, he's half the human race, and I particularly like them twenty-plus with a gleam in their eye.

I'm not fussed about age. I've had it sensational from the forties, sweet from the twenties and really, really dirty from the guys in their sixth decade. I'm a girl who'll try most things once and some of them again and again if the trying is nice.

Life's OK. I roll with the punches. But this was something new.

'You want me,' I said, trying to get things absolutely clear, 'old flame that I am, to spy on your wife in her house when you aren't there.'

'I knew you were quick in the mental sphere.' Rog tongued my sex.

'When she finds me she'll get the police,' I pointed out.

'She won't find you.'

'She's stupid?'

'The loft. She thinks it's more or less closed off but I can open the hatch, let you in and then seal it closed again. That is, I can make it look sealed.'

'The ceilings in your house are one way glass?'

It took him a moment but he got there. 'I see what you mean. I'm going to drill holes at strategic places so you have spyholes. There'll be a couple for each room. They won't show. We've got this fancy plasterwork, artexing, they call it.'

'She won't notice an adult human being clumping about the loft? She'll put the noise down to deathwatch beetle?'

'You'll have to be quiet,' he admitted. 'Wear slippers or something.'

'The time factor troubles me. How do I get out?'

'I put you in. I go away for three days. I let you out. You take everything necessary up there with you.'

'It sounds foully insanitary.'

'I'll rig up a chemical loo. They still use them in caravans and boats where they don't have plumbing. They're OK for short spells.'

'You're going to fit me up with a primus so I can cook?'

'Only if you promise not to set light to the roof.'

He continued to play with my pussy, just delighted to be back with an old friend. I thought he had gone absolutely off his trolley. He was seriously proposing I live like a gipsy in his loft and play peekaboo with his wife. I'd get six months if I was caught. He said he'd give me a letter proving I was there at his instigation, hired by him. That way, it might be unpleasant but I'd be safe from the law.

I don't know to this day why I did it. It was a crazy thing to do. Perhaps underneath I trusted Rog. His story might be weird, his request perverted, but I knew him of old. If he wasn't seriously worried, he wouldn't be suggesting it.

On the other hand maybe I agreed to do it because it was so breathtakingly awful. As a kink, I'd never met anything like it. Rog was proposing to get his jollies off getting his girlfriend to spy on his wife. The guy was one step short of the funny farm. Only, the thing was that the very idea got him so steamed up he was prepared to stuff his cock into me in lots of very interesting and exciting ways. You don't get the enthusiasm for sex nowadays that you used to. But here was Rog taking me back to the good old days when sex was an exciting adventure. These smart young designer males today with their obsession with name tags, they're coffee table sex. You know? All glossy and put out for show. There's not a decent read, as in fuck, in any of them.

What followed all this changed my life. I had taken things very light-heartedly up to this point. I found life pleasant, its little ups and downs adding interest and excitement. Sex was definitely the highlight of my life. I enjoyed sexual encounter and I enjoyed sexual variation. Despite all the noise made about sex, I think the average person is prudish. I'm not, and I enjoy myself finding people like me, people prepared to go just that bit further, do just that little more. Like Rog.

I haven't lacked for men in my life. I'm a definite type, tall, big-breasted, I have long red curly hair. Enough men go for this to keep me well pleased. But I had missed Rog after his marriage. We went so far back, he had been important in my development. I was fond of him.

I was glad to have him back parting my creamy thighs, tasting my juices, burying his face and his cock in my breasts. Rog had a way of turning me over and making me kneel. He would hold open the cheeks of my arse and kiss what he found there, real sucky probing kisses. He was a male capable of wallowing in sex and I am a female with the same capacity.

He started me on something that day. He got me going and things are different now. I look at life differently. I feel afraid. There are things we don't understand, things that can't be explained and they are frightening things.

Rog's strange request, to spy on his wife, opened doors into this other world for me. I did it because he asked me to. I did it because he screwed good. I did it because he was the first man to get it up me. I did it, I guess, to spite Janie.

'I'll want paying,' I said maliciously.

'Yeah,' he said, sounding sour. He didn't care about the money, he was pretty loaded. He saw it as a reflection on our friendship.

'In kind,' I added softly.

'In what?'

I took his cock and held it. I looked him in the eye. I was naked, sitting with my knees apart and my legs crossed at the ankles in front of me. My pussy gleamed from among its fiery curls. My breasts jutted forward. 'I've missed you, Rog,' I said deliberately.

He rolled over and lay on his back with his head in my naked lap. He held my breasts apart and looked up into my face. 'I've missed you,' he said.

I looked down his body and saw that it was true.

'If I do this for you,' I said, 'you have to show me some gratitude.'

He grinned. A thumb strayed over one of my nipples. 'I don't know if I can manage that,' he said wickedly.

'You have to. It's my payment. And the first thing I

have to do is to check you've told me the truth.'

'I'd never lie to an old friend like you,' he assured me.
He pulled my right breast hard and managed to get the
nipple into his mouth.

'You told me you managed it five times with Janie.'

'Mm,' he agreed, sucking.

'So do it five times with me.'

My nipple popped wet out of his mouth. 'If the feeling
I had that night was real,' he said solemnly, 'I mean if
there was really something outside me and Janie that was
being imposed on us, then I swear to you, Red Marsden,
that if we ever come across it I'll do you ten times in a
row. I'll screw each of your pretty orifices twice just to
get started. Then I'll come in between that really luscious
pair you have. Let me see, that's seven, isn't it? Then I'll
shoot my load in your hair and make it all smeary. That's
eight. You can give me a hand job in the shower, that's
nine. Have you got any suggestions for the tenth, sweetheart? You used to be quite inventive if I remember
rightly.'

'I'll tie you up and whip your arse,' I said softly, putting
my nipple back in his mouth. 'I'll whip you till you spout
all across the room.'

He bit me. I deserved it, I guess.

As lofts go, it wasn't bad. There was a rooflight, the place
was wired for electricity and I had all modern facilities
laid on including a double mattress made up with classy
bedlinen. Rog had tried hard not to make it so that I
was slumming.

Janie had a part-time job. The house was isolated from
neighbours. Rog found it easy to arrange to work at home
for a day while he prepared things and showed me round
the place.

It was as he said, a long low house made up of a terrace
of three workmen's cottages. They had been farm cottages
once, I think.

In the dull wintry weather I found it unattractive. I'm not the rural kind, preferring urban pleasures, but Rog was evidently proud of his home and it certainly was beautifully fitted up.

Their bedroom was in the middle section. The walls were papered dark blue with little silver stars. The carpet was silver grey, the curtains plain dark blue and the bedlinen matched the wallpaper. Very nice, I thought, but cold. The only warm note came from the vase of red roses on the dressing table. Apparently Janie always had red roses in her bedroom.

I'm ashamed to admit that when I'm screwing a man I often don't notice the surroundings. My attention is on the male, what I'm doing to him and what he's doing to me. Not every man likes his lady to be active but I was born that way and I need to involve myself with the male body very vigorously and in a variety of ways.

Rog lay on the bed in the loft. 'I don't think you will be too uncomfortable,' he said. 'It's very firm, of course. It should do your back good.'

I fixed up my mirror over the bed. Then I knelt across Rog. I looked down into his face. We had dropped a blind over the rooflight so that light couldn't shine out and alert some passerby the house wasn't empty when it should be. A sidelight shone and the loft was a strange shadowy wooden cave, clean smelling, dry, warm, full of beams.

I hoisted my skirt up revealing brief panties and a garter belt. I have a very white skin to go with my red hair. My thighs gleamed like marble. My dark stockings were misty in the poor light. I rubbed my hand across the front of Rog's trousers and felt him hard within. I pulled the crotch of my panties to one side, licked my finger and slid it into myself. Rog lay with his hands folded behind his head. I lifted myself on my knees and smiled. I wriggled on my own finger and let him see I was enjoying it. While I masturbated myself I began to unzip his trousers. I eased the belt undone. I began to frig my clitoris. My tongue came out from between my parted lips. I undid my blouse and let my breasts show. I hooked one out of its support. It hung heavy, the bright nipple elongating as it pointed down at Rog. I caressed it, making the nipple grow longer. I continued to frig my little clit, squirming slightly as excitement built in me. I lifted my hanging boob and bent my head. I was just able to slip the nipple between my lips. I sucked myself there. I stopped masturbating myself long enough to unfasten Rog's trousers completely. I reached in, still sucking my own tit, and felt for his hard pole. I eased it free from his hot hairy jungle.

I released my tit. I used two hands to push his trousers down, he lifted up slightly to help me do this. He was so hard and horny his cock stood up and brushed my swollen vulva. I wouldn't let it come in. I put my own fingers back inside myself and began to bring myself to climax leaving him out in the cold.

He gripped my hips and began to push up with his cock, thrusting to get in alongside my fingers but he was so big there wasn't room.

'You stay there, Red,' he snarled, 'and I swear I'll find some other entrance.'

You can tease a man enough. I took my fingers out and felt him thrust up.

My head went back exposing my white throat. I felt my hair hanging down my back. My boobs lifted and I felt Rog catch them with his hands and begin to knead them. I gasped as his rod went all the way in. The man seemed to get bigger every time. His cock was lusciously hard, squeezing me out, making me feel tight and hot just how I liked it.

Above me were the sloping roof beams. I reached up and grabbed them. Now I could lift myself and really control the amount of cock impaling me and how heavy I came down on it.

Rog thrust hard upwards again and again. He fucked

like a maniac, revelling in having me swinging from the rafters as he poked my sex. He seemed to have some kind of twist to his cock. He was winding me up, closer and closer to orgasm. My juices ran and I started to cry out. The bastard was hitting some particular spot, I couldn't control the convulsions of my flesh. I was coming and my contractions on his cock were making him come. This wasn't fair. I wanted it to go on and on for ever.

I bent over him, shivery with the release of tension. My hair brushed his face. He took my swinging tits one by one into his mouth and sucked them as if they had cool beer on tap. All the time he moved slightly in me, making little after-tremors of sex shake through me. I kept squeezing my cunt on him, feeling myself wet all around his softened sliding cock.

I came off him by falling off the bed and lying on a rug he had placed over the floorboards of the attic. I looked up. The mirror on the beam above was well placed. It reflected his torso, the hairy belly revealed where his shirt was pushed up, the strong thighs revealed where his trousers were shoved down. It showed his cock, gleaming damply, big and soft and lying to one side where I had slid off it.

'Lick it,' he ordered. 'I want to watch in the mirror.'

I bent over the soft sluggish thing. I could get the whole of it in my mouth because it was bendy. I ran my tongue round and round it and I licked all the spunk off it. I licked it up the way and I licked it down the way, pulling the foreskin down off the glowing head.

Five times he said he had come with Janie that night, five times in her sleeping body. I could remember him coming nine times one long hot summer night with me, when he was nineteen and I was younger. Every time his cock had hardened we had turned it into a full-scale fuck. He had orgasmed nine times in my sweet strong greedy hole. Now he bragged about just over half that number. *O tempera! O mores!*

He lay with his hands folded behind his head, smiling. 'That's very good, Red,' he said. 'I like it when you do that.'

We checked out the loft together. He had thought of everything. You could tell where the old house divisions had been because once they were walled apart. Now they were knocked through. This made three connected loft spaces with dividers. Up the far end were my primitive sanitary arrangements. In the middle was my bedroom and general purpose living room, over his bedroom in the house below. Then I had yet another area where my cooking facilities were. I had a microwave oven, water, all manner of drinks including whisky and beer. There was a stack of food, and more to come that he would put in a freezer bag at the last moment.

I could eat, sleep, relieve myself, wash, read and listen to music on a personal stereo. When I came back the next day he would install me. Then he would go away for work, as he so often did.

I would be on my own, watching Janie.

Janie spent each morning away at her job and she was leaving before Rog. She kissed him goodbye the next day knowing he would be spending the next two nights in the Midlands. Half an hour after she was clear, I turned up. Rog was going to drive my car away and get a taxi back to pick up his own. We decided this was better than me arriving by cab. We wanted there to be no way that Janie could ever find out I was there, and whereas a passing car wasn't unusual, the house was isolated enough for a single woman arriving with luggage by taxi to be remembered, in the event of some unlucky future coincidence. Rog taking a taxi to his own house could be explained, if ever it became necessary, by pretending the car had broken

down in some trifling way. It was the firm's car. Janie
drove the one they owned themselves.

Rog took me in and kissed my neck, holding me by the
waist and rubbing his body against mine. 'I want to make
love to you,' he said, 'but I don't have time. The business
with the cars will make me late.' Though as he said this,
he ran a hand up my skirt and felt me. He loved his
fingers inside a woman. He loved the warm sliding feel of
a woman's cunt. He particularly liked it when both parties
were fully dressed and it was an inappropriate time and
place. It made it dirtier somehow, and Rog liked his sex
spiced this way.

That's why we got on so well, of course. I liked it
outrageous myself.

That as it for now, though. Leaving me as horny as he
was himself, Rog installed me in the loft and carefully
closed the hatch. For the next three days I would have
water tanks for company.

I heard him there for ten minutes while he made it look
as though the hatch hadn't been opened in a long time.
Then it all fell silent. I crept along the loft tracking his
movement from spyhole to spyhole as he prepared to leave
the house. The two interior walls to the loft were each of
raw brick, showing how it had once been three separate
dwellings. There were crawlways between the three lofts.
I damaged my stockings seeing Rog go away. I came
back to the middle bedroom section and stripped off the
laddered stockings. I thought for a moment. Then I stripped off everything else. It was warm in the attic. If it got
too stuffy I could risk opening the rooflight though I
mustn't do anything that Janie would notice and I mustn't
attract burglars to the house.

Meanwhile it was warm and I took everything off. This
pleased me. I stroked my body, enjoying its curves with a
narcissistic pleasure. I was a pale figure in the shadowy
room. I was a ghost.

I liked it. I liked being secret in this secret place. I had everything around me that I needed, the way a child imagines. It was a miniature world.

I remembered riding Rog's pole and feeling it big and swollen in my soft pussy. I hadn't told Rog, but in my luggage was a dildo. I would use it soon. When he came back and this was over, he would owe me. I would make him give it to me here, in this place. I began to think of the ways I wanted him to fuck me.

So the time passed.

Janie came home mid-afternoon. She went into the kitchen after garaging her car and unpacked some shopping. She hung up her coat and then put up her feet for half an hour, drinking coffee and reading.

She did a little housework. She watched the news. She spent some time on what looked like the family accounts. She phoned a friend and chatted. I could see her sitting at the phone. It was hard to hear what she said, though it was just possible.

Naughty Rog. If Janie ever found out what he'd done, she would leave him. Any woman of spirit would.

I enjoyed my spying role. Secretly I observed this wife of my lover. I wasn't bored, I was fascinated.

She spread a mat on the sitting room floor. She went into her bedroom and took off all her clothes. She came back into the sitting room and lay naked on the mat, facing upwards. I watched her. Her breasts were flattened, their rounded nipples dark. Her pussy fleece was dark also though she bleached her hair blonde. It was an interesting contrast, the pale head, the dark sex.

She lay flat like a starfish relaxing. I stared down at her nakedness and was aware of a warmth between my legs.

She began to put herself through a set of yoga positions, stretching and holding positions for five seconds or so. She had a good figure and she kept it trim. Her slow controlled movements, her periods of stillness when she held a pose, were like a balletic dance. Some of it she did flat on her back. Some she did lying on her front or kneeling. Some she did standing.

It was curiously erotic. Once or twice I actually saw between her legs, but that wasn't it. She was sure she was alone and she was entirely open. I found myself stirred. The sight of Janie's nakedness aroused me. I envied Rog his right of access to that lissom body. I began to fantasise being with him in bed, with Janie. What would Janie and I do? What would we do to Rog? What would we do to each other?

After some time Janie went to the bathroom, where she showered and washed her hair. She came out of the bathroom still naked, I loved seeing her so, and went into her bedroom. She dressed and tidied up the clothes she had been wearing when she came in.

In the kitchen she put on a load of washing, dried her hair and fixed a meal. I could hardly bear to stop watching her long enough to get something for myself. My eyes hurt and it was good to rest them.

The evening was quiet. The phone rang a couple of times, one was obviously from Rog. She phoned out. She watched television. She listened to music. She flicked through a magazine. Then she did as Rog said she did.

She went to bed early.

All my lights were off. When Janie put her light off she mustn't see a tiny spark in her ceiling.

I arranged myself comfortably. I had the bed to sleep on but that would be mostly in the day time, when Janie was out. For my night-time watching I had a thin single upholstered mattress that was made in three sections. It folded twice to make a large stool. For now I could stretch my length on it and move it easily around the loft to different spyholes should that become necessary.

I lay on my front propped on a pillow watching. Before

I did this I crept over to my luggage and found the thing I had brought with me. Back on my spying bed I lay down. I inserted the thing in my pussy. I didn't switch it on, I just left it there as a passive reminder of what I enjoyed.

I lay on my front, alternately watching Janie below me and resting my eyes. The slug of warm plastic in me pressed my soft places and squeezed my sensitive flesh. It kept me aroused and awake. I wriggled slightly on it from time to time. It was like having a very slow fuck. Hours could go by. I liked it very much.

Janie read for a while propped up in bed. Then she switched off the light and snuggled down to sleep.

Time passed.

I think I must have dozed off. The pressure in my sex was continuous. I had a succession of mildly dirty dreams. I dreamt of men inserting their sex into me. I dreamt I lay on my back in extreme comfort, somewhere warm. My legs were up and held open by two gorgeous young men. They held me gently and stroked my skin from time to time. They smiled at me.

Looming from the mists of fantasy a man would approach, a vast cock stuck out in front of him. The young men would hold my legs apart, someone would stroke my breasts to soothe me, and the cock would slide magnificently into my cunt and begin to shaft me.

I did nothing. My body moved up and down yieldingly to the slow rhythm of this dream sex. I would be shafted with exquisite pleasure till my pussy melted with happiness.

I noticed it was women who stroked my breasts. That made it nicer. They had breasts of their own and understood what was nice. They stroked me and stroked me and occasionally they oiled me and they bent their heads and sucked my nipples.

The young men smiled and stroked my legs. Another

great cock loomed up and slid into my eager pussy. My body moved up and down to my unseen lover's thrusts. The women massaged me and kissed my nipples.

I woke up squeezing on the dildo up inside me. I was incredibly aroused. My pussy jerked and gulped in its crying need for sex. It took me a moment to sort out reality from dream, for reality was very strange.

The warm wood-smelling dark pressed down on me. My body felt silky bare and charged up for sex. I remembered Rog and lusted briefly for him. Then I remembered Janie.

My pussy ached for the living thrust of a man. My breasts ached to be caressed. My mouth craved to taste a man's sex. But there was work to do and no man anywhere near me. I applied my eye to my spyhole.

The covers were flung back. Janie was rolling on the bed writhing almost as if she was in pain. Her hand kept going between her legs so she could frot herself.

Her long pale straight hair was spread out on her pillows. She moaned slightly and I saw her lips were parted. Her eyes were closed. It was hard to see detail, but her curtains weren't quite drawn and there was a big moon.

She drew her knees up and began to jerk on her fingers. She made little cries. Once she rolled right over and went on her knees, her face down in her pillow and turned to one side. Her fingers were in her pussy scrabbling frantically. Her hips worked as if she was shafting something.

Now she was lying on her side. Still her hips bucked. She looked for all the world like a woman who wasn't getting it, a strong sexy woman who needed it but couldn't get it.

With Rog as husband? This was impossible. Rog could keep all but a nympho serviced and have time left over. He was a greedy lover.

Was Janie a nympho? Was I witnessing an affliction? I had no idea.

I was in trouble myself now. I had woken out of sexy dreams very much on heat. My stupid trick with the dildo was working too well. The sight of that lovely slim girl in sexual torment below me aroused me still further. The whole secret bit, the spying, had a frisson all of its own.

I couldn't get satisfied. I began by playing with myself, I'm good at this, but it wasn't enough. I shoved the dildo in and switched it on. It was a pallid experience, I needed something stronger.

I stopped watching Janie. I became desperate to satisfy my inordinate lust. The moon poured cold through the rooflight and I searched in frantic silence for something to help.

I tipped my handbag out over my bed. There it was. I picked up my hairbrush, a circular one with bristles all round. Sobbing with relief I removed the smooth plastic dildo and inserted the hairbrush. I squatted on the bed holding on with one hand to a sloping roof truss. With the other I held the handle of the big hairbrush. I had the business end, the bristles, shoved up inside my tortured pussy. I jigged up and down hard and let the bristles frig me to peace.

When I had come I hung onto the roof beam sobbing slightly with the easing of the torment. I left the hairbrush in place. The stiff bristles sticking into my pussy flesh on the inside were absolute heaven. I moved slightly on their abrasive coarseness. I had never known such intensity of feeling.

I remembered what I was supposed to be doing. Leaving the hairbrush in situ I crawled across the floor to the single mattress. I collapsed down on it relishing how my movements made the brush prick and stick into my pussy flesh. I applied my eye to the hole Rog had drilled in the floor.

Janie was balled up on her back. She had her knees drawn up so far they were either side of her ears. She had something stuffed up inside her but I couldn't see what it was in the uncertain light.

Plainly she was fucking herself with it even as I had fucked myself with the hairbrush and was still enjoying its prickly presence. She was calling out softly and moaning as she frigged herself. One hand held her knees up, the other held the object and moved it in and out with short violent stabs.

She came to climax and relaxed, uncurling, leaving the thing stuck up inside her. It was quite big. I saw something thin and snakelike laying across her thigh. She lay with her eyes shut moving slightly, sort of settling after her frenzy.

Then I saw what it was.

She had fucked herself with the telephone receiver.

I became aware of pain in my pussy. Gingerly I removed the hairbrush. I rolled onto my back holding it. It would require some quite special washing.

Janie and the telephone receiver. Me and the hairbrush. What the hell was going on?

The rest of the night was quiet. I dozed and watched from time to time. Then I made myself something to eat and ate it. I washed and put myself properly to bed in the dawn.

I was very tired.

I slept till late morning, a deep sound dreamless sleep. I woke slowly, peacefully, coming round feeling very relaxed and calm. My limbs were heavy, as though my muscles were so pleasurably at ease they were reluctant to rouse themselves and get into action.

Gradually the events of the previous night came back to me. I squeezed my pussy but it felt normal, as if I'd had a man, I so often do, but nothing out of the ordinary.

I lay very unworried, thinking how nice it was having a man. How satisfying it was when he slid his engorged muscle up into my yielding clinging warmth.

I thought about Rog. I thought about some other men

in my life. I have a fondness for old things, old possessions, old flames. I like my lovers to last for years with occasional meetings. I like to have a dozen or so on the go and to see them each from time to time, when we feel like each other's company. I hate the boyfriend situation, having one man who religiously takes you out several times a week and screws you upon occasion. That's mini-marriage and I've never wanted marriage in any form.

I have a stable, you might say. I like to ride different horses in any one week and I also like something new and unknown between my legs from time to time.

Eventually I washed but I didn't dress. I liked having nothing on and it was warm, so warm. I washed my brush as best I could. Only then could I brush my hair.

Naked with tousled hair, slumber-slow, I was the gipsy in the attic.

I ate and did some exercises while Janie was out of the house and the noise didn't matter. I remembered her yoga. It looked a good thing to do. I read for a while. I lay listening to music and painted my fingernails and toenails deep red. I compared the colour to the colour of my pussy hair.

Then I watched Janie after she came home. The routine was much as the previous day. Finally she went to bed.

This time I didn't fall asleep. I watched the peaceful sleeping woman gradually begin to wrestle with her night demons, her demon lovers. I could see nothing in the moon-flooded room but I could feel the presence. He was naughty, licentious, greedy, a shade cruel.

I wanted to see him. I lusted after him. I could feel him with my mind, with my emotions, but I couldn't feel his flesh nor see his person.

He was there all right. I knew he was there and he knew I was there and soon it would be my turn, when he had finished his naughty doings with Janie below.

Then he would turn his attention to me.

She had changed her sheets in the daytime and they were pale. Her body was dark against them. She had cast off all covering and from directly above I looked down on her squirming and writhing in sexual frenzy. The tension in me built unendurably. I was trying not to sob aloud with my need for sex. I groped across the dark loft and found my hairbrush again. Squatting on it I took myself rapidly to climax. I fumbled back across the room to watch Janie. By the time I was there I was frantic again.

He was calling me.

I stared at Janie. She was mewing in her sleep, the fingers and thumb of one hand bunched together as she tried to frig herself.

He called me downstairs.

I rammed the hairbrush even harder into myself and worked my pussy savagely.

It didn't satisfy. He wanted me downstairs. He wanted me with Janie.

I was mumbling apologies to Rog. I unbolted the attic hatch. I was about to bust his marriage and I couldn't help it, I had to do this, I had no freedom of choice.

Now I lifted the wooden square out. As I did so I broke the tape Rog had used to seal the edges, the white tape that blended with the white-painted ceiling. Every movement was bliss because of the prickling thing full of spikes in my pussy.

The air below was cool. This was the far end of the house. Janie was in the middle section. I sat on the edge of the hatch and then I eased myself over. Clinging to the edge I lowered myself until I hung.

For a moment I was suspended hanging from my hands. I felt him then, quite close to me. I was naked, my body completely exposed.

My legs opened. The hairbrush came out. I felt a rush of cool air inside me. I wanted to scream at the emptiness.

I hung, twisting slightly. My breasts tingled as if fiery

33

hot. Moaning faintly I let myself fall.

For a moment I crouched there where I had landed. The middle section of the house, where the bedroom was, was before me. In my section was a spare bedroom, a study and a second bathroom. They were dead. They contained nothing, no life. It was all concentrated in the middle section.

I stumbled through the dark house till I came to Janie's room. I opened the door.

She made no acknowledgement of my presence. Rog was right, she was asleep. I slid into the room and felt at once as if I had walked into something solid.

The air was thick, almost tangible. It pressed on my skin. I tried not to sob. It was sexual static. Every nerve in my body was on end and every cell in my body demanded sex.

Janie was uttering little cries, her eyes closed and her eyeballs rolling. I reached out a trembling hand and touched her breast.

It was warm and smooth as satin. My hand slid over its pillowy softness and I allowed the nipple to rest in the centre of my palm. I rotated my palm and felt the nipple enlarge. I caressed the whole thing and then I gently squeezed and tugged the yielding flesh. I drew it into a cone and I bent over the sleeping frenzied woman and I kissed her nipple.

I sucked it between my pursed lips. Stroking the skin of her breast back from the nipple, I sucked harder. Janie arched her back, thrusting up at me, groaning with pleasure.

I put a hand on her stomach. It was very flat. It fluttered under my hand. My fingertips touched her dark fleece. I sucked her nipple with my head turned sideways watching my hand. I slid it further down. I could feel the hard bony mound. I could feel the soft layer of skin over it. I could feel the soft curly fleece. I went further. Now my fingers could feel where her flesh divided, where the fruit was split. I could feel warmth. I could feel dampness. My fingers trembled.

I touched her clitoris.

Her body arched sharply with such a jerk that she slapped me in the face with her breast. She cried out harshly and thrust her sex into my hand. I rubbed the clit with one finger and let the others go on.

She was very wet. I separated her sticky flesh and felt for her entrance. She was liquid slidy and hot.

I released her breast and went round the bed. Her legs came wide open. I knelt down and looked into her cunt.

She smelt wonderful, warm musk, spice, oozing fruit. I put two hands in and opened her vulva wide.

The moonlight fell across her body in a silver flood. I saw her hole a black entrance into bliss. I saw her silver flesh shine wetly in the cold light. The whole thing pulsed and throbbed. I slid my fingers into her cunt and felt the flesh close octopus-tight on me.

It was warm and spongy and muscular. She squeezed my fingers in rapid pulses. With my other hand I found her clit again. I began to frig it.

I frotted her button. I penetrated her pussy and thrust vigorously, in and out. I felt her come, a fantastic velvet convulsion that left my fingers dribbling wet with her luscious flow of musk.

I took my fingers out of her and put them into my mouth. I sucked the lovely juice. Then I knelt forward over the bed and began to suck her pussy.

I had a hand on each of her breasts squeezing them and manipulating her nipples. My hair fell over her belly. My face was driven in between her parted lips. She had her knees drawn up and her legs wide open. I sucked her moist swollen parts, I sucked and licked and nibbled and all the time she thrust into my face with gentle rhythmical movements.

The hairbrush had fallen out of my pussy when I hung from the loft hatch despite it being rammed hard into me. I had left it there. Now I felt it inside me. As I sucked Janie I felt a great prickling brush thrust hard into my urgent pussy and it began to fuck me with something close to violence.

The insane prickling and spikiness went on. My abraded flesh flowed thick with juice of my constant orgasm. I had a sexual orgasm in my mouth, mine or Janie's I didn't know, but her juices flowed and I sucked and her flesh stretched and quivered and pulsed of its own accord.

I was dazzled. My mind was in starburst. My body was overloaded with sensation.

I woke up lying across the bed. Janie was on her front with one knee drawn up. I had the fingers of one hand still inside her body. My head was against her side.

Very gently I disengaged. She was sleeping peacefully. Instead of being alarmed I was utterly peaceful myself.

It was still dark but I saw from the time that dawn was not far off. I went out into the corridor and walked down it till I was under the hatch. I took the stepladder from the cupboard as I had seen Rog do. I climbed it and replaced the hatch door. Then I fixed the tape back into position so it wouldn't show.

I was very calm. Although the house was cool and I was naked, I was comfortably warm. I tidied away the steps and found my hairbrush lying on the floor. I picked it up. Then I went on silent feet back into Janie's room.

For a moment I stood looking down at the sleeping girl. Her spread hair, her chubby buttocks, one hand up at her face as though she was about to suck her thumb, all these things made her look so sweet. I loved the long smooth line of her back. I admired how graceful it was.

Very gently I covered her. Then I slid myself under the bed and I lay on the soft silver carpet. I heard the heating come on. The floor throbbed gently as the house came awake. A grey light filtered in from outside.

It was morning. The alarm went off. Janie awoke and switched it off. After a few minutes she switched on the bedside light and her radio. The new day had begun.

I slept a little down there under the bed. It was about an hour before she went out. I went into the bathroom and had a shower. I took a mirror off the wall and squatted over it inspecting my sexual parts. They looked quite as usual. I felt inside myself but I was not especially tender nor sore.

Rog would be back in the afternoon but Janie would probably be in before him. I went up into the attic and tidied up and collected some clothes. I was extremely reluctant to dress but I knew I had to. I came out of the attic and fixed the tape back in place. When it all looked innocent I had to find somewhere to hide.

I chose the fitted wardrobe in the spare bedroom. I settled in it with my case. I had made myself something to eat upstairs and felt completely at ease.

I knew something very odd was happening but I felt little more than a warm friendly interest in it. I felt no fear, no unease, no worry.

I thought it would be nice to see Rog again.

I heard Janie come home and move around. I could guess what she was doing since she seemed quite happy to follow a routine after getting in from work. She was cheerful, singing to herself as she moved about the house.

Later Rog came in and they exchanged affectionate greetings. They sat and talked for a while. Then Janie went out.

I heard Rog get the steps out. I came out of my cupboard and went to the doorway. He was opening the hatch.

'Roger,' I said huskily.

He all but fell off the ladder. When he had himself

under control again he demanded to know why I was downstairs. There was a real fear in him. This was hardly surprising. He must have thought more than once about the risks he was running with his marriage, hiding me in his house.

I couldn't feel afraid. I laughed. 'It's OK,' I said. 'She doesn't know I'm here.'

'But why, Red? Why the risk?'

'I've got a lot of explaining to do. When does Janie come back?'

He checked his watch. 'She's playing squash. Sometimes she has a drink afterwards, sometimes she comes straight back.'

'I can't tell you now then. I probably can't tell you at all. I mean, I can't explain anything. I can only say what happened.'

'You're driving me mad. I have to take you to your car. I need to be here when Janie gets back. Can you tell me on the way?'

I hesitated. 'Look,' I said. 'What's the score tomorrow? Do you go off before Janie or after?'

'Generally I work in the house for a day after one of these sessions,' he said.

'Keep me here, then,' I said. 'I'll go back upstairs. Come up with me and I'll explain what I can. Then you can see for yourself tonight.'

What was there to explain? Some weird sexual force took over his wife every night. That was hardly an explanation. It took me over too. I had felt it but I couldn't explain it.

'Is this a ploy?' he said impatiently. Then he saw my expression.

He moved in close. 'You know I'm crazy about you,' he murmured. He put his hands on my waist and drew me into him. 'I'd have married you, you bitch, only you didn't want me.'

'I wanted you,' I corrected. 'I didn't want marriage.'

'Do you want it now?' he asked. 'I don't mean marriage, sweetheart. I mean do you want me to fuck you? I'd like to, believe me, I'd like to.'

He was rubbing himself against me and nuzzling my neck under my hair. I did believe him. He wanted me all right.

'It isn't a ploy,' I said. 'Something really, really strange is going on here. I can't explain it in any sensible terms but I think I ought to be here tonight. Perhaps if you and me see it together I won't think I'm mad.'

'See it together?' he echoed. 'You mean a ghost?'

'I don't know what I mean,' I said impatiently. 'I don't have the words. It defies sense. Put me back in the attic with my stuff. After you've gone to bed with Janie tonight do whatever you normally do on these occasions. Then get the hell out of the bedroom as soon as she's asleep. Don't stay with her. Come and let me out. Maybe the two of us will be able to sort things out.'

'What if she doesn't fall asleep?'

'She will. She always falls asleep. She won't know anything's different so of course she'll fall asleep just like normal people do. But you mustn't, Rog. Get out of the bedroom as soon as you can without waking her.'

'What happened while I was away?' The poor man was frantic.

'It was like you told me. She has these hot dreams and she doesn't wake up. But I was awake, Rog, and it affected me too.' I stopped and I looked him in the eye.

'You've got something in the house, Rog. It isn't just you and Janie here, with me as a temporary visitor. Someone else has come to stay. Or something else.'

I shivered suddenly, feeling scared for the first time. My sense of well-being was wearing off. 'I don't believe in ghosts,' I whispered.

For a moment there was silence between us as my words

hung in the air. It was time to pull myself together. The strangeness was definitely wearing off. 'Look,' I said sternly. 'You do it plenty tonight. You'll be able to quench anything but the most perverted appetite. Let's get this sorted out. Perhaps I'm suffering from being locked in a loft for two days. I'm a randy bitch at the best of times and seeing Janie writhing about like that when I couldn't get it has maybe turned my mind. She's very pretty, your wife, and I'm thinking I like looking at pretty women which is a very odd thought when you've been as heterosexual as I have, Rog.'

He kept a hold of me. He kissed my ear, my neck, under my hair. 'Are you going to watch me, Red?' he murmured.

'You bet. I'm dying to see how you do it with someone else.'

I felt him shiver. 'I think I'll like that,' he whispered. 'I think I'll like it very much. The only promise is that I'll want to give it to you too and perhaps I won't be fit for it after I do as you say with Janie.'

I pressed against him and stroked his hair and his neck. 'You have to do as I say,' I said silkily. 'Those are the rules. You do it as often as you can with Janie tonight, as often as she'll let you. And I'm going to watch every move you make.'

With what I know now it's strange recalling these events. I have to record what we did, the three of us. I have to remember it as it was. I have to know what happened.

It's relevant, what happened. The precise details are relevant. I was proposing to watch a man make passionate love to his wife, knowing that he was likely to make love to me straight afterwards, as soon as he could muster the energy. At that point in time I found the idea wickedly exciting. I liked ordering him to have sex with another woman and I wanted to have him reeling between the pair of us.

Perhaps part of me wasn't as amoral as the rest. Perhaps by bullying Rog in this way I was punishing him for having two women and deceiving one of them. I wanted him to suffer for his sex. I wanted him reduced to an exhausted rag as he struggled to satisfy two rapacious women.

At the time I wasn't worrying about my emotions other than to feel that they existed. I was looking forward to bedtime.

It came early. Rog had a bath and afterwards he sat on the edge of the bed in his towelling robe talking in a low voice to his wife. They were chatting, catching up, talking ahead about this and that.

Janie undressed and brushed her hair. Then Rog took the brush and did it for her. His hands came over her shoulders afterwards and he slid her robe down so that her breasts were exposed.

He began to fondle them and to kiss her. She responded readily by leaning back into him so that he could run his hands all over her front and down into her lap.

I settled cheerfully. The guy had style. I knew he'd put on a show because he knew I was watching. Janie would benefit from all this by-play, of course, getting the dream lover, the screen lover as husband in her own bedroom.

This business of Rog's was teaching me all sorts of things about myself. I hadn't known I liked spying, never having guessed at the secret charge it could give. Watching Janie had made me feel powerful and superior. I was shocked at the pleasure of it. The security services must be full of people addicted to this particular high.

I suspected it was bad for me.

I hadn't known I liked seeing women nude. I hadn't realised the sensuous attractions of a pretty woman's body. I hadn't known it would wind me up sexually.

I'd never realised I could go with a woman. I didn't know before this that I could bury my face in the sexual flesh of a woman and drink there. I hadn't realised I

41

wanted to feel inside a woman's cunt, not my own. I knew now that I liked it, that my appetite had barely been touched yet. There were many other things I wanted to do with Janie and in some of the scenarios I imagined I was the passive partner.

I'd never consciously admitted to having the desire to see a couple copulate before. Certainly I enjoyed a little bumping and grinding on television but that had been the mildest of thrills. But the scene below me now was electric. I was seeing a man hard for sex about to give it to a willing woman. That they were both sophisticated people made it better. Might they get up to tricks? If they did I was greedy to watch.

I was bisexual. I was a voyeur. What else might I be?

Rog laid his wife on her back on the bed. She had removed her robe and they had the light on. I saw her long slim body with its dark thatch. I saw her nipples. I saw the expression on her face.

She smiled as she opened her legs wide. She put her hands under her hips and lifted herself. Then she got her heels on the bed and lifted her hips up. 'Give it to me, Rog,' she cried. 'Do it, darling. I want you in me now.'

He was stood by the bed looking down at her. She had her buttocks close to the edge of the bed but lifted high. She was balanced on her heels, her elbows and her head. Her whole body was straining towards Rog's erect cock, coming between her thighs to enter her and fuck.

He leant right forward, putting his hands either side of her body. He thrust hard with his hips and she gave a gasp of pleasure. With her straining up and him leaning in, he did it then. He thrust hard, with powerful jabs that had her crying out in delight. I could see her face. She tossed her head from side to side, beside herself with excitement.

I could see his cock. I could see the gleaming wet pole sliding in and out of his wife's sex. I could see the swing of his heavy balls underneath it.

It was a very pretty sight.

He thundered into her and stopped. She wriggled slightly on the end of his rod as her orgasm took her. I could see the red flush to her belly and her breasts. The lady did no faking.

He took her under her buttocks so she could let go herself where she had held herself up. She lifted her legs one at a time and wrapped them round his hips. He stood there laughing down at her, still penetrating her, with her legs tight about him. She was almost upside-down on the bed.

He released her and they got on to the bed together. I think she would have been content then to go to sleep but Rog wouldn't let her. He caressed her back and her hair as she read for a little while. Then he pulled back the covers and began to fondle her buttocks. Finally he moved himself down the bed and opened her buttocks. He began to kiss her there and bite her. She wriggled and laughed. Then he moved round to kiss her vulva.

I stared down at his head buried in her thighs. She lay on her back writhing with pleasure. The light was still on and I could see her eyes were open.

I was sure Rog was enjoying a double-edged excitement. He would know I must be as horny as hell up here on my own with the two of them satisfying their lusts in such delightful ways in front of my eyes. Rog knew I adored being sucked, I always had, and now I was watching it being done to another woman. She was really enjoying it too.

I saw him bring her to orgasm for the second time. The signs were unmistakable. He only used his mouth but then I knew what skill he had with his mouth and how well he could use it. He had done the same for me on other occasions.

Now she was definitely satisfied. She went off to the

bathroom and when she came back she made all the moves for going to sleep. During the period she was out of the room Rog lay flat on his back with nothing on and no covers over him. He stared up at the ceiling. His legs were quite straight and very slightly apart. I had an excellent view of the man's sexual organs and I knew that this was exactly what he intended.

It takes a real man to screw one woman twice and then flaunt his sex to another, making tacit promises. Rog was all that and more.

They kissed. They put out the light. The moon was waning and it was dimmer than it had been.

I waited patiently, resting my eyes at intervals. I must have nodded off because I came round to hear Rog making his way into my eyrie.

'My God,' he breathed.

I stirred sleepily. I hadn't told him how his attic made me a nudist. Once in it alone again I had stripped off as before. It was the only way to be.

He had put on the light as he came up through the hatch. I lay languorously disposed on my spying mat, my bottom curving lusciously and my long rounded thighs very much in evidence. As I rolled slightly to look at him I raised myself on one elbow. A large white breast was revealed.

'You look like something Rubens might paint,' he said.

'I hope you don't mind.' My voice was low. 'It's the most comfortable way to be.'

'You're a beautiful woman,' he said sincerely. 'I'm afraid the sight of you makes me want to get in among that plump flesh and bite it while I fuck you.'

'You've already made it twice,' I pointed out.

'Once, gorgeous. Janie made it twice or weren't you watching?'

I rolled on to my back and opened my legs. 'I was watching,' I said.

He came over to me and knelt by my mat. He laid a hand on my stomach. Then he deliberately slid two fingers straight into my pussy. The pleasure was so pure I closed my eyes. He wriggled his fingers and found how damp I was. 'I can't believe how lucky I am,' he whispered. 'Janie down there and you up here. Red, you are so beautiful you take my breath away. You're like treasure. I want to plunder you. I want to dip my hands in and feel you cascade through my fingers.'

Deliberately I lifted my knees and opened my legs wider. His fingers slid further in. I lay with my hair haloing my face, my big breasts hanging one to each side, my white belly and thighs glistening up in the shadowy light under the eyes of the eager man. He bent almost reverently and kissed my nipples. He kissed my throat. He kissed my eyelids. He kissed my belly. He bent right over and keeping his fingers moving inside me, he kissed my clitoris and bit it.

He sat up on his heels and began to stir me with gentle rhythmical movements. 'What happened on those two nights?' he asked quietly. There had been no time to talk.

I settled with my eyes closed feeling the man's hand deep up my cunt. Occasionally I moved slightly on him to intensify the pleasure.

'The first night I fell asleep watching,' I said. 'I had put a dildo in my pussy and I was naked as I am now. I hadn't switched the thing on. I just wanted to feel it in place. I found spying on your wife very exciting. I have to say that. I was already excited just by watching her. Then I emphasised that by inserting a fat plastic slug up my pussy. I fell asleep and had very hot dreams, dreams that I was being poked again and again by glorious fat cocks while women loved me and kissed my breasts.'

'Jesus,' said Rog weakly.

I squirmed a little. 'When I woke I was so randy it was hard to think. I remembered what I was supposed to be doing and peeped down at Janie. She was freaking out.'

'What?'

'She was writhing and going at her own sex like she was a nympho and no man would let her have it. She was frantic. She frigged herself madly but all the time she looked as if she was asleep. I became almost hysterical myself. I had to have something to fuck me. I found something and shoved it up. I made myself come and that calmed me down a little. Janie was going crazy. Then I saw that she had found something and put it in her. She was bringing herself off. I only saw what it was when the fit passed and she calmed down.'

'What was it?'

'The telephone receiver.'

His fingers jerked in my pussy. 'Don't play games,' he hissed.

'I'm not. I swear it. If I was awake and not dreaming, she managed to get the whole thing inside her and she brought herself off on it. The evidence might still be there. You can check it out tomorrow.'

'I don't believe what you're saying,' he whispered as if dazed.

'The fit passed and that's what it looked like. A fit. A frenzy. But I felt it too. I went mad up here.'

He stirred doubtfully. 'Are you sure that wasn't just because you were horny anyway and seeing Janie made you more so?'

'I'm not sure of any damned thing. I tell you for what it's worth.'

'That was it for that night?'

'That was it. The fun and games started again on the second night.'

'Tell me.'

'This time it was like there was someone else.'

His fingers stilled. 'A lover?' he said in a cold voice.

'I saw no one. I think no one was here. I felt a presence, though. It was male. It was dirty. It was cruel. It was laughing at me. It was going to have Janie and then it was going to have me.'

Rog stirred uneasily and said nothing.

'Maybe he didn't know I was there the first night,' I said. 'Maybe it's hard for him to become aware of us. Perhaps we are as shadowy to him as he and his world are to us.'

'The ghost?' asked Rog gently.

'Yes. The ghost. He had Janie in coils down below. Then he told me to come down. He watched me when I dropped out of the hatch. He didn't come into that end of the house. I went to him, joining him in your bedroom. Then I made love to Janie. I kissed her breasts. I kissed her pussy. I frigged her. I sucked her. I made her come. Then I fell asleep with her. I woke near dawn knowing I was released. I felt fine. I felt good, if you want to know. I fixed the hatch so it looked OK and then I hid under the bed till Janie went to work. Then I wandered around a bit. Finally I came back up here and got my stuff ready. Then I waited in the cupboard in your spare room.'

Rog stirred my pussy. 'Red,' he said presently. 'You never played practical jokes before.'

'I don't now. I don't understand this thing. I'd like to. At the moment the best I can come up with is that there is a spirit here, a sexy spirit.'

'You said cruel.'

'I felt it to be cruel. Even malevolent. It's having fun at our expense. But you feel very good afterwards. If this is happening to Janie every night, no wonder she is a little odd and wayward in her manner.'

'Could it happen when I'm here?'

'She doesn't wake. Maybe you haven't been waking.'

Rog peered through the spyhole. He had to stretch to keep his fingers inside my sex but he did so. I felt a tremor pass through me. I was going to need more than fingers

soon. I reached between Rog's legs and found his cock.
It was up.

'Can you see her?'

'Yes. She's moving a little. Not much.'

'I think we ought to be downstairs,' I said. I stirred as
I did so. My need to be poked was becoming urgent.

Rog sat back and looked at me. 'The telephone
receiver,' he said gently. I could see his eyes glitter.

I spasmed on his fingers. Lack of proper penetration
was becoming painful. 'What did you put up yourself,
Red?' he asked in a silky voice. Evidently he had been
paying close attention to everything I had said.

I realised he wasn't believing me. I spoke with difficulty.
'My hairbrush,' I said.

'What?'

'Get it. You'll see. I'm ready for it now. For God's sake,
Rog. Get it and make me come.'

He emptied out my bag and came over with the fear-
some thing. 'You don't have to do this,' he whispered.
'Don't do it.'

I pulled it out of his hands. I drew up my knees and
opened my legs wide. Holding the handle with two hands
like a dagger, I stabbed myself viciously in the vulva. The
brush drove hard right up into my pussy. The sensation
was so exquisitely relief-giving I nearly orgasmed immediately. I fell forward and put a hand on Rog's shoulder to
support myself. With my other hand I began frantically
to wank myself.

Rog gaped at me in horror. I clung to him, masturbating
myself viciously. His body shook with the violence of my
self-inflicted actions. The relief was bliss. I began to shake
with orgasm. I could feel my love juices spurting and my
pussy shuddered harshly as my climax erupted. My belly
went in and out, my breasts stood out hard and my mouth
was wide open.

The frenzy eased. I looked at Rog. 'What's Janie doing?'

I rasped. He peered over me and looked through the spyhole.

He took my breast in a trembling hand. 'I don't believe it, I don't believe it,' he said monotonously. Leaving the hairbrush in my pussy I put my eye to the peephole. Janie had the rose vase driven far inside her. The roses lay scattered on her breast. She was rubbing them, thorns and all, into her naked breast while she brought herself off with the crystal vase.

She was still asleep.

'Fuck me,' I moaned.

'I can't,' he said hoarsely. 'You've got that thing in you.'

The hairbrush must be projecting obscenely from my body. 'Hold it,' I ordered. 'Frig me with it. And shaft me where you can.'

'*What?*'

'Do it,' I moaned. I held my buttocks open. 'Do it. I'm begging. Put it up me there, Roger. And make my pussy hot with the brush at the same time.'

The hairbrush handle got in the way. It wasn't easy for him. He managed though. He took me up my rear with his oversize stiff cock till I was split and moaning with perverted sexual bliss. At the same time he frigged my needy pussy with that coarse bristly brush.

I felt quite literally as though my body was on fire. It seemed to melt and cave in on itself. He withdrew when he had come, I must have been painfully tight on his cock, but I made him find the dildo and shove it where his cock had been.

'Red,' he whispered. I was kneeling in dizzy delight, my face down and turned to the side. From my upthrust rump protruded two artefacts, one designed for sexual pleasure sticking out of my arse and the other most definitely not designed for any such thing sticking out of my pussy.

I was dribbling, my mouth lax. I kept clenching the muscles of my arse and cunt. I'd never been so coarse or so violent before.

It wasn't going to be enough. I was silly with pleasure at the moment but it was waiting for me. It was there, about to pounce.

'Can't you feel it?' I whispered drunkenly.

'Feel what?'

'The force. The sexual strength of it.' I moaned suddenly. 'Rog, do it again. Please.'

'We've got to get down to Janie,' he said.

'Yes. Janie,' I mumbled.

He got me up. I stumbled across and into the end section of the attic to the hatch exit. I felt a bit better but I wouldn't take my friends out. I needed my orifices filled. I needed my friends.

We went down the ladder. Rog led the way to his bedroom. Having seen the state of me he was desperate to get to his wife.

I pushed past him as he went into the room. I rushed straight across to the bed and fell on my knees. I plunged my face between Janie's legs. I began to suck her poor needy pussy. The vase lay smashed against the far wall where she must have thrown it. As my mouth closed over her pulpy throbbing sex she lifted herself hard and began to sob softly with relief.

Rog must have watched us for one long stunned second. Then I felt the brush pulled roughly out of my pussy. A moment later his huge shaft was in me. He began to hit my sex, fucking me so violently it was hard to suck his wife properly.

I tasted her divine come and came myself as Rog jetted into me. He came round and knelt beside me.

'She's sleeping,' he whispered hoarsely.

'Am I dreaming?' I quavered. 'This is hotter than last night. Can't you feel it?'

'I can feel it,' he said. He took the hairbrush and began to scrub gently at his cock. It came back hard almost immediately. 'I'm going to have my wife,' he said. He slid it in but still she slept, wriggling and smiling in her sleep as she got what she wanted.

I bent over her and began to kiss her breasts. Rog made it in her watching me sucking and kissing her. Even when I kissed her wide sweet mouth she didn't wake and he didn't object. Then I kissed him while he shafted her. He stroked my breasts and kissed my mouth passionately and all the time his cock was inside another woman, doing it with her as he kissed me and fondled me.

And something in the room found all this very funny.

As before, I woke up peacefully sometime shortly before dawn. I stretched with slow luxuriousness. I felt warm friendly limbs disposed around me.

Sleepily, I opened my eyes. There was Rog, old friend that he was, asleep with his arms wide and his legs apart looking as if he would sleep on just the same until the millenium. The hair on his chest rose and fell. His breathing was deep and regular. I laid my hand on his chest and felt the steady boom, boom, boom of his heart. There was nothing wrong there.

I saw his cock lying pale across one thigh and thought to myself with a silent chuckle what a very long dongo my dear friend Roger had. I'd never told him but it had been a disappointment to me at first, finding out that most other men were shorter. Then I found out what fun men could be, regardless of whether their cocks were long or short, fat or thin.

Rog was long and fat though, and he erected to a highly satisfactory length. I mean he had a good expansion. It has always seemed to me that man should carry a little certificate around with them. It isn't the expansion of their chests that we females give a damn about. It's their ability to expand elsewhere that matters, and what the ratio is, slack to hard, limp to erect.

Rog had a good ratio, it has to be said.

I moved my leg gently. It was resting across Janie's thigh. I saw her dark thatch and rounded limbs. Her face was peaceful, her breasts rising and falling as regularly as her husband's.

I was definitely de trop. Unfortunately I lay in the middle of them. Carefully, I began to ease myself out from between their warm sleep-wrapped bodies.

Not carefully enough. As I moved Rog stirred and put his arm across me.

I lifted it and tried to continue my escape. He mumbled something and put his hand on my breast. His lips grazed my chin.

He thought I was Janie. It must be like this for marrieds, used to sleeping together all the time. I saw his cock slip off his thigh and start to grow.

I put one hand over his mouth and with the other tried to find some soft flesh to pinch. His arms closed round me and he rubbed my face with his, kissing my hand.

I pinched his thigh hard. His eyes opened in astonishment and I watched him as sense and memory flooded back.

I resumed my stealthy movements. Rog reached out and stroked my thigh in passing. I looked down in surprise, he was the one who had so much to lose, but his eyes glittered and he was grinning. As I climbed off the bed he slid his fingers into my pussy.

I tried to retreat but he only pushed them up harder. The man was a lunatic, to gamble so much for so little.

I stifled a snigger. At that precise moment Janie murmured in her sleep and rolled across the bed to Rog.

He turned to her instantly and as her eyes came open

he plunged into a passionate kiss. His free hand waggled dismissively behind his back. He rolled on top of his wife holding her head between his hands and kissed her with fervent passion. Hiccuping with laughter at this sudden descent into farce, I dropped to my hands and knees and crawled out of the room.

In the corridor I tidied up the hatch and put away the steps. In the wardrobe in the spare room I found a fur coat. I wrapped it round my naked person and settled myself to await the new day.

We were back where we had started, in the wine bar moodily drinking cheap alcohol. I was edgy because we sounded bonkers and Rog was edgy because I was asking awkward questions.

'You see, if Janie herself is the focus for this,' I was saying, 'then maybe she should see a doctor.'

'You make her sound like a witch,' grumbled Rog. 'Or a nymphomaniac.'

Since I agreed with him I shut up.

'Did so much happen?' he argued sullenly. 'I mean, just having you two hot numbers available for me, one not knowing about the other, is enough really to make me capable of prodigious feats.' He smirked faintly in memory.

'You haven't accounted for Janie's strange behaviour nor for mine,' I said patiently.

'Janie was asleep. Maybe she is taking sleeping pills, after all, and all this repressed sex comes out. It could be as simple as that.'

'And me?' My tone was arctic.

'Aw, come on, Red. There's no woman like you.' He laughed uneasily. 'You always have wanted it hot and strong. Sex with you is chilli and red peppers. Isn't that right?'

'The hairbrush,' I said in a soft voice.

His eyes slid away from mine. 'It's been a while for us. People tend to like their pleasures stronger as they get older.'

I gave up. 'It's your wife,' I said. 'You do what you think right. All I'm saying is something damned odd is going on and either it stems from Janie herself or it comes from the house. I felt it, Rog, whatever you say. I felt a presence.'

'Ghosts,' he said and snorted.

The silence stretched between us.

'So what would you do?' he asked.

'Get Janie out of the house and see if it still happens,' I said promptly.

His mouth opened and he looked at me like a dead fish. 'Oh,' he said blankly.

'Not so hard, eh?' I asked. Men are awful dumb, sometimes.

'Why didn't it used to happen?' he asked. 'If anything is,' he added hastily.

'I don't know, Rog. The house has been there a long time and Janie has been around quite a time as well. What should trigger this business, I have no idea. But if someone I loved was involved, I'd make it my business to find out.'

Again there was a silence. Then he said: 'If I got Janie out of the house, would you be prepared to spend the night in my bedroom?'

He was in such a state he didn't even see the humour of this proposal.

'No,' I said flatly. 'It isn't that I don't like the sex because I do. But I like having some say in the business. I like it to be a pleasure, not a necessity. It's all the difference between a meal in a posh restaurant when your appetite is pleasantly sharp, and being given food when you've starved for sixty days. It was over the top, Rog. Something was going on in your house I can't explain. I'm not easily frightened, but your bedroom scares the pants off me. In every sense,' I added.

He grinned. 'I'd be there.'

'Sweetheart, anywhere but your place.'

He frowned. 'So I'd have to stay there alone.'

I thought about this. 'It recognised me,' I said slowly. 'I mean, it became aware of me. It felt masculine. How was it for you?'

He stirred uncomfortably. 'Not like that. I mean, I felt something, but it was far more general. There was an atmosphere, I admit. You've got it labelled as a person. To me it was just a feeling.'

I was busy following my train of thought. 'If it is male, then it will make itself known to women, assuming it wasn't gay when it was alive. Or rather, it will be more conscious of women itself. Men won't interest it. I told you I felt our world might be as shadowy to it as its world is to us.'

'I don't like to hear you speak like this,' protested Rog.

'I felt it in the loft more than I felt it at the ends of the house. Even there it was only at night, between certain hours. The effect didn't carry on all the time. It concentrates in the centre of your house, in the middle of the night.'

'They were three houses once,' said Rog.

'Did anything happen in the middle one?' I asked.

'How should I know? I bought them as the three in one, ready converted. We've only been there two years.'

'When did all this start?'

'It's hard to say. It isn't an on-off thing. I became aware things were different only very gradually. A month past, maybe. Maybe longer. We went to my mother-in-law's for Christmas. I'm sure everything was normal before that.'

'How do you feel?' I asked diffidently, 'about getting one of these psychic research groups involved?'

His jaw dropped again. 'I feel horrified,' he said. 'Janie

will think I've flipped. I'm not aiming to explain any of this to her, you know.'

I looked at him. 'Get your priorities straightened out,' I said. I stood up. 'See you around.'

'You can't be going!'

'Why not? I've done what you asked. What you do next is up to you. I've given you my advice but you are choosing not to take it. Fine. Let me know what happens. Toodle-oo darling. It's been lovely catching up.'

I felt like Albert, I thought. It's hard having a lover called Albert. It's an unsatisfactory name in lots of ways, but he was a terrific lover. Once every two or three months we would go away together for a weekend and bonk ourselves blind for two days. Then we would return to our entirely separate lives.

I thought about Albert as I made my way over to my office to pick up my accumulated mail from the last few days. Our last weekend together had been taken in a hotel on the front at Brighton. There in a room lit by a vast window that let in a flood of sea-reflected light, Albert had dressed himself the way he liked, in a woman's old-fashioned girdle. The tight elastic webbing encouraged his cock to stand up hard and I enjoyed sitting on his lap, facing him, astride his legs, while he put it in me and made me squirm. I found the slight awkwardness of his peculiar fondness for restriction rather pleasant. Further, he liked me to strap on a dildo and come at him from behind, giving it to him up his rear between his tightly squeezed buttocks. Sometimes he just knelt with his bottom elevated and I played with his balls from between his thighs. These simple pleasures gave us much mutual entertainment and I was fond of my curiously-named lover.

A week went by. Then Rog phoned. He'd persuaded his mother-in-law to encourage Janie to stay with her on

the pretext he thought the house had something wrong
with it, an infestation of insects or something, and he
didn't want to alarm her unnecessarily. He would call in
the experts while Janie was away.

Now he wanted me to come so he could see if anything
would happen while Janie was out of the way.

'I said I wouldn't do it,' I said. 'The place gives me
the creeps.'

'It was your idea I got her out of the way.'

'That doesn't mean I have to replace her.'

'How can I get anyone else to come?' he asked. 'Be
reasonable.'

'Haven't you any other ladies on the side?' I enquired
sweetly.

'For heaven's sake, Red.'

'What you need is an innocent couple.'

'I haven't got an innocent couple. I don't keep people
in my back pocket. I need you, Red. Come on,' he wheed-
led. 'You used to be fun.'

I could feel myself weakening. Aside from anything else,
I had an itch to know. Passing time had made the experience more blunt. It was hard to believe my appetite had
been so terrifyingly ferocious. Anyway, I'd been all right,
hadn't I? I mean, no harm had come to anyone.

Rog would be there, safe old Rog. It was odd to think
of him like this. Rog had always been the dangerous one.
That is, we had been dangerous together.

When I was sixteen I had given him a hand job once
on the front seat upstairs on a bus. The bus had been
crowded. We had had schoolbags on our laps. We'd used
his scarf and my beret and the bags to mask what we were
up to, and with the sublime ease of youth Rog had come
very quickly.

Another time we had made it up a tree in a park. It
was full summer and the tree was very leafy, but even so
if I had fallen off the branch I clung to I would have

broken one of my necessary parts, quite apart from the indecency charge.

We'd been on the motorway another time and I'd put my head in his lap while he was driving. I sucked him to climax without him wandering from his lane. It had impressed me at the time and I admit it still did.

Then there was the holiday job I'd once had. I sold cigarettes from a kiosk so small it was like being in a cage all day. Rog had seen this as a challenge and while my top half had been engaged in performing my duties, he had been crouched at my feet with his eager strong mouth clamped over my sexual equipment. I had orgasmed during a transaction concerning pipe tobacco. Talking to people and taking money while my pussy was sucked and probed with a muscular tongue had remained a sexual highlight with me for several years thereafter. I could remember the entire experience in great detail. Afterwards Rog had lain at my feet while my nude lower parts felt cool and wet. My own sexual juices had dribbled down my inner thighs while I served businessmen with packets of cigarettes. It only needed one of them to peer over the high counter and he would have seen my pushed-up skirt and lack of panties. But no one did.

Rog and I went way back. It's true I felt a louse letting him down now. 'Well, er . . .' I said.

'You sexy lady,' he said softly. 'I knew a leopard couldn't change her spots. You are the best, lady. You are unique.'

Despite this flattery I decided to add a little wrinkle of my own.

'I'll let you know whether it's to be you or a man of my own providing,' I said sweetly. Two could play at exhibitionism. What was sauce for the gander could perfectly well be sauce for the goose. I might enjoy going through my sexual paces with Rog up above watching.

He gulped. I had him fairly caught. 'Right,' he said, with a notable lack of enthusiasm.

I arranged to come round that evening.

The thing was, who could I bring and how much should I tell him? I didn't want him predisposed to expect a sexual maelstrom because part of the point of the experiment was to see how external and objective the phenomenon was, if phenomenon there was at all. But some account of why we were in someone else's house for the night would have to be given.

I let my mind range lovingly over my stable of lovers. Not Albert, obviously. Not Charlie, either. He dealt in scrap metal and was one of the last romantics, always taking me to posh restaurants and the like. We usually went racing together, he was a great one for the gees and was an inveterate gambler.

He had a hard side, though, and could turn violent if he felt threatened. Not with me, I mean, but with other men. It had better not be Charlie.

James was married and couldn't spend a night away very easily so that let him out. James was a bit kinky, too, and we always made love on fur. I found it very erotic. I had a fur mitten I used to stroke his cock with and he would wear a fur hood and mask and lick my pussy, rubbing his face gently between my legs as he did so.

Then I had it. Nick. Nick was a victim of the City's retrenchment in personnel. He was some kind of economist or financial forecaster and he was taking unemployment hard. Lately he had seemed a little more prosperous and I was trying not to work out the possible sources of his new-found income.

The thing was, Nick was young, dirty-minded, inclined to take risks and unbothered by other people's opinion.

I gave him a call.

'It's Red Marsden,' I said. 'Can you talk?'

I knew he had other ladies and I didn't want to embarrass the guy.

'She'll have to lump it, won't she?' he said genially. I

heard an indignant female squeak in the background. What a bastard he was, I thought cheerfully. I knew he kept the phone by the bed.

'You fixed up tonight?' I asked directly. You didn't need to flannel with Nick.

'Possibly. It depends what you're offering.'

I heard the female in his bed expostulate.

'I'm sitting someone's house,' I said. 'There's been trouble with squatters in the area and he doesn't want to leave it empty while he's away.'

'Any cash in it?'

'He's a friend.'

'His bed, eh?'

'That's it,' I said softly. 'I fancy having you in his bed.'

'Been a bit naughty, has he? A bit possessive, maybe.'

'You're sharp, Nick, you know that?'

He laughed. 'Where is this pad?'

'In Kent. It's a bit lonely.'

'Much of a drive?'

'Forty minutes from my place. I'll provide transport.'

'Tonight?'

'Yeah. Take-off would be about seven, if that suited. It's the dark that frightens him.'

'It frightens all of us. OK, Red. Pick me up about half six, then. I'll have my toothbrush ready.'

I called Rog back. 'I'll have company,' I said in dulcet tones. 'You'll have to leave the wherewithal for a spanking meal, booze included. And you'll have to stay out of sight.'

'You bitch,' he said, gasping a little.

'I'll have to come over and get you fixed up in the loft, won't I?'

'Since your friend doesn't know what the house normally looks like, the hatch doesn't have to be sealed,' said Rog coldly.

'All the better. Can you swing yourself up into it without using the steps?'

'Yes. You'll owe me for this, Red.'

'No, I won't.' I was indignant. 'I'm doing you a favour, remember?'

'So you are,' he said and I grinned.

And that was that. The only thing now was to turn up.

FILE THREE

The man in the loft saw his old girlfriend and her lover enter his bedroom. They were full of food of his providing, high on booze he had paid for, and now he was going to see the woman he lusted for used and penetrated by another man.

She was laughing. She opened her blouse and let her big white breasts spill out. She lifted them and pointed them at her lover. A moment later his hands were fondling her and his lips were touching her exposed flesh.

He began to suck her breasts, coiling his tongue round her long nipples and sucking the chestnut-pink aureoles deep into his mouth. She put her head back so that the man in the loft could see her throat. She thrust into the mouth of her lover and moaned with pleasure.

He pushed her to a chair in the room and made her bend over it. Slowly he hoisted her short tight skirt, inching it up over her rear. Now her bottom clad in tiny panties was revealed. The man fondled this appreciatively for a moment, as if comparing it to the feel of her breast flesh. Then he hooked his fingers under the edge of the panties and pinched the tight white skin.

The woman squealed.

Her skirt was round her waist. She was doubled over the chair, her hair all tumbled forward so that her head and face were hidden. The man with her bent down and took the material of her panties between his teeth.

Deliberately he tore the delicate stuff. He twisted the shreds of lace out of the way. Then he pinched her buttocks again.

He opened her buttocks and contemplated the vision before him. Then he reached in and pinched her, her labia, parts of her vulva, her unhooded clitoris.

She cried out and writhed on her uncomfortable perch.

Her lover laughed. He picked up a tube of something from the bedside table. It was a jar of deodorant or a shaving stick or something similar, the man watching from above couldn't tell exactly.

Her lover deliberately pushed the fat tube into her pussy. He laughed to see it sticking out of her. Then he swiftly slid a finger into her softly pouting anus. With his free hand he smacked her on her buttocks.

He smacked harder. The tube in her pussy wobbled. His finger up her rear slid further in and his hand moved as he wriggled it. He smacked her on both buttocks really hard so that her flesh stung and all the time she shouted out.

Suddenly the tube shot out of her, expelled by her orgasmic contractions. Immediately her lover fell to his knees and sucked at her wet pussy, keeping his finger in place and working it cruelly. Moments later he pulled her roughly off the chair. She rolled over as if she was drunk. Her hair was all over the place. Her breasts thrust out lewdly from her opened clothes. Her skirt was still wrinkled up around her waist. Her legs were gawky, like a foal's. She didn't seem able to stand up properly.

Her lover forced her over to the bed. He threw her on it and immediately jumped on her. He took hold of her wrists and held them with one hand. With his other hand he loosened the knot of his tie. He got his tie off and then he used it to tie up the woman's wrists.

He tied her to the pine bedhead. He bit her breasts and then he opened his trousers. He put his erect penis into her breasts and rapidly bought himself to climax, holding her breasts tight so that they squashed his prick as he masturbated himself.

After this he sat back. He reached lazily over to the bedside table and found his cigarettes. He lit himself one, watching the woman tied on the bed with his sperm trickling between her breasts. He was sitting astride her so that her lower body was pinioned by his weight.

The woman shook her head to get her hair out of the way. For a moment they spoke together, low-toned, so that the man in the loft couldn't hear what they said.

Then he saw it. At one moment the man sat astride the ravished woman casually smoking, laughing down at her helpless position. In the next moment he was frozen, stiff with tension. The woman slack under him went rigid. She uttered a low keening noise and her body began to lift from the bed, pushing the man seated on her up at the same time. She strained against her bonds, using her shoulders and legs to heave upwards. At the same time she rubbed into the man on her.

She was begging for it.

Clumsily her lover moved back so that he was between her legs. He put his cigarette in a saucer he had brought through with him. The woman stayed lifted, her back raised clear of the bed, her feet dug well in and her legs wide apart. Her lover made a grunting noise and then he dropped his trousers to his knees. Still kneeling he thrust himself forward. He didn't use his hands. His sex was ramrod stiff. He simply plunged it in and used what was in front of him to relieve his need. Leaning back he shuddered at his hips hard against her raised vulva. Then he was done.

Five minutes later the woman took him again, in her mouth this time. His trousers were round his ankles and he lay over her face as if he were doing a press-up. Again the man in the loft could see his shuddering hips. His buttocks were tightly clenched. Below him the woman gobbled eagerly at the stiff penis in her mouth till the man came again. They lay a little dizzily after this, then he jerked up again and pushed helplessly at her sex, as though he was a marionette and not in control of his strings. It was some time later that the watcher in the loft saw that he had entered her by a different way, in her rear, not in her pussy at all.

By this time the watcher in the loft was in a sorry state himself. His hand worked his sex constantly and it was as if the flow could never be stopped, only temporarily interrupted. He felt a fire in his penis and he struggled to put it out, to relieve himself. He struggled to satisfy his insatiable lust. He tried to bend himself double and suck his own sex. Finally he laid his hands on a piece of copper tubing cut by a plumber some time in the past when the plumbing was modernised. The tube was barely two inches long. The cut edges were rough, very rough. The man in the loft pushed his tender delicate bulging penis through the tube and jerked himself against its confinement and abrasion. Even that was only a partial easing of his need.

The woman also was consumed by lust. As the panting man came once more in her and hung for a moment, gasping with exertion, she began to move again, needing him to make it in her, needing him to satisfy her.

He did his best.

FILE FOUR

Testimony of Nick Farrell

At first Mr Farrell swore he had no recollection of the events hereinafter described. He admitted his mind was fogged, stating that he 'must have had sex with Ms Marsden, that's what they always did' but that he only remembered falling asleep.

When pressed, he said that he had faint memories of dreams, sexual dreams, which he had disregarded. Finally he agreed to describe these 'dreams' which he then recalled in considerable detail. He maintained to the last, and indeed still maintains, that he did no more than sleep and dream in the room in Roger Greaves' house. Red Marsden, he says, is 'one hell of a lady' but for himself, he can only tell the truth as he remembers it.

He refuses to spend another night in the room, however. He states this is because it is a futile exercise. He has nothing to be afraid of.

My name is Nick Farrell and I'm a market analyst temporarily freelance. I'm friendly with a woman named Red Marsden. She's older than me, I think, but she is real dynamite. I always have fun with Red and she is a lady who doesn't seem to have the word 'no' in her vocabulary. There's no romantic nonsense either. She's like a man in that respect. She knows what she wants and she goes for it, bald-headed. I admire her.

She asked me over one time to house-sit, she said. I guess she was getting one over some dumb lover who had been too possessive, or maybe he had given her the runaround. I don't know and I didn't care. The thing was, I was in rather low financial water and she offered me for free a big lush meal with all the alcoholic trimmings plus her generous body to play with afterwards in this other guy's bed. It tickled my fancy, I admit, and I went along with it out of devilment and because I like a good time, and that's what you get with Red.

I thought the house was creepy. It was old, stuck out in Kent down some go-nowhere lane and it was that dank dripping time of year when the countryside is wet and cold and nothing looks as if it'll ever grow again. It was dark as hell, too.

You could see a woman lived in the house. It was prettified with all the expensive little decorations women seem to think important. There were lots of artificial cottage ambience in stripped pine, all set off with fancy dried flower arrangements and little woven baskets full of smelly dried leaves. Rural Hampstead, I call it.

Red and I fed well and we sank some booze. The guy kept some decent wine and we reduced what he had on hand by a noticeable amount. Then we went through to the bedroom and made it a couple of times and we went to sleep. At least, I did.

Now that's all that happened. But I've been pressed on this and certainly I had some very peculiar dreams. I don't mind describing the dreams though I don't see the point. I admit I've never quite had a dream like it before but I don't see how that proves the room was haunted or anything so stupid. I didn't like the house, it's true, but then I don't like the countryside anyway.

They were dreams about some man and Red. I dreamed he tied her wrists to the bedhead, one to each corner of the bed. Then he sat astride those great white breasts of hers till he could feel them soft and cushiony between his thighs. He had a fat erection and he laid his cock between her breasts and he began to rock backwards and forwards. Red didn't say anything. She tossed her head from side to side till all her hair was a red tangled mess round her face. Her pointed tongue kept coming out from between her lips. At one point the man on her was so inflamed by this that he took his cock from between her breasts and stuck it on her tongue and rubbed it there for a while. Then he put it back between her breasts and he held each breast and pushed them together while he went urgently backwards and forwards.

All the time she kept pushing up into him so he felt her writhing up against his balls, egging him on, wanting to see him come. When he did come it was good. His spunk went all over her breasts and her upper chest, dribbling out across her shoulders. She twisted her head up as best she could and she licked at it. Her red hair got sticky with it. The man knelt up then so his cock hung limp between his legs. Red sort of gobbled at it, sucking it into her mouth and tonguing it till it was inflamed again, all in no time at all, in the way it goes in dreams.

Now he moved off her and sort of took a look at her. Still she didn't say anything. But she moved all the time, squirming and pushing her body up. He could smell how much she needed it.

He laughed then, I think. He was certainly amused by what was happening. He took one of those long shapely legs and he doubled it over her body, tying it to the bedhead where her wrist was. Then he tied the other ankle in the same way. Because her legs were held open, he could look straight into her sex and he really liked this.

He looked at it for a bit. She was wriggling but she couldn't move properly at all. She kept squeezing her pussy muscles though and the man watching could see this. He found it fascinating. Her clit wobbled about, her pussy entrance squeezed shut and came open and all the shapely bits in her cunt waved around. He poked in a curious finger and found her warm moist squeezing pussy very nice. Her thighs were flattened and squashed against her body. Her breasts strained, crushed between her strapped and bound legs. Her vulva pushed up in the confined space allowed it, tufts of red springing hair crushed against the white thighs. The dark pink of her interior sex was exposed and it made a striking contrast. All the time she moved, pushing to get him to do something with her sex.

He took a shoe, one of hers with its high four inch heel, and tipped wine from the bottle by the bed. It was red wine and he tipped it from the shoe to dribble over her straining pussy. Then he licked up the wine, licking her crisp squashed sex flesh as he did so. He enjoyed the mixture of tastes and he enjoyed the sight of the dark wine, the red public curls, the white thighs and the pink throbbing vulva all squashed together.

He nipped her clitoris a couple of times. Then he inserted the neck of the wine bottle in her anus.

This he found really interesting. He tipped the wine up carefully and let it fall back. He pulled the neck of the bottle out of her anus and licked the winey hole. Then he put his finger up it.

Red began to pant and bounce up and down, straining against her bonds. He saw her pussy foam as he idly worked his finger backwards and forwards in her grapey hole. He bent down and ran his tongue lazily along her bubbling slit. Then he tipped some wine on to her orgasm, holding her cunt open as best he could so the wine went into her body even as it climaxed. He put the neck of the bottle back into her anus, carefully stretching the puckered flesh and easing the dark green blunt glass in as far as he could make it go. Her pussy bulged now. It occured to him to slide his fingers into her vagina and feel the bottle from within her body, how it penetrated her rear.

He worked it in a bit more. He had three fingers in her pussy and it convulsed hard around him. He screwed the wine bottle round and round and then back again, enjoying the sight on her little brown bottom hole distended and distorted by the intruding blunt object.

Looking round him he now picked up the shoe again. Red wore shoes with long pointed toes. Almost absently, as with a detached curiosity, he fed the point of her shoe into her body. Now she was penetrated in one orifice by the wine bottle which protruded like a vast green pupal sac from her rear, and in her other orifice by her own shoe. It was amazing how much of the toe he could insert into her pussy.

For a while he screwed the bottle round and back watching her buttocks quiver and strain, while simultaneously he pushed the shoe in and out to masturbate her eager sex with it. It seemed to him she was in constant orgasm and he felt he played her like an organ, pulling out and pushing in stops.

Red had been wearing a necklace of fat wooden beads which she had removed before getting ready for sex. The man's idle fancy saw these now. Abandoning the bottle and the shoe, he picked the necklace up from where it lay on the bedside cupboard.

The shoe slid out almost immediately but the bottle stayed where it was, trapped by the tightly constricting muscle ring it had penetrated. The heavy bottle waggled slightly as the woman rolled in her sexual frenzy.

The man took one end of the necklace after undoing it, and began to feed the wooden beads into the woman's vagina. He heard her make a noise now, a formless inarticulate noise that was the essence of pleading, or so it seemed to him. He fed the wooden beads in one after another with a growing fascination at how many her sex channel could contain.

After a while he stopped, the last bead he had managed

to push in ejecting itself even as he watched. He pulled the necklace gently and another bead oozed out. He continued his gentle pulling. A third bead, shiny with love juice, oozed out. He revelled in the sight of the string of beads vanishing into her. He was enjoying this slow emission, one bead at a time, each distending the entrance to her sex as it squeezed out. It was nice to see her pussy entrance grow bigger, show its wet wooden pearl, let the wet wooden pearl begin to ease out and finally plop free of the pink creamy flesh.

When all the beads were out he looked thoughtfully at her straining sex. He took the bottle out of her anus and drank some wine out of it. Then he began to feed the beads into the passage the bottle had vacated.

It was a long necklace. He fed as much as he felt was right into her rear. Then he fed the other end back into her pussy. When this process was complete, he was delighted. The necklace had almost entirely disappeared save for the beads on display leading from out of her pussy between her wet red curls and her dark pink labia, straight to her little puckered arse. He fingered the wooden beads and rolled them about. The beads bulged wetly, glistening from her two orifices. He pulled slightly. In synchronisation, two beads, one from her arse and one from her cunt, oozed out with a gentle plop.

The man laughed. He pulled again. Again her body disgorged two beads, one from each orifice. He went on with his game until all the necklace was out.

Absently, while he planned what to do next, he lifted her taut buttocks on to his knees and entered the violated rear with his penis. It was a luxury to satisfy his own need and he held her helpless body while he went quietly about his business, emptying his cock into her rear when he was done. Her rear was agreeably tight and he enjoyed the crushing sensation on his hard member.

He stood up after this and watched, standing by the

bed for a bit. The woman was a mess now. Her face was slack and blunt with sexual need. Her hair was tangled all over the pillows and caught in sticky dreadlocks with his spunk. Her breasts were smeared with a membrane of drying spunk, her nipples projecting oddly from between her bound legs.

Her wet lust-dark furry sexual slit stuck up swollen from constant use between her bulging thighs. The sly fruity arsehole below it seemed to invite further ravishing.

The man wandered through the house into the kitchen. Here he found a length of clear soft plastic tubing in a cupboard. He took it to the bedroom and inserted one end into the vagina. He inserted the other end into that delectable, bitable arse.

For a moment he looked at the clear hoop of plastic joining her holes. He moved it a bit, sliding the ends further into her. Then he fumbled in his clothing and took out a penknife. He cut the tube. Now each of her orifices had a waving piece of tube sticking up.

He picked up the wine bottle and with infinite care tipped some wine into one end of the tube that led into her pussy. After several tense seconds, wine bubbled out around where the tube vanished inside her. He bent his head and licked up this wine. Then he put the tube end into his mouth and sucked.

The woman screamed. He saw her come, bubble into the tube, her love juice. She liked it. He sucked again. With a considerable effort he was able to suck the juices of her orgasm up the tube into his mouth. He tipped some wine in to flavour them vinously and then he drank from her climaxing body.

Next he tipped wine into her rear. Again it began to bubble around where the tube disappeared inside her. He arranged his head carefully by her rear and tipped gently again. Now he could lap the wine even as he poured. It was cooler than her body temperature and he wondered in an abstract way what it felt like, pouring cool into her heated parts.

Another man joined them at this point. He had no clothes on and he took no notice at all of the man whose dream it was. He went straight for Red strapped and doubled up on the bed. He pulled out of her the two tubes sticking obscenely from her body. With some difficulty he then worked his erect sex into her squashed and bulging sexual orifice. The dreamer, who had not closely inspected a couple having sex before, watched with interest as the cock went in and out, first pushing the pussy flesh and then dragging it out as it moved. He saw how the two colours of pubic hair mixed. He saw how the balls moved and what happened to them as the penis was thrust into the woman. What he found really interesting was that the woman's rear pulsed all the time her pussy was invaded. He managed to insert a finger between the struggling pair and he slid it into the woman. He was thrilled to feel within her the regular filling and emptying of her vagina. It was very interesting, a unique sensation and he savoured it. He wriggled his finger around in her elastic flesh and felt her wall of slippery muscles tremble and vibrate.

The man's actions, as he moved to climax, were sufficiently violent to make it necessary that he moved his hand away. He thought a finger might be broken at the least. He watched as the penis erupted and, after it was withdrawn, craned forward eagerly to see the man's spunk bubble from the sobbing vagina of the woman.

Even as a dream, the next sequences were hazy. The woman was released and for a time there was a considerable invasion of various bodily orifices by various bodily parts and with objects that came to hand. The dreamer felt every drop of spunk drained from his body, as though he were one vast manufactory and with its delivery (into the man as well as the woman, he fancied) he was sucked in and shrivelled. He felt smeared and saturated on his outside even as he felt drained and dry on his inside. He remembered sleeping, lying on his back exhausted with the woman's thigh between his own and her foot on his chest. He held her foot and he remembered the feel of it, the feel of her toes, before he slept.

FILE FIVE

Testimony of Roger Greaves
When my mother-in-law phoned up to say Janie had had
an accident, I felt a certain tenderness in my conscience
at having deceived her. I felt I was being punished. This
was stupid, I know that. I had deceived her for her own
good, to find out what, if anything, was wrong with our
house or with Janie herself. When she broke her leg I was
very sorry.

I spent a week living with my mother-in-law after this.
Janie was suffering from a bad break and had to spend
the first night in hospital. They brought her home to her
mother's because I had to be out at work all day and
her mother was free and willing to take care of her.

I don't get on with my mother-in-law and Janie is very
sympathetic about this. After an increasingly tense week
she suggested I say that I was worried about leaving the
house empty and I had better move back home, at least
for part of the time. I agreed gratefully and we were able
to present it to her mother without giving offence.

Strangely, during this time, I had forgotten about the
goings on in my bedroom. I think by now I had settled in
my mind that there had been nothing really, I had imagined
it. Then I brought Red Marsden on to the scene. I should
have remembered about Red. She is the hottest lady I
have ever known, utterly without shame, utterly ruthless,
and a total tiger for sex at any time of the day or night.

I had gone to her for help but I couldn't resist her when she came on at me. She had eyes of jade green, very wicked. I could only remember those wide thighs, those luscious fruity breasts, that ever moist clinging pussy. And I could remember all the dirty tricks she used to pull. She had the dirtiest mind of any woman I've ever met and she took some keeping up with.

She seduced me. There's no other way to describe it. She had done it as a little girl when we were at school together. By the time we hit sixteen she knew more about my cock than I did. She used to play with it wherever we went, in the park, on buses, in school. She couldn't leave it alone. I was obsessed with it myself, wanting to come again and again like any normal teenager. But Red made me come, she literally took me in hand till I was her slave, needing her to masturbate me on a daily basis.

I remeber groaning as I stood behind a tree with her, my trousers open and her hand flashing as she made me cream. She would put my hand up into her knickers, too. She had the pussy I felt first. She made me put my fingers inside her and wriggle them about. She made me play with her bottom, even at that age. She showed herself to me and she took a good look at me, in all the states of which I was capable.

Later she seduced me fully. She fed my trembling prick into her greedy hole and I've never known a moment like it. I knew I'd come home. I knew that's where I belonged. I've enjoyed being up inside women ever since and I swear I will till I die.

You don't marry women like Red. They eat men for breakfast. You just drop in now and again for the excitement and the experience, and then you escape and take it easy for a while, recuperating.

So over this strange thing that happened in my house, I decided that Red was to blame. Something might have been going on. Janie might have been having hot dreams, but the weird behaviour that involved myself with Red and then myself with Janie and Red, and finally that awful Nick guy Red picked up from somewhere, all that was caused by Red herself and her bizarre sexual temperament infecting us momentarily.

That's what I thought when I came home after Janie's accident. The only strange phenomenon was Red herself. Now I had met up with her again it might be nice to go and warm myself by her fires from time to time, when I felt a little jaded, but basically, for my sanity's sake, I shouldn't get too close.

Half way through my first night alone in my bedroom I woke up. I was rigid and sweating. I had been dreaming dreams so hot I couldn't handle it. I found that in my sleep I had got hold of Janie's sweatband, the one she wears when she plays squash. It was in the bottom corner of the linen basket, waiting to be washed. I had found this thing and then wound it round my cock and I was masturbating myself with it.

I left my bedroom feeling trembly and ill. I showered, gradually reducing the temperature till I was shivering under the cold needle spray. Then I went into the kitchen and poured myself a whisky. I sat there in my towelling dressing gown cuddling my drink like a sleepless child. Finally I went into the sitting room and bunked down on the sofa. I spent the rest of the night there.

I managed to find time to put in half an hour in a library the next day. That evening, armed with the information I had obtained, I contacted the number of an organisation that claimed it investigated paranormal phenomena.

Waiting until the evening to phone had been deliberate. I reckoned these organisations would be pretty one-horse. If they ran to daytime offices manned by permanent staff I would have to readjust my ideas.

No readjustment was needed. I got through straight away. I was dealing with a set-up run from someone's home address, just like I had thought.

I had taken some time to think what I might say. I didn't want to look foolish, yet having made the decision to call in the 'experts' I should at least suggest they had something to investigate.

When the man on the other end of the line asked me what I was calling about, it occurred to me that his less than enthusiastic tone might be the product of innumerable hoax calls. I hastened to make clear that that was not the case this time.

'My name is Roger Greaves,' I began. 'I think something very odd and unpleasant is happening in my house. I can't explain it. I should say that I am not someone who believes in ghosts.'

'Have you had any dealings with our organisation before, Mr Greaves?'

'No.'

'Or with any like us?'

'No. But this thing is so odd it defies rational explanation.'

'All explanations are rational, Mr Greaves. It is merely that some things cannot be explained by the ordinary laws of mainstream science.'

'You mean there are non-ordinary laws?'

'Just so. The National Health Service does not recognise certain medical practices known colloquially as alternative medicine. That doesn't prevent alternative medicine from curing many people and alleviating the symptoms of many more. You might say we consider we deal in alternative science. It has rational laws which have to be obeyed. It is just that they are imperfectly understood, or even not understood at all.'

'Can you deal with problems or do you just look at them and then go away?'

'It depends on the problem. We have relieved some unpleasant situations. Perhaps you could let me know just what your problem is.'

It was difficult to get the words out now it came to the point. 'I have, uh, a presence, um, in my house.'

'Yes,' said the voice on the line, gently, like he was encouraging a child.

'It's quite an old house. The presence is just in one part.'

His voice sharpened. 'One room?'

'Mostly my bedroom, but all the central area of the house. It's three cottages knocked into one, all on a line.'

'How does this presence manifest itself, Mr Greaves?'

'Uh, we feel it.'

'We?'

'My wife acts odd. I feel the strangeness and act odd myself.'

There was a long silence. 'You feel it physically? Or just emotionally?'

I was hating this. 'Emotionally, I guess. But very strong. It's creepy. I can't sleep in my bedroom any more. I wake up with strange dreams and feel very het-up. I only calm down when I get out of the room and into another part of the house. A female friend of mine felt it as a malevolent male presence, someone sly and given to cruel jokes.'

'Do things move?'

'No. Nothing like that. We don't hear noises, either.'

The guy sighed audibly. 'Can you give us your address? We'll come and make some preliminary readings.'

'What does that involve?'

'We set up equipment and monitor the infected area. We also see if we can subjectively experience the phenomenon as well.'

'Right,' I said blankly. I gave him my address.

They turned up, three of them, the next evening. I explained I couldn't feel the effects in the daytime except that I had now got nervous enough hardly to judge. They arrived at about five, with dark falling on a clammy cold November night and I had to arrange to leave work early to meet them.

I groaned when I saw the fanatical gleam in their eyes. The one woman and two men all had a kind of hairy out-at-elbows look. One guy wore a bow tie. The woman was plump and dumpy with her hair strained back in a bun. She was only about ten years older than me but it felt like a generation at least, so great was the difference between us. She kept blinking at me through her glasses.

They explained their equipment to me. One piece was little more than a radio receiver to receive, naturally enough, any radio waves emanating from the phenomenon. They would be searching up and down the frequencies later on. It was a weak receiver intended to receive only the most local of sources.

They had something to search in the infrared. And they had a simple video camera which they could link to a screen in a different part of the house.

All of this was fairly understandable. They had also some really whacky stuff for picking up psychic radiation. 'Psychic phenomena,' said the guy with the bow tie whose name was Andreas, 'distort the ether, much as gravity waves distort space. This instrument measures etheric disturbance.'

I didn't ask what ether was. I was just glad Janie couldn't see all this. She'd think I'd flipped. And if Red Marsden ever got word, I'd never hold my head up in public again.

They went all round the house waving receivers everywhere like paranormal vacuum cleaners chasing psychic dust. When I poured myself a whisky and offered everyone a drink, Andreas-bow-tie expressed as much horror as if I'd proposed eating babies.

'Alcohol disturbs the enamations,' he hissed.

'I'd have thought it relaxed you and made you more receptive,' I said sweetly.

'It fuddles the brain. We have to deal with unbelievers,

Mr Greaves. It doesn't help our case as researchers if we imbibe while on the job.'

They weren't interested in me. They had brought sandwiches and ate them in the kitchen, huddled together eagerly discussing cases they had known. I found them incredibly alien, like things from another planet.

Time went on and I relaxed in the sitting room with my feet up glowering at the news till they told me to switch the TV off. That distorted the emanations as well, it seemed. I was gloomily convinced by now that all this farce was for nothing. Whatever it was that Janie and Red and myself had felt, it wouldn't come while this nonsense was going on. No right-minded spirit would.

At half-past eleven the phone rang. I answered it, thinking it would be Janie. But a high squeaky male voice asked to speak to Andreas.

He took the phone eagerly and listened for some time to the torrent of words from whoever was phoning. The other two, Arthur and Kathryn I was supposed to call them, listened with their ears almost visibly pricked. They had been expecting this call, then.

When it was over Andreas turned to his followers, it seemed the msot adequate word to describe their relationship to him, and rubbed his hands in quiet glee. However, he spoke to me first, courteous indeed but enjoying the sensation he hoped to create.

'Well, Mr Greaves, this is most interesting, most interesting. That was Paul Reynolds, our local historian. Paul always researches the specific location for us. He is an archivist, you understand. He investigates the history of the place in which we are conducting our researches.'

'Has he come up with anything?' asked Kathryn. Her glasses gleamed with excitement.

'He has hardly had time to do a full investigation,' said Andreas pompously. 'But preliminary researches indicate that when these farm cottages were indeed three separate dwellings, there was a scandal attached to one of them, some unfortunate girl and the local miller, after which the girl was found dead. Burned.'

'Burned,' echoed Kathryn reverently. Some hairpins fell out.

'When was this?' I asked.

'Just a hundred years ago. Almost exactly. There was another death by burning earlier this century. That was during the war, the Second World War. It was certainly the middle one of the block, only the block had four cottages then so there were two middle ones. I gather one end cottage has since been demolished.' He looked at me enquiringly. I shrugged my shoulders. I had no idea. I was more interested in who might build next to me in the future than I was in what had existed in the past. 'How come he gets this information late at night?' I asked. It seemed to me they might be making this up. No one had asked me for a fee but I thought a financial touch might be in the offering. Their equipment might be daft but it didn't look cheap.

'He has access to parish records because of his work, but he can't use work time. So he does it after hours. He has found out who is listed as having died here and then, having their names, he tracks back through the written record to see if they are mentioned in life, or this place in connection with any event. It's very hard work,' said Andreas severely.

'Two deaths in a hundred years,' I said incredulously. 'Dozens of people must have died quite naturally in these cottages. He can't only have found two.'

'He's found two referred to elsewhere,' corrected Andreas. 'So far, that is. These things take time.'

'What was the scandal?' asked Kathryn.

The French clock on the sitting room mantelpiece chimed midnight. Despite myself I was getting interested.

History might be bunk, but hearing about times past under this very roof, the roof I owned, was strange and not unpleasant.

'Sexual,' said Andreas briefly. Kathryn blushed.

'Why should that rate an entry in parish records?' I asked almost absently. 'What was special about it?'

'The miller was a lay preacher, an important man locally and much looked up to. The man who lived in this cottage was the grave digger. The suggestion is that the miller came here about respectable business and somehow was alone with the girl. I don't know whether she was some little servant girl or a daughter of the house or what. I don't suppose the grave digger was rich enough for a servant,' added Andreas dubiously. 'Anyway,' he hurried on. I could see the discussion was distasteful to the company. 'They were caught in flagrante, as it were. The miller was hounded out of the district.'

'How unusual,' said Kathryn. 'Normally the man would say the woman tempted him and he would suffer nothing after such misconduct.'

It was fun to see the latent feminist in dull little Kathryn.

'It shows how shocked they were,' said Andreas. 'The girl lived here, apparently. But days after there was a renewed scandal.'

'What was that?' I asked.

'Paul didn't specify. The record was coy, as if it was too shocking to put down in print. But after that the girl ran out on the street in flames. She died shortly after.' Andreas was reading his scribbled notes from the phone conversation.

'Urgh,' said Kathryn. 'They must have attacked her.'

'Unless she committed suicide.'

'The presence is male,' I said and a silence fell.

Kathryn ran her fingers round the collar of her dress and undid the top button. Her face was a little red. 'Let's sweep the house,' she suggested abruptly. She wasn't talking about housework.

They walked up and down, going into each room and twiddling knobs and earnestly reading dials. Now it was Andreas' turn to look a little flushed.

'The bedroom,' he muttered. 'You said there was something odd in the bedroom.'

'That's where it's strongest,' I agreed steadily.

'Would you mind going into the bedroom and telling us whether you experience anything?'

'Yes, I would mind.'

He stared at me. 'Put one of your own people in,' I said curtly.

'Let it be me,' urged Kathryn. I shut my eyes.

Kathryn went into the room.

FILE SIX

A description of the video recording of psychic researcher Kathryn Pentecost

'I am hot,' says Kathryn. 'I'm very hot. Is the heating very high? I don't think I've ever been so hot in all my life.'

She removes her cardigan.

'I feel restless. I know I should loosen my clothes until they are comfortable and then lie on the bed and allow natural sleepiness to overtake me. That's what I normally try to do in these situations.'

She roams up and down the room.

'I certainly feel something. We are trained to disregard feelings prompted by a sense of expectancy or the cruel delusion of hope. But I certainly feel hot and restless. And not alone.'

She undoes some buttons on her blouse which has a high neck.

'My clothes are an unbearable restriction. A distraction. I feel I should welcome a presence and not show it fear. How we must frighten messengers from the other kingdoms. Yet we are afraid of them. Ridiculous. We could learn so much.'

She unfastens the waistband of her skirt and giggles suddenly. 'I'm like Alice. She grew very large and she grew very small. Perhaps I'm growing fatter, that's why my clothes feel wrong.'

She hesitates. 'I'll put out the light and lie down,' she

says craftily. She does so. The camera can record in the infrared and continues to present an image. The image is very strong. If there is a second faint image in the room, it cannot be seen. Kathryn glows strongly.

'Andreas!' screams Kathryn. Outside the men make a concerted move for the door handle. Only Roger Greaves keeps still.

'No,' sobs Kathryn. 'Don't come in. Don't break the spell.'

The men stop and go back to watching the screen.

'I feel it,' she whispers. 'I feel him. Mr Greaves is right. He's a man.'

She titters. 'He's a naughty man.' She takes off her blouse and skirt. She wears a nylon slip over her underwear and remains decently covered. She lies on the bed. She strokes her bare arms on their upper flesh. Then she rolls on to her face and loosens her hair.

Her hair was grey at the temples. When it was pulled back the greyness showed. Now it is forward and tangled around her face, it looks darker and she looks younger.

She begins to hum. She lies on her back propped slightly by the pillows. She raises one leg. The slip falls back. She undoes the stocking and begins to roll it off her raised leg. She strokes the leg which is smooth and young looking in the strange image. Continuing to hum she unfastens the other stocking and removes it.

Outside the room Andreas and his acolyte Arthur discuss in an undertone whether to intervene. Both men loosen their clothing. Only Roger Greaves seems relaxed though a closer examination would show that his hooded eyes are bright with anticipation. He has one hand casually in his lap.

Kathryn lies on her back and lifts each of her bare legs in turn. Her slip has fallen back to the top of her thighs and her briefs can easily be seen. She continues to hum in a droning, tuneless way, now loud, now soft, and from time to time she puts her fingers in her hair and feels its luxuriance as though it were a novel experience. She moves her body gently from side to side. It is a slow writhing, wriggling movement, almost voluptuous. It is as though she squirmed in fur so that the cool soft silkiness of fur caressed her skin. So powerful is the illusion that Roger Greaves blinks and looks more closely at his own bed on the screen, as if the coverings have somehow metamorphosed.

It is the woman, not the bed, who is metamorphosing in front of the men. They are silent now and frozen as rabbits in car headlights. They say nothing, watching.

Kathryn strokes her body. She lifts her hips and smiles, tilting herself invitingly to one side. She begins to wriggle out of her slip.

She is revealed in bra and briefs. Her body is not ill-made. It is square and strong with wide hips and a deep bosom. Kathryn removes her brassière and throws it to one side. She caresses her breasts.

Andreas and Arthur stare at the screen goggle-eyed. Roger Greaves walks over to them.

'Has she ever behaved like this before?' he asks. He has a hand deep in one pocket. He has to repeat the question before the men respond.

'No,' says Arthur hurriedly in a low voice. 'No, no.' He wriggles on his seat and emits a faint bleat.

Roger Greaves moves back behind the men till there is some distance between them. He opens his trousers, takes out his naked erect sex and begins to masturbate himself. The two other men don't notice because they are so absorbed in the events being depicted on the screen.

'I said you shouldn't watch from this part of the house,' says Roger loudly. He had wanted them to have been out of the central area altogether but they had insufficient length in their cables.

They take no notice of him.

Kathryn sits up. She leans forward. She feels her breasts, apparently admiring how they fill her hands, how they fall forward heavily.

She swings her head round so that her hair falls first forward and then round and streaming down her back. She laughs, falls back and hooks her panties off.

Arthur is bent double over his lap servicing his sexual need. Andreas takes no notice. Sweat rolls in large droplets from his brow. He ignores it.

Kathryn rolls about the bed totally naked, throwing her arms and her legs into different postures in a kind of erotic dance. She raises her chest, then her hips, a leg here, one arm there, pushing each part of her body into visual prominence.

Her breasts fall and roll heavily. They are very large. Kathryn finds some night cream on Janie's side of the bed and begins to put dollops of white cream on to her naked breasts. She rubs the grease into her skin. Her breasts shine dully. The nipples enlarge to saucer size. Kathryn comes on to all fours and looks directly at the camera. She shakes herself like a dog. Her breasts swing from side to side. The nipples are very long.

Kathryn looks between her legs. Her pubic hair is a dark erect fuzz at the top of her legs. Between her legs something can be seen hanging down. Kathryn makes an audible crow of delight. She plucks her own hidden flesh. Now her labia droops in to view. She comes up, still on her knees, and faces the camera. Deliberately she pouts at its unwinking eye. She runs her tongue round her lips. She straddles a little further apart. She puts the fingers of one hand between her legs and plucks at her labia. She pushes her hips forward. Her breasts slide stickily, shining with grease.

She puts the light on.

In normal vision she is startingly clear. 'Andreas,' she says in a high voice. 'Andreas.'

Wordlessly he abandons his seat and walks stiffly into the room.

The two watchers see him appear on camera. He goes over in front of Kathryn but she moves so that the camera is not blocked by his back. Andreas stands with his head bowed, quite dumb in front of the naked woman.

'Touch me,' she whispers.

A hand comes up hesitantly. Before he touches her, his second hand comes up. He makes a grab. A moment later he is grasping the two great sliding shining breasts. His fingers sink into their gleaming depths. He kneads at them desperately. Kathryn pulls her hair about her face and then hangs her head back till it all falls down her back again. Andreas sinks to his knees and begins to kiss her breast flesh.

He takes her nipples into his mouth one after the other. His free hand finds her thigh. Her inner thigh. His hand begins to slide up.

Kathryn holds her breasts up towards Andreas who sucks deeply on her right nipple so that the two men watching see Kathryn's breast stretch, the dark skin of the aureole disappearing into Andreas' mouth. He sucks very hard. The skin stretches. Kathryn leans back, arching her spine with her knees wide apart and her hair brushing the bed behind her. Andreas' hand comes up to where her legs meet her body.

Arthur, watching from outside, stands up with a muffled noise. He takes out his erect penis and begins to masturbate himself clumsily. He takes no notice of Roger Greaves who is standing just behind him.

On screen, Andreas crumples on to his knees. He begins to push his fist into Kathryn's unseen vagina. She makes a strange gurgling cry and falls backwards, splaying her legs wide and arching her back, inviting the man to come as deep into her as he can.

His fingers burrow urgently. He removes his hand and

stares at his fingers, almost with disbelief. Then he sniffs them. Then he pulls his clothes aside and falls foward on to the plush eager body on the bed before him.

Once joined with her flesh, Andreas grunts loudly as he works himself to climax. Outside the room Arthur removes his trousers and underpants. He flings the door open and rushes over to the bed. He gets astride Kathryn's face and pushes his thick sex into her face and mouth. Andreas makes no protest nor any sign that he has seen or noticed Arthur. Kathryn's body flexes up and down, despite the weight of the two men on her.

Outside, Roger Greaves trembles and holds his aching cock as if for support.

Andreas achieves climax and staggers back from the bed. Arthur pulls away from Kathryn's face and begins to seek a way into her body. It is as if he doesn't know how to perform the act of sex. He doesn't seem to be able to get the two correct body parts together. He hauls up one of Kathryn's legs revealing her swollen wet sex, but he is still kneeling across her face, twisted awkwardly round.

He feels into her hole and then licks his fingers. He pulls himself off her face, disregarding her entirely. He falls down her body facing the wrong way and then hunches himself and grasps his own swinging sex.

Panting and apparently bewildered, he collapses on Kathryn with his face in her groin. Then convulsive movements occur at his hips. He struggles down the bed and at last begins to turn round. He now has his face at Kathryn's sex again, but the rest of his body is falling off the bottom of the bed.

Kathryn lifts her legs up and catches them behind the knees. She holds them wide apart. Her sex is frothy with use. Arthur crawls into her.

First his face bumps her vulva. He opens his mouth in a howl and then plunges his face into the fruiting woman's body. There are loud slurping and gobbling noises. Then he crawls up until his hot wet face is in her large slithery breasts. He rubs his hot cheeks there. At last his penis is somewhere in the region of her vagina. His hips buck helplessly. Kathryn lies holding her legs up, grinning and humming.

Andreas comes heavily forward. He takes his colleague's beleagured sex and forcibly feeds it into Kathryn's gaping maw. The suffering body organ disappears with an audible slurp up into the orifice. Arthur's bottom begins to waggle and bump. He turns his head sideways and pillows it in Kathryn's breasts. A look of stupified pleasure replaces his anxious expression. He settles down to fuck peacefully in blissful contentment.

He finishes quite soon and bears all the appearance of a man intent on going to sleep. Andreas stares at him for a long puzzled moment. Then he bodily hauls him out of the sex of the willing woman and allows him to drop to the floor. Kathryn releases her legs and rolls slowly over. She elevates her body so that her bottom is high in the air but her face on the pillows. She reaches round behind her in what to Roger Greaves is an oddly familiar gesture. She uses her two hands to hold apart the cheeks of her bottom. All her sexual area is displayed, as is her anus. Andreas grunts and pushes his penis forward. For a moment it slips. Andreas keeps pushing. Now his sex has disappeared inside the woman again. He begins to jerk himself hard inside her.

Watching them, Roger Greaves has allowed his trousers to fall to his ankles. He has penetrated his own rear with an Etruscan effigy he bought as an antique. He now squats, staring at the screen, buggering his own arse with a fine and rare old artefact.

The video camera faithfully records Andreas falling heavily on to Kathryn's body. She lies on her front, twisted slightly to one side, one hand between her own legs and the other outflung, as though to welcome a new lover if one should chance by. Andreas sleeps. So too does Kathryn. On the floor Arthur is curled like a dog, also asleep.

Roger Greaves walks heavily to his bathroom and showers. Then he goes to his sitting room where he drinks a large whisky. Then he too falls asleep, stretched out on the sofa. His rather grim mouth relaxes.

The other three, in his bedroom, sleep with smiles on their faces.

FILE SEVEN

Testimony of Roger Greaves continued
Andreas and his people went away. They wouldn't talk to me, they wouldn't discuss what had happened. Andreas said that if I attempted to contact Ms Pentecost, he would set the police on me.

They didn't know that while they slept stupified by sex, I had copied the video tape they had made.

I now had a real problem. Janie was talking about coming home. I was frightened to sleep in my own bed. I was too embarrassed to tell anyone that something was wrong with my house. Even if I put the place up for sale straight away, I could hardly prevent Janie from coming home. I did not want her in the house. I did not want her in the bedroom. I did not want her under that baleful influence again.

It wasn't that with time and distance it hadn't been one hell of a thing. But I had the not-in-my-backyard syndrome really bad. I might have found the idea exciting in someone else's house, but I didn't want the problem within my personal four walls.

I did the only thing I could think of doing. I contacted Red Marsden again.

I've explained that Red is one frightening lady. You don't go to her to have your hand held and you don't go to her when you are feeling weak. She is a woman who sucks out of a man (often literally) what she wants. She's

95

powerful, gorgeous and greedy.

She is also crafty as a fox and under that mass of red curls she keeps dynamite instead of brains.

That cool lady hadn't stopped thinking about my problem. She listened to my description of the paranormal group's experience and we watched the video together, at her place.

We were both a little lickerish afterwards, I guess. I mean, the video was quite something.

Red looked at me archly. 'So how do you feel, lover?' she asked.

There was never any need to beat around the bush with Red. 'Getting inside your panties would be most agreeable,' I said.

'I could manage some male fruit up me,' Red murmured. 'But it isn't like it was at your place, is it?'

'No,' I said gratefully. 'I mean, I feel I could take some time over the business. I could employ a little subtlety. I could enjoy being teased a little. I want your gorgeous body but I'm not about to die if I don't get it.'

'Mmm,' she said, smiling. 'I know what you mean. If you were to rush off for an important appointment right now, I'd happily get out my toys and satisfy myself. By the way, do you know what I've found lately really turns me on?'

'No,' I said cautiously, bracing myself.

'I get a real kick out of having a man, and then knowing he's going off somewhere straightaway to have it with another woman.'

I stared at her.

'I mean,' she said deliberately, 'that what I like is, for example, having a really good session screwing with you here and now, and then you pulling your things on and going straight off to screw Janie. You know? You poke me and then you put the same thing in Janie while you're still warmed up. You get me?'

'I get you,' I said huskily.

'There are all sorts of variations,' said Red dreamily. 'I mean, I'd like to watch a man who's just had me have someone else. I'd like to be there, watching him pull his cock out of me and posting it in some other lady's mailbox, with it still hot from my body.'

'I understand,' I said.

'To get back to your problem, why don't we see whether we can reach the peak of desire we reached in your bedroom in some other set-up? Why don't we see just how unique the whole thing is?'

'How?'

'Well, I said I liked the idea of having you fuck me and then immediately fuck another woman.'

'Yes. You said that. We did it, though. I had you and Janie together.'

'We did it under that strange compulsion that operates in your house. Let's do something equally dirty we haven't done before. Let's see how worked up we get.'

'In my house, you mean.'

'In your house in the daytime. Not at night. Not after midnight.' Red looked at me soft and sly as a pussycat. 'It would be a scientific experiment,' she suggested.

I drew breath. 'What dirty thing do you suggest?'

'I've got this friend,' said Red and smiled. 'She likes really elaborate games.'

This was to prove to be no understatement.

FILE EIGHT

Game, as played by La Demoiselle Virginie and as told by her

I had been sent to this house in the country by Madame who had commanded me to take some comestibles to the old man who she said lived in the house. I had my basket full and, like Little Red Riding Hood, I went to the place Madame described, but I did not like it.

It was a very cold time of year and my little hands became chilled on the long journey, as did my toes, and I longed to sit by a fire and warm myself. But Madame is very strict with me and so I hurried on my errand and I hoped the old man would be kind to me and let me rest a little before I set off back to Madame.

The house was very dark and gloomy when I arrived. It was raining and the empty wintry countryside was bleak and bare. I shivered on the doorstep and at last I heard the slow shuffling step of the old man coming to open the door. I knew it must be him because Madame had told me he lived alone.

He opened the door. I felt very nervous, he was a big man, bigger than I had expected. 'Monsieur Plongeur-Profond?' I squeaked, hardly daring to raise my eyes and look him in the face.

'Yes,' he grunted.

'I come from Madame La Directrice. She asked me to bring this basket of food for you.' I curtseyed. I felt very

99

tired and hoped he would not send me straight away. I was tired and hungry.

'You had better come in,' he said and, though I was nervous, I was so grateful that I stepped straight indoors brushing against him in the narrow passage as I did so.

He took the basket from me. I peeped up and saw he was younger than Madame had led me to believe.

'What tasty morsels Madame always sends me,' he said. 'Are you new in her care?'

'*Oui, M'sieur.*' I curtseyed again out of politeness. Because we were still in the passage this meant that by accident my face came level with the front of his trousers. I saw that his buttons were undone and I fell right over with surprise. The next moment I felt his hand on my arm. He helped me up.

'You are cold and tired, child,' he said gruffly. 'Come in here by the fire and I will give you some milk and a biscuit.'

'Thank you, sir,' I said faintly, and the next moment I found myself in a sitting room beside a glowing wood fire, seated on a comfortable sofa.

Monsieur Plongeur-Profond went away and I sat happily by myself stretching out my toes to the fire and warming them. I slipped my shoes off and I rubbed my hands together. I soon felt much better.

Someone came into the room. I started back from the fire guiltily. Then I saw it was a lady.

'Don't be frightened, child,' she said. 'See, I've brought you something to eat and drink. Monsieur is very grateful for the things you have brought and he is writing a letter of thanks for you to take back with you.'

'I thought he lived alone,' I said.

The lady smiled sweetly. 'I come sometimes to help him here. Gentlemen don't manage very well by themselves, you know. So we ladies have to help.'

'Yes, Madame,' I said. 'Thank you for my food.' I began

to nibble a biscuit. It was very sweet, very good.

The lady bent down and felt my feet. 'Your stockings are quite wet,' she said. 'You must take them off. Here, let me.'

Without further ado she knelt down and reached under my skirt. Quickly she released the elastic that supported my thick wool stockings. She rolled each one down and slid them off.

'Now warm your bare toes,' she said. 'I'll put these to dry on the kitchen range. You stay there.'

She went away and I drank my milk and finished the biscuits, wishing there were more. I began to feel drowsy afterwards. The afternoon was wearing on to an early dark. The fire was warm and I was very comfortable.

I must have slept. The next thing I knew was that Monsieur and Madame were both in the room with me, talking quietly.

'See,' said Madame in a soft voice. 'The poor little bird sleeps. She is tired out.'

'My buttons have come undone,' said a gruff voice.

'If you were to take your trousers off, Monsieur, I could sew the buttonholes smaller so that the buttons did not keep coming undone.'

There was a rustling of clothing. Then I felt the sofa I sat on dip and bounce. I peeped under my lashes pretending I was still asleep. It was not Madame with her sewing box who sat beside me, but Monsieur in his underthings.

I saw something curious on his lap. I lay pretending I was asleep and watched all the time to see what the strange thing was. I had not meant to deceive these kind people but somehow I was pretending to be asleep and I didn't know how to end the pretence.

Madame spread the trousers on the floor and knelt with her needle and thread. It seemed a curious way to sew but I am only an ignorant young girl and it is not my place to question the activities of my elders and betters.

The thing in Monsieur's lap grew bigger. It was tubular, slightly shiny and a purplish pink colour. Ridges of smudgy blue ran along it. Then I saw there was another thing inside it, peeping out of the end. The shiny stuff was an outer case and something redder and angry-looking was beginning to poke out.

I was so interested in this strange object that I almost forgot my pretence of sleep. Monsieur Plongeur-Profond was reading his paper all the time, rustling it as he turned the pages, taking no notice of this fat tube thing in his lap.

After some time, a very quiet time apart from the rustling of the newspaper, Madame lifted her skirts and put them up over her back.

This made me very startled. Madame wore black floor-length skirts and now they were up her back as she knelt and sewed. Was her underwear wet so that she must expose it to dry at the fire? Were her legs so cold that she wanted them heated by the fire? Did she believe Monsieur would not notice, so engrossed he seemed in his paper? It was very odd.

Next the sofa moved. Monsieur was getting up. He put the paper on Madame's bent back and knelt in front of the fire. She took no notice of him. Then he began to undo her knickers, her long knickers, where they were buttoned. All her petticoats were already up out of the way with her skirts, on her back, under the newspaper of Monsieur.

I knew enough to know that this sort of behaviour was supposed to be very rude, yet Madame made no complaint and Monsieur said nothing at all. He seemed quite abstracted, hardly aware of what he was doing. The thing that made my eyes open wide, that almost made me gasp out loud, was that the big pink tube was now projecting forward with its angry red inner part pointing directly at Madame's bottom.

Was Monsieur a doctor? Was Madame in need of medicine for her bottom?

Very carefully, Monsieur opened Madame's knickers till parts of her buttocks were exposed. Reading his paper, and with one hand on the paper to keep it in place, he put the other hand into the gap in Madame's knickers and began to feel her buttocks.

Madame knelt, bent forward, and sewed with small careful stitches, making each buttonhole a little smaller.

Monsieur felt Madame around the region of her bottom for some time. He poked in a curious finger. Then he raised the large and heavy tube and began to push it into Madame.

This is a most hard thing to describe. The tube seemed to be slung on his front like a very low stethoscope. To put it into Madame, he had to come right forward between her legs and push his hips in. As a piece of medical equipment it seemed to me to be inexpressibly clumsy. I wondered if Madame was constipated, poor lady. Was the good doctor giving Madame an enema?

He grunted a little as the tube thrust into Madame. When it was driven home, his stomach was pressed against Madame's buttocks in a way I thought most rude. He then used both hands and opened Madame's buttocks wide. Now I saw that he had not put the tube in her bottom at all. I was very pleased because it was a fat tube and I could not but think that such a thing in one's bottom must be most painful. I would be most afraid of constipation if it meant such a large weapon would be placed in my little derrière. Nor could I see how it could scoop out what was stuck. Perhaps it was a little suction pump, I thought suddenly. Perhaps Monsieur could suck out Madame with it, and so cleanse her inner parts.

Now Madame took no notice at all of all this activity. Perhaps she was too embarrassed and that was why she pretended nothing was happening. It is hard for a lady to exhibit parts of her body to a doctor. Maybe the sewing was a little pretence, so Madame could behave as if nothing rude was happening.

The doctor had put his tube somewhere, however, so much was plain. Now he began to withdraw it and I saw part of its length come back into view. Madame had red hair, a bright copper red, a most beautiful colour, and I saw little red hairs cluster about the tube as it withdrew.

Suddenly, painfully, I blushed. I knew what part of Madame had received that tube. It was even more horrible to imagine than thinking the tube went into her bottom. It went in that very tight place that ladies have, the part right underneath us between our legs where we do our pee-pee from. Monsieur had his tube in that hole and now he was pushing it in again.

I watched with scarlet cheeks. Monsieur kept pulling the tube back until it was nearly out and then pushing it right in again. I had just decided that he did this because it must hurt Madame so much to keep it there, so deep inside her, when he started to do it harder, so that Madame was pushed backwards and forwards by the slam of his body.

She had to stop sewing. He stopped reading the paper. He moved his hips to which the tube was attached very energetically. I saw it looking wet or greasy, I couldn't tell which. What a terrible treatment. I wondered what could be wrong with Madame that this should be the cure.

Monsieur was now grunting with the effort of his medical care. His face was red and I could hardly accuse him of being a doctor who did not work hard on his patients' behalf.

Suddenly he pushed extra hard. He juddered slightly and then he relaxed, slumping forward a little as if to rest on Madame's back. Slowly he began to extract the tube. I saw to my amazement that it had gone quite small and soft. Now it hung down, floppy. Somehow he had emptied its contents into Madame. I looked at her exposed bottom and what was underneath, now that Monsieur was out of the way. I saw her flesh all bumpy and red between her fiery curls. A kind of froth dribbled down.

It seemed to me I must help. I stood up and fetched a clean napkin. I knelt down by Monsieur and began to pat and clean the parts Monsieur had been medicating.

Monsieur said nothing. He stood up and picked up his paper. The limp thing hung from his front lower belly. It glistened slightly. He walked out of the room.

Madame turned her head round. 'Why do you do what you do, child?' she asked.

'I thought you might be sore where Monsieur Le Docteur was treating you.'

'Monsieur is not a doctor,' she said.

'Then I do not understand,' I cried.

She was silent a moment. I continued nervously to dab at her underparts.

'What is your name?' she asked presently.

'Virginie, if it pleases you, Madame.'

'How old are you, Virginie?'

'Seventeen, I think, madame, though I am small for my age, I believe.'

'You have not been with Madame La Directrice very long?'

'No, Madame. I was in a convent but I did not have the vocation, they said. So I left. Madame La Directrice will train me to be a lady's maid.'

'You do not know what Monsieur was doing?'

'No, Madame. I thought he was a doctor. I thought something was wrong with your bottom, till I saw it was not your bottom that he put his tube into.'

'There is nothing wrong with my bottom. Come here, child. Kneel as I was kneeling.'

I did as she said. She came round beside me. She lifted my skirts as hers had been lifted. I wore no knickers and she had already removed my stockings. She touched my buttocks. Then she did what Monsieur had done to her. She parted them.

'Feel my fingers,' she said. 'This is your bottom, is it not?'

'Yes,' I said breathlessly. Her fingers fluttered in a tickly way on my skin.

'Now this is your woman's place.' She touched me lower down. She tickled me. The sensation was very nice.

'Yes,' I said obediently.

'A man puts his part in this place in you and that is how the act of sex is performed.'

I was silent. I did not know how the act of sex was performed. The nuns had never said anything about it. I thought only married people could do it and I suppose I thought you were given something to do it with when you got married.

Meanwhile Madame continued to caress my underparts and tickle them, a sensation so pleasant that for a time I was quite content just to kneel there with Madame.

I heard the door open and felt the floor move slightly.

'You don't mind if Monsieeur Plongeur-Profond is in the room, do you, Virginie?' asked Madame.

It was embarrassing, of course. He was not a doctor, Madame had said. And yet he had just seen Madame like this and all of her bottom without either of them seeming to be troubled by it, so how could a little servant-girl like myself complain? Meanwhile the tickling and stroking was so pleasant that I didn't want it to stop.

'Do you know what a man looks like without his clothes on?' asked Madame.

'I have seen pictures of the saints and martyrs,' I said.

'Without any clothes on at all?' said Madame.

'No, I have not,' I said.

'Perhaps Monsieur would be good enough to show you,' she said.

'But it will be a trouble to Monsieur,' I said timidly.

'No trouble,' he said gruffly. Then I looked up and he removed his underclothing and I saw the tube was part of his body. I think I knew now it was the male part.

He began to stroke himself and then he took one of my hands and made me stroke him. Madame continued to tickle me and I wriggled a little from time to time with the delight of what she was doing. Meanwhile I felt how strange was Monsieur. His male part was soft and silky smooth with the harder ridges and bumps of what I now knew to be veins. It was all nested in a cloud of dark curly hair. As I stroked his tube became bigger and bigger. At first, as it hung, the baggy things behind it were longer than it and it seemed to rest against them. But as it grew proud it stood forward and became long and fat. It was nice to touch, warm and silky, and I thought Monsieur most agreeable to permit this from me.

'Now, when a man and a woman copulate,' said Madame, 'he puts his male organ in this place.' She slid a finger inside me. That was very nice indeed and I found I could squeeze myself and attempt to trap her finger and keep it where it was.

I laughed. 'Monsieur is too big,' I said. 'He could never fit inside my hole. Why, Madame, even your finger feels tight, does it not?'

'Your hole will stretch and Monsieur finds it agreeable to have his organ squeezed,' said Madame. 'Try it.'

I did. I put my hand round the big purple thing and I squeezed. The red bit stuck out and Monsieur gave a pleased grunt. I squeezed a bit more. Then I remembered. 'But ladies and gentlemen must not do this thing unless they are married,' I cried. 'Monsieur cannot put his thing inside me until I have got a husband.'

Monsieur Plongeur-Profond laughed out loud. 'The little maid has the rights of it,' he said. 'I had much better not put myself into her until she has a husband, eh?'

'But what about me?' asked Madame and she waggled that finger inside me.

'The nuns never said anything about ladies,' I answered and rolled over on my back.

Madame pushed my dress up till my belly and little furry part were exposed. Monsieur Plongeur-Profond knelt by my head, watching. Madame came forward up my body, on top of me, and kissed my mouth. Then she slid my dress off my shoulders and exposed my breasts. She kissed them.

This was very strange. Monsieur reached out to the sofa and picked up a cushion. He lifted my head and placed the cushion under it so that I was pillowed and more comfortable. Then he bent over my face upside-down and while Madame kissed my breasts, he kissed my mouth.

I felt his hands on my face and neck, smoothing my hair. His lips were warm. Madame made my breasts tingle. She kissed me and kissed them and then she went back down my body and lowered her head in between my legs.

Monsieur came round beside me. He began to kiss my breasts and my face the right way up. At the same time I felt something hot and wet and tickly between my legs. Madame was kissing me there.

It is hard for me to describe the next part because all the sensations and activities were so new to me that I could hardly separate one from the other. Monsieur reached between my legs and held my flesh apart. Madame sank her tongue into my hole and prodded me with it where her finger had been. She placed a finger over the little projection I had and waggled it. Then she gently bit and kissed my bottom-hole. All the time Monsieur kissed my face and shoulders and breasts. My whole body felt very marvellous, sort of excited and pampered all at the same time. I could not help wriggling as they kissed and bit me with the pleasure of the thing, and then Monsieur actually wriggled my dress right off so that I was completely naked on the hearth rug between them.

I let them do whatever they wanted. Madame took me in her arms and kissed me very sweetly, opening my mouth and putting her tongue round mine. She kissed my eyes and my brow and she stroked my hair. Then she took all her clothes off, even her shift, and she lay so that our naked bodies were entwined in the firelight. Monsieur Plongeur-Profond took all his clothes off and then sat watching us.

I began to kiss Madame back. She let me kiss her anywhere. Her woman's breasts were very lovely and she let me play with them, squashing them, holding them apart, rubbing them and then, with great daring, kissing them, especially the nipples.

I was charmed when the nipples grew longer as I kissed them.

I kissed her side and her back as well. Then I ran my hands down over her bottom as she had done with me. I began to feel her there, to look at her and to touch what was normally hidden by buttocks and legs.

She opened herself wide and let me play and look and kiss where I wanted. She kissed me all over. She put a finger up inside my bottom. She began to kiss my sex and suck.

Now something strange began to happen to me. I felt myself grow very red and hot. A sort of bursting feeling started to grow inside me. I began to whimper. I needed something and I didn't know what it was. Monsieur came and held my hair out of the way and stroked my brow. I rolled from side to side but Madame kissed harder, biting my flesh, sucking on it, stabbing it with her tongue.

My belly grew tight and then suddenly it was as though a dam burst inside me and I went all soft and weak. I felt runny and wet at my sex. Monsieur left my head and went to look at my sex. Before I knew what was happening, he had bent his head and kissed my wet excited parts as well.

Madame turned away from me. She bent forward submissively and put her brow to the floor. Monsieur took his sex which was very big and fat again and began to slide it into her body.

'Let the maid kiss me,' she begged.

He withdrew with a grunt and I realised I was to kiss Madame where she had kissed me.

She was musky and strong. Her hair tickled my face. I bit her gently and tugged on the sticky-out bits of her flesh. Then Monsieur reached in and opened her sex hole for me. I pushed in a finger, and then I pushed it some more. Madame was very wet and very stretchy. I kissed that place and I sucked as hard as I could. Then Monsieur moved me gently out of the way and, where I had been tonguing Madame, he slid his sex-tube in right in front of my eyes.

I was fascinated as Madame's flesh expanded to admit such a proud intruder. I watched breathlessly as he pushed and pushed, seeing his tube squeezed by Madame's sex-hole, seeing it vanish into her body. He took my hand and made me hold the baggy things hanging down. He squeezed them using my hand and I understood that I was to caress and fondle them as he did his plunging business with Madame.

It was a very interesting process. I felt his nuts swell hard inside their soft baggy flesh. I tickled his hairy belly. I even stroked his buttocks. Meanwhile he pushed his sex in and out of Madame. He opened her buttocks and indicated I could play with her still. I put a finger in and began to slide it a little way into her bottom. She made a small howling noise and her sex-hole gripped Monsieur very tight. Then she grabbed for me and I slid myself under her body. She raised her face from the floor and soon I was lying right underneath her, each of my legs

110

wide to each side. She swayed backwards and forwards all the time as Monsieur thumped into her sex-hole. My face was under hers. Her breasts swung against my chest. She began to kiss me.

She kissed me very lovingly, also kissing my neck and shoulders and hair. All the time Monsieur continued to copulate with her. Madame reached a hand down and began to tickle my sexual parts again. They began to feel empty and forlorn. Then she juddered sharply and I heard Monsieur cry out. A few short jerks later and he was done.

He pulled me out bodily from beneath Madame and I sat up and looked at her pouting wet sex. I kissed it carefully. It tasted different now. Madame rolled over and sat up. She clasped me to her bosom and kissed my face passionately, ignoring Monsieur Plongeur-Profond absolutely. She cuddled me and kissed me, kissing my breasts and making my nipples grow. Her hand roved down and she tickled me and penetrated my body. She pulled my legs wide apart. Then suddenly Monsieur Plongeur-Profond began to put his half-hard sex-tube in my female place.

I wriggled and made faint cries of 'no'. I was sure the nuns would not approve. Monsieur was wriggling inside me in a very determined way and if the truth be told, I wanted him to do to me what he had done to Madame.

All the time Madame caressed me and kissed me. She opened my legs wide and helped Monsieur to push his sex into me. She even held my sex-flesh wide open to permit his easier ingress.

When he was in I felt very stretched and not entirely comfortable. Madame let me lie back in her lap so she could stroke me and help me to take his manhood in the proper way. She kissed my lips very lovingly and called me a good girl. Monsieur watched her kissing me and then he began to do the backwards and forwards movement he had done with Madame.

I felt I entered heaven. The sensation was utterly

delicious, better than the best chocolate, the most creamy cake, better than anything I had ever known. Monsieur pushed his fat thing into me, Madame kissed my mouth and caressed my breasts, and I lay between them doing nothing and letting my body sway deliciously as Monsieur surged forward.

It went on for some time, longer than it had each time with Madame. I laughed to think I had mistaken Monsieur for a doctor, and yet this felt very health giving and entirely charming. All sorts of wriggly feelings ran up inside my body and I even thought how nice it would be to have a finger inside my bottom again. This was most strange as only a short while before I had thought putting things up one's bottom very rude.

That bursting feeling grew in me again and suddenly I was gasping and burning up as my belly collapsed and wet flowed all around Monsieur's tube of sex. He then pushed very hard into my body and I felt him squirting great creamy jets into me. He began to ease his sex out of me and by bending awkwardly over I was able to see how my little pale pink place had become a great swollen sucky mouth, all frothy with sex-juice, and a deep rosy red.

I was so very happy after all this. We all sat a little while in front of the fire and then Monsieur stood up and put his clothes on, including the trousers that Madame had sewn for him.

'Shall I put my clothes on, Madame?' I asked shyly. I didn't know if everything was over or not and I had not yet been given the letter to take back to Madame La Directrice.

'No, no,' she cried gaily. 'I will make us all some tea. Perhaps you will like to eat some honey and spice cake before setting out on your journey home.'

'That would be most pleasant,' I said. I found that I was hungry and some tea would be much appreciated.

She glided out of the room and I sat very happily without a stitch on staring at the flames of the fire. Monsieur had put some more wood on it and it flickered madly now sending great sparks flying up the chimney.

'I will fetch the letter of thanks, child,' said Monsieur and then he too left the room.

Some time went by. I think I leaned back against the sofa and began to nod with sleep. The next thing I knew was that Madame La Directrice was in the room shaking the rain off her umbrella. She was very very angry.

I wrapped my arms round my naked parts and crouched frozen with astonishment on the floor. Neither the kind Madame nor Monsieur were to be seen. Or so I thought at first. Then I saw that Monsieur was standing quietly by the door into the room. He must have admitted Madame to the house.

'Where have you been all this time, Virginie?' demanded Madame La Directrice.

'Why, nowhere but here, Madame,' I said timidly. 'Where you told me to come.'

'I told you to come home as well,' she said wrathfully.

'But I was going to come home,' I stuttered. 'The kind Monsieur offered me tea.'

'Why have you got no clothes on?' shouted Madame.

'Because Madame kissed me and Monsieur put his sex into my sex-hole and it was very nice,' I said.

I was frightened of Madame La Directrice. We all were, at the house where she kept us and trained us. She was very strict and I had seen her being most cruel to the other girls when they did something wrong or made a mess. Now I saw that she was more angry than ever I had seen her. Her face was white in the flickering firelight. I became very frightened and would have shrunk myself to the size of a mouse if I could.

'Stand up,' she hissed. She removed her wet cape and stretched her leather gloves tight on her hands. Then she reached into the big bag she always carried.

I stood up feeling all my naked parts shamefully exposed.

'You slut,' she hissed in the same tone of voice. 'Look at you, naked as a harlot, your breasts and your sexual parts all exposed and on show.'

I felt the juice Monsieur had put into me begin to trickle down inside my thighs.

'Turn round and bend over,' roared Madame.

Monsieur Plongeur-Profond made no effort to intervene. The kind Madame seemed to have vanished into the regions of the kitchen. I turned round and bent over. I knew what was about to happen.

Madame beat us when we were bad. She had an 'instructor', as she called it. Sometimes she called it her 'corrector'. Now she would instruct and correct me with it. I would call it a whip.

It was more a cane than a proper whip. It was flexible, about some three to four feet in length and Madame liked to spank us on our bottoms in front of the other girls to humiliate us, when she thought we had done wrong.

It was my turn to be humiliated. I had to bend over and hold my ankles. I felt Monsieur watching me. Suddenly the whip struck my poor bottom and I gave a yelp.

She struck me again. I heard the whistling noise the corrector made as it came towards my tender flesh. Then there was the terrible stinging feel as the blow fell. I even heard the smack of it against my flesh. I knew my bottom would be smarting, with great red stripes across it. She did it again.

I began to cry hanging there upside-down having my bottom whipped. Madame interrupted herself to insert her gloved hand between my legs and open my sex-hole. 'I can see a man's copulatory juice,' she roared. 'You filthy little slut.'

I heard her give a queer moan. The next blow fell and all my bottom blazed as if on fire. I risked a peek between my legs and I saw, upside-down as I was, that Monsieur Plongeur-Profond had walked up to Madame La Directrice and calmly lifted her skirts. Even as she whipped me again, he put his sex up into Madame, bending his knees in order to adopt the necessary position.

This seemed to me to be so unfair that I fell to my knees. Madame whipped me again so that my skin smarted and tears sprang to my eyes. Madame bent forward and Monsieur began to push very hard with his sex, very fast indeed, as though he was specially eager to get the business over quickly. If I looked up I could see Madame La Directrice with her face red as a turkey-cock, her arm raised to beat me, and all her skirts up over her back.

Far from making her happy, his sex in her seemed to drive her to new frenzies of beating. My bottom stung and burned as the whip descended again and again. I roared and cried in pain. Madame thrashed and thrashed, bouncing to Monsieur's sexual thrusts even as she screamed 'slut' and 'whore' at me. Monsieur thrust and thrust harder, crying out himself so that between the three of us we made the most terrific noise.

Finally Monsieur was done. He pulled out of Madame's sex-hole, wiped his sex on the tail of his shirt and put it away. Madame stood straight and let her skirts fall back into her place. She stopped hitting me but I continued to howl dismally on the floor.

They picked me up and put me face down on the sofa. 'Pah,' snorted Madame in disgust. 'I haven't even broken the flesh. To hear the girl howl you would think she was half-dead.'

'You should be kinder to your tender charges,' murmured Monsieur. 'The poor child was only enjoying what all natural adults enjoy. Yet you blame her for such pleasures.'

'And if she gets with child?' said Madame acidly. 'What will become of her then?'

But Monsieur was not listening. Instead, he felt my

burning cheeks and his cool hands on my bottom were a great relief. He slid a finger between my buttocks and probed a little. I was surprised to find that with all the pain of my smarting cheeks, I still found his questing finger very pleasant. 'Will Monsieur do it to me,' I begged, snivelling and crying, 'to take away the nasty pain.'

He looked at Madame to see if she would permit such a thing. 'You might as well,' she snapped crossly. 'The damage is probably already done.'

He looked at me and I saw his eyes were merry. 'You will have to help him get up,' he said to me gravely.

'Please,' I sniffed, 'I do not understand.'

'I have just used my sex-organ in Madame as she beat you. He needs time to recover, or he needs some special stimulus. Perhaps you can supply this, child.'

'Oh, do what he wants,' said Madame La Directrice in tones of disgust.

'But I don't know what he wants,' I cried miserably.

Monsieur knelt by me where I lay on the sofa trying not to put weight on my bottom. He had his sex in his hand, very soft, barely standing out from his clothes. 'Open your mouth,' he said.

He got himself into a position where he could kneel over my face where I lay on the sofa. His sex hung down. Obediently I opened my mouth. He put his sex into it and began to instruct me in how to suck strength and firmness of purpose back into his organ. Simultaneously I was to caress his dangling balls which he hooked outside his clothing, in the way he had already taught me.

I worked hard at my appointed task and in so doing began to forget the enormous pain in my stinging bottom. I felt Madame La Directrice lift my legs and look into my used sexual parts. She prodded me with disgust. Then she slid the end of the corrector inside my body and began

116

to simulate the male sex-organ.

I couldn't have stopped her because Monsieur had me effectively pinned on my back with his great thing in my mouth. But I found I didn't want to. It was very agreeable to have her do this to my sex-hole while Monsieur came up to the full military stiffness he required from his sex-soldier.

My bottom stung. My sex tingled. My mouth tasted the heavy man in it. His balls were baggy soft outside and firm and nutty inside. I tickled and sucked and wriggled and suddenly I thought I might be having that tight feeling in my belly again, the one that preceded the exploding feeling of release.

Monsieur moved down me and Madame La Directrice removed the corrector from inside my body. Now Monsieur slid his mighty weapon deep into me. Madame pulled my legs wider.

Monsieur began to plunge rapidly into my tight place so that I was gasping at the extremity of the stretched feeling. As he did so he pressed down on my sore bottom which rubbed into the sofa. It began to sting fiercely again but in a way I can't describe, this had the effect of making me more desperate for the fullness of his mighty sex in my hole. Indeed, when Madame La Directrice found a way under Monsieur's bottom to reach my body, and then under my body to reach my little bum-hole, I found the insertion of the corrector into this orifice astonishingly pleasant.

I gasped and panted as my bottom stung. The object up inside me rubbed agreeably, making me feel saucy. The huge sex-weapon of Monsieur filled my sex-hole and stretched it with painful tightness, but it was a pain I enjoyed fiercely. My little breasts bounced around. Madame La Directrice was saying that perhaps I should not be a lady's maid, there were other professions where my natural talents could be better exploited. She did not seem angry any more, as though this of the sex-holes pleased and appeased her.

Tea would be coming soon with honey and spice cake. I was very happy.

As a result of this experiment conducted in the late afternoon and early evening in the sitting room of the 'haunted' house, both Red Marsden and Roger Greaves state unequivocally that despite performing the sexiest scenario they could envisage with the help of a third party, the degree of arousal and the ability to perform remained within what they would describe as 'normal' parameters, that normality being defined in terms of their previous experience. The red-hot need for continuous and ferocious copulation was absent, though this was the determining feature of sex in the bedroom in the house past the hour of midnight. They have allowed the girl who played Virginie to describe the scene in great detail to emphasise that although they indulged in what might be called an orgy of sex, it was nevertheless qualitatively and quantitatively different from the compulsive 'haunted' sex.

FILE NINE

*History of Lane End Cottages: report of local
historian*

There is evidence of dwellings at Lane End, Fibsey, Kent,
for some two hundred and fifty years. All the original
buildings have long since vanished and their precise nature
is no longer known, though it is presumed they had agricultural connections.

The present houses were initially constructed in plaster
and lath on an oak framework around a century and half
ago. Later the plaster interstices were infilled with brick
giving the basic construction still existing, though the
houses are now extremely modernised.

There were six cottages at this time though only three
now remain, knocked into a single long dwelling. Earlier
this century they were tied cottages belonging to Lane
Farm which has since been incorporated into the Marfleet
estate. It was at this point that the cottages were sold off
and moved into private hands.

There is little local history connected with the cottages.
Checking the parish registers for deaths, as requested, has
produced the following list, herewith included as Appendix A. Appendix B is drawn from this master list and is a
list of all the deaths about which some further mention
was made in the annals of the parish. The relevant information is included though there has been no cross-checking
as to its accuracy.

Appendix A: not included in this report because of its subsequent irrelevance. The deaths listed fall into three main categories. The first is that of infant mortality. The second is that of death from disease, including the devastating effects of periodic scourges of, for example, scarlet fever, typhoid fever and so on. There is a third category of death from agricultural accident. Apart from these categories, the deaths from old age are few and far between.

Appendix B: deaths not belonging to the above categories about which some mention is made in the historical record.

1832 Martha Jakes of Lane End murders her husband, Thomas Jakes, during drunken celebrations following the passing of the Reform Act. She alleges that he attacked her and she was defending herself when the accident of his death occurred. When questioned concerning the nature and purpose of the Reform Act, claims she thinks it will make poor folks richer. Sentenced to death at Tonbridge Assize.

1841 Chimney collapse at Lane End, causing the death by head injury of William Makepeace. Landlord admonished and told to repair said cottage.

1843 Death by burning of Jenny Wilkes. Eliza Jakes taken for trial to Tonbridge Assize after neighbours attest that John Jakes and Jenny Wilkes did 'abandon themselves to lewd and licentious practices before the eyes of Eliza, John's wife, and several neighbours including the parish beadle who was visiting at the time.' [NB This was evidently a great scandal. It is hinted that the beadle and the neighbours who were present actually joined in whatever happened and something of an orgy of vice took place. One can only assume this was inflated by gossip since it seems to be inherently incredible. However, see 1893 below for a curious repetition of this case.] Eliza Jakes was released presumed innocent and the death was blamed on the new chimney installed the previous year.

1855 Death of James Tubey of Lane End in drunken brawl with a tinker. Tinker arrested and subsequently condemned to death at Tonbridge Assize.

1893 Death of Alison Makepeace of Lane End by fire. Facsimile of newspaper cutting appended:

> *Scandal at Lane End, Kent*
> *There was horror and disbelief expressed at the Coroner's Court convened to investigate the Death of Alison Makepeace who died in flames in front of several witnesses on the last Monday in November at Lane End Cottages, in the Parish of Fibsey, Kent.*
>
> *Alison Makepeace was a young woman who was the eldest Daughter of Arthur Makepeace, Farm Labourer, of the same address. Altho' the family were known to be quiet and sober People who always attended Church, Alison had become increasingly wanton in her ways to the great distress of her family and neighbours. Her father serves as Gravedigger for the Fibsey Parish Church. She had been visited by her Priest and was the subject of much Prayer but had become so enamour'd of her Vice that few men were safe in her presence, it was attested. In particular, the local miller, a most worthy man, was corrupted by the girl's voluptuous depravity. This was so extreme that in her latter days, some said, she expos'd her Private Parts to anyone who wished to see and though many good men came to Remonstrate with her, there were none that succeeded in breaking her addiction to Vice. Her Priest, the Reverend Samuel McAlister, in particular spent one whole night locked in with the afflicted girl attempting to Exorcise the wicked Spirit he believed possessed her, but to no avail. He was afterwards very exhausted, he confessed, though he remained willing to try again for her Soul's Sake.*
>
> *The Coroner commended the Good Man for this strenuous activity with the lost girl.*
>
> *All Fibsey was in an uproar at the girl's open and lewd*

behaviour. On the day in question Alison ran out into the road in front of her Father's house burning like a Torch. Neighbours attempted to smother the Flames and save the girl's life, but the attempt was to prove hopeless. In the cottage were found three strange men, believed to come from a neighbouring Parish, in various states of undress, who claimed to have been asleep at the time. They could not account for the girl's catching Fire and were themselves unharmed, as was the house.

The Reverend Samuel MacAlister opined that God had struck the girl down by means of a Thunderbolt, and was himself earnest in Prayer that all should learn that the Deity could not be flouted.

A verdict of Death by Misadventure was recorded.

1904 Death of Edward Grey of Lane End Cottages from Cholick. [NB This death should possibly be included under death by disease but indigestion seems an inadequate reason to die, among the poorer classes. Possibly it was food poisoning.]

1914–1918 Deaths relating to war or war wounds.

1932 Cottages sold off after Lane Farm absorbed into Marfleet Estate.

1939–1945 Deaths relating to war or war wounds.

1943 Death of Linda Campsey, land girl, boarding with Mrs Martha Makepeace, No 4, Lane End Cottages, Fibsey. According to newspaper reports, Linda was found reduced to ash apart from her feet and ankles in the kitchen of No 4, Lane End Cottages. Only a very intense heat could have produced such an effect. The kitchen was substantially undamaged by fire though an unpleasant oily vapour clung to the walls and furniture. The floor beneath Linda's remains was found to be scorched and the vinyl tiles were partially melted. The hearthrug, some eighteen inches from the remains of Linda's head, was undamaged.

Enemy planes had passed over in the night and there

was talk of a new weapon, some kind of fire device being dropped as a bomb but no evidence was found for this.

Linda was a south London girl who had been in the area for six months. She was very popular at the Marfleet Arms, the local public house, where she had many friends, especially among the young men of the area.

1951 Death of Martin Johnson of No 2, Lane End Cottages, Fibsey, in a car accident in Tonbridge.

1965 Death of Martha Makepeace, No 4, Lane End Cottages, Fibsey, as a result of a bone being lodged in her throat.

1984 Death of Jeremy Tubey aged 14, No 3, Lane End Cottages, Fibsey, struck by car while riding his bike.

FILE TEN

Testimony of Roger Greaves continued
It was typical of Red that she should set up her so-called
scientific experiment to involve sexual excess. Yet she
had a point. We had been experiencing very curious
sexual effects and there had been times (they are in
this record) when I had doubted the evidence of my own
body. Red was so electrifying that it would be hard for
someone who did not know her as I do to separate the
two effects. I mean the Red Marsden effect and the
house effect.

Red turned me on. She worked me up. She encouraged
me to do amazing things, dirty things, and then to repeat
them. She encouraged me to experiment. She made me
come and she made me come again. Her body was like
a great ripe mound of fruit. She made a man want to
crawl naked over her and cram her fruit into his mouth
till the juice and the pulp dribbled out. I wanted to
squeeze her fruit and crush it with my body. I wanted
to stuff myself with her and then some. She was for
plundering, she demanded excess – but this was the
normal Red. She'd always been like this, even as a
little girl teasing me and putting my hand in her
knickers.

What happened in the bedroom was not like that. It
was more. It was more violent. It was more compulsive.
My body became a robot almost, or a puppet. I jigged

helplessly, frantically, to the demands of my cock. I think there are insects that indulge in mass copulations. I felt like that. I was submerged in sex and my body jerked away doing what it needed to do without sense, without control, almost without me being there, in the sense of my mind controlling my body. It must have been like that for Janie, too. When I saw my wife wriggling hotly in the bed, I didn't like it too much. I mean, I liked it to be me who worked her up, not her own imagination though I can see that this is selfish of me. But Janie performed all her acts of sex while she was unconscious. Asleep. The mind wasn't needed at all. The body could go through the motions without its assistance. I mean the conscious mind, of course. The awake mind.

What use is anything if you can't remember it? If it happened in your sleep? It's creepy, acknowledging the existence of this other life where your body obeys a different set of rules.

I don't know much about dream theory but I've heard that dreams are supposed to be a way of our unconscious reorganising the experiences of the day and assimilating them into the persona. Dreams express anxiety too, and we get mentally ill if we can't dream on a regular basis. If this is so, then dreams are in part a kind of mental housekeeping, like a subconscious Filofax. And in part they are a release of tension because they allow us to work through alternative scenarios that express or release fear in harmless ways. They vacuum clean emotion spilt in the day and allocate it to artificial events so the slate is clean the next day.

If any of this is close to the truth, what was Janie dreaming about? Was she having very sexy dreams, and if so, why? Had she become amazingly worried about sex? Had she become amazingly deprived?

I find this hard to accept. It's not an ego thing, I hope. I took trouble to make sex good for my wife and we made it together frequently and she seemed happy and satisfied.

So the problem wasn't Janie at all.

This seems obvious now with hindsight, but it was far from obvious at the time. However rampant Red was between the sheets, she felt the room had an effect on her that was not natural, and she was awake at the time and able to remember it. I felt this myself. Red described it as a presence. She felt someone was there. She felt the active force of someone's control, or at the very least, their manipulation.

The trouble was, all this was hard to accept because of my fundamental disbelief in ghosts. They provided the perfect explanation, but I didn't believe they existed.

But Red's scientific experiment had more or less proved the effect was external to us, the players in the game. She had set up this really sexy episode at a time we knew the 'presence' was an absence. It was a time when we felt normal. We had all behaved as very sexual people and we had all indulged ourselves, but Red and I knew it was different. We were constructing the Virginie game. It wasn't constructing us.

I wasn't cold-blooded during the game. Far from it. I'd never done anything like it and it was a fantastic experience. Compulsively screwing Janie and Red together had nothing of the flavour and gorgeous taste that the game had.

What man wouldn't enjoy a beautiful young girl like the one acting Virginie to offer her body as a playground to tantalise his senses?

The girl, I never found out her real name, was only about eighteen or so. She was very slight and young. Normally I like women to have something of a figure, but this little creature, pretending a naïvety that wasn't hers, was altogether delectable. I can't describe touching her and then touching Red. I can't describe the movement from full flesh to spare, from luscious curves to fragile bone and skin. I can't describe the glory of sinking my cock into one woman's eager hot place, and then sinking it into another woman's. That they should both see, both watch, me having them!

My balls were caressed by one woman as I plunged my cock into another. I saw the women kissing, I saw them playing with each other's breasts, I saw their open mouths pressed together and I knew they tongued each other.

I saw one woman suck another to climax, and then I could ease my hard cock in where her face had been. I could do what I wanted. To have a small scented female hand pushing your cock into another woman's body is an experience I want to have again. I can recommend it. It is superb.

Part of how good the game was was the fact that we made it up as we went along. We had agreed on our characters beforehand and we had devised the basic set-up, but that was all.

There was all the difference in the world between my frantic grabbing at anything I could plunge my cock into, and the almost intellectual pleasure of teasing the senses sexually into further and more delicious byways. I keep relapsing into food imagery. The Virginie game was a delicate banquet, a series of flavours that made up a sensual feast. We made it happen.

The activity in my bedroom was like force-feeding a starving man. You were desperate for it but pleasure was the least of your worries. Afterwards you felt knocked out and uncomfortable. The Virginie game is something I'll dwell on and relive, though, as often as it continues to please me.

So back to ghosts.

There was no evidence in the historical record as why the central part of my three cottages should be haunted. I even fed the deaths by disease into my computer and ran a programme to find patterns in it relating to one cottage or another. There was nothing.

As for the other deaths, they were a mixed bunch. The two that stood out were the deaths of Jenny Wilkes in 1843 and Alison Makepeace in 1893, because of the sexual scandal associated with them. They were both deaths by fire, too. But the suggestion that Jenny had been attacked by the angry wife was very clear. It was irritating not to know what happened to the husband and what he had said at the time. Presumably he was absent when Jenny caught fire, or Eliza wouldn't have been sent for trial. Who was Jenny? How did she come to be the house? And which house was it?

And what about Alison Makepeace, fifty years on? The newspaper report was stuffed with innuendo, or at least it was to modern eyes. One could hardly help imagining just what the Rev MacAlister had got up to all night with the lewd and licentious girl. No, it was Jenny who was described as being lewd and licentious. Alison was addicted to vice.

I spared a moment to consider how little newspaper reporting had changed. Even the land girl who died was subjected to smutty hints.

Jenny and Alison. Both girls had been accused of sexual behaviour. Had our ghost been abroad at the time, or was one of the girls our ghost?

Red felt it as male. What if it was Jenny, even though Red said not, and then Jenny haunted poor Alison. Red went both ways, it should be remembered. Red liked girls as well as boys.

It was strange having some history relating to the house. I became someone on a list, in a line. I was no longer myself but merely an interlude in the forward march of events where the house itself, rather than me myself, had the greater reality.

I didn't want to be an interlude. I wanted out of the house. I wanted no connection with it.

Meanwhile, Janie my wife was coming home. I couldn't explain about seeing her in a silent sexual frenzy. I couldn't tell her about Red and the things we had done together. I couldn't describe to her the Virginie game which had proved to us the uniqueness of the experience in my bedroom.

I set fire to the bedroom carpet and burnt an ugly great hole in it, marking the wall above with scorched stains and smoke damage. Then I moved our bed and all our personal belongings into the spare bedroom at the end of the house. I filled it with flowers including Janie's favourite red roses and I sat tight with my explanation for the shift all ready and waiting. And I had the house valued. We were going to sell it. Come hell or high water, that's what we were going to do.

I went to fetch Janie home and found her unaccountably nervous. Her leg had been broken very badly and she had some weeks to go before they removed the plaster.

It transpired that her mother had decided to visit us to look after Janie and drive her to the shops and so on. There was the housework to consider. I worked too hard and men weren't any good at housework. Janie's mother said so and Janie's mother was always right.

I looked at the two women. Janie had her case with the clothes and personal things I had taken across for her. Her mother had an alarmingly big suitcase. 'Uh,' I said. 'I had an accident in our bedroom. It can't be used till it's redecorated. Meanwhile we're in the guest bedroom, honey.'

'I've never understood why you only have one spare bedroom in that house,' said Janie's mother.

It was always an effort to address her by her name. I made the effort. 'Violet,' I said. 'We had to raise the ceiling level downstairs to comply with modern planning requirements. That meant we lost the opportunity of using the loft for proper living accommodation. We also put an en suite bathroom with the end bedroom, using up what would have been room enough for another bedroom, which we didn't want. There's the study and we have a walk-in cupboard there as well. They were small cottages. It isn't a big house.'

I had explained this before, needless to say. I think she wanted to move in with us. I couldn't risk us having a bigger house.

'What sort of accident?' asked Janie.

'I burnt the carpet. It's a hell of a mess, darling. I'm sorry, it was really stupid of me. I've got on to the insurance people and they are sending out a loss adjuster.'

'You don't smoke,' said Violet accusingly. 'How did it happen?'

'I smoke cigars occasionally.'

'Is the room unusable?' asked Janie.

'It looks terrible. It needs repapering, and of course there's a big hole in the carpet with scorch marks round it.'

'It won't worry me,' said Violet. 'You know I'm not one to make a fuss. You can put the spare room bed over the hole and I'll hang a cloth on the wall. So there's no problem, is there?'

'No,' I said. 'No problem.'

So Janie's mother Violet was going to sleep in the haunted bedroom. Now there was a thing.

Don't get me wrong about the woman. She was fifty-five years old and if Janie aged like her mother, I was going to find myself married to a handsome woman for very many years. Violet was slender, graceful and always beautifully dressed. Her dark hair had gone grey but it was immaculately kept and very attractive. She used make-up skilfully. Other people found her charming, I know. She was cultured, well-read, and had a sense of humour.

That she wasn't like this with me was because I was married to her daughter, I think. Had we met in any other circumstances I think she would have liked me. I certainly would have admired her and perhaps even got a little itchy in my pants. She retained some sex appeal and she and Janie were sufficiently alike for me to feel attraction for the one because I was attracted to the other.

She was widowed and had been for several years. She didn't look the sort of woman to enjoy celibacy and I had long taken for granted that she made discreet use of men friends. She had plenty, that I knew. The problem with me, that is her problem with me, was that I fucked her daughter. If Janie disliked thinking about her mother and sex, Violet disliked thinking about her daughter and sex even more. I might have been Janie's father, the way Violet radiated disgust at me. I was obscene, wanting to paddle in her daughter's vagina. She couldn't like me whatever I was like, because I put my cock inside her daughter's body and moved it about.

So much for Violet. I couldn't help grinning at the thought of her shut in with whatever had moved into our house.

Suddenly I had an idea. The thing had moved into our house. It hadn't been there when we came. Perhaps we should be researching the past deaths in local houses that had recently been demolished. Maybe the ghost in one house had tramped across the fields or hitched a lift down the road and dropped off to spend eternity with us.

The very fact that I had this screwy idea shows how far gone I was at this point.

I took the womenfolk home and they unpacked. Janie was doggedly determined to do all she could and hopped about in a pathetic way with a crutch hooked under one arm, putting her things away.

She said one interesting thing. 'I don't think this wallpaper is as nice as the paper in our bedroom.'

'No,' I agreed. 'I'm sorry about the mess in there.'

'And this bathroom isn't so nice as our one. The main one, I mean.'

'It's too small,' I said. 'We can use the other one when your mother has gone home.'

'But I'm actually very glad we've changed rooms.'

'Are you?' I was thunderstruck. 'Why?'

'I was finding our room quite creepy,' Janie shuddered. 'I was having amazing dreams before my accident. I didn't really like it. I kept waking up all sweaty and stiff, as though I had been running races in my sleep.'

She knew. It was obvious she knew she dreamed sexy dreams. I didn't blame her for not coming clean with me. Why should she? I didn't own her mind any more than I owned her body. She was entitled to her privacies, her reticencies.

'You were a bit restless,' I admitted, with nicely calculated casualness.

'I think that's why I fell. I was physically tired a lot of the time. Because of the disturbed nights, I mean. I think it made me clumsy.'

'Did you wake up a lot?' I murmured.

'No. Not really. It was like the edge of nightmare. I couldn't wake up. I mean, I dreamed I was asleep dreaming and I dreamed I couldn't wake up. Does that sound silly?'

I gave her a hug. 'It sounds as though I should be home more.'

She ran her fingers down my chest. Even through my shirt it made me shiver. 'There's a better reason for having you home more,' she said and laughed.

I kissed her. 'Let's move house,' I said. 'This place is too isolated with you so much alone. Let's move into Tonbridge.'

'Right in?' Janie was doubtful.

'A nice town house,' I said. 'We can walk when we go out or take a taxi. No problem with drinking and driving. Most of our friends are there.'

'We had a dream about living in the country,' she said wistfully.

I undid her blouse and kissed her breasts hungrily. 'There have been too many dreams,' I said. 'Let's access some reality.'

I cooked a meal. We watched some television. We went to bed. I made love to my wife and felt her go to sleep. I waited in the darkness.

It turned midnight. The night wore on. The house remained quiet. Was I mistaken? Would nothing happen?

Then I heard a muffled noise. There was silence again, and then a thump and a shuffling noise.

My conscience stirred. I grinned and told it to lie down. I was looking forward to this.

The one thing I didn't dare do was go to Violet's room. I had no intention of fucking my mother-in-law and I knew the sex-compulsion was irresistible when at full force. I had to stay clear.

I wished I was in the loft. The trouble was that Janie slept peacefully beside me. I would risk disturbing her if I got out of bed now and started moving furniture about. Nor would I be able to explain why I was in the loft. I should have jimmied the plumbing, I thought sleepily. Then I could have gone up and done mysterious things with ballcocks.

I heard some more subdued noises. Poor Violet. Did she know what was happening to her?

Time passed. I sweated a little. I hoped she would be OK. The thing didn't seem to do any actual physical harm. It was just sex.

I wished I knew what was going on. Should I put Red back in the loft? Then she could spy the following night and report to me what she saw.

Two drawbacks to this occurred to me immediately. The first one was that Red would succumb herself and come downstairs and the thought of Red having sexual congress with my mother-in-law was a little strong for my stomach. The second thought was that Janie would be around most of the time and I couldn't sneak other females in and out of the house at will, as I had done before.

Quietly the solution came into my mind. Video camera. I could record what Violet was doing.

At that moment car headlights swept the house and I heard an engine come to rest. Startled, I sat up. I still made sure I didn't disturb Janie. She looked a little drawn from her accident and she needed her sleep right now. She was convalescing.

It could hardly be a burglar coming so openly. Was it vandals or hopheads, youths who didn't care?

Not by the way the car had been driven, quietly and smoothly. Now I saw the lights were being switched off and I heard the door clunk quietly shut.

I put on a dressing gown and slipped from the bed. Outside the room I drew breath. I ran down the corridor at the gallop, not wanting to be deflected by incestuous activities in my old bedroom. Perhaps sex with your mother-in-law isn't incest, as there's no blood relationship. I don't know. I wasn't going to do it, though. About that I was completely certain.

I went to the kitchen and collected the largest of our Sabatiers and the knife sharpener. Viciously armed in this way I waited behind the front door.

The car driver knocked on the door. At the same moment Violet came through from her bedroom.

She didn't put on any lights. She swept past me in the dark and opened the front door wide. I stood back amazed. She had passed within twelve inches of me and had been unaware of my presence.

She wore a full length nightdress and some floating thing, a negligé of some kind. I smelled her perfume as she went by me. It was good.

'Frank,' she said to the man on the doorstep.

'I came when you phoned,' he began. He sounded bewildered.

That was as far as he got. Violet put her arms round his neck and kissed him on the mouth. She released him after a moment and made a little moaning noise. 'Quick,' she whispered. 'Quick. Come to my bedroom. I need you. Right now.'

'Violet,' protested the poor guy.

'Now,' she hissed.

I stood grinning in the dark as they went by me. Frank was in for a surprise, that was for sure.

Wasn't Violet an enterprising lady? I'd forgotten the phone in our old bedroom. When she needed a man, she dialled for one. The fact that he'd turned up as commanded proved she was one hell of a lady, even if she was pure bitch to me.

I'd have given a lot right then to know what was going on in that bedroom.

I didn't see Frank in the morning. The man and his car were gone and Violet made no reference to him. When Janie asked her mother how she had slept, her mother replied that her first night in another house was always a little restless but by the second night she would be completely relaxed. This was good news to me because by the next night I had made arrangements. I had had to be careful, both women were in the house most of the time, but I had set up the camera and arranged for it to tape for four hours. That way if we went to bed at eleven to eleven thirty, I could make some excuse to come in the room and switch it on and then leave it to record over the crucial hours.

Would she have arranged for Frank to come back? How would she play it on Night Two? Just which way would Violet jump?

I was rubbing my hands in anticipation. This was going

to make up for several years of barbed and unpleasant remarks. I didn't want Violet ever to know what I was doing, but I would know and that was enough. She would have no power to get at me in the future.

FILE ELEVEN

Description of video recording

'Did you bring it?' asks Violet. She seems agitated and impatient.

'Yes, of course,' says Frank and he puts the big parcel on the bed.

Violet begins to unwrap it greedily. As the contents are revealed she caresses them happily. A look of pleasure has spread over her face.

Frank looks uneasy. 'It doesn't seem right, my being here,' he mutters.

'Don't be silly.' Her tone is absent. Plainly, they have already discussed this issue.

'It's the sort of thing teenagers do,' persists Frank gruffly. 'I'd feel embarrassed to meet your daughter or your son-in-law.'

Violet eyes him coldly. 'Embarrassed?' she snaps. 'Why?'

'Abuse of hospitality, and all that.'

'Stuff and nonsense. I can do as I please. Do you think *she* hasn't done as she pleased all these years?'

'What do you mean?'

'She married that man she calls her husband for what he can do for her in bed. Their relationship is no deeper than that. They aren't a married couple. They are philanderers. Their only point of connection is when he puts his sex inside hers.'

'Violet!' Frank is clearly shocked.

'He's one of nature's gigolos. He's a bellboy, a chauffeur, a lifeguard on a surfing beach.'

'I thought he held down a very good job.' Frank is stiff and outraged.

'He has some fancy sales manager's job. The man's all charm and surface sex, no stamina, no ability. He's a sponger, Frank. He might be earning now but the time will come when he lets my daughter down. I bet he pops it in every little secretary who'll have him.'

Violet is magnificent in her contempt. But it seems Frank is not entirely naïve. A considering look on his face indicates that he might be detecting a subtext here. It certainly is a fact that Violet's son-in-law is a very good-looking man.

'Now,' says Violet with a change of tone. 'Let's talk about us. Come here, Frank. Take off your clothes.'

She sits on the bed and watches him, smiling faintly. The time is eleven forty-five at night. Frank has driven to the house and been admitted by Violet as he was the previous night, though that was at a much later hour. This meeting is by arrangement. Violet has made no frantic phone call for help this time.

Frank's body is in good physical trim for his age. The wiry hair on his chest has turned grey and his belly is softer than it would have been ten years ago, but he looks fit and ready for action.

Violet sweeps the package and its contents onto the floor. She wears a pale green silk nightdress extravagantly trimmed with lace with a matching silk negligé on top.

Frank lies on the bed on his face. He spreads his arms and his legs wide. His face is turned to one side. He relaxes and closes his eyes.

Violet stands a moment watching him. Then she says softly: 'The orchestra is about to play. First we hear one great drum beat.'

140

She takes from the package a table tennis bat and smacks Frank sharply once on his buttocks. He jolts but otherwise makes no sign that anything has happened.

'Now the violins come in with the first rendering of the melody.' Violet takes a large ostrich feather and begins to sweep it up and down Frank's back.

'The melody is sweet and soothing,' Violet says. She strokes Frank with the giant feather, up and down his back. 'Then there is a little harmony in a lower tone, or perhaps it is another melody, a counterpoint that weaves sinuously with the first.'

She continues to stroke Frank with large sweeping gentle strokes all across his back. With her other hand she takes up a fur glove. She runs her gloved hand up Frank's thighs. She feathers his back and plays with his thighs, running lightly inside and outside them, coming high towards his groin and then dropping back down to below his knees. She sweeps more strongly with the ostrich feather and runs its tip along the crevice between Frank's buttocks. At the same time her fur-clad fingers enter the region at the apex of his legs where his penis lies slack under his testicles.

For several moments Violet is silent, concentrating on the movements of her hands. She tickles Frank between the cheeks of his rear and she tickles his balls with her furry hand.

Frank wriggles slightly.

'Now the drums sound a warning note,' says Violet. She drops the glove and takes up the bat. She smacks Frank very violently on his buttocks several times.

She stops, panting, to admire her work. Frank's buttocks are red. Violet drops her negligé off her shoulders, revealing her long slender arms and her naked throat. Her nightdress is supported by two thin satin straps.

Frank says nothing. His eyes are tight shut.

'After the warning notes of the big drum,' says Violet,

'comes a strange little tune, very uneasy, played on, I think, an oboe. Or maybe a clarinet.'

Violet picks up a pair of tongs. She touches Frank quickly up and down his legs making sure that the tongs slightly nip his body hair each time she touches him.

'The main tune re-establishes itself.' She strokes his back again with the ostrich feather. 'But the uneasy tune is still there, sometimes more clearly heard, sometimes less so.'

For some time she feathers and nips Frank. She nips closer to his sexual organs so that occasionally she plucks at a little pubic hair.

'And then the uneasy tune is drowned out as the full orchestra rushes in and plays gaily altogether,' cries Violet.

In rapid succession, having abandoned the tongs, Violet smacks Frank's bottom, fur-strokes him, feathers him and runs wooden wheeled objects up and down his flesh to massage and stroke and soothe him.

'But the little evil tune hasn't gone away,' says Violet. She takes up a meat skewer and pricks Frank all over his back and buttocks and thighs. She seems to concentrate particularly on the cheeks of his bottom. She pricks carefully, not breaking the flesh but causing it to indent sharply. The only conclusion the observer can reach is that she has done this before.

She stops. 'The drums beat softly,' she says. She smacks Frank gently with the bat, but not so gently that he doesn't mark from the force of her blows.

Violet slips one strap off her shoulder and allows the lace cup of her nightdress to drop below her breast. She stands for a moment looking down at Frank prone on the bed. Her one breast protrudes, the other still being covered.

She pushes her hair back. Its grooming has become less than immaculate in her strivings.

'The violins play.' She feathers Frank's back.

'The music swells.' She runs a fur-clad finger hard between Frank's buttocks.

'The orchestra settles into its stride,' says Violet.

She sits on the bed beside Frank. She takes a nail brush and scrubs gently at his back. Then she wipes him softly with a length of silk, letting the cool material flutter across his skin and soothe it. She feeds the silken length under one of his thighs and pulls one end so that it slips slowly through. She does this again at the very top of his legs so that his swollen penis is touched and tugged.

'The music plays,' says Violet dreamily. She patters down Frank's body with the backs of two spoons. 'But always underneath there is the suggestion of something not quite right.' She takes an ice cube and places it against Frank's anus, hard between his buttocks which grip to hold it there.

Frank shudders and his skin shivers and trembles.

'Those big drums,' shouts Violet. She hits Frank hard on his buttocks using two table tennis bats now.

It is just past midnight.

'And other instruments,' sobs Violet. She rubs an object like a multi-tined fork hard down Frank's back. His flesh is scored.

Violet releases her other breast. Unsupported, her nightdress slips to the floor. She is naked now apart from a pair of fluffy mules on her feet.

'And more stirring music,' cries Violet. She takes an object like a beaver's tail. It is flat and paddle-shaped and appears to be made of leather. It has a certain weight to it. Violet begins to slap Frank with this object. His body jolts and bounces on the bed.

Suddenly he cries out. He crawls up onto his knees, still with his face down on the bedding and with his arms helplessly outspread. It can now be seen that his sex is very hard and large.

Violet moans slightly and smacks his upraised buttocks

and the backs of his swinging balls. She drops the paddle and picks up the fur gauntlet. Not bothering to put it on, she wipes the fur over his mortified flesh. Moving down the bed she scrubs gently on the penis with the nail brush. At the same time she tickles his sex with the large feather.

Frank makes a stifled noise.

Violet puts a cup underneath Frank. She wraps the length of silk around his penis and pulls it tight.

Frank groans. There is blood where he has bitten his lip.

With the penis tightly strapped by the silk, Violet tickles Frank's balls with the feather and then strokes them with the silk. She scrubs his inner thighs with the nail brush and then she puts a fresh ice cube between his straining buttocks.

Frank whimpers.

Violet removes the silken bond. Frank's penis vibrates. Violet takes a bottle of water with a spray attachment, such as is used for spraying houseplants, and sprays Frank's penis. Water drips down it and into the cup. He squirms as the ice melts against his anus.

'Now,' pants Violet. 'Now for the climax to the piece. There's plenty of noise.' She smacks Frank with the paddle on his buttocks. She puts the nail brush against his penis and rubs it, not holding the penis itself so that only its own weight holds it against the abrading bristles.

Frank's hips jolt. Violet slips a rubber band onto his balls so that they bulge tightly below the squeezed scrotal sac. Frank's buttocks open helplessly and the ice cube falls out.

'Naughty,' shouts Violet. She puts the ostrich feather into Frank's dripping anus so that it stands up and waves about as he moves.

Violet laughs. She takes a wet cloth from amongst her store of ice cubes and wraps it quickly round Frank's penis just as he comes to climax. He jerks helplessly, out of control. Spunk shoots irregularly from his frozen urgent cock into the cup below. The ostrich feather waggles. His confined testicles bulge, unable fully to do their proper job.

Frank falls on his side. His face is wet with tears and his nose is running. His penis has shrunk rapidly and it is clear he is in pain. Violet takes the cup and puts it to one side and removes the ostrich feather.

Frank rolls onto his back. Violet has a towel and she wipes his face and cleans him. She dries his wet places with exquisite gentleness. Frank lies passive under her ministrations.

Violet stands up. She replaces the fluffy mules with black high-heeled shoes. They are very high heeled. She puts on a nurse's apron and a nurse's cap. She sits beside Frank.

'Not feeling too good?' she asks in a professionally sympathetic voice.

'Not too good,' acknowledges Frank.

Violet holds Frank's wrist and using the nurse's watch pinned to her apron, takes his pulse.

She then attaches a strap to his arm and takes his blood pressure.

'Temperature,' she says brightly.

'Do you have to, nurse?'

'I'm afraid so,' Violet smiles.

Frank looks into her face. Violet separates his legs. She lifts his penis and moves it to one side. She gets a pot of Vaseline and carefully greases the thermometer. She smiles all the time, looking into Frank's face. She reaches between his legs and fumbles down between his buttocks, under his body.

'Up a little,' she says brightly.

Frank lifts himself at his hips. Violet holds his buttocks apart with one hand and slips the thermometer into his anus with the other.

'Hold the position,' she says. His flopping penis has regained a little substance, up in the air as Violet penetrates his rear.

She reads her watch. Three minutes go by. Frank wriggles very slightly.

'Now,' says Violet and removes the thermometer. She reads it and pops it into a cup of disinfectant.

'I think you need some therapy,' she says warmly to Frank. He lowers his hips and lies flat on his back. Violet takes an elastic band and puts it onto his penis. She takes several more. Frank's penis grows, bulging between each restrictive band.

Violet takes the loose foreskin between finger and thumb and holds it away from the penis. She begins to prick it with the meat skewer. Frank trembles visibly.

Now Violet climbs astride Frank on the bed, facing down his body. Her starched apron rustles and her naked bottom is in front of his face. When he bends forward he can see her entire sex just in front of his eyes.

She puts the meat skewer down and begins to twang the elastic bands against the firming member. Then she places a little suction cup over Frank's testicles and begins to pump so that the skin of the scrotum is tugged into the suction cup with each stroke. She does this quite hard.

Frank begins to perspire.

Violet releases Frank's penis from the rubber bands which have become very tight as his sex has swollen. Violet wraps his penis in a rubber tube. She attaches another pump, like a miniature bicycle pump, to the end of this tube and pumps air into it. The tube goes round and round Frank's erect penis. As Violet pumps, the tube fills with air and constricts the member it surrounds.

Frank becomes very red in the face. He has bitten his lip again. The open sex in front of his face has swollen slightly and is very wet.

Violet stops pumping and disconnects the pump. She

now begins to manipulate the air in the tube so that it goes up and down (and therefore round and round, spiral fashion) Frank's sexual member. Under this elaborate masturbation Frank begins to exhibit distress. Violet bends over and fits a fat glass tube over the end of Frank's penis, pushing the head in as far as she can get it.

Frank moans and bares his teeth.

Now Violet returns to playing with the air in the tube. Frank's penis spurts clumsily, the liquid caught in the tube which is marked in millimetres. As it spurts Violet reaches under Frank and tickles his balls as though to encourage him.

When he is done she briskly releases the end of the tube to let the air out and then takes the whole thing off.

Violet sets the glass tube with Frank's spunk in it upright on the bedside table. She takes the cup she used earlier to catch his semen and tips the contents carefully into a second glass tube. She scrapes out with a spoon as much of the thickish milky fluid as she can.

Frank watches. He is slack and relaxed. Violet still sits across his chest so that her naked underparts contact him there but he can see what she does as she puts it on the bedside table.

Violet reaches right down and finds a notebook. Frank looks into her sex as she leans forward. Violet then reads the measured quantity of semen in each tube and enters the results in the little notebook.

Having done this she looks up. For the first time she looks uncertain. She moves slightly so that her underparts rub on Frank.

Violet frowns. The time is ten minutes past midnight. She touches one of her breasts where it rubs against the starched material of her apron.

Frank, who is in his fifties, has come twice in less than half an hour. He has come lavishly. There is an air about him of having completed some pre-arranged activity.

147

Then Violet's slight restlessness begins to infect him also. Violet is holding herself very rigidly. She bends forward suddenly and puts her forehead on the bed between Frank's legs.

'Punish me,' she sobs. She is muffled by the bedclothes and not completely distinct.

'What?' asks Frank, as if he wants confirmation. He is alert. This might be a new departure.

'Punish me,' says Violet, audibly grinding her teeth.

Before his eyes Frank sees her vagina pulsate. The labia swell and seem to reach towards him. The clitoris has unveiled itself and keeps moving slightly, up and down. The vagina bulges softly, inviting him to enter.

He does so. He gropes over the side of the bed and when he brings his hand back he has something like a policeman's truncheon. He licks the head of it. It has a dull sheen and appears to be made of plastic or rubber.

Frank prises the soft flesh in front of him open. The inner flesh of the vagina is visibly convulsing. Frank pushes the fat blunt end of the truncheon into the soft elastic moist entrance.

Violet gasps. Frank ignores this. He is smiling now, just as she smiled earlier. He pushes harder so that all the soft wet flesh is squeezed tight. The head of the truncheon slips inside the vagina. The labia close round it, like petals clinging. Frank smiles coarsely and pushes.

Violet eases her splayed knees even wider apart. It is clear now that the truncheon is made of leather. Frank withdraws it slightly before pushing it in again. The leather is stained dark where it is wet.

Frank pushes the truncheon very deeply into Violet's hole. He holds it there for a moment. Then he twists it, watching the flesh drag as he does so. Then he pulls it back until it is almost out of Violet's body.

He pushes the truncheon back in. He gropes over the side of the bed again. He finds a dripping ice cube. He opens Violet's buttocks and for a moment watches her pouting strawberry-shaped anus. Then he puts the ice cube against the hole and closes her buttocks over it.

Violet makes a yelping noise. The end of the truncheon moves. Frank continues to hold her buttocks shut against the ice cube but watches in fascination as a steady drip of ice cold water runs down over the hot swollen flesh below.

He gropes again over the bed. It takes him some time but he comes up with a small soft leather bag. He unzips this one-handedly.

The truncheon wobbles. The ice drips. Violet's clitoris is an angry red and it is in constant movement as her vagina strains around the invading object fixed in it.

Frank takes out a lipstick. He slips off the cap and winds the waxed colour out. He begins to paint Violet's vulva.

The lipstick is a deep purple colour. As Frank gets colour onto Violet's flesh despite the dripping water, it begins to look black.

Frank admires his handiwork. He finds another colour of lipstick in the bag. This is a bright sugary pink. Frank carefully paints the leather truncheon where it enters Violet's body.

Now be begins to masturbate her. The pink lipstick on the truncheon smears and mixes with the purple of her vulva. There is pink smeared on her vulva and purple smeared on the truncheon. Frank must be enjoying these effects because he is smiling.

Violet sobs tightly with relief as he masturbates her.

Frank stops and considers. Then he reaches into the little leather bag and comes out with a small slender object.

Its true purpose is a mystery. It has a small wooden handle. Set into this handle as if it were a blade is a thin strip of flexible metal divided into two near its end. There is a tiny ring around the base of the metal strip, resting against the handle. The entire object is perhaps two inches long.

Frank places the end of the divided strip so that one part is above and one part is below Violet's clitoris. He slides the tiny ring up the strip so that it clamps the divided end tight over the clitoris. He lets go. The little object stays in place. It nips Violet's clitoris tightly, and hangs from it. Frank flips it. Violet shudders and the end of the truncheon moves so violently that Frank sees her muscular contractions are now enough to eject the truncheon.

He masturbates her briskly for a moment, deliberately knocking the tiny instrument of torture clamped to her clitoris each time.

Now he takes the metal cap off the end of the truncheon. It reveals a screw thread. Frank reaches over the side of the bed and comes up with a flexible rubbery object, smaller than the truncheon but very like it otherwise.

It too has a screw thread but it is inside the end of it. Frank screws the one object onto the other.

The truncheon is now vastly longer but its newly attached part is much softer. Frank bends it round and opens Violet's buttocks. The ice cube has melted and she is wet in the crevice. Frank finds the Vaseline and greases the end of the object. Then he forces it into Violet's bottom.

Her anus distends. Her fists drum against the bed between his legs. All this time Frank has lain on his back with Violet kneeling over him, facing down the bed.

Frank forces the rubbery object deep into Violet's body. She is tearing the bedding with her teeth. Frank now pulls the truncheon partly out of her vagina. Then he pushes it back in while simultaneously withdrawing the rubbery object in her anus.

He sets up a rhythm. He masturbates Violet in her vagina and her ravished arse simultaneously, pushing one object in as he pulls the other out.

Violet's body bucks and heaves. Frank is laughing soundlessly. He sees wet ooze all around the truncheon.

Violet is in continuous orgasm. She is staring forward with her face raised from the bed. Her mouth is wide open and her eyes are bulging. Her arms are outspread, supporting her. The double violation of her body is causing her stomach to ripple sharply. There is no doubt she is in orgasm but she can't stop. She doesn't seem to want Frank to stop.

It is half past midnight.

Frank's cock is up under Violet's heaving straining body. As she moves her breasts rub his penis. He spurts into her breasts but she doesn't seem to notice.

There is sweat on Frank's brow and he has become very red-faced. He pumps Violet frantically. Violet suddenly emits a shrill squeak and collapses, going at the knees and letting her face hit the bed. Her eyes are shut.

Her sudden action has caught Frank by surprise. Both objects have been jerked from her body. He looks a little surprised but after a moment he smiles.

He begins to lick the truncheon.

There is a brief interlude during which Violet appears to sleep. Frank stops licking his truncheon and lifts one of Violet's legs. He inspects her sex. The little clitoral clamp is still in place pinching her hard. Frank flips it idly.

He relaxes himself. He too appears to go to sleep. Ten minutes pass. Violet opens her eyes. She looks blank. She gropes round Frank's inert body. She turns herself round and finds his penis is slack. She hits him in irritation. Frank wakes up and stares indignantly at her. Then he grabs her and pulls her breasts into his face. They are slimy with his spunk. He sucks her nipples and then reaches between her legs. He tugs the clitoral clamp and watches her face change.

Violet bares her teeth and sinks down with her face over Frank's penis. His body jerks sharply and when Violet raises her face it is a mask fixed in a malevolent grinning rictus.

Frank's penis is hard.

Violet reaches between her legs and without bothering to release the clamp, she tugs it off her body and throws it to one side. Then she drops herself on Frank's upright sex and begins to bounce up and down hard.

After a few moments Frank grasps her hips and holds her. He pumps up vigorously. She throws back her head, arching her back, letting him slam up into her.

Suddenly she drags herself to one side forcing Frank, if he is to stay inside her body, to roll with her. After a short complicated shuffle she is underneath. She bends her legs right up and throws herself up onto Frank's penis. She is so vigorous that he need do nothing except support himself over her and let her make all the running.

They both come rapidly to climax. Violet moans slightly. She appears to slip into unconsciousness and indeed, for the duration of the tape after this point, makes no voluntary move again.

Frank appears to doze. Then he wakes and after a moment he drags himself from Violet's body.

He looks round the room. The light has been on all the time and the debris of their sex games is very evident.

He looks down at his own sexual member. It is smeared and streaked with pink and purple lipstick. He touches it curiously.

Then he looks at the measuring tubes with his semen in them. Slowly he reaches over and picks of them up. He examines it. Then he upends the cold contents over Violet's supine sprawled body. Idly he rubs the spunk into her flesh. Then he takes the second tube and empties it over Violet as well.

He smiles and wriggles slightly, as if remembering what has happened to his body that night.

He lifts one of Violet's legs and looks into her sex. He bends over and begins to kiss and suck what he sees.

Violet makes no response. Frank sinks his face into her

vulva and rubs it there. When he lifts it his face has purple staining on it. He lays his face on Violet's stomach, smiling. He goes to sleep.

FILE TWELVE

Report by Red Marsden and summary of the evidence so far
We weren't as bright as we might have been, but then the whole thing was so incredible it takes some believing even now. There were things going on at this time that we didn't know about till much later. If we had have done, maybe we would have arrived at the truth a little faster than we did.

So where were we by now? Well, we knew there was something really screwy with Roger's house. We knew it affected only the central part of the house and it was strongest in his bedroom.

We had some evidence that it affected women more than men. That is, women became more extreme in their behaviour. Why this should be so, we didn't know. It might be that women are physically weaker than men or even emotionally softer, and so more open to influence. I doubt this, frankly. The emotional softness, I mean. I think women appear emotionally softer because society allows them to express their emotions in public without being ashamed. If anything, though, this makes women tougher, I think. They are physically weaker, of course. I can't deny that.

Maybe it affected women more than men because although women are allowed to express their emotions fairly freely, they are not historically allowed to express their sexuality as much as men. I mean, I know things are changing but there are plenty of men about who get scared when a woman comes on hard or makes specific sexual demands. I should know, I'm that sort of woman. I don't want to get deep into feminist dogma and all that crap, but if women are more repressed, letting go for them might be a bit wilder than it is for the average man.

I don't know. I'm just throwing out ideas. I felt the influence was male, myself, and I felt he got a greater kick out of making women jump through sexual hoops than he did out of making men do the same.

The trouble was, I couldn't discuss it with Janie and I couldn't discuss it with Roger's ma-in-law.

Now that was some lady. I saw the video and it had quite an impact. It gave me some ideas about games to play in the future as well. She is a very inventive person, there's no denying.

It could have been Frank but he didn't seem to be the leader of the pair. It struck me, going by the video, that he was the more passive partner. Again, I couldn't discuss it with him and that was a lot of the trouble. The subject, that is sex, is such a tense one in our society that it's hard to get an honest account of it. We've done our best here in these files in the interests of scientific research, but who else is this frank about what they get up to in private?

Yet it's entirely natural.

There was that girl, Kathryn Pentecost, the paranormal researcher. She was another one we should have talked to. But we couldn't. We've had to do the best we could in the circumstances and let the facts, the record, speak for itself where we weren't personally involved.

So, to get back to what conclusions we were tentatively drawing at this stage.

In Roger's bedroom was a kind of sexual aura that developed after midnight and affected all the people in or near the room, so that they indulged in a sexual mania.

It appeared to affect women more than men.

Younger women (that is myself, Janie and Kathryn) appeared to go more out of control and be more affected than older women. That is, Violet. She actually continued to perform elaborate dirty tricks rather than just stuff her needy pussy with anything the right shape.

We couldn't tell whether this was a true age effect or whether Violet is a woman with a lower sex urge or was somehow less affected. But Frank went less manic than Roger or Nick, and Roger and Nick were more manic than Andreas, the paranormal guy. So it did look as if increasing age reduced a person's vulnerability.

You didn't have to be a sexy person in the first place to be affected. The evidence for this comes from the paranormal group. They sure as hell weren't sexy before the effect hit them.

The effect wore off in an hour or so and resulted in deep slumber. Whether this was caused by the effect or whether the need to sleep was a simple result of the intense physical activity, we didn't know. But certainly the second explanation is quite adequate. If you screw very hard, you get very tired. You don't need spooky explanations.

The effect induced sexual mania and provided the complementary physical prowess. The ability to orgasm frequently, not to say continuously, came with the package. Even men had no problem producing spunk as often as required by their feverish lady. Or ladies.

Janie claimed not to remember what was going on but the rest of us did. Andreas forbade Roger to get in touch, so he remembered. He was protective concerning Kathryn so we can assume she remembered. Violet remembered because she got herself organised to exploit the effect the following night, so she must have had some kind of sexual hangover after the first night, which she had to spend alone or commit incest by involving Roger whom she evidently fancies like mad. Nick remembered though he pretended not to but he recalled what happened under the guise of having dreamed it. Roger remembered and I remembered. So the effect didn't play any permanent mind games with us. We all reverted to being normal people when the effect wasn't affecting us.

None of us was hurt, physically hurt in any way. We might have been stiff and sore from violent exercise, but no one suffered any worse effects than that. Yet I at least felt the presence as malevolent.

The best description we had for the effect at this stage was that it was a ghost. I don't think that either Roger or myself or the person who became the compiler of this dossier later on really thought of it as a ghost. We had a language problem. We had to call it something. The human instinct is to relate present experience to past experience, to fit into the pattern, as it were. It doesn't matter whether you relate what happens to you to yourself and your past or to other people's experiences, but you have to relate it to something or you're not part of the human race any more. If you think your experience is unique and unnamed, then either the men in white coats come along and carry you off to the funny farm or you found a new religion. Much the same thing really, except the food is generally better in new religions.

Having sort of decided the house was haunted, we investigated its past history. We didn't really think it was haunted because neither of us believed in ghosts, but it was the logic of language again. Ghost was the best description. That meant a haunting. That meant some poor bozo dead in a nasty manner in the past.

There was nothing special about such history as we unearthed. A normal amount of people had died given the level of occupancy over the years of the cottages, and they had died from regular and ordinary causes that were prevalent at the time. Such people who had died seemed singularly ordinary. This was where we discovered a kind of snobbery about ghosts. Usually they are lords and ladies, or clan chiefs or their cruelly treated offspring. Little servant girls and scrubbing woman and peasant women hoeing the fields don't become ghosts. They aren't important enough, it seems. The only conclusion I drew from this was that we were tripping over the age old belief that the poor don't feel things like the rich. They don't have the physical and emotional tenderness of important people and their tragedies are mysteriously less tragic than rich people's tragedies.

I could be very vulgar about this, but let's just say I don't believe it. When someone said slaves aren't properly developed human beings, a scientific fact isn't being expressed. It's just a moral get-out for human cruelty. When you know you treat your servants badly and they are overworked and hungry, it makes a Christian conscience less queasy to pretend they don't feel hunger and cold and pain so much.

All the antecedents of Lane End Cottages had been humble folk. They had suffered very many distressing and distressingly common things at the time. Nothing stood out except the couple of girls, Jenny and Alison, who had both died by burning after a sexual scandal. The strong suggestion was that Jenny had been the victim of a murderous attack, and perhaps Alison had suffered the same fate. The people around at the time of Alison's death would know of the previous history. They'd know all about Jenny. The scandal was only fifty years old at the time.

As I recorded this thought, it brought to mind the land girl who died, also by burning. The cottages must have been fire traps in those solid-fuel days and we had no figures for how many fire deaths there were in society in general so we didn't know whether the incidence at Lane End was normal or exceptional in some way.

The land girl, Linda Campsey, had died fifty years ago. Someone in the area might remember the events surrounding her death. It would be worth finding out the local long-term inhabitants and seeing if any of them recalled the incident, though no doubt the war had swamped such a trivial local event as a good-time girl coming to a nasty end.

The detail concerning Linda's remains was very odd and because it was in the 1940s, and for that very reason more believable. The girl was reduced to ash apart from her ankles and feet. This was a disgusting piece of information. However, it improved my chances of finding someone who could remember Linda. If the newspaper report had it correct, it was a bizarre death.

Fifty years ago. 1943. A hundred years ago. 1893, when Alison Makepeace died. A hundred and fifty years ago. 1843 when Jenny Wilkes had died.

Odd. A coincidence, of course. But the dates were odd.

FILE THIRTEEN

The Theatre of Dreams

There were four women in the room. It was a curious room. Though it had a carpet and a bed and a door which locked, which was locked, it had only three walls. It was not triangular and there was no conundrum.

It was a stage.

The four women were on stage in a theatre. The carpet, at close quarters, was dull and threadbare, laid over the naked boards of the stage. The door was a theatre carpenter's artefact, no real door but set within the system of flats.

The women were actresses, but they were not acting. What they did was for real.

The provincial theatre had a chequered history having been destroyed by fire some twenty years earlier. It had been known as an unlucky theatre before that time. Touring repertory companies that used it found the atmosphere uneasy. Plays that had been in production for weeks took on nuances in performances in this theatre that they had lacked elsewhere. Sexual nuances. The most innocent play gained a salacious tinge.

It was something neither the director nor the producer seemed able to control. The theatre gained a certain reputation. Not unnaturally, this reputation adhered to the actors.

The actors. The technicians. The stage manager. The

director. The theatre management. None of these had an untarnished reputation, even though the actors came and went for the most part. The town did not consider itself particularly strait-laced but the scandals from the theatre were so regular that when it burned down, it was considered a virtue and collectively the town wiped its brow with relief.

The seventies had a wild reputation. The stories that were once attached to the theatre became attached to the period. Time moved on and a new civic centre was planned. And a new theatre. On the site of the old one, because it was a good site and it seemed fitting to continue the tradition of a playhouse in precisely the same place. The architects were combining the past and the future when they planned it so.

They gave the new theatre a new name. They called it The Phoenix. It was opened to civic éclat along with the new shopping precinct and the leisure centre by minor royalty.

The Phoenix management appointed a director for the season and he began to organise the schedule and employ actors. And actresses.

Acting is an overstaffed profession and, except for the fortunate few, most actors spend a considerable proportion of their lives unemployed. To the underworked actor a director is the man who pulls his strings. Actresses have been known to have sex with a director in order to secure their standing with him. No doubt actors have done the same where the director's sexual proclivities have tended that way.

There are few women directors.

Actresses have had sex with a director because they liked him, or because they are attracted to power or because they feel they need all the help they get in their careers and will use any means to get a part.

Not four actresses, though. And not simultaneously.

The director of The Phoenix Theatre was called Joel Bannerman. Joel Bannerman had four women who didn't seem to want to leave the theatre and go home.

The first production of the new season didn't open for another three weeks. The stage should have been bare. Joel had had it set roughly for the auditions.

Emma. Robina. Sandy. Carol. Each had made it very plain they would like to service their director's sexual need. He had responded positively to each. He hadn't expected, he couldn't have dreamed what would eventually happen.

Testimony of Joel Bannerman
Sandra Cooper is a handy little actress if you don't give her anything too complicated. She always looks good on stage and she is an even-tempered and biddable girl, a director's dream. Although not very creative in a part, she accepts direction well and throws no temperament.

I didn't think she put out, though I know nothing of her personal circumstances. I don't think she is married. Despite her generally placid exterior she is as ambitious as the next actress and as anxious to succeed in her career.

But I didn't think she would go to these lengths. She caught me in the wings. In The Phoenix the wings are curiously designed and create a great deal of separation between backstage and on-stage. They are a tiny private halfway world. Sandy caught me in this no-man's-land and pressed close against me in the confined space.

'I'm glad you wanted me, Joel,' she said.

'I'm fond of you, Sandy. It's good to be working with you.'

She pressed closer. I stiffened. Then, unmistakeably, she rubbed her body against my groin.

I felt a real thrill of pleasure go through me. It was sharper even than usual though Sandy is no more than averagely good-looking. She put her hands up on my shoulders and pushed herself hard into me.

'Sandy,' I said in tones of mild surprise. Then I kissed her. As I did so I felt desire so sharply I slipped a hand under her jumper and slid it up to hold her breast. Her response was to lay her palm flat over my groin and then grip me tightly.

I practically had her then and there. There were people all around us but we had gone from first approach to the moment of insertion in something under thirty seconds.

'Not now,' I said in a muffled voice. 'Um, at six. Yes, make it six o'clock, honey. Then all the others will be gone.'

I honestly wondered if she'd turn up at six but she was there. I felt a little nervous. We hadn't got to know each other at all. It was hard to believe she was as brash as her crude approach made her seem.

'Do you want to come to my office?' I asked. We were standing in the front of the auditorium. The stage working lights were still on but otherwise the theatre was in darkness.

Sandy came towards me soft-footed. She had long dark hair and a sweet, rather young face. I couldn't decipher the expression on it though my life's work is the expression on people's faces, you might say.

She looked ready to faint. Her hand was trembling as she reached out for me. I couldn't understand the depth of her emotion. Was she fancying herself in love? She'd never shown any personal interest in me when our paths had crossed before.

Her hand slid unromantically for my trouser belt. I smiled.

'On stage,' she whispered.

'What?'

'Can I have you on stage?'

I was grinning now. 'Sure,' I said. I was looking forward to this. She was promising to be something special.

I had had an actress come on like this once in the past.

She had just been dumped by another member of the cast. She was using me to show him she didn't give a damn and I found I was more than willing to oblige. I don't care why they get into bed me, as long as they keep doing it. I'm a man who enjoys variety and who dislikes the settled life.

Sandy ran her nails down my shirt front. 'I'll go first,' she said. 'You wait here.'

Bossy. That needn't be a bad thing. A commanding woman in bed can be a pleasant change.

She disappeared backstage and a moment later appeared on the far side of the footlights. She peered down at me. Then, in that heavy warm dusty atmosphere, without sounds or music or the relaxing effect of alcohol, she began to take off her clothes.

She didn't do me a strip. It was better than that. She took off her clothes one by one slowly, with hesitation. As if she was shy. She couldn't even see me properly through the lights. She took off her clothes on stage as if she didn't really like it.

I did, though. She took off her clothes as if we were in my bedroom and she was shy. It was our first time, after all. It was hard to believe I was watching. I should have been up there, helping her, kissing her, warming her up. She didn't seem to need all that, though. This was what she had chosen for herself.

When she was quite naked she turned to face me. She folded her hands together so that they lay against her little rounded belly. She was longer limbed than I had realised and very pretty nude. She looked very young with her long dark hair framing her face and her body drained of colour by the unflattering lights.

She came downstage as far as she could. She unlocked her hands and opened them. I wondered what part she was deep in. The girl was acting, that was for sure.

The triangle of her dark fluffy sex made my loins burn.

'Make love to me,' she said. She gasped slightly. It was a beautiful delivery. She sounded desperate.

I vaulted up on stage and took her in my arms. She didn't want that, though. She began clawing urgently at my clothes.

We fell to the ground. She wrenched my trousers open and pulled my swollen sex out. She got her legs round my body and pushed her sexual parts at me. I was still wrestling to loosen my tie as the head of my cock felt her vulva.

I jerked convulsively. My cock thrust forward. Her cunt was sliding paradise and I went all the way in and felt her squeeze me and suck at me. I think I called out. The floor was hard, I remember, and not very clean. Her body began to move with incredible energy. I felt my spunk was being sucked out of me. I couldn't resist the power of her muscular strokes along my cock. My climax started to come and it was too soon. I wanted this to last longer, she was extraordinary. She wouldn't let me hold back, though. Her cunt demanded, it's the only way to explain it.

I began to orgasm into her wonderful dark hole. It seemed to suck my climax from me in great mouthfuls. My cock felt wonderful and tingled with release. I wanted to laugh with pleasure.

She released me and stood up. Her chest was heaving and I watched with appreciation as her breasts went up and down. Her nipples were very dark. Her pubic hair had flattened and was damp. She was flushed and bright-eyed.

'The bed,' she said. She appeared to have trouble speaking.

I stood up with some difficulty because my clothes were all over the place. I pulled them together and followed her over to the bed. I used to do a bit of acting years ago and it was most strange being on stage and doing this. I knew there was no audience. The theatre was closed and locked, empty but for our two selves. But the rows of gaping seats disappearing back into the velvety darkness were oppressive. I felt spied on.

Sandy threw herself on to the bed. At this point it was not made up and had only an old bedspread slung over the mattress. Sandy rolled on to her back, opened her legs wide and grinned up at me.

I felt my damp cock harden. I stepped out of my clothes. She had pearls on her thighs. I took hold of my cock and stroked the pearls with it, smearing them as though they were paint and her thigh the canvas, my cock the brush.

Her breasts flattened into soft mounds on her chest. I reached over her and touched her nipples with my cockhead. I played for a moment, rubbing her nipples, letting my balls swing against her breast flesh and caress it.

She drew up her knees. She opened her legs wide. Once more she contrived to wrap them about me. She jerked upwards. I felt her sex against me. I tried to feel down and play with it but she was thrusting vigorously up. My fingers slid in the goo and went round and touched her bottom. She jerked harder and my cock slid into her body for the second time.

Her cunt sucked me and squeezed me. It gripped, twisted and drew my second climax out, with me hardly being involved. I wasn't insulted, the sensation was too terrific, but the lady was like heroin. The more you had, the more you wanted.

She wouldn't let me go and she wouldn't let me lead in anything. She threw me violently backwards and plunged down on top of me. My wet limp cock went into her mouth. I yelled out loudly as she sucked me. Her teeth were sharp. She took me to the edge of pain and held me there. Then she sucked me to climax.

I had come three times in rapid succession. My brain told me that was it for a little while. My body told me different.

The bed was wooden with a shaped carved knob on each of the four corner posts. Sandy climbed off my body leaving me gasping. She stood by the bed end and lifted one leg. She hopped slightly and arranged herself so that the pointed knob projected upwards. She had one foot on the floor. She had the other foot up on the bed. She grasped the wooden rail that ran along the bottom of the bed. She lowered her body, watching me all the time. The varnished wooden knob pushed up into her body.

She began to bob up and down.

I had never seen anything like it. She was masturbating herself on the furniture before my eyes. She frigged her gaping hole with the bedknob as an artificial penis. Her face looked transcendently wicked. She kept watching me and I guess I looked as astonished as I felt.

At first. My cock began to rise up again. Sandy's breasts kept joggling up and down. Her dark hair was in tangles. Her lips were swollen from where she had bitten them in her frenzy. I knelt up and reached for her. I gripped her hair and put my mouth against hers. Her tongue was slithery and wet. I stood up. I put one foot on the rail she was holding. I grabbed a handful of hair again to steady her head as she moved up and down. Then I put my fat cock into her mouth.

I don't know yet how I kept my balance. I had to go up and down with her to a certain extent. She managed to time how she moved to satisfy her own sexual urge on the bedknob while allowing my cock to slide in and out of her sucking mouth. I held her hair and pushed her face into my groin. I didn't care if she suffocated. I had to have her take me like this.

Moments later I had fallen back on the bed dragging Sandy with me. Her face was strained and for a moment she was limp. I pulled her legs open and looked down into her sex.

It was very dark, a deep crimson colour. The edges of

her labia were dark grey, almost black. Her sexual fleece was spunk soaked and flattened. Her clitoris stood out, twice the size of the girls I had had before. Love juice bubbled from her vagina.

I put a finger in and moved it around. I felt her elastic walls throb and tighten on the little invader. I found her panties and began to wipe her. I wiped her gently, entering her hole and mopping up the excess of come. Then I wiped her hard, rubbing along the length of her vulva and frotting her little arsehole.

She wriggled and squirmed. I bent my head and began to kiss her sex. She had a musky ripe taste, like fermenting fruit. I licked her and kissed her. Then I sucked her sweet parts and her hole and I plunged my tongue deep into her and licked her cunt inside. It throbbed as it had when my finger went in.

I sucked her to climax. I'd never known a woman orgasm like Sandy did. My own cock couldn't lie down.

My memory gets hazy at this point. We fucked again, me on top. Then she sat astride me, I think. I remember facing her bottom and poking between her cheeks. The session seemed to go on and on.

I woke up stale and exhausted. I was alone. I pulled my clothes on. I was hungry and thirsty. As I laced my shoes Sandy came in.

She was fully dressed and the hair fringing her face was damp, as if she had been washing. I went to her clumsily and kissed her. She trembled.

'I'm tired,' she whimpered.

'I'll see you back to your digs.'

'I'll have to have you again.'

I wasn't used to women speaking to me like this, especially not little second-rate actresses. But it was flattering in its way. The girl was absolutely crazy over me. Her pussy was pure delight, so full of pleasure it almost tortured me.

169

She seemed dazed as I saw her home. That suited me. I didn't feel like talking.

The next day Carol Stanhope came to see me in my office. She appeared to be ill-at-ease. I didn't know Carol very well. I had hired her through her agent after a friend of mine told me she was a useful actress who did a little television now and again. I had needed a tall good-looking blonde for the part and Carol was a suitable physical type.

She was also my type. If I was to go for one of the females in the company, it would be Carol. She had a kind of smoky look about her, yet she was all cool elegance.

That was her appearance. She seemed less sure of herself now.

'I was wondering, Joel,' she began, 'whether you wouldn't mind running me through my solo scene again.'

There was nothing wrong with her solo scene which we had blocked that day. Rehearsal would give it the authority it currently lacked. I had no worries about it.

Carol was something else, though. I couldn't stop my eyes from flickering up that long slender body of hers. I forgot about horny little Sandy and had a brief fantasy about Carol.

'Sure,' I said easily. 'Now?'

She licked her lips. 'I'm nervous about it,' she confessed. 'I'd rather do it when no one else was here.'

I was delighted. The dirty little bitch. I chuckled to myself. I was really going to enjoy the run of this particular production. Usually I had to make some of the running myself. This time it appeared I could just lie back and have them flocking to me.

She had it all worked out. She made me come on stage and physically move her. The minute I touched her she twisted to face me and lifted her eyes to meet mine.

I kissed her on the lips. I could smell her perfume. She shivered with sexual excitement and untucked my shirt.

Moments later I was on top of her on the bed pumping away for dear life. She writhed like a snake under me and my cock felt as if it was being gobbled in her eager cunt. This theatre certainly had ambience. I'd never known sex like it. I could feel with exquisite clarity each little muscular flicker so that ripples of sexual pleasure built in me like the headwaters of a damned river. Then the damn burst. We were both shouting eagerly. We had made it simultaneously.

I relaxed, marvelling at my good luck. I had two eager bimbos and I was in excellent sexual trim. Then Carol twisted under me. I came up onto my hands and knees. A moment later she had fastened her mouth onto my hanging cock and her sweet juicy cunt was just underneath my mouth.

I groaned. It was almost too much of a good thing. I sank my mouth into her body and gave her all I could. I felt her pussy respond to the probings of my tongue. It was as though a kind of supersensitivity was filling both of us. It had the effect of making me come easily and often. It had the same effect on Carol. Again we climaxed simultaneously and I tasted her juices in her quivering little pussy as I bucked hard into that beautiful mouth of hers.

I fell on the bed laughing. 'You're fantastic,' I said. She stood up and fumbled with her clothes.

The next moment I saw she had a leather belt in her hand, taken from her jeans. She wrapped it round her hand and looked at me.

'Hey no,' I cried. 'I'm not into that.'

She looked wonderful. Her blonde mane was tossed and tangled by our violent love-making. Her long elegant body looked pale and wanton. Her cherry-red nipples made me want to bite them. Her face was sly and sexy.

She tossed me the belt. Then she turned her back on me. She bent forward and put her hands on her thighs. She peeped over her shoulder at me and then turned away again.

She was inviting me to strap her long white haunches.

I could whip her rounded white buttocks. I could mar her bottom and paint it with red strokes.

I did it. I made the leather sing and smack against her lovely flawless skin. I stood up to get a more powerful swing and she cast herself on the bed. I whipped her a couple of times and then I saw she was jerking. I prised her legs apart and looked. She had a finger in her pussy and was frigging herself as I beat her.

I smacked her then. She retaliated by spinning round and biting my cock. I pulled her off but as I did so I ejaculated without any preparation. I knocked her over and smacked her in earnest. Her bottom quivered and shook. Then she was jerking and gasping and I knew she had come.

I stopped and sat there for a little while, breathing heavily and wondering what the hell was going on. Carol rolled onto her back and took the belt from me. She lifted her legs in the air. With a quick wriggle, she looped the belt between her legs and held the end, one behind her and one in front of her. Holding her legs apart she began to rub the belt backwards and forwards so that it abraded her delicate sexual flesh.

A fatuous look of complacent bliss settled over her face. I hardly seemed necessary to her any more. This made me so angry I thought I'd teach her a lesson. I put my hand between her buttocks. The belt rubbed against me as she sawed backwards and forwards. Then I fumbled in the tight cleft between her rounded cheeks and found what I wanted. I sucked my finger for a moment and then I pushed it back. Her tight flesh yielded. I was inside her, hot and pulpy and squeezingly tight. I began to frig her little rear.

She came almost instantly. I saw her bubble and froth. The leather darkened. She began to moan softly. Her eyes were unfocused. Her hips jumped and shook. She stopped what she was doing with the belt and coiled it up. Then she fed the inner part of the coil into her orgasming pussy. I had never seen such a sexy sight. Her cunt was bubbly and kept convulsing as she continued to orgasm. The end of the belt was fed into this cauldron of activity. Because it was still partly rolled up, she was feeding it coiled into her body. She kept pushing it in until she reached the buckle.

She let go. The metal buckle gleamed against her dark pulsing flesh. Unable to resist, I reached out and took hold of the buckle. I began gently to pull.

The leather came out of her soaked in sexual juices. Fleetingly, I remembered Sandy. I pulled the belt until it was free of Carol's sex. Then I put my cock in and fucked her as hard as I could.

Again my memory becomes uncertain at this point. I know we had it together again, several times. We slept. When I woke up the fever was over. I was exhausted. I was lying with a beautiful desirable woman but I was exhausted.

I dressed slowly. I woke her up. 'You'd better get dressed,' I said.

She looked at me as though she didn't believe I was real. Then she blushed.

The blush was something terrific. The girl was really embarrassed. I wasn't. The music we had made together was crazy, but it had been an experience not to miss.

We left the theatre together.

The following night Sandy begged to see me again. It had to be the stage. She wasn't interested in anywhere else.

I agreed, more in surprise at my own libido than anything else. We had just got our clothes off and my cock had just sunk its full length into her divine pulsating cunt when Carol appeared through the wings.

I couldn't stop. Far from being inhibited, my cock wouldn't give me any peace. I simply had to go on banging into Sandy though if I was forced to choose, it would be Carol whom I preferred.

Nor would Sandy release me. She was giving everything she could to our frantic congress. It was disgusting, the two of us going at it like animals with the furious Carol a witness.

She didn't turn on her heel and go. She took off her clothes and joined in.

This had been a fantasy of mine from adolescence. I was beside myself with happiness. I rolled onto my back laughing. My wet penis flopped on my naked thigh. The two women looked at each other.

I put out my arms. 'I want to feel you both,' I said. 'I can satisfy you both.'

This was a boast. Of course I couldn't satisfy them both. They were the two women most rabid for sex that I had ever met in my life. That they were here together was the most astounding coincidence.

I couldn't believe it when they lay beside me, one on each side. I put my arms round them and hugged them. Carol kissed my mouth. Sandy kissed my chest. My mind went into a spin and I felt them all over my body.

Testimony of Carol and Sandy
Carol and Sandy agreed to talk to Red Marsden when this dossier was being compiled and all possible evidence was being collected. By then some time had passed since the incidents they describe had taken place. They were both shy at first, merely agreeing that they had had an affair with Joel Bannerman. Red persuaded them to relax and tell the truth by informing them of some of the other events described in other parts of this dossier. When they understood the importance of their testimony and why it was wanted, the girls proved very willing to help.

Carol: I can remember being with Joel and Sandy. I came

in and saw them there together. My first feeling was acute disappointment.

Sandy: Not jealousy?

Carol: No. Disappointment. I absolutely had to have sex. If Joel was giving it to you, Sandy, he wouldn't have spare for me.

Sandy: Are you usually so tolerant of your lovers having other women?

Carol: I'm not tolerant at all. On any other occasion I'd have scratched your eyes out. As it was, I decided to join you.

Sandy: Have you fancied being one of two women before?

Carol: Certainly not. I've fantasised being one woman with two men, maybe, but that's all. How did you feel?

Sandy: Horny. I couldn't stop screwing to worry about you being there. I was crazy for Joel.

Carol: So was I. I was burning up to have him inside me. I tore my clothes off watching you two going at it. I've never seen live sex close up before. Then I was on the bed too. I felt Joel take a hold of me. I was kissing him but that was a nuisance. I wanted him inside me. Then he was inside me. It was bliss. The tension of being empty was unbearable. Joel's sex inside me was perfect. I could have died happily. I was full of energy, pumping it out. I hardly knew you were there.

Sandy: He came out of you floundering like a beached fish. It seems funny now but all I was really concerned about was getting him in me. I began to suck his cock. It leapt into life though he'd had it twice in rapid succession.

Carol: We fought then. You remember?

Sandy: I remember. We both kept trying to throw each other off and stuff Joel into our own bodies.

Carol: I'd get him in me and feel that hot quivering gorgeous sensation and then you'd haul him out.

Sandy: He settled it, though, didn't he?

Carol: He slapped us both till we let go. Then he turned us on our faces and made us put our backsides up in the air. He put his finger in my pussy and his cock into yours.

Sandy: He fucked me for several minutes. I was moaning and dribbling into the bedspread. Then he pulled out of me. He put his cock into you. I got a finger instead.

Carol: He was wet and hot. He slid into me greased and slick. I felt every nerve in my pussy, it was a completely novel sensation. I poked out my rear and tried to squeeze him hard. I could feel his balls swinging against me.

Sandy: Then he was out of you and into me. I was maddened at the lack of him and driven crazy with desire at the same time. Part of me knew that he was handling the situation with great inventiveness and flair.

Carol: He's a director, remember. He can orchestrate a scene.

Sandy: He handled us, all right. Oh, he was sweet in me. I loved it. I wish it could be like that again.

Carol: Don't. It'll never be like that again. That's the point.

The two girls admitted that neither normally went in for joint sex in this way. Both described their passion for Joel as unnatural and seemed relieved when Red told them that their experience was not unique, that they needn't feel responsible for their actions. Both said that they couldn't resist it, nothing could have prevented them from behaving as they did. Sandy described how she felt the man, licked him and kissed him, how she sucked his mouth and his cock and his arse, how she put a finger into his body even as he slotted his cock into the other girl.

She described how she saw his glistening sex as it went in and out. She stared at the other girl's sexual parts as they were in use, she'd never seen such a sight.

She felt she could do anything to the male body. She hit it. She grasped the swinging testicles and gently tugged them. She ravished the male arse as he had sex with the other woman. On later occasions there were to be three other women. On this occasion she kissed his mouth and rubbed her breasts on him. When he was done she pulled him out of Carol's body and stared fascinated as Carol's sex pulsed in the aftermath of orgasm. She licked and sucked at the wet cock hanging down. Then she kissed Carol's sex. She put the cock between her breasts and twisted awkwardly till she could kiss Carol. Then she kissed her sex again.

She felt the man watching her. She felt his arousal and she kissed Carol between her legs, where she was wet from the man. Her hand snaked out and she grasped the lovely dangling member. It swelled in her hands. He was inexhaustible. She rolled over on to her back and lay so that her head rested on Carol's stomach, lying between her parted legs. The man bent forward over her so that his cock stroked her face as he kissed Carol. He kissed Carol, on the mouth and on the breasts. He sucked her nipples and pulled them with his mouth. All the time Sandy had his cock in her mouth. Her fingers were up playing in his balls. When he was firm she brought herself into what was almost a shoulder stand. His sex dropped heavily, happily, into her open hole. It closed tight around him and she felt her own cunt muscles work the male organ in their grasp. Meanwhile he kissed Carol and murmured to her even as he fucked Sandy.

Carol wriggled out from beneath their straining bodies. She fetched her belt. Their sex was bland. It needed a little salting. She could provide that.

She whipped him as he shafted Sandy. Sometimes she whipped Sandy. Their flesh bulged. They prodded it against each other. Their bottoms quivered under the lash. Their hips jerked. She could almost smell burning.

They stopped, panting. Carol dropped the belt and the two women crawled up the man and lay each to one side of him. Then they kissed his sex, the blonde hair and the dark tangling together. They kissed his sex together, one each side of his cock while he lay between them with his eyes squeezed shut. Then they kissed each other. They hauled themselves up over the man like beaching seals. They wrapped their arms around each other and kissed mouth to mouth.

The man's eyes were watching them now, watching everything they did.

Slowly they swirled on the bed until they were head to tail. They ignored the man completely. Each of the two women began to kiss with sweet delicacy the sex of the other. They were calm now. Their pink tongues extended and licked carefully at each other's sex. The watching man saw their vulvas licked clean, saw their clitorises swell and move, saw their labia sucked and pulled. He saw pink female pointed tongues sink into sweetly pulsing holes of cushioned sex flesh. He saw long slender fingers plucking the sexual flesh apart so that those tongues and lips and teeth could have easy access.

He saw everything.

FILE FOURTEEN

Red Marsden made extensive enquiries in the vicinity of Fibsey, Kent, trying to find someone who could remember the death of Linda Campsey in 1943. Linda was found burned to death in the kitchen of No. 4 Lane End Cottages.

Billy Toomer was found when Red was told that after the demolition of The Marfleet Arms, which had been his local public house, Billy and some other old hands in the district began to drink in the Green Man.

Billy is now seventy-four years of age and he is a widower. He appears frail but he is a wiry old man with considerable vigour despite his rheumatism. He was stationed in Kent for a while near to Fibsey in 1943 as part of a slow recovery from a severe leg wound. Later he settled there.

The following account is an edited version of the interviews Red conducted with Billy. There was considerable repetition which has been omitted for the sake of clarity. Billy's memory appeared to be excellent though he became vague on recent events, especially those occurring in the last five years.

Testimony of William Toomer
There was five of us, good pals, and we used to drink regular at the Marfleet Arms. Sid Johnson was the barman, and he knew how to keep his ale well.

179

We was young lads with no sense of responsibility. None of us was married and we all enjoyed having a bit of cash in our pockets. We'd seen the war for ourselves and we didn't reckon we'd live to see the end of it. We was just interested in having a good time before it happened to us.

Some of the girls didn't feel so very different, though perhaps they didn't expect to die themselves. But they had seen enough young men go away and never come back. If they was to have any fun out of life, they had to have it now. There wasn't going to be no fun in the future. There weren't going to be any young men left.

Anyway, a lot of them girls had never had so much freedom. Decent girls had a dreadful stuffy kind of upbringing in them days and here they were, working, away from home and with a little money in their pockets. They felt it their duty to entertain the lads, if you know what I mean. We was fighting and dying for these girls, and they felt it.

They was good girls with a bit of fun in them. No one meant no harm. The older people, they didn't understand. It was our life that was being blown away over in France and Belgium. We took what we could.

Linda was the gayest of the bunch. I suppose she was no beauty because then girls were supposed to be very glamorous, like the screen stars. Linda was a big rough girl with a freckled face and a great wiry mass of blonde hair that stuck out all round her face. She knotted it up in the daytime but I've seen it down, I have, and I wasn't the only one.

She liked wearing the shirts and trousers that land girls wore. She'd come striding into the pub and drink her pint like the rest of us. She was so good at darts the chaps let her play in the team. She was good at all them bar sports, dominoes, shove 'apenny, skittles. She was a pal.

Word soon got round she didn't make a fuss. I remember the first time I went with her. I saw her in the bar and her hair was coming down. It had been a rare hot day and she was all flushed and sunburned. Her shirt was undone halfway down her chest and girls didn't wear so much then so her bosoms, they was clear, and big and floppy. I really fancied her, what with the heat and two or three pints of strong ale inside me.

I said it to her straight. I asked if she'd pop outside into the fields for ten minutes. I whispered it so the other chaps wouldn't hear, but she gave a great laugh and took my hand.

We went out. The night was all heavy and hot and sticky. We walked down the lane and turned into the field. Linda undid her shirt and put my hand on one of her breasts, just like that.

It were lovely. She was a big-made girl at a time when skinny girls were in fashion. But I liked them big. She had great big soft squeezy breasts and I can remember them now, clear as clear. That's funny, because I can hardly remember Susan, my wife, that's been dead fifteen year. Linda was very alive. She wasn't one a man would forget easily.

Well, what followed was what you could imagine. Linda undressed me, all matter of fact, and we lay down making a bed of our clothes and had it there and then under the stars. It was good. We went back into the bar afterwards and the chaps joshed me a little but Linda didn't care, so why should I? I felt good and I knew I'd be right pleased to go with Linda any time, even if she did go with other chaps.

I know you want to know about Lane End Cottages. Linda was boarding there with Martha Makepeace. Martha was on her own by then, her man having died, I think. I don't clearly remember. I was a young fella and not very interested in old women, nor in history.

Anyway, one day one of my mates, Cyril his name was, he said to me that Linda was letting some of the chaps come to her digs and have her in the bed there. Now that was a great thing in them days. We had the freedom of the hedgerows, you might say, and we could have what we wanted gipsy-fashion. That was normal. But having a girl in a proper bed when you weren't married, that was different. That was special. That was Sin with a capital S and that was what we all wanted. It was something to boast about, if a girl let you into her bed.

I don't remember precisely how many cottages there were. Linda was in one about the middle of the row. That night or the next one we threw stones at Linda's window and sure enough, out pops her head. We'd had enough sense to make sure we didn't wake Martha who slept at the back. There was a sort of grapevine among us chaps for important information like that. It was like a little war, you see. The landladies were the enemy. The girls were the territory we aimed to capture.

Linda giggled and come down to the kitchen and opened the window so we could slip over the sill and get in. We was a bit shy, then. I wanted Cyril to go so I could have a kiss and cuddle but Linda wouldn't let him.

The kitchen seemed very hot though the fire was out and it was a cool night. I began to feel very funny, I remember that. Linda had all her hair down and unplaited, she'd been getting ready for bed, she said. She wore this long white cotton nightdress down to her bare toes. Her hair was a great fair crinkly mass that came right down her back to her waist. In the half-dark she looked lovely, really desirable, you might say, and I didn't care if she went with the other lads. I just wanted her to go with me, whatever else she did.

Cyril's standing puffing and gasping beside me. He's goggle-eyed at the lovely thing she is in her white nightie, all innocent with that smashing hair. She stands up on tiptoe and strokes his hair back, pretending it was out of place all playful, see, and suddenly I can't bear it. I reach out and slide my hand up her leg at the back scooping the nightdress up as I go.

I see her naked thighs and her lovely rounded bottom. She's taking no notice of me at all, playing around with Cyril and pulling his ears and teasing him to kiss her. But I'm burning, see. So I outs with my John Thomas and I just slips it between the cheeks of her arse and it slides into the right place just as easy as pie and two seconds later I am going at it for dear life and Linda is all the while kissing Cyril just as if nothing is happening at all.

I stagger back when I'm done and her nightie slips back into place. Cyril has the buttons undone now and is fumbling in her gorgeous titties. I stroke her hair and begin to button myself up. Then she's falling backwards and I'm catching her so she won't fall. Cyril has his business friend out and Linda is pulling up her nightie and Cyril is putting it into her, just where I've been.

We weren't bad lads. We didn't go in for any of this kinky stuff. We had it clean with a girl, without anything fancy or peculiar. We'd all been with girls up an alley or whatever, with a mate standing guard in case anyone came, but that was as near as we got to what you might call perverted sexual practices. We wasn't sophisticated and we didn't care to be. We just liked it hearty with a willing friendly girl as often as we could get it.

Two of us sharing a girl like this, at the same time – well, I mean I knew it was done, I knew it happened, but it wasn't the sort of thing I did or my mates did. But here in Martha's kitchen, we all went kind of mad, I think. Linda finished with Cyril and bent over and touched her toes. Then she pulled her nightie up. She didn't have to say anything, I'm ready unbuttoning again and then I'm in her, with her bent double in front of me. The second I'm finished and pulling out, sort of dazed at the way things are turning out, Cyril has filled her just the same as me. I mean, I'm doing up my buttons and Cyril is in her already going hell for leather. Linda's rocking about trying to keep her balance but she can't get enough of us boys. She wants us both all the time. The three of us are going frantic.

I can't say how many times we did it that night and I wouldn't be believed if I did. I'm too old to care what anyone thinks now and if it tickles me to remember, I don't see why I shouldn't tell the truth. Linda was a good strong lively lass and we were lads who'd looked death too close in the eye. We did it till we bust. It was like we were possessed.

We got tired or the madness passed, I don't remember. The heat stays with me, though. When we finally crawled over that window-ledge more dead than alive, I shivered in the night air because it felt so cold. We was burning in the kitchen.

Maybe my mind has invented that because of what happened to Linda. It was three weeks later she was found dead. That was horrible. I think she was killed, myself. You can't carry on like she was in a country parish like Fibsey was without getting someone very upset. Linda was going mad with having lads round at night, she was the talk of the camp and some of the lads, me included, had stopped going. I think I was a bit frightened at how peculiar that night with her and Cyril had been.

Word must have leaked to the women. Anyway, the gossip was that one night Martha had come down and caught her at it. Martha had laid about her with the frying pan but one fella had upped her nightie and poked her and all. I don't believe this, mind, but that was what was said.

Next we knew Linda was dead. Turned to ash, barring her feet. It was gruesome. I think Martha took revenge, or maybe one of the other women whose husband had gone with Linda. Nothing was said though. That was the end of it at that time.

You might wonder why I remember all this so easy and clear. Well, it was a strange time of life and things were very vivid then, living in the shadow of death all the time like we were. You kind of fixed each experience in your mind so you could savour it, in case there weren't many more. We aren't anything, are we, more'n the sum of our experiences?

About three years ago someone else came looking to hear about Linda. It was a fella from some society or other. They sounded like loonies to me. He was researching into people who'd died by being burned. Not just everyone who'd been burned, but special ones like Linda who'd kind of turned to ash. Ones where the house didn't burn down and kill the people in it, but the people died and the house wasn't harmed.

[NB Toomer is referring to a researcher into the phenomenon of spontaneous combustion, in which human beings appear to self-ignite and, as a rule, burn to death.]

FILE FIFTEEN

Testimony of Red Marsden

Roger and I had an argument after I did the interviews with old Billy Toomer. I wanted to follow up the business about self-igniting humans but Roger said it was spooky rubbish and we shouldn't waste our time over it. He'd had enough of paranormal groups when he'd called the ghost hunters to his house. He wasn't having any more weirdos.

I was very struck at this point by the accumulating coincidences. We hadn't reckoned Linda's death to be anything but the potential for a ghost. Yet the interviews with Billy Toomer had turned up all this sex stuff. Linda had been hot, very hot. I couldn't blame her and I didn't blame her, though if Billy had the rights of it she was going a bit over the top towards the end.

Now Linda's death had similar aspects to the death of Alison Makepeace fifty years earlier, and that of Jenny Wilkes, fifty years before that. The three girls had a certain reputation, a sexy reputation. Each girl died by burning. There was a suggestion of foul play each time.

There was another factor linking the three cases but I didn't like it. It had to be coincidence. It had to be irrelevant. I mean, we didn't even know if these events had taken place in the same cottage since the historical record didn't identify which cottage it was for Alison or Jenny, and we didn't know if No. 4 where Linda had died was part of the modern house owned by Roger and Janie.

Jenny died in 1843. Alison died in 1893. Linda died in 1943.

Was there a significance in the fifty-year intervals? How could there be?

I think all this was so scary Roger didn't want to know any more. He had the house up for sale now and was prepared to take a loss to move fast. He wanted to forget the problem, to escape from it. He and Janie wouldn't use the room though I don't know what he told her at the time. He didn't tell me what went on between them any more and he certainly didn't tell her what had gone on between our two selves. The way I saw it we were just investigating a phenomenon the best we could when Rog and I screwed, but I didn't think Janie would see it like that.

So Roger vetoed the self-igniting humans thing as a weird byway we didn't need to explore. But I had an itch to know. Linda's death was odd if the details were accurately reported. Martha, the landlady, hadn't been accused at the time, nor had anyone else though Billy Toomer suspected foul play. In a way he was right. If your behaviour is extreme you unleash strong emotions. Linda was plunging into deep waters by offering her sexual favours so freely in a tight little rural district at that time. The wives and mothers wouldn't have been sympathetic, not by a long way. Some of the men might have been quite ugly about it too, especially if Linda rejected some and allowed others, as would have been likely.

Without telling Roger I went ahead on my own. I didn't think it would take much time and I didn't think we should neglect any possible lead at this time. My job is investigation, of course, and Roger's is sales. Perhaps that's why our attitudes were different at this point. Another reason we had different attitudes might have been that Roger had a lot of money tied up in the house. If he found out something too awful he might feel guilty about selling the place.

I had no such problem.

It didn't take me long to trace the SI-Humans organisation. That's what they call it, self-igniting humans being long-winded though descriptive. I said I was seeking information on behalf of a client and they agreed to let me come and meet someone and have a talk with them.

The person they sent me to meet was called Sonja. She was little and skinny with huge dark eyes set in a dead white bony face. She had black hair cut short and spiky and she wore lots of eye make-up and jangly jewellery.

She turned up at the meeting wearing harlequin tights, a bomber jacket in black leather and little red leather ankle boots. She was really thin and her clothing revealed that she had a small flat arse, a big bump at the base of her belly that was her sexual mound, and she had little pointed breasts. Her nose was pierced too.

She wasn't what I expected at all and she could see I was surprised.

'I'm the daughter of a fireman,' she said. 'He was convinced in the reality of SI-Humans but it simply wasn't allowed as an explanation. He used to talk to people about strange cases and some agreed with him, there was something peculiar to investigate, something they didn't understand. But most firemen were frightened that they'd lose their jobs or their promotion if they spoke about something so strange, so they denied it. The police denied it and coroners deny it. They just blame cigarettes or bring in death by misadventure.'

I had my own story ready. 'I've been investigating the history of some cottages in Kent,' I said. 'A friend of mine lives in them. We found out that a girl who died in 1943 was considered by a member of your organisation to be a possible SI-Human case. But that's all I know. I don't know anything about the subject at all.'

Sonja was happy to enlighten me. 'The victims are all ages and both sexes, without any one group being special except that the very old seem exempt. They burst into flames spontaneously, by which I mean that there is no outside agent. They aren't ignited by their clothes catching fire and then burning them, for instance. If anything, it's the other way round. The victims can be awake or asleep. They can survive if they are rescued either by their own actions or by someone else's. If they aren't lucky enough to survive, you can often tell an SI case because the condition is characterised by them being substantially reduced to ash. That's the key factor. If they burn completely without interference, the bulk of their body can be so fiercely burned that it is calcined.'

'Calcined?'

'Turned to ash. It's actually very hard to reduce the human body to ash. You ask anyone at your local crematorium. The temperatures needed are fantastic and even then the bones remain and have to be ground down before you get your loved one in an urn.'

This was gruesome. 'In the case I'm thinking of,' I said politely, 'parts of the feet remained.'

'Yes, that's very typical. Often the legs and ankles and feet are almost undamaged, as if there was a blast area.'

'So what causes it?'

'Ah.' Sonja smiled. 'There are several schools of thought. The short answer is that we don't know. Some people point to the fact that the human being is essentially a candle with the wick on the outside and the wax on the inside. Our clothes are the wick and our body fat the wax. Given a high enough starting temperature, we burn like a candle despite all the water we contain.'

I gasped at this revolting idea.

'Other people think something goes wrong with our gut flora,' said Sonja comfortably. I think she was enjoying shocking me.

'What is our gut flora?' I asked in horror.

'The microbes and bacteria that live in your gut and help digest your food. If they are upset and fail to function properly, you build up gas inside. Like for instance, methane. Highly inflammable when mixed with oxygen. Some people have caught fire up their backs when lying in bed on their fronts. We wonder if escaping gas hasn't spontaneously ignited in these cases.'

She was silent while I digested the implications of these horrible ideas. Did flatulent people die enflamed or was Sonja having me on?

'Biochemists have pointed out that the process whereby we turn all our food into glucose releases a lot of heat,' Sonja went on. I wanted her to stop. I'd heard enough. I felt quite green at these revolting details. 'All chemical reactions either release or absorb heat and breaking down carbohydrates into glucose releases heat. The body does it in many stages releasing heat in little amounts all the time. That's how our body is heated by our food. But if that process went wrong occasionally, perhaps we could literally burst into flames.'

'I don't like this very much,' I said queasily.

She took me seriously. 'No. I understand that. But you don't make bad things go away by ignoring their existence. If something is going on, we ought to know about it, don't you think. Then we can set about dealing with it and controlling it, if that is possible.'

'Yes. I see,' I said feebly.

'If you were to tell me about the case you have in mind, I can look it up and see what we have on it. If we have anything, that is. It depends upon whether this previous investigator thought it was one suitable for the records or not. We have to distinguish between SI-Humans and ordinary house fires and so on. A typical SI-H does minimal damage to the surroundings. The floor might be scorched and often there is an oily vapour or an oily deposit over everything. But nearby furniture and even clothes often survive.'

I told her about Linda Campsey. She said she kept

copies of the records at their office. If I'd like it, she would look up Linda and see if she was on file.

I said I'd like that and we arranged that I would come round to her house in two evenings' time. If she had anything, she'd let me know then.

I was disturbed by this information and it made me very uncomfortable. I didn't want to see Sonja again, not because I hadn't warmed to the girl, but because I didn't like the subject. However, my personal feelings were irrelevant. I was working, trying to help Roger even if he didn't want helping. And I was itchy to know what the hell was going on in Lane End Cottages.

I met Sonja as agreed. She did have Linda on file as a possible SI-H victim but the file contained no new information for me. Linda remained just one more fact in an inexplicable situation.

Sonja and I drank some wine and I began to tell her a little about what had been going on. This was indiscreet but I didn't think she'd go running to the newspapers crying scandal. It wasn't in the interests of her organisation to have the dreaded word sex associated with the phenomenon they were investigating. They were seeking credibility, not notoriety.

Sonja's huge eyes got bigger and her white face got whiter. 'You'll think I'm crazy,' I said. 'This girl Linda was really putting it about. Then she died horribly in the cottage. I think Roger thinks she's the ghost haunting his house. But I don't believe in ghosts and anyway, if the thing is anything, it's male.'

'I can't follow this,' protested Sonja. 'Tell me what the thing is, again.'

I laughed. 'Sex. You want to make love all the time. Making love puts it too nicely. You go crazy to screw.'

The bony face in front of me relaxed and smiled. She looked like a pussycat. 'You mean Linda went mad making love and now you go mad making love.'

'You have to be in the room to experience it. It's indescribable. It's like your pussy eats men and can't get enough. Rog and his wife won't sleep there any more and the house is up for sale. The paranormal group threw off their clothes and had an orgy the night they were there.'

Sonja's eyes glittered. 'So who's going to catch fire?'

'What?'

'Sex and flames. That's it, isn't it? Linda had sex and burned. Is that going to happen to you?'

'No,' I said indignantly.

'You look like you enjoy sex,' said Sonja rapidly.

'I do.'

'How can you tell the difference between normal enjoyment and this extra that you describe? You fancy this Rog guy anyway.'

'Roger and I go way back. He's a tasty man. But the room makes you crazy. You go frantic.'

'I guess you'd go pretty frantic anyway, once you were aroused,' said Sonja in that same peculiar rapid voice.

I looked at her in silence. She was maybe five feet tall. At the moment she was coiled down on a big cushion on the floor. She wore a black croptop with a low neck over leg-hugging black tights.

I thought about my big full body, my strong thighs, my broad shoulders, my long luxuriant red hair. 'Why don't you find out?' I said coolly and waited.

She stood up. She pulled her top over her head. One of her nipples was pierced. Under her bust she wore a wide black elastic band stretched tight round her ribcage.

'What's that for?' I asked lazily. I had narrowed my eyes and I was watching her.

'I enjoy restraint.'

She slid her lower garment off. Under it she wore no panties, but there was a similar band stretched tight round her hips. She also had one round the top of each thigh.

The effect was extraordinary. Her white thin body with

its hard black bands looked anything but alluring. But I was turned on. She had something. The black spiky hair of her head, the black hair in her armpits, the crop of black hair at the base of her belly, were all flaunting her femininity. She was a harsh little creature but she was all female.

And delectable, in a fierce way.

I stood up and removed my blouse and skirt. I wore a lacy bra, black net panties, a red garter belt and black stockings. I reached into my bag and found a little pair of manicure scissors. Carefully I snipped through my mesh panties until I could remove them and throw them to one side. Then I fluffed up my pubic hair till it glowed with copper lights. Deliberately I cut a shining curl of hair. Then I walked over to where Sonja watched me. I reached into her groin and took some of her black pubic hair in my fingers. The texture was coarse and strong. I smoothed out a curling tuft, deliberately pulling slightly against her skin. I snipped the curl free and put my red and her black hair together.

'That's nice,' said Sonja evenly. 'You want to take it all off?'

'All?'

'You can shave me there if you like.'

'I think I like,' I said.

Sonja fetched towels and a basin of warm water. She had an ordinary wet standard sort of razor. She had a man's shaving brush and a stick of shaving soap as well.

She lay down on the floor. I knelt beside her. 'Should we take the belt off?' I asked huskily. I wanted to see her buttocks and they were partly covered by the elastic webbing that constrained her.

'If you like.' She released it. Her flat little stomach was marked where the thing had bitten into her flesh. I touched her there for a moment and her stomach fluttered under my fingertips.

194

Now I touched her pubic hair again. I stroked it and gently teased it a little. Sonja parted her legs and I investigated between them. She was a very hairy girl, there was lots of the coarse strong stuff. It came down alongside her vulva framing it and masking it till I held the hair back and looked.

I made no move to touch her sexual parts. I exposed them to the air, to my own sight, but I did not touch them.

'I'd better cut the hair first,' I said.

Sonja smiled.

I had this tiny comb in my bag. I took it out and began to comb Sonja's pubic hair. Then I decided it needed a wet cut. So I fetched a little shampoo and I washed her hair.

It was wonderful wetting it and then shampooing it thoroughly. I let my fingers investigate all of the area I was cleansing so that I could do a very thorough job. When the hair was all soapy I made it stand in strange shapes and had some fun with it. Then I rinsed it letting the water trickle into Sonja's vulva, so that it might tickle her there.

Now I pulled a small hank of the hair and snipped it off. I snipped some more and that left me with a long piece in the middle of the area I had been cutting, with short hair all round. This was on a very miniature scale, of course. I teased out the long hair and plaited it into a tiny plait.

I did this all over till her whole pussy had little tight plaits sticking it out, held by elastic bands. Sonja admired the effect very much.

'Can you shave round the cut areas?' she asked.

I brushed shaving soap on till her fleece was white with foam. Then with exquisite care, I began to shave around the plaits I had made.

The skin protested slightly and squeaked as I dragged

the blade over it. I rinsed the blade carefully and repeated the operation. Wonderful smooth skin was appearing, interspersed with hairy projecting plaits. I ran my finger along the nude grooves among the plaits. The skin felt like silk, baby fine without its strong covering of coarse hair.

Sonja stood up after I rinsed off the shaving soap and admired herself in a mirror. She was very pleased, I think.

She turned to face me. 'Will you do the rest now?' she asked. 'I'd like it all off.'

She lay down and I undid the plaits. Then I snipped them off. Then I shaved the little bristly tufts remaining. She lifted her legs and held them wide apart. I shaved between her legs as close as I dared to her sexual flesh.

As she became nude, so her vulva seemed to bulge forward. It was the sweetest thing. I cleaned all the soap from her skin and then I washed it gently in warm water. I patted it dry. Then I took some baby lotion and very carefully worked it into the shaven skin to soften it. I kept my fingers away from the enticing mysteries of her vulva though it was so close. I just worked and worked that lovely skin freshly revealed by the blade of the razor.

Sonja lay quietly, her legs wide apart. Her face was closed, its expression enigmatic. I stroked her naked skin and thought how removing the hair made her mound of Venus bulge towards me, as if inviting the caressing palm. I found I could place my whole hand over her mound. If the heel of my hand was on her stomach, my fingers curled naturally down and round till they slipped into the divide between her legs.

After a while I began to stroke her inner thigh where the white flesh was cool and silky and firm. I ran my fingers up to the top of her thighs again and again till she shivered. With no discreet covering I could see her vulva laid entirely bare. Her labia trembled slightly. Her clitoris moved as she worked her inner muscles. Her secret entrance squeezed shut as her level of excitation grew.

My own excitement was growing. The girl was delicious. She was spicy and appealing. At the moment she was passive and apparently submissive but I didn't think that that reflected her real character. I reckoned she was a real box of tricks but she would only open the box if I made her think it was worth her while.

I'm not used to being challenged. After a thoughtful moment I slipped away into the kitchen and looked in Sonja's cupboards. I found what I wanted and made a little mix of ingredients in a cup using cold water from the tap.

I took the goo I had made and sat myself down by Sonja's exposed sex once more. She eyed me like a cat from slitted eyes. I dipped my fingers in the sticky mess I had made and very carefully began to paint Sonja's sex.

It flowed white and thick. The flour and water paste began to set quite quickly. As it dried it shrank slightly, pulling in her skin. I knew she liked restraint. This tiny, small-scale, intimate restraint should appeal to her.

It appealed to me. I saw the white caking on her sex harden. I found that where it had dried I could pick it off with my long polished fingernails. Sonja's lips parted and she began to pant slightly. I guessed the sensations I was inflicting on her vulva were wonderful.

She began to writhe slightly. I painted the paste really thickly right from her strawberry arsehole to her mobile swollen clitoris. I was careful not to lay it on too thick and when she was thoroughly plastered I bent forward over her.

I brushed her lips with mine. I kissed her pierced nipple and tongued the little gold ring, tugging it slightly. I kissed her armpits and tasted her musk there. I kissed her ribs above and below the curious strapping she enjoyed. I trailed my tongue down her body and then I went back to her breasts and squeezed one hard with my hand while I kissed the other.

I kissed her neck and I opened her mouth with mine and I kissed her so that I could tongue her tongue and taste her saliva. I allowed my big breasts to crush between us so that they were caught by our bodies and trapped.

I sat up and caught her under her narrow waist. I lifted her middle. She arched like a bow. Her slender body was lovely, whippy and thin. I kissed her stomach. Bits of hardened paste cracked and fell off from her vulva. I lowered her and looked at what I had done.

It was crazed like old concrete. I slid one long shapely red nail under a flake and picked it off. Her clitoris poked out at me. I laughed and pinched it lightly. More hardened paste flaked off as Sonja convulsively squeezed her vaginal muscles.

I grasped the tiny stick of flesh and pulled it around a little. More paste fell off. Then I scratched some away with my nail. I enjoyed running the nail edge along parts of her vulva as they became exposed. Its colour was lovely as it came into view, raw and red and excited.

I chipped delicately into the paste. It became slimy and I knew I had the right place. I chiselled my way into the vaginal entrance. The natural wetness of the place had prevented the paste from hardening. I cleared the area some more. Only small flakes now still adhered. I cleared the bursting little arsehole holding the bumcheeks apart as I did so. It too was slightly slimy where the paste hadn't hardened. I put out my tongue and began to lick the little orifice clean.

I used the extreme tip of my tongue, making it with very tiny short licks so that the cleansing process took some while. Under my probing tongue tip the arse fluttered and trembled like a leaf. I ran my tongue round and round the puckered hole. Then I poked it in.

Sonja groaned. I smiled to myself. Then I bit her.

'I'm going to come,' she said weakly. They were the first words she had spoken since I began playing with her body.

'I'll punish you if you come before I'm ready,' I said calmly. I ran my nail round her arsehole and scraped the delicate flesh. She gasped slightly and I licked where I had scratched.

For a moment I played like this, licking her softly with velvet wet licks and then scratching her with my nail. Then I carefully inserted a finger into the hole and licked again, as best I could, and scratched again.

Sonja began to pant. 'Oh, oh, oh,' she cried. She was moving all the time, lifting her hips and squirming as the excitement threatened to overpower her.

I laughed. Leaving the finger inside her body I flaked the remaining hardened paste away. Then I licked her clean, harshly, like a cat.

She was jolting now in sexual stimulation as she struggled to hold her orgasm back. I touched her clitoris with one fingertip and pressed hard. I began to revolve the finger in her bottom. I adored the feel of her, soft and hot in there. Now I began to revolve the fingertip on her clitoris, going the opposite way. I pressed hard as I went round and round.

Sonja whimpered tightly for a moment. I watched her vagina closely. Then her belly went up and down, her tiny pointed breasts flushed and the thin runny juices of her orgasm began to trickle out of her cunt.

Its muscles contracted sharply and then released. I plunged my face in and bit the pulpy flesh as it shuddered. Sonja twisted and writhed and gasped. She began calling out. I released her body completely and sat back, watching her.

After several long minutes her eyes fluttered open. 'I couldn't help it,' she said.

'I'm going to smack your bottom for what you've done.' She looked at me. Then she rolled over.

'No,' I said sweetly. 'Stand up.'

She stood up.

'Bend over the arm of that chair.'

She bent over as commanded. I saw a glistening streak on one of her thighs. She was a lovely juicy girl. I picked up a flat leather sandal I had seen earlier. Sonja had been barefoot when I arrived but these embroidered leather sandals had been pushed to one side of the room where she had evidently kicked them off.

I tested the sandal lightly on my palm. It was very flexible. I placed it against Sonja's narrow white pointed buttocks. I drew it back and took aim. Then I smacked her as hard as I could.

The leather sole hit her flesh with a resounding whack. She gave a startled scream and I saw how the area I had abused began rapidly to glow a deep red. It must be stinging terrifically. I drew back my arm and let fly again. This time I hit the other buttock.

Sonja sobbed slightly. Her little body shook and trembled. I smacked her very hard rapidly two or three times in swift succession. She cried out but she didn't attempt to move away.

Now her bottom was fiery red. I touched it with my palm. It was hot. I had a idea and left her for a moment, telling her sternly to stay right where she was.

Back in the kitchen I rifled the fridge. It was the freezer compartment I needed. Moments later I was back in the room.

I took the ice tray and broke a few cubes out. Cradling them in my palm I applied them to Sonja's bottom.

'That burns,' she cried out.

I laughed and rubbed the cold ice across her flaming rear. The trouble was it made my hand hurt, it was so cold.

I thought for a moment. While I thought I slid a freezing finger into Sonja's rear once more. Then, as the ice melted and the edges softened, I slipped a rounded cube into her arse.

She screamed and jumped sharply, ejecting the ice.

Instantly I smacked her with the sandal again. She bent over miserably.

I had seen something else in the kitchen. I went back and I took a bag of frozen peas from the freezer compartment. I brought them back with me and applied the whole thing like a poultice to Sonja's glowing posterior.

This was better. Now I could smack her with the sandal and then freeze her pretty rump. To her it was burning, the cold was no different from the heat. Trying not to laugh out loud I told her to lie down on her back. I allowed her to have a cushion under her spine and under her thighs so that her tortured bottom was raised from the floor.

She lay down. 'You've been a naughty girl,' I said.

'I'm sorry. What you did was so wonderful I couldn't wait.'

'That's no excuse. And I don't think you've been punished enough.'

She whimpered. I tore the corner off the peas with my teeth. I emptied some into my palm.

'Open your legs,' I ordered.

She obeyed.

'Lift them up and hold them open.'

She did this. I knelt by her. I began to feed the little frozen pellets into her vagina.

She began to cry. 'That's enough, that's enough,' she pleaded.

'I'll check,' I said. I poked a finger back inside her strawberry bottom. I could feel the wobbling little pellets from that part of her body.

'I don't think it's too full at all,' I said, and put some more peas into her.

When I decided she truly had had enough I released her little arse. I stood up and took a hold of her ankles. I closed her legs and began to move them about. Sonja kept them quite stiff. I moved them intending the peas to move inside her as I did so.

201

She gasped and cried out with the pain. I released her legs and stood astride her. I bent over her and caught her under the arms. With one magnificent heave I hauled her to her feet. As I was still in my high heels and she was in her bare feet, the discrepancy in our heights was even further exaggerated.

'You may let one pea out,' I said.

She whimpered. She stood straddle-legged and opened her body. Several peas fell.

I walked round her and smacked her lightly with the sandal on her stinging bottom. 'I said one pea at a time,' I repeated.

It took her three goes to get it right. As the pressure inside her eased and as the peas themselves warmed up, she became better able to control their release. I lost my excuse for beating her lovely cheeks but I admired the fierce control she had of her own body.

When all the peas were out I knelt in front of her. 'We'd better make sure,' I said. I reached inside her body with my long fingers. I groped as best I could all round inside her poor tortured pussy, but it was indeed truly empty.

'We'd better warm it up,' I said. Sonja said nothing. She looked at me.

I made her lie down again. I fetched hot water from the kitchen and a long-spouted can I found there, for watering house plants.

I filled the little brass can and tested the temperature. Hot but not burningly so. I carefully inserted the long spout into Sonja's cunt. Then I slowly poured.

She sighed and gasped and began to relax. The hot water bubbled out of her pussy and dripped onto the towel underneath her. I bathed her frozen parts and warmed them in this way. Then I made her roll over. I slid the nozzle into her arse and I began to pour water into her there. She squeaked and squirmed and water ran out of her. I laughed heartily. It was a lovely sight.

I allowed her to lie on her back again and relax. I had a good look at her. The naked sex was truly beautiful.

'I have a dildo,' she said, watching me. 'In the drawer over there.'

I fetched it. It was a splendid thing, but it looked far too large to enter such a slender girl. I felt its artificial balls and ran my fingers lovingly over the shaped soft plastic. It was a wonderful representation of the male organ. It even had retractable skin over its bulging head. Moreover, it was a shining ebony black, gleaming silkily and satin smooth. The swollen head revealed by the retracted rubbery skin was a deep rich gold colour. I'd never seen anything so glorious. Even the veins on a man's penis were beautifully modelled.

I took some grease and for the pleasure of the thing I greased the whole wonderful length of it. Then I nudged it between Sonja's sexual lips. I pressed it against the mouth of her cunt. Her flesh began to yield. I pressed harder, fascinated. The fat head slid inside Sonja and vanished. I waited a moment and then I pushed the object further in. It slid easily. I pushed further. A look of strain appeared on Sonja's face. I pushed further again and then withdrew the thing till only the bulging head was clasped within her straining body.

'Could you put the belt round my stomach,' she panted.

I picked up the wide elasticated webbing strip and fastened it around her stomach. She winced as her sore buttocks were squeezed and small tears of pain trickled from the corners of her eyes. I groped in my handbag and found a tube of mascara. I inserted this between her buttocks and tightened the belt so she would feel the tube pressing against her bottom.

Now I began to fuck her in earnest with the dildo. I took my time and tried to simulate the best sort of fucking I'd had from a man. Sometimes I plunged it in hard and fast, and sometimes I just teased and tickled her by working the tip backwards and forwards, and sometimes I fucked her with long slow strokes.

She loved it. She lifted her hips to admit the thing further into her body, as deep as it would go. Doing this forced her buttocks to clamp the tube tightly under the restraining webbing. This must have hurt but she didn't care. She was given over to the exquisite sensations in her cunt.

I saw her move to orgasm. I controlled her and I loved it. I was kind and brought her all the way using all the skill and knowledge at my command to make it as good as I could.

When she orgasmed I fed it with deep plunges until she calmed. Then I slid the great plastic slug out of her body. I bent over her pussy and began to lick her, cat-fashion, licking her juices and tasting her. I licked her clean, feeling the little after-tremors as I did so and she purred in satisfaction.

I sat back holding the massive weapon thoughtfully. Sonja sat up, wincing as weight came on her buttocks.

'Well, well,' she said. I smiled.

All this time I had been wearing my pretty underwear. Now Sonja snapped at me to remove it. I did so, feeling startlingly vulnerable without it.

She made me stand naked in the room and she walked round me. The only things I was allowed to wear were my shoes. She flicked at me a couple of times.

'You're fat,' she said coldly.

'I'm not,' I said indignantly. I was certainly full-fleshed where it mattered, at my creamy bust and where my bottom provocatively pouted, but I was narrow waisted and I had long slim shapely legs.

'Fat,' she said scathingly. 'We'll have to do something about that.'

She went off to her bedroom and came back with a box. She opened it and took from it a large stiff garment.

It was a corset. She put it round my body and I felt the boned garment press into my soft flesh. She went round the back to where the laces hung and began to pull them tight.

My breasts rested more or less on top of the strange garment where a frou-frou of stiff black lace topped the crimson satin corset. Wide black stripes emphasised how the garment would pull in the waist. At my back Sonja began to pull the laces.

She pulled as hard as she could so that I staggered and almost fell. Then she put a foot up against my back and pulled harder.

I began to gasp. I couldn't breathe. My waist was so tightly held I felt faint. My ribs were squeezed so that I thought they would break.

Sonja pulled tighter and then tied the thing so I couldn't loosen it. I had to rely entirely on Sonja for release.

She came round to face me. I must have been red-faced with the struggle to breathe. 'Walk up and down,' she said, and smiled.

I walked across the room and back again several times, getting used to the restriction and adjusting to it. My breasts were bloated balloons squeezed up almost under my chin. I felt distanced from the rest of my body, my lower areas. They were the other side of the corset and I could hardly see them.

My bottom felt funny, half-crushed by the corset as I walked. It came up at the front to end at the base of my belly. My red hair fluffed out, tangling with the black lace that edged it all around.

'Good,' said Sonja. 'Now sit down.'

I couldn't, I was too stiff. I couldn't bend my body at the appropriate places. I leaned back and my body lay at a stiff angle instead of conforming to the shape of the chair.

'That's no use,' said Sonja. 'Sit here, on this chair.'

She pulled a wooden chair forward and turned it round

so that I could sit upright astride the seat and hold on to the back of the chair. I could manage this, just. I had to sit bolt upright and my legs were straining against the tight clasp of the corset where it attempted to constrict my buttocks. But the position was at least possible.

Sonja fetched a long leather belt. I struggled to keep my expression calm. She wove the belt through the wooden chairback and then fixed it round my body so that I was strapped to the chair with the buckle at my back where it was impossible to reach it. I couldn't twist at all, the corset held me so stiffly. I was now completely at Sonja's mercy.

Next Sonja took a leather thong and bound one of my wrists to the chair back. Then she bound the other wrist so that my hands couldn't touch each other. She bent down and tied my ankles to the chair legs in the same fashion.

I continued to sit. The harsh wooden seat pressed into my swollen excited sexual flesh. I couldn't understand what Sonja intended to do. She couldn't reach any part of me except my bulging breasts.

When she was done she stood back in satisfaction. Then she went all around me and tested the bindings to check that none of them were loose. It seemed to me she was expecting me to struggle. But I still couldn't understand what was going to happen.

She paused thoughtfully. Then she knelt by the chair again. She reached up under the seat. My vulva felt itself being twisted. I yelped slightly. Then cool air rushed against my heated flesh.

Sonja had removed the seat of the chair from underneath me. I sat astride a hole now, and my sex gaped through it while the wooden frame of the seat dug painfully into the soft flesh of my underthighs. So, Sonja could do as she pleased. I was securely bound and my most vulnerable parts lay open for her pleasure.

I remembered how I had tortured her and shuddered.

'I think it's time a friend came,' said Sonja. She looked at a watch she had resting on the mantelpiece.

'A friend?' I gasped.

'You look ready for company.'

'No,' I said.

'I asked him round to talk about SI-Humans with you but this is much more fun. He's quite a guy.'

'No,' I said more strongly. 'I go with men on my own terms. You can't do this.'

She laughed and checked her watch again. Sure enough the doorbell rang at this point.

She wore nothing except her curious webbing. She went out of the room without bothering to put a robe on. I knew she had a peephole to her flat, but even so, she must be on very good terms with the man coming to the door. It gave me a sadistic pleasure to see how red her cheeks were as she turned her back to me.

All too soon she was back. Silently she showed a male into the room. My face burned with humiliation. I could do nothing, nothing at all. And there didn't seem to be anything to say, either.

'This is Red Marsden,' said Sonja. She smiled. 'She's come to play.'

'No,' I said forcefully.

He was tall and blond, a complete physical contrast to the little dark Sonja. He wore a T-shirt under his jacket and I could see his muscles bulging when he slipped his jacket off. He was wide-shouldered and narrow-hipped. His bronzed face glowed with a healthy tan. He looked at me almost idly.

'Has she been like this long?'

'No,' said Sonja. 'I haven't had time to do anything yet. But she needs chastising. She's a very naughty lady.'

The man sat down. They hadn't told me his name. Sonja picked up a fly switch and flexed it. Then she reached under the chair and swatted smartly upwards.

A sharp stinging pain erupted through my tender parts. I shouted in dismay and Sonja smacked upwards again.

The man laughed.

'It hurts, dammit,' I said indignantly.

Sonja hit me again.

She hit me several times. An enormous burning pain grew from my tortured vulva. Tears poured out of my eyes. I flushed a deep horrible red. I sobbed and squirmed uselessly. I was strapped fast to the dreadful chair.

The man got up and came over to the chair. He bent underneath and had a look. A moment later I felt his probing fingers.

My flesh shivered and juddered away from the intrusive fingers. 'Don't do that,' I yelled. For an answer Sonja popped an ice cube up under the corset so that my buttocks held it against my arse.

She beat me some more, the switch stinging all my open sexual parts so they flamed. Almost I could feel them writhing away from their abuser, as though my sex was an animal with a life of its own.

The man had an idea. He rocked the chair over so that I lay on my back on the floor, the chair back on top of me. Now my exposed sex was easy for them to see and to get at.

The two of them squatted, looking into my bruised and beaten vulva. 'Look at my new toy,' said Sonja. She picked up the dildo and began to slide it into my body.

I cried out. I was swollen and sore and the dildo hurt.

'Do you want to do this?' Sonja invited.

'Sure. I'll just get more comfortable first,' he said.

He stood up and came round to where I could see him. Nonchalantly he stripped. He was staggeringly beautiful, a marvellous male, all gleaming muscle and tight skin. His sex bulged forward in a very interesting way. He was a proper man in every respect.

When he was quite naked he went back round to Sonja

and knelt by my poor sexual parts. I felt him slide the dildo in. He began to fuck me with it quite rapidly.

I was sore and it hurt. But I was also very excited. I hadn't realised this. Suddenly, grossly, I found I was in orgasm. I strained and panted in my bonds. I thought I would suffocate, it was so hard to get air into my lungs. I felt my pussy was turning inside out. The pair of them were laughing at what they could see. They took the dildo out and watched my final spasms closely.

'Nice,' commented the man.

A moment later I felt probing fingers elsewhere. The ice had melted and they easily found my bottom. The cheeks were held apart and the corset pushed up slightly. Fingers investigated. I felt tears of humiliation on my cheeks. I lay quietly trying to relax. I wanted to draw deep breaths but I couldn't. I tried not to think.

More fingers went inside me. I clutched my buttocks as best I could and whimpered through set teeth.

My buttocks were held open against my will. I felt something huge and blunt push against my arsehole.

'No,' I cried out in agony.

'You know, I don't think it'll go in,' said the man conversationally.

'Sure it will,' said Sonja and laughed.

She pushed harder. My bottom felt split open. I didn't know if she was pushing his cock into me or the dildo. Either of them was far too large for my tight tender place.

'You'll tear me,' I gasped.

Sonja snickered. She pushed harder. I gasped and stopped resisting. The huge invasion slid right in and my mouth fell open, my head back, my eyes bulging.

It was the dildo. The two of them stood up and took a leisurely look at me. I lay with my arse split wide and ravished and the two of them smiled and looked me over as if I was meat.

The man was erect. His vast golden wand stuck out in

front of him. He ignored it, though he glanced casually at Sonja's sex. 'What happened?' he asked.

'She shaved me.'

'It looks nice.'

'I think so.'

They contemplated me in silence again. Then Sonja sighed. 'We'd better get on with it,' she said.

They went back round to my opened sex and stuffed bottom. Sonja played with my clitoris while the man fucked my bottom with the dildo. The real humiliation was coming. I couldn't prevent myself from moving to orgasm once again.

Then they abandoned me. They left the thing in me, sunk deeply between my buttocks, but left me on the rise to orgasm without having been satisfied. They came round to the side and Sonja knelt down on all fours. The man knelt down and hefted his cock. Before my astonished eyes he slid his cock into her pussy.

'Why is your bottom so red?' he said, working his cock deep into her.

'She beat me.'

'Naughty lady.' He began to move to Sonja.

I lay with my head cranked sideways watching them. He began to fuck her quite slowly and gently, though as time passed he went faster and made love harder to her. They were only about twelve inches from my face. I saw his fat balls swinging. I saw her hairless pussy. I saw his gleaming rod powering in and out of her and I felt jealous.

Moments later she was sighing with release and he was extracting his softening member. He pulled free and watched her pussy with appreciation. I could see it too. His spunk bubbled from her hole and steamed faintly.

He looked across at me and smiled. Then he stood up and turned round. He dropped himself so that he was kneeling astride my face. His musky sex-soaked prick lay on my face. I could feel its damp stickiness. Sonja crawled round to my rear. I felt her kiss my pussy and again there were tears oozing from my eyes. She kissed my pussy and sucked the trembling flesh. She ignored the huge dildo distending my bottom. She settled to kiss and suck me, licking my clitoris, and the man put his used sex into my mouth.

I didn't know his name. His sex lay soft and heavy on my tongue. I could taste his spunk, Sonja's musk. I rolled my tongue round his sex. It felt a little firmer. He knelt all golden and beautiful, his cloud of pubic hair tickling my face. He joggled his hips slightly. I sucked harder. He began to fuck my mouth and I sucked him as he did so, and brought him all the way to climax.

He spurted freely into my mouth but then drew back slightly so that he messed my face. I lay panting, hardly aware of whether I was in orgasm or not. Sonja appeared and began to lick my face, licking my tears and the man's spunk impartially. The man laughed and stroked her bottom while she licked me. He had sat back down on me and this time his limp cock rested on the black lace of the corset top and my straining breasts.

When Sonja was done the man turned round so that I had his bottom in my face. Sonja made him tea and he drank this, smoking a cigarette and talking with her about various people they knew. After a while he arranged his cock so that it lay in my tight cleavage. As he sat relaxing, I was able to feel his cock slowly grow.

He put his cup carefully down to one side and raised himself slightly and edged back. His big hairy bottom was now over my face. Sonja came round behind my head and held his buttocks apart. His large puckered hole was revealed. He lowered this over my mouth and they waited for me to begin.

'No,' I whispered, muffled by his arse.

He sat up. Sonja let me go. She walked round and took the dildo out of my arse. Then she smacked my sex with the fly switch. I was swollen and tender from her kissing me to climax. I screamed. She came back to behind my head and squatted there. She opened the man's cheeks and he put his bottom over my face again.

'No,' I said again.

They repeated the procedure, saying nothing. My vulva stung dreadfully and again I felt the weak juices of orgasm run without any control on my part.

This time I gave way. Gingerly I reached up with my tongue. I didn't even know his name, I knew nothing about him, but here I was kissing his arse and preparing to lick him there.

Sonja squatted patiently above me. If I looked up I could see straight into her beautiful underparts. Their baldness was fantastic. I must consider having it done to myself. Meanwhile almost all of my vision was blocked by the great male arse hanging over it.

I began to kiss his bottom.

After a while I felt his cock harden and lengthen. He began to move. He had it trapped between my breasts again and he was fucking his cock into my cleavage as I sucked his rear and teased him there. All the time Sonja squatted by my head watching intently and holding his bottom open so I could penetrate it properly, not being able to use my own hands for anything.

He took a long time. He was enjoying himself and in no hurry. Finally I felt him groan and jerk. Sonja stood up and went round to see. He was spurting into my breasts, pushing hard against their resistance and bringing himself to a full and fine climax.

He stood up and looked down at me. I couldn't see myself properly at all. I could feel the warm wet spunk oozing over me though.

He sighed. 'I'd better go,' he said to Sonja. He began to get dressed.

She saw him to the door. Then she came back and

released my ankles and my hands. She undid the belt and pushed me on to my side away from the chair. She loosened my stays.

I lay gasping like a beached fish. Air sucked and whooped into my tortured lungs. Sonja helped me to sit up and offered me a glass of wine.

I clambered painfully to my feet and hobbled over to an armchair. I slumped gratefully into its soft curves. I drank the wine and felt some kind of comfort return to my body.

After a while Sonja sat on the edge of the armchair and stroked my freely-swinging breasts. 'They're lovely,' she said.

'I'm fond of them,' I said, 'but you are something quite special in that department yourself.'

I sat up stiffly and kissed her breasts and sucked them. They were so tiny they were sweet and I loved the feel of them in my mouth, especially the one with the ring piercing the nipple. I even felt the faint tickle of arousal again, tired and sore as I was.

'Is he in the SI-Humans organisation?' I asked eventually, my investigative curiosity becoming rearoused as my body relaxed.

'In a peripheral way. He's a journalist. Sometimes he writes a piece for us if his editor lets him.'

I was alarmed. 'He won't write anything about what I've been asking you, will he?'

Sonja smiled. 'He wasn't interested in what you had to say,' she commented.

She had a point. Anyway, what did I have to say to these people? They believed that under certain circumstances humans could self-ignite. I'd come to them with three case histories where girls might have self-ignited but more probably were attacked for their sexual behaviour which would have scandalised their neighbourhoods. They had investigated at least one of these case histories already, since that was how I'd got on to them in the first place.

'Could you let me have a list of some of the deaths you think are examples of SI-Humans?' I asked.

'What for?'

'Just to see if there are any similarities with the deaths I'm interested in.'

Sonja laughed. 'You reckon self-igniters haunt, do you?'

'Maybe,' I said, embarrassed. Some sort of idea like that had occurred to me, it was true. I figured I might check one or two, if it wasn't too difficult, and see if any funny goings on were going on where the so-called self-ignition had taken place.

Sonja laughed at me but she gave me the list. I saw at once there were many American examples on it and I could hardly investigate them. Americans are less resistant to new ideas than the British, of course.

I was thoughtful when I left Sonja's flat. It had been a most interesting evening. I had thoroughly enjoyed myself.

FILE SIXTEEN

Three incidents where I behave oddly, by Red Marsden

Incident One – Planefields School

I chose the school because I felt that it was a place where absolutely nothing weird could be happening. If there was a rule to be proved, something I strongly doubted, this would be the exception. Some twenty years earlier when the building was still a private house, the then owner had rushed into room full of his wife's guests. He had been engulfed in flames. A rug was hastily torn off the wall with great presence of mind on someone's part and thrown over the burning man. He had received third degree burns over a fifth of his body but he had survived.

His story, as it was recorded, was that he had been standing in the flagstone passage that led into the house from the kitchen garden into the servants quarters. He had been in conversation with a gardener, and had then come in to remove his rubber boots and jacket.

His stomach had suddenly felt very uncomfortable. He had opened his mouth to belch and flames had issued from his mouth, burning his tongue and lips. He had clapped a hand over his mouth and the hanging sleeve of his unfastened shirt had ignited.

Meanwhile a sharp pain had caused him almost simultaneously to double over. His stomach had a terrible cramp. To his undying horror flames were coming out of the front of his trousers.

He insisted afterwards the flames had started inside him but the hospital rejected his story as the subjective reaction to shock and fright. Certainly there were incredibly deep burns on his body.

A year later he was found dead in the same passage, burned to ash.

The wife had sold up and the large country house had become a small private school for girls. The ugly reputation of foul goings-on had clung to the building for some time but now all seemed peaceful, if a building full of teenage girls can ever be so described.

The wife had remarried very soon after her husband's death and again there was that faint hint of foul play.

I intended to visit the school in the guise of a remote relation of the original owner, come from abroad to see the old family home. The school had been initially very sympathetic to this nostalgic approach and I had hinted over the phone that I had pubescent daughters who might be sent here. I decided I was an Australian for the occasion. The school fees were very high.

I dressed in my most fabulous suit, a Paris design that screams haute couture though it is a copy. It was beautifully cut and designed and it clung to my curves in a flattering and seductive manner. I wore it to make men drool and women feel jealous. Though incredibly smart, it was mysteriously sexy. I looked wonderful in it, not sluttish but mouthwateringly edible. I knew the effect drove men wild.

This time however I was wearing it to impress women.

I hired a Porsche and drove up to the front entrance on the gravel sweep with something of a flourish. I went inside and found the secretary's office. Her room overlooked the entrance. She could see the vehicle I had arrived in.

She led me into the headmistress's room. It was large and square with dark panelled walls hung with gloomy oil paintings. The room would have been gloomy itself but for a pair of vast windows that ran from dado to cornice height. From them one looked over playing fields stretching into the distance. Girls could be seen running about slowly in the dull cold weather.

I had a fur stole wound round my neck in which my chin nestled. My red hair gleamed foxy above the deep brown tones of the fur. I looked impossibly young to have teenage daughters but I adopted a haughty manner more suitable to a rich woman in her mid-thirties than the feckless free spirit of independent mind and inadequate means that was what I actually was.

I swooped on the headmistress with a faint Aussie twang and settled myself in the padded chair opposite her to the sumptuous accompaniment of rustling silk as my stockings and suit lining rubbed together.

'You have daughters who might wish to attend Planefields?' said Miss Houghton, getting down to the matter at one.

'I thought it would be cute if they came here, where cousin Roger once had the family seat,' I said. 'I mean, we feel we have connections with the place. Know what I mean?'

'Yes. Quite. A charming thought. You must regret the property having left the family.'

'I guess I do. But it's all nostalgia, really. I mean, my home is the world, Miss Houghton.' I stared at her earnestly. 'We live on the yacht mostly.'

'The yacht?'

'The hubby and me. He can handle all the day-to-day business affairs using the satellite link to our Sydney office. He takes the seaplane if he needs to get home in a hurry.'

I didn't need to do all this but I was enjoying myself. I needed some excuse to go poking my nose around the school and this had seemed to me to be one she couldn't check up on.

'How have the girls been educated so far?'

'Teachers,' I said succinctly. 'We hire 'em and fire 'em.'

'You fire them?'

'The girls are forward for their age. And real pretty. I guess they need a little discipline.'

'We believe in discipline at Planefields.'

'Great,' I said genially. 'I reckon a good spanking is all a kid needs when she's out of line. I don't like to nag, see.' I smiled and rustled my clothes again. Miss Houghton looked a martinet to me. I could well believe in the discipline of Planefields.

She began to show me round. I saw a bunch of classrooms that almost obscured the gracious origins of the house. I saw science labs and computer rooms and music rooms (with a recording studio), the theatre, the language centre and so on until I was bored stupid. It was the old kitchens I wanted to see. That was where the unfortunate man had twice caught fire.

After a while I said: 'How about the chow department, Miss Houghton? A girl needs good grub in her to face the rigours of the academic day. I mean, I wouldn't want Morningstar and Sally-Anne to get peaky, now. They're shapely girls, Miss Houghton. I want none of this anorexia nonsense.'

Her eyes flickered. I was enjoying the picture I was building up of a pair of flirtatious little madams. I only did it to entertain myself during the dreary round of the school.

We went down to modern kitchens. The place must have been extensively refitted when it was made into a school. In desperation I became nosy. I wanted a flagged back entrance, or something that might once have been such a thing. I marched forward and flung open a door. 'What's through here?' I asked with Aussie brashness.

'The punishment room,' said Miss Houghton. She was panting slightly in an effort to keep up with my free and long stride. 'As I explained, we believe in teaching the girls self-control. That means in rare circumstances we resort to physical punishments. All parents sign a disclaimer, Mrs Kesteven-MacBride. We believe in the power of the admonishing hand, when used with discretion.'

I'd seen the cold showers with no cubicle doors and the cloakrooms with an almost equal lack of privacy. Poor little cows who came here, I thought. But Miss Hougton was proud of her uncomfortable regime and plainly the school was flourishing. Enough wealthy parents sent their offspring here to make her unashamed of the spartan lifestyle the girls had to suffer. The whole school was a kind of punishment block, to my mind.

'Please don't go in,' she began, as I reached for the next door handle. The decor had suddenly taken a leap back in time with thick old plastered stone walls and a quarry-tiled floor. I had the feeling I was near to my goal.

I stopped with my hand on the door.

'There are some girls being punished right now?' I enquired, smiling.

'Possibly, possibly. Mr Findhorn administers correction.'

'You have a guy smack the girls?' I raised my perfect eyebrows, still smiling.

'It teaches them obedience to men,' hissed Miss Hougton. 'Our girls do not get divorced. They are happily married. This school has no modern ideals. We believe in solid family values.'

I bet you do, I thought cynically and opened the door.

What a sight met my eyes. The room was very dark, long and narrow, but it took me a minute to see the flagstone floors. I had reached my goal.

The sight was dazzling. A long rail ran along one white-washed wall at knee height. Another rail ran parallel to it at waist height some eighteen inches away from it. Bent over this rail and holding on to the lower rail were six girls.

They were all upside-down and red faced but they looked about sixteen or seventeen years of age to me. They wore school uniform but it had been disarranged for their punishment. The man who was to punish them, Mr Findhorn, was standing with a slender birch rod in his hand. He had looked up at me, startled, when I burst in. Now he eyed Miss Hougton nervously, waiting for what she would say.

'This is Mrs Kesteven-MacBride,' she said, between gritted teeth. 'Mr Findhorn, our master of correction. Mrs Kesteven-MacBride is connected with the family who used to live here,' she added for Mr Findhorn's benefit. 'She has two daughters who might be interested in coming here, Morningstar and Sally-Anne.'

'Morningstar?' asked Mr Findhorn. He laid the rod lightly in his palm. 'That's an unusual name, Mrs Kesteven-MacBride.'

'It's the name of the first mine that did good for my husband,' I said. I winked at Mr Findhorn. He was about my own age, my real age, I mean, and he was a honey with wild Byronic locks tossed across a broad brow. His eyes had a kind of storm-tossed look about them too. I looked with interest at the girls being admonished by this dark and sexy specimen of brooding manhood. They had remained upside-down obediently in place during this conversation.

They all had naked bottoms.

I could see their thick school knickers down about their ankles. Their skirts were up over their heads. Some of the girls wore socks and had bare legs. Some wore thick stockings held up by garters and these pinched into the soft flesh of their plump young thighs. Some wore proper pretty little garter belts and good stockings. Their naked bottoms were all the juicier.

Some of the bottoms had red stripes across them. 'Don't mind me, Mr Findhorn,' I said, with great good humour. 'If the girls have been naughty, whack it to them. I'm all for it.' I smiled into his eyes and ran the tip of my tongue along my red lips. Then I pouted slightly and waited.

'The girls are being taught obedience,' said Miss Houghton in a stifled voice. 'We find this the quickest and surest method. The girls have voted for this sort of punishment rather than being confined to the school grounds or being set extra homework. They appreciate the virtues of punishment and true repentence.'

I now saw we weren't alone. At the far end of the passage near to the door to outside, beyond the row of pink naked bottoms, another man sat on a high stool. He was holding a leather-bound book.

Miss Hougton saw where I was looking. 'The Reverend Brightwater oversees the punishments and reads from the Scriptures,' she said. 'The girls' minds are edified as their persons are chastised.'

'Well, carry on,' I said. 'Morningstar and Sally-Anne will want to know all about this. They'll need some warning if they are to drop their knickers every time they're bad girls.'

Mr Findhorn turned back to his work. He flexed the rod slightly and looked at the pouting bottoms lined up in front of him. 'Where had I reached?' he asked. Even his voice was dark and sexy. I could have stood to line up with the girls to have such a dish chastise me.

'Me, sir,' squeaked a voice. The girl was half-way down the line. Her bottom gave a tight little wriggle as she prepared herself. Mr Findhorn looked at me, looked at Miss Houghton, drew the rod back and thwacked the little female arse in front of him.

The girl shuddered and sighed. He went to the next girl. The Rev. in the corner started reading again, from the Old Testament I think. Mr Findhorn whacked and the girl moaned. Just hearing it, you wouldn't have known she was objecting.

I watched with pleasure as he played his birch rod along that lovely pulsating female flesh. It was clear to me the girls adored him. I could smell sexual juices on the air and I was sure that some of the girls were in orgasm. Miss Houghton and the Rev. might be missing the byplay, but Mr Findhorn certainly knew what was what. I could see the bulge in his trousers.

He smacked his way up and down the line. After a while, he put his palm on the bottoms in front of him, one after another, and felt them.

'He makes sure the flesh is chastised but not abused,' said Miss Houghton. I mentally hugged myself. People's capacity for self-deception never ceases to amaze me.

Mr Findhorn stroked bottoms and then birched one or two of them again. The rod made a lovely thin whistling noise as it approached a glowing rear.

He stood back and coughed slightly. 'That will be all, girls,' he said. They began stiffly to stand themselves up. They rubbed their bottoms and groaned. Now I could see little thatches of pubic hair, some pale and some dark. The girls made no attempt to cover themselves. Far from it. Some of them turned round with their skirts hooked over their arms showing all their sweet little bellies and pussy fur, and groaned in complaint to Mr Findhorn.

'Oh sir, you did it much harder than usual.'

'Sir, I'm sure you gave me an extra one.'

'Am I all red, sir? Take a look and tell me.'

'It hurts everso, sir.'

Miss Houghton stopped this girlish chatter and reluctantly the girls hauled their drawers up their legs. Some of them wore delicate inner panties under their uniform knickers and they carefully separated the two garments and hauled the flimsy little things up first over their mortified cheeks.

'Does it show red through my panties, sir?' one girl asked, turning round and bending over again in front of the master.

Miss Houghton shooed them away. Then she turned to me. But I was ready for her. 'Perhaps you'll let me poke about a bit by myself,' I asked cheerfully. 'I can talk to the girls and see if it's a happy school. I want my girls to be happy, I guess.'

'Certainly, Mrs Kesteven-MacBride,' said Miss Houghton. 'I'll see you in my office for coffee in, say twenty minutes? Will that be sufficient?'

I glanced at Mr Findhorn. 'That'll be just dandy, Miss Houghton. Thanks a bunch for the inspection. I'm real impressed. I think my hubby'd like this place no end, you know that? He kinda approves of girls getting an old-fashioned upbringing.'

Miss Houghton took the Rev. off with her. I advanced on Mr Findhorn and held out a hand. 'Thanks for letting me see your work,' I said. As I did this I put my other hand over the front of his trousers. He was hard erect. I smiled at him and squeezed his cock. 'I guess you're a happy man, doing right by these little girls all the time.'

He licked his lips. We were still holding hands as if we were shaking them and my hand was clamped like a terrier over his sexual equipment. I squeezed some more. 'Why did you choose this gloomy little hole to do the business with young ladies?' I said, my accent getting broader and broader. 'You'd have had a better view in a nice sunny room.'

He licked his lips and I felt his cock move in my grasp. 'It seemed the right place for it,' he said.

I closed up to him so that my boobs brushed his chest. 'Ever felt any strange presences down here while you're giving it to the girls?' I murmured.

'What do you mean?' His lips brushed my brow.

I rotated my hand full of trouser front and male sexual

parts. 'My cousin died down here, you know. This mansion used to be in the family. My family. Does my cousin haunt you ever, Mr Findhorn?'

'No,' he said and undid his trouser belt.

'How about you chastise me a little,' I murmured in his ear. I put my tongue out and licked into his ear. I felt him jolt in my hands. 'I had a suspicion the girls kinda liked it, you know that?'

'They do seem to come back,' he said, his breath coming short. He reached down and caught the hem of my skirt. He hauled it sharply up. I pulled away from him and keeping up the eye contact I slid my silky panties down to my ankles. Then I turned round and bent over the punishment rail.

I felt him palm my buttocks. He caressed them, his breath coming noisily, for several long moments. Then I heard the whistle of the birch. My stomach muscles tightened involuntarily. The sharp sweet sting of the rod cut my flesh. I cried out and held on to the other rail.

He brought the switch down again, and again. The pain sang thinly through me and I felt the delicious hot burning glow from my bottom spread outwards through my pussy till I was feverish for entry. Then I felt that cool caressing palm again. I let go of the holding rail and reached behind me, pressing forward into the rail I was bent over for balance. I held my bottom cheeks apart.

His hand came between the plump mounds of soft flesh. I felt him touch, flutteringly, my arse, my clitoris, my pussy entrance. Then a finger was momentarily in my body, feeling my juicy inner heat. A moment later I had the full engine inside me, his naked cock thrust deep into my needy cunt, and he began to pump me rapidly.

His belly struck my sore buttocks and the quick sting of pain with each blow added fire to the fuck. I could feel his soft hairy balls swinging against my thighs. I squirmed back into him. He thumped really hard and the next moment I felt him jetting into me.

My thighs became all messy with spunk. 'I haven't come yet,' I said indignantly. His response was to stand back and remove his softening cock. He then began to beat me again, but this time they were feathering blows, little short rapid twitches against my skin, each a tiny stinging pain that built into a glorious glowing whole so that my cunt swelled and my orgasm ran free at last.

I hung panting. My Findhorn was divine. I worked myself upright and turned round, pushing my hair into place and allowing my cheeks to cool. The cheeks of my face, I mean. Then I took his face between my leather gloved hands. I kissed the young man hard on the lips and as I did so, he put the switch between my legs and drew it up so that it pressed on my tender dribbling parts. For a moment I rode the rod. I wriggled on it and then I allowed my weight to press down so that it fell away and I knelt in front of my chastiser.

His cock was noble in semi-repose as it was now. I took it into my mouth and kissed and sucked its soft length. Then I stood up, savouring the taste of the man as I did so.

I felt in my handbag and found mirror and lipstick. I patted my hair into place and fixed my make-up. All the while my panties stayed round my ankles and my skirt up around my waist. All my private charms were visible.

At last I pulled my clothes together and checked my watch. 'I'd better see Miss Houghton, I guess,' I said and sighed regretfully.

He watched me go, his dark and sombre face indecently handsome. The amenities of the school were really very good indeed.

I did speak to a couple of the girls and I asked them if the building was haunted but they said no, not to their knowledge. Also, there had been no fires or other incidents of any kind. There was a limit to how much I could ask without seeming odd, but it seemed to me that apart from the delicious punishment routine evidently enjoyed by the master and girls alike, there was nothing odd about the place at all. No ghosts, no incidents – all was peaceful. Here was no repetition of poor Linda Campsey's experience at Lane End Cottages, nor the feverish sexual excitement that had almost torn Roger and myself in two when we experienced it, though we were hardly novices in the field of sexual practice.

Whatever was going on in Roger's house wasn't happening here. I went away none the wiser.

Incident Two – Musgrove Hill

The conflagration in this case had occurred five years earlier. The victim was a fireman, curiously enough. He had been a very fit man and was only forty-five at the time of his death. He had died in bed from a terrible scorching heat that was also very localised. The house suffered extensive smoke damage but little else had burned. The bed was not burned though some of the bedding was scorched, nor was a newspaper burned that had been on the bedside table. When help finally reached the body some bones remained and three and a half pounds of ash.

So much I knew. What I didn't know, beyond his name, was the business of the current occupant of the house. I had found out his name from the electoral register but I knew nothing else. It was difficult to prepare a story, therefore, as I had done for the school. I would just have to use my wits.

When I finally arrived at the door I held a clipboard in one hand very ostentatiously. I also wore glasses perched on my upturned nose secured with a little gold chain so they could hang from my neck if necessary. I had ready a dazzling smile and when the householder opened the door, I let him have the full effect.

'I'm so sorry to bother you,' I said. To my relief I saw

he was a personable man, in his fifties perhaps, with grey hair kept rather long. He had piercing blue eyes which were all the more apparent because he wore a blue denim work shirt and blue jeans. His forearms were muscular and hairy and he looked lean and fit. I couldn't place him at all.

'What is it?' he said. His eyes flickered down me and up again. I couldn't tell if he approved or not.

'I'm doing some social research,' I said.

He interrupted. 'I don't have time, Miss, er . . .'

'Fulsome,' I said sweetly.

'What?'

'Miss Fulsome. It won't take long, I promise, Mr Bulgar.' I thought he deserved a better name. His was dreadful.

'Geoff Bulgar used to live here. Then I bought the place.'

'I'm so sorry,' I cooed. 'Your name is?'

'None of your business.'

He didn't shut the door. I guessed he was playing games. He was a man who liked to have people plead.

'Of course not. And the survey is confidential. But we note down all the names so that we don't sample the same person twice. The names are preserved only for a short time and then they not kept with their corresponding questionaires so that the anonymity of your replies is absolute. I wish you could find ten minutes to help.' I smiled winningly.

'What is the subject of the questionnaire?' he asked coldly.

I had four prepared. I chose the one I thought most suitable for the specimen I had before me. 'I'm a sociology graduate from the University of Southend,' I said. 'I'm doing a PhD on a grant from the Zenith Foundation to investigate common sexual practice by housing type.'

He gaped at me. Then he grinned. 'You're not serious.'

'Certainly I'm serious, Mr, er . . .'

'Jason Wells.' He looked at me keenly and suddenly there was a tense silence.

Jason Wells. He expected me to recognise the name. I didn't and I had the feeling that to admit as much would get the door shut in my face.

Jason Wells. Good-looking. Arrogant. Rude. Apparently well-heeled. At home in the daytime. Working.

'I've seen your work, Mr Wells, though I'm too busy to be as familiar as I'd like with it,' I said cannily.

He shrugged. 'It's written for men, mostly, though I believe I have a small but fervent female readership.'

I let my eyes walk admiringly up his person. 'If I'd have had any idea I was going to meet you . . .' I said. I hesitated. 'Look, do you mind letting me do the survey with you? It really won't take long. I'd be honoured.'

He couldn't resist the flattery. He obviously reckoned it was his due. He stood back opening the door wide and I trotted into his house like the fly into a spider's parlour.

Suddenly he seemed to have all the time in the world. He made a cup of coffee for me muttering his housekeeper didn't stay there all day.

'Are you married, Mr Wells?' I asked.

'The hell I am. I was, of course, but it didn't work out. I guess you know what I mean.'

I didn't, but I was going to antagonise him now. I looked round the place as best I could. The fireman had died in bed, upstairs. I could ask to use the bathroom or I could pretend I was a fan and yearned to see where he worked. I had heard him thumping down the stairs to answer the door so I had good reason to think he worked up rather than down.

I wondered what he wrote. I had looked at bookcases as I went through behind him to the kitchen to see if there was a row of pristine uniform editions that would signal his own work. Maybe he wasn't as arrogant as I had taken him for. I saw no such thing.

We came back carrying the coffee to a room at the back of the house with patio doors opening to a small garden beyond. They were closed against the cold weather, a fog was coming down, but an artificial log fire kept the room comfortably warm. Jason sat himself in an armchair one side of the fire and gave me the benefit of his blue eyes.

I sat in the other chair, crossed my legs to make my skirt slide up and arranged my clipboard. There were books all round the room and no sign of a TV. Again, I could not see anything that suggested his personal oeuvre.

'What was it again, Miss Fulsome?' he said. 'Sex by house type, I think you said.'

I took my glasses off, opened my eyes wide and leaned forward earnestly.

'It's a small part of the continuing investigation into the true nature of sexual behaviour in an advanced democracy,' I said. 'The subject is such a difficult one and people are inclined to say what they wish was true rather than what actually is true. Image is all, Mr Wells.'

'Jason. I don't agree. We aren't all screwed-up failures dogged by out-of-date and insufficient morality. Some of us act naturally and tell the flat truth.' He smiled and bared his teeth.

'My name is Charity,' I said. 'That's marvellous, Jason. I'd really like to do you, you know.'

'Do me?'

'For the survey. Once we have a true reflection of society, then public health can be more sensibly addressed and campaigns can be directed to where they matter.' I was getting carried away with my own fantasy here. Jason was almost openly sniggering at me.

'I think sex should be dirty,' he said. 'Or it's no fun.'

As it happened I agreed with him, but I didn't think Charity Fulsome would, as I had presented her character.

'Now then,' I said busily, wielding my biro. 'Male,

single, aged, um, thirty-five to forty-five?' I looked up in query.

'Older,' he said briefly. So he was prepared to tell the truth at this stage, was he?

'Occupation, writer.' I marked my sheet of paper. 'How would you describe the nature of your books, Jason? I mean, would you say they fell into a particular genre?'

'Yes,' he said.

I looked at him expectantly. He said nothing. 'The house, then,' I went on. 'You have lived here for how long, Mr Wells? Um, Jason.'

'Eight months. Why don't I show you my work and then you can fill in for yourself?'

'OK. All right.' I nodded slowly. There was subtext here I wasn't getting.

'We'll have to go upstairs.'

Good. I wanted to see upstairs. I wanted to see the room where the fireman had died.

I stood up and took off my glasses. 'I'm ready,' I said.

He led the way. At the top of the stairs we went into a room lined with books like the one below. However, there was a difference.

'This is my working library,' Jason said. I drifted over to the shelves and looked.

Fanny Hill. The Golden Ass. The Decameron. The Complete Works of The Marquis de Sade. And many, many more.

'My own work is over here,' he said, watching me.

I went over to where he stood. At last I saw the shelf that contained his own work.

Sex and Sorcery. The Maidenhead Revisited. Castle of Knowledge. I picked out this last one and opened the pages. I readily saw the nature of the knowledge the castle contained. Esoteric. Arcane. Sexual.

I carefully replaced the book and turned to face those blue piercing eyes. He was watching me carefully. I saw his nostrils were flared.

I felt crazy. 'A man died in this house once,' I said. 'Do
you ever feel his presence?'

'Come next door,' he said. I followed meekly. My heart
was thumping and the glasses resting on my bust bobbed
up and down.

The suburban room was papered to look as though it
was built of raw and almost undressed stone. Attached to
the walls were some very real artefacts. I saw handcuffs.
I saw chains hanging down. I saw a brazier in the centre
of the room, unlit, with a metal rod like a poker lying in
it. A rack filled one side of the room, all heavy wooden
gears and polished framework. Bizarrely there was a
word processor set up on a desk against another
wall.

The guy was off his trolley. I turned with alarm and
tried to get to the door.

He caught me and held me, one hand on my wrist, the
other lightly round me. We were chest to chest.

Those blue eyes looked down at me. 'Don't be afraid,'
he whispered. 'It's for my work. I'm not a cruel man. I
don't torture women.'

Carefully I stood back from him. He let me go,
watching me all the time. 'I'm about to ask you how many
different women a month, a year, you sleep with,' I said.
'I'm going to ask you how many times you make love in
an evening of sexual activity, and how many times on
average you make love a month. I'm going to ask you
which sexual practices you favour in fantasy and in fact.
I'm going to ask you about your reading and your viewing
on the subject. I'm going to ask you . . .'

'Be quiet. Ask me in bed.'

'I can't do that,' I cried.

'Why not?'

'You frighten me?'

He ran a finger up my bare forearm. I had long since
removed my jacket. 'Fear is a useful adjunct to sex,' he
said softly.

I shook my head violently.

'For some people,' he amended. 'Miss Fulsome, will you really not get between the sheets with me?'

I don't know what came over me. I seemed to cling to the character I had created. 'I have a fiancé,' I said and blushed, dropping my eyes.

'So? Will he know? Will he care, as long as he doesn't know?'

'But it's so, er, abrupt,' I chirruped.

'The best sex is,' he murmured. 'The best sex is unexpected, unprepared for, unimpeded . . .'

'Unimpeded?'

'By petty morality and restraint. You have to let go, Charity. You have to risk all. You have to release your inhibitions and fuck for the glory of fucking and for nothing else.'

I blushed. I was beyond caring whether he was an arrogant bastard or not. I reckoned he would be hot between the sheets and I aimed to spend time with him there.

Yet I acted oddly, as if I was really bashful and afraid. 'Could we go downstairs again,' I asked.

'If you kiss me first,' he said.

I smiled and came closer. Just as I began to lift my face to his, he pulled the front of his shirt open. It had metal fasteners rather than buttons and came undone quite easily.

His chest was tanned and broad and quite hairy. 'Kiss me here,' he said.

His flat nipples sat surrounded by hair. I ignored them and kissed the base of his throat.

It was warm, the cupped skin between the bones satin soft. I felt his pulse jump as my lips brushed his flesh. Then I walked by him and out of the door.

Immediately I felt cooler. The creepy room with its dungeon-like appearance had been getting to me.

He caught me up and pushed by me on the stairs. He turned to face me, looking up. His face was on a level with my hemline.

He took hold of one of my feet. I grabbed for the bannister. Jason lifted the foot clear of the stair and slipped off my high-heeled shoe. My stockinged feet sat in his hand. He bent his handsome head and kissed the foot, the arch resting in his hand. Then he released it and slid his hand up my leg and under my skirt.

'I like it best in my ideas room,' he said.

'Your ideas room?'

'The one we've just been in. I find young ladies very inventive in my ideas room.'

'You like them young,' I said.

'No older than half my age,' he said softly. 'I think I'm safe with you, Charity.'

Now I was out of the ideas room I wanted to go back in. 'You write sexy books,' I said. 'Do you always act out the things you describe?'

He kissed my foot again and then he lightly bit it. 'All first hand experience,' he said. 'It has to be that way.'

I sat down on the stairs and hitched my skirt up a little. He sat himself at my feet and prised my legs open. He ran a hand between my legs until he touched the crotch of my panties.

'Wet and warm,' he said. He reached up and kissed inside my knee.

The man had some style. I settled to enjoy myself. I turned onto my knees and pulled my skirt up. 'Can you make it on the stairs?' I asked.

I could feel his eyes boring into my lace-covered rump. A moment later he bit the fine fabric and tore it with his teeth. He came up the stairs and gave me a perfectly straightforward hearty fuck.

Afterwards, quite naked, he found a bottle of wine and opened it. He poured the red liquid into two beautiful long-stemmed glasses. I too was naked by this time apart from my shoes and I began to roam the house and look at it. All this sex stuff might be very nice but it was quite beside the point. I wanted to see the room where the fireman had died and ask about strange feelings and possible presences in the house.

His bedroom was predictable for a bachelor, navy silk sheets, extra large bed and some explicit pictures on the walls. The bathroom off the bedroom was very clean, I guessed his housekeeper did that. There was a bland and innocent spare bedroom. I've described the other two rooms already. They were the upstairs library and the ideas room.

I liked standing in the ideas room almost naked. I held my wine and felt the manacles and articles of restraint. I almost fondled them. I took a length of chain and put it between my legs. Putting my wine glass down, I held the two ends of the chain and pulled the cold hard links up against my sweet damp vulva.

Jason came in. His broad hairy body looked good with nothing on. He was stockily made and his belly was flat and his shoulders well muscled.

He saw me pressing the chain into my sex. He smiled. 'Have you ever tried this?' he asked. He made me stand straddle-legged. Then he put the end of the chain inside my pussy and moved it about.

I looked down at him and smiled in my turn. I liked standing like this, arrogantly naked, my legs apart, looking down at the naked man kneeling at my feet and fiddling with my cunt. 'Just a moment,' I said. I made him remove the chain and then I sat down. Still keeping my shoes on I rolled onto my back and then went into a shoulder stand. Very carefully, so as to keep my balance, I opened my legs wide so that I was doing the splits.

'Now put the chain in,' I said in a muffled voice.

Jason had gravity working with him this time. With my

cunt gaping open and upside-down, he was able to feed the links in till I felt the weight and coldness of the steel inside me.

He allowed the free end of the chain to fall down my front, over my breasts. He sat down at my head and opened his legs wide so that his erect cock rested on my forehead. He reached forward and fondled my swinging heavy breasts. Then he gently pulled the chain so that one link edged out of my stuffed and bulging cunt.

I whimpered with excitement. I couldn't stop flexing my cunt muscles against the hard steel. The cock on my head thumped softly. He grasped it with his free hand, the other was holding the chain, and he began to masturbate himself.

I was dizzy with the effort of keeping my balance upside-down. Jason eased another link out. I squealed slightly. His cock-head kept appearing upside-down in my field of vision. His foreskin was pulled back and I could see his bulging fat red head. I could smell it. His balls kept hitting my head, my hair must have been tickling them. I love to see men masturbate, I love to see their hands working on their own sex and I can feel their rising excitement by proxy, as it were.

I had my own excitement to deal with too. My weird position and the strain it imposed on me prevented me from climaxing too quickly. Every time one of the large hard links was eased out of my trembling hot sex I wanted to sob with release. The smell of the turgid cock just above my face was driving me wild. I felt my mouth watering. I wanted to suck it fiercely.

One more link came out. This time my own sex bubbled hotly, I couldn't resist the fire in my belly any longer. I moaned as my sweet honey flowed and I felt the inside of my sexual hole flex itself helplessly against the unyielding metal.

My mouth was open though my position meant my

chin was driven into my chest. My breasts ached, the nipples reaching my cheeks the way I was doubled over. Jason was close to climax. I would see his lovely sperm soon. I saw the vein throb between his feverish fingers. He pulled the chain, savagely bruising my clitoris. My orgasm redoubled and then he came.

He covered me. His love juice hit my breasts in a hot sticky cream. Some fell on my face and I ran my tongue round my lips greedily. I fell flat despite the pain of the chain jerking harshly into my tender swollen vulva. I twisted over like a snake and took the throbbing male organ between my teeth.

I worried and sucked the lovely thing, drawing the last of his juices into my mouth and swallowing them down. I pushed my face into his groin so that I felt his belly with my forehead. His pubic hair tickled my face. His balls were trapped by my chin. I sucked him so fiercely I felt him howl with shock.

My hands came round him as I pushed myself harder into his body, butting him in the stomach. I caught his buttocks and rammed my fingers between his cheeks. I took his balls into my mouth and sucked. Then I pulled myself forward and wiped my breasts, sticky with spunk, onto his belly and ribs.

He fell back under this assault and I crawled up his body. The chain was still held within my body and it came too. I reached under me and caught a link and thrust it between his buttocks. He shouted then and stopped me. I would have stuffed it into his rear if he had let me, but he didn't. Shakily, he told me he didn't like that. Somehow I didn't believe him. I made him go over onto his hands and knees. I fetched the poker thing that rested in the brazier. I put the end against his puckered arsehole and began to push the weapon in.

He moaned, grinding his face into the floor. 'You like boys, don't you?' I said, screwing the cold metal deeper into his arse.

'How did you know?' He was panting, almost begging me to stop.

'Because I'm clever,' I said. I didn't know the answer. I had just felt he went both ways.

'You bitch,' he said and I released him then, having abused him enough, I thought. I laughed and took the poker out. Then I bent down and kissed his ravaged hole. I opened my legs and made him look at me. 'What do you like best?' I asked. 'This or what a pretty boy has?'

He didn't answer. He was regaining his composure. He took the chain completely out of my pussy and wound it round my wrists. He padlocked it shut. Then he made me double my body, drawing my feet right up until he could put them through my chained hands. Now my hands were behind me. Suddenly I realised what I had let him do. I knew I must stop taunting him now. He was a man with a big ego and I was at his mercy.

He hauled me to my feet and held me while I wriggled my feet into my high-heeled shoes again. He liked me like that, raised up and slightly unsteady on my feet. He pressed me back against a wall, kissing and licking my breasts as I tottered backwards. Once there, he manacled my bound hands to the wall.

Now I was really his prisoner. I stood uncertainly as he backed away from me, considering me.

'I'm just answering your questionnaire,' he said softly. 'This is the kind of thing I like to do.'

He went out of the room for a moment. When he came back he was looking very pleased with himself. He settled himself at the desk and fired up the word processor, having calmly plugged it into the wall socket for all the world as though plugging in electrical equipment and chaining a naked girl to his wall were much the same sort of thing.

He changed the disc he had used to start up and began to type rapidly. I stood where I was. After some time I interrupted him. He kept looking at me as he typed and I guessed he was describing me and my nakedness for his work.

'How long do you propose to keep me here?' I asked.

'Patience, Charity,' he said, and giggled. 'Have faith.'

'I have other people to interview,' I said. 'It's been fun but I have to be getting along.'

'In a while,' he said cheerfully. He typed rapidly as he spoke. 'Now be quiet, dear. There's a good girl.'

All this sex was distracting me from my real purpose. 'Do you ever get a creepy feeling in here?' I asked presently.

'What?' He had hardly heard me.

'Do you ever feel someone is looking over your shoulder?'

'No.'

'No ghosts in the house?'

'Not that I know of. With my mortgage, they'd have to pay rent if they wanted to live here.'

'Do you ever feel you go over the top about sex?' was my next question.

This actually caused him to break the flow of his typing. He looked up from the keyboard. He smiled, baring his teeth. 'No,' he said softly. 'Do you think I am going over the top?'

'That remains to be seen,' I said. I didn't mind a kinky man. A maniac was something else.

I heard a distant ring. 'Excuse me,' said Jason politely. He stood up. 'I think there's someone at the door.'

'You can't go like that,' I cried. He was stark naked. His cock had swollen a little since he sat down and now looked interesting, standing forward of his hairy groin a little.

He laughed and went out of the room. I heard him thump downstairs. Then I heard the murmur of distant voices. Moments later I realised they were climbing the stairs.

A hot flush began to cover my body. I suddenly knew what was coming. I heard male voices laughing and seconds later my worst fears were realised. Jason, quite naked, had brought two more men into the house and into the room.

I was bound and chained naked to the wall. There were three men in the room all looking at me in an interested manner. Their eyes ran hot and gloating up and down my curvaceous body. I was hot with embarrassment. I couldn't cover myself at all, my hands being tied behind my back. They could see everything.

They began to take off their clothes. Through my confusion and dread I could now see that they were young, very young. Maybe they were only eighteen or nineteen. They hardly seemed to be older. They still had some of youth's thinness, their muscles were not fully developed for manhood yet.

Their sex was. I saw a pair of large male sexual organs swing into view. Both young men had white soft bodies. Their cocks were large, partly erect, and purplish in colour.

Jason sat at his typewriter. He shut his eyes, his hands hovering over the keys. He stayed quite still as if he was in a trance. When he opened his eyes I saw they were glittering with excitement. He opened his knees wide. One naked boy dropped to all fours and crawled under the desk. He put his face to Jason's groin. He took the partly erect cock into his mouth. Jason's face became dreamy. His cock vanished deep into the sucking mouth. Jason began to type.

His fingers flew over the keys. The other boy advanced on me. I shrank back against the wall. He had found something and was putting it on round his waist. I was astonished. Despite his own erect sexual member, he was strapping an artificial one on as well. This was a great black plastic thing with gold fingers painted on the side. I flattened myself against the wall but with effortless strength he lifted one of my legs, hooked it over his arm and wiggled dexterously.

I felt the plastic thing press at my open soft sex. I felt

weak with surprise. Jason was radiant, typing as he was sucked. He watched us, his fingers flying over the keyboard. I felt the big plastic dildo slide up into my sex. The real cock below it brushed against my thighs. Now the boy's hips began to jerk. His cock rubbed silkily against my inner thigh. His false cock plunged up into my hot cunt. I moaned slightly and Jason laughed with excitement.

Our bizarre tableau was over in less than ten minutes. I was sobbing and biting my lip, unable to restrain my orgasmic pleasure at the violation of my cunt. Jason was jerking violently into the sucking mouth attached to him like a leach. His fingers were still at last. Even he could not type while he climaxed.

The two boys crawled across the room to each other. They kissed, open-mouthed, so that one tasted the spunk in the other's mouth. Then one turned round. The boy with the dildo slid it, slimy from my body, into his friend's nether orifice. Calmly the two of them practised their strange pleasure with Jason and myself watching. Jason typed frantically. The ravaged boy indicated he was ready to come. They moved so that his erect and unused cock was against my foot. He grasped his cock and held it against the thin high heel of my shoe. He frotted it urgently and the artificial thing up his rear added to his own masturbation brought him to climax.

His spunk oozed hot over my foot. I stared at Jason with dilated eyes. The man was really kinky. I felt excited at what might happen next.

I was soon to find out. I was released from the wall. They forced my feet back through the circle made by my bound wrists so that I had my hands in front of me again. Then the three men lifted my hands high. This raised my breasts and they all took the opportunity to finger me and prod my soft flesh. One boy sucked my nipple so his friend had to do likewise with the other nipple.

I thought how exciting it would be to have three men make love to me simultaneously. I had two pulling at my nipples and I was loving it, though part of me was frightened at their extreme behaviour. Another part of me was suffering from *déjà vu*. I had experienced this, or dreamed this at some other time.

They put leather cuffs on my wrists and undid the chain. Now my arms were held captive high above me by two broad wrist cuffs in thick leather. The leather cuffs were on the end of chains which in turn were held by ringbolts into the ceiling.

Suddenly I was lifted. I squealed and wriggled but the three men held me tightly. The two boys held my legs open in front of me so that I hung from the ceiling in a sitting position. Jason walked between my legs and with my groin at cock level, he was able to insert his sex into mine just standing there.

He bumped forward. He was still quite soft, only firm enough to get in me, not yet firm enough for real fucking. As he bumped me, I swung slightly and came back against his body. I felt red-faced and foolish. I was totally helpless. My legs were held open, I swung from my arms.

Jason began to fuck me softly, grinning unpleasantly. I felt my nipples sucked again, one by each young man. Suddenly I cried out and jerked onto the invading cock.

Jason laughed and I heard one of the boys titter. I cried out again.

Underneath me, using their spare hands, the two young men were sticking pins into my vulnerable bottom cheeks. Each time they pricked me, I jerked on Jason's cock. He had only to stand still. My movements to escape the torture were giving him all the movement he needed.

One of them picked up a bat. All these implements were behind my back and I couldn't see what was coming. I was smacked now and I could not help but jerk sexily on Jason's cock, lying idle in my spongy cunt. I even squeezed my sexual muscles in involuntary attempts to escape the pain. It was futile. Every time I began to get used to something, they changed it. Now one of them was tweaking my pubic hair while the other put the poker in my bottom.

I cried and wriggled and squirmed, a regular dance as I desperately fought against their torture. In front of me, inches from me, I saw Jason's face grow tight with pleasure as my frantic efforts to escape pain redoubled the delicious movements I made on his cock. The boys bit my breasts and stuck pins in my buttocks again. I felt the poker released and its own weight caused it to fall out of my bottom to the floor.

Tears of rage and humiliation stained my cheeks. Jason had his mouth open as he neared climax and his eyes bulged with excitement.

I screamed. They were putting something hot against my sore bottom cheeks. They were burning me. I leapt convulsively like a suffocating fish. Jason's face showed that he had entered bliss. My cunt gripped fiercely at his pole. He began to climax. I shuddered hard into his body to escape my torturers.

Jason came sobbing, bending forward in the excess of his emotion. Immediately the two youths stopped abusing me. I cried, hanging there, but they laughed.

'You burned me,' I sobbed.

Jason was trembling, unable to move, his face ecstatic from the intensity of the experience he had had.

'No, we didn't,' crowed one of the young men. 'We froze you.'

I saw then they had ice. I don't know why I hadn't realised before that they were fooling with ice, especially after my experiences with Sonja. I knew that ice and fire felt much the same to ignorant flesh, and I had been unable to see my torturers' instruments.

Jason slowly withdrew from my body. As if in a daze he

went back to his chair. He began to type rapidly.

The boys lost interest in me. They tied my ankles up in cuffs and attached them to ceiling chains. I now hung from all four limbs like dead meat. My bottom was sore. Inside my arse felt stretched and trembling. My pussy felt huge and tender. Jason's spunk bubbled from my open hole.

The boys went away. Jason typed. I was cold, sore and afraid. Finally he stopped.

He seemed to come out of the daze he had been in since he entered me. I had spoken to him several times, in anger and pleadingly, but he had ignored me. Now he stared at me as though he had forgotten my existence.

'You're still here,' he said a little blankly.

'How could I get away?' I said, still tearful with mortification.

'Do you want a bath or something before you go away?' he said uncertainly. He glanced at his word processor. This was the final humiliation. I had served his imagination and now I could run along.

'Yes,' I snapped. 'I also want to see what you've done to me.'

He released me limb by limb. I stood tottering for a moment. Jason led me through to the bathroom. There was a long mirror there and I knelt stiffly on all fours and peered over my shoulder.

My bottom glowed a soft cherry-red but otherwise looked none the worse for its adventures. Jason bent over it solicitously and felt the tiny pinpricks. 'I'll put some antiseptic cream on after you've bathed,' he said. He prised my bottom cheeks open and fingered my little bumhole. 'Not too sore?' he asked.

'You bastard,' I hissed. 'Do you always treat women like this?'

His abstracted manner left him abruptly. He stared at me and then slapped his thigh and laughed. 'You loved it,' he cried. 'You danced on my prick and you loved it. I could feel you in constant orgasm.'

I stood up. It was hard to say with certainty that he was wrong. I had been aware of convulsive pussy movements on his cock as I was abused, but had assumed it was part of my futile efforts to escape. Was he right? Had I adored that crazed and painful method of bringing a man off inside my cunt?

I turned to the bath and began to run the taps. I had to sit and have a pee. I told Jason to go but he said no, he wanted to be sure I wasn't hurt. His face kept sliding into a blank, bland dreamy expression. He was a man who had experienced catharsis and he was at peace.

I crawled into the foamy water and felt it ease me immediately. Jason washed me, being very gentle about my sexual parts. He plucked at my labia and washed every little part of me.

I stung pleasantly and let myself relax. Then I remembered why I had come. 'Do you only play games like you did today in your ideas room?' I asked sleepily. 'Or do you use your bedroom too?'

'Sometimes the bedroom but it isn't so much fun,' said Jason. 'I get my best ideas in the room I have so designated. That's where I write, too.'

'Did you do this before you came here?'

'Did I write? Yes, of course. You know I've only been here a short while.'

'Did you have an ideas room in your last place?'

He was silent a moment, washing my breasts. 'No,' he said slowly. 'Not really. I was working towards it, I suppose. But it is since I came here that I got really organised.'

'Do you ever feel odd at night here?' I asked.

'What the hell are all these questions?' he said, bewildered. 'You aren't a journalist in disguise, are you?'

I opened my eyes and looked down my naked body in the aromatic water. 'Some disguise,' I said. I looked up at

Jason. I could see he was getting bored with me. I guessed he wanted to go back to writing up the afternoon's experiences.

'I'm psychic,' I lied. 'I could feel something in the other room. As though someone had died there and was making his presence felt. I just wondered if you felt anything.'

'You're crazy,' he said. He stood up and looked at me.

Obediently I got out of the bath. I took the towel he gave me and he went away while I dried myself.

I looked at my body critically in the long mirror. It looked fine.

Was I any the wiser? I didn't think so. I was glad Roger didn't know what I was up to. He had not thought this a fruitful area of research and it was true, I was turning up no coincidences. If self-igniting humans had anything to do with the phenomenon at Lane End Cottages, it was escaping me.

Incident Three – The Clinic

Despite the feeling I had that I was wasting my time, I wanted to make a third visit to a place mentioned on Sonja's list. I had decided to check up on three incidents and my failure to make sense of two of them would not stop me from persevering.

I tried to reason with myself. I would expect the girls at the school (how lovely their bottoms had looked, all lined up – lucky Mr Findhorn!) to be easily seduced by the notion of a resident ghost. Teenagers are notoriously volatile and if anything was going on suggestive of the paranormal I would have expected them to pick up on it.

Perhaps they had. Perhaps they had and the school authorities, as personified by the formidable Miss Houghton, had clamped down on the incipient hysteria and forbidden all mention of spiritual activity. It was funny they should have chosen where the former owner had died to be their punishment room. Perhaps girls had felt a ghostly presence and squealed and been afraid there. Then they had been punished.

Suddenly I was aware I had an idea. Roger and Janie (and myself, for that matter) had nearly fucked ourselves to death where Linda Campsey had died. Maybe Linda wasn't the ghost, I always felt it to be male, but an earlier victim of the ghost. Maybe the ghost had been a sex-crazed man and so that was the aura he projected. We all, Linda, Roger, Janie, myself, Nick and the unfortunate paranormal group, and Janie's mother and lover, all had felt his baneful influence.

This was a crazy idea but a neat and original variant of the tedious haunting theme. Here I was suggesting we had a ghost who didn't haunt to punish those alive for his (or her) own unfortunate death. I was suggesting he haunted because he had a bizarre character to begin with and this had kind of spilled over after his death to affect the living, where they were in the place of his death. The essence of the dead person's character was floating around on the ether, as it were, ready to soak into likely candidates who subsequently occupied the same space.

Intellectually I kind of liked this idea but I could feel in my bones I didn't believe in it. It was screwy. Nonetheless, I continued the line of thought to see where it would take me.

To get back to Planefields School, maybe the ghost there had been heavily into punishment. Maybe the owner of Planefields when it was a private home had been a sadist. So the aura he projected was one of crime and punishment.

Those delicious bottoms! Would I ever forget their youthful exuberance of pink rounded flesh.

Jason Wells, the writer. Perhaps the fireman who had died in his house (well, it had been the fireman's house then) was a writer manqué. Jason had moved in and was imbued with the dead man's spirit, so he had lots of ideas.

As for Roger's house, it was obvious what the salient feature of the ghost there had been. We were dealing with the Casanova of Fibsey down at Lane End Cottages, or rather his raunchy spirit.

I sighed. It was all very well having all these smart thoughts, but I lacked all the information necessary to prove my hypothesis. I didn't know if a sex-crazed man had died in no. 4 Lane End Cottages and I didn't know if the middle of Roger's house corresponded to the old no. 4. I also didn't know if the sometime owner of Plane-fields had been a cruel man. I didn't know anything about the dead fireman including which room of the house he had died in. It didn't have to be Jason's ideas room at all.

As a theory it was so full of holes it was more like a sieve. Yet it was hard to get upset. I was having a good time. I had got frightened at Jason's house but needlessly, as it happened. Planefields had been pure pleasure. Whether it was me or whether it was coincidence I didn't know, but this was proving to be a very sexy adventure.

This was just as well. No one was paying me for this investigation and I was devoting quite some time to it. There had to be a pay-off somewhere.

As for what had gone on in Roger's house, with a little distance it seemed all to the good. I'd blown my mind over sex and it had been one hell of an experience. It had been creepy at the time because I had felt out of control. But that was what appealed to me now. It's good to lose control once in a while. We British are an up-tight nation. If some of our Cabinet ministers could spend a few nights at Lane End, I was certain we would be better governed as a result.

The place I had chosen for my third visit was a health farm, or clinic. It advertised itself as offering whole body health but since I had that anyway, it struck no sparks with me.

Someone had died here, at the clinic. I had bothered

to find the newspaper report in the local paper. According to Sonja's list the incident had occurred a bare three years earlier.

The death had nearly caused the business to founder, that was clear from the reports that I read. Yet there was no accusation of negligence and no blame had been attached to the clinic in the course of the police investigation. A woman, Helen Bellman, had burned to death in an otherwise empty room. Her feet had remained and I saw a photograph in the paper of the grisly mess Helen had become. She had reduced to nearly nothing with her feet and shoes clearly distinguishable. No cause of the fire had been found and there was nothing but smoke damage to the rest of the room. It was the gymnasium and it was hard to imagine what might have caused the flames.

I guessed the clinic would be edgy at any enquiry. They would feel I was unearthing old scandal that could only do them harm, when at the time they had been completely exonerated from blame. I must be very careful at what I said.

Obviously I must go as a client.

I was blooming with health, my adventures had left my hair glossy and my skin creamy, so I decided to lie and say I was too fat. I certainly carried some weight but I didn't want to lose it. What girl well stacked up front wants to be flat and saggy instead, just so the bathroom scales can approve? Bathroom scales don't come male-shaped, warm and strong, with a mind full of dirty ideas and the body to carry them out.

I hired the Porsche again, it was fun to drive, and arrived unannounced at the Clinic. It was out in a broad sweep of countryside that was a dull green with naked hedgerows this late in the year. It was damp and chilly and I wore my cute little fur as I walked up the white steps into paradise.

The lobby was huge without being intimidating. It had been broken into comfortable areas by the clever use of seating units and greenery, and it conveyed an intimate and luxurious atmosphere. Only the extreme cleanliness stopped it feeling as I would expect an upmarket whorehouse to feel. The soft warm air was faintly on the move as it was wafted between the groves of rainforest. That was the only description I could give the plants scattered about. If the clients came out as healthy as the greenery, the place earned every penny of profit it made.

I negotiated the deep pile and the tropical flora and presented myself to the starched receptionist.

She was reassuring. The way she strained her white coat up top showed they didn't believe in slimming away a girl's natural assets. She was so loaded she must have seriously considered becoming a Country and Western singing star.

We went through the routine. She asked if she could help me, I asked about the fees and the courses. I then went into shock and pretended I was seriously considering the merits of the various options for health and beauty that I was being offered. She asked if I'd like to look the place over and I said yes.

She pressed a button on her desk and whiled away the time before any response came by handing me some leaflets. Then a perfectly lovely young man arrived and was detailed to show me round the place.

He was in his very early twenties, I guessed. He had a gorgeous figure and I could see most of it because he wore a T-shirt that strained across his marvellous pectorals and deltoids. His very brief shorts told me he had superb legs and I itched to confirm that his buttocks were as tight and hard as they looked. I could see clearly the bulge of his penis which hung to the right. I wondered if the tip ever came below the bottom of his shorts. It looked as if it might.

'What is your function here?' I cooed, following him through the lobby mangroves.

'Massage and some physio,' he said. He smiled. His

teeth flashed white in his sun-tanned face. I could bear to
have him handle me and pull me about, I thought.

The next thirty minutes lacked excitement apart from
my idle fantasies about my companion as I furtively
inspected his virile charms. We saw various facilities and
we strolled about the grounds and shivered a little. That
is, I shivered. My companion was magnificently impervi-
ous to the cold despite his brief clothing.

We were coming back to the lobby and his sales pitch
was becoming more obvious.

'You don't appear to have a gym,' I interrupted. 'Is there
no exercise training down here as part of the health and
fitness regimes?'

'We have an Olympic standard gym, refitted in the last
couple of years to the highest international safety regu-
lations. Our approach to the body's health is based on the
latest technological understanding of the way the body
works as a natural biological engineering marvel, if you
see what I mean. We understand the body in terms of its
flexibility, its shock-absorption, its strength and its
lubrication.'

'Lubrication?'

He smiled. 'You want a good fluid movement with no
abrasive interfaces. You want to feel easy. Yes?'

I agreed heartily. 'I haven't seen the gym,' I said.

He hesitated. 'Have you read our literature?' he asked.

'There hasn't been time yet.'

'I want you to know that we think the body is beautiful.'

I looked his over. 'I so agree,' I said.

'All bodies,' he corrected gently. 'That is, all bodies can
be beautiful when their harmonies are balanced and they
are in tune.'

'I'm with you so far,' I said. What the hell was he leading
up to?'

'The gym represents the core of our work where we
reshape the distortions caused by unhealthy living.'

This sounded ominous. Did they use scalpels?
'Reshape?' I asked delicately, not wanting to spoil our
budding relationship by rudeness.

'So we have to see the body. The clients have to see
themselves as they harmonise. They have to learn not to
be afraid of their natural shape. Rather, they must glory
in it. We teach our clients that their bodies are wonderful
places to be in. We make them proud of their bodies and
happy and comfortable.'

I was with him at last. 'You do it nude,' I said.

'No clothing in the gym. That is correct.'

'Staff as well as clients?'

'Naturally.'

I smiled. 'It seems hard I'm not allowed to see what
you call the core of your work before I've signed up.'

'You are allowed to see,' he said.

I looked at him. 'Then lead on.'

We turned back and climbed a broad curving staircase
with an elegant wrought-iron handrail picked out in gilt
paint. The resemblance to a high-class brothel became
more marked. Something light and classical was oozing
tastefully out of the walls. I watched the neat tight arse of
the man leading me and felt like laughing.

He took me through a door. It was a room with cupboards down one side. He turned to face me. 'You may
retain your clothing but I have to shed mine,' he said.
'House rules.'

I waved a hand. 'Go ahead,' I said airily. I sat in one of
the chairs and crossed my legs. I watched.

He pulled off his T-shirt and revealed his massive muscly
chest. It would be liked cuddling a wardrobe, I reflected,
an old-fashioned wardrobe in warm wood. You could
bounce coconuts off his sternum. Then he slipped out of
his sneakers. He wore no socks. Lastly he gave a seductive
wriggle and dropped his shorts.

The cloud of pubic hair was fluffy and golden. His

darkish prick lay peacefully at rest against the dangling balls, the whole delightfully nested in his wiry hair.

He wasn't in the least embarrassed. His blue eyes twinkled. He held out his hand. 'Shall we go through?'

I took his hand and we went through the further door.

We were high up, on a gallery that ran round the top of a large room. My guide had told me the place had been refitted in the previous couple of years. I had to believe this was the old gym where Helen Bellman had died.

I'm a physically lazy woman except between the sheets with an active male, so the various pieces of high-tec machinery had all the flavour of a modern torture chamber to me. There were racks and frames, pulleys and hydraulic rams, belts, moving floors and sinister boxes and beams with plenty of padded flooring between. I guessed there were some thirty clients down below, attended by another dozen or so members of staff.

I rested my chin in my hand and my elbow on the guard rail and feasted my eyes.

The clients, male and female, were all shapes and sizes. Breasts quivered and wobbled. Bottoms were slapped and hips shook. Penises flopped up and down. Women and men ran on endless floors, jumped, were stretched, lifted weights, cycled – all the usual activities and they did them nude. Some of them had meters attached to their skin, or probes or monitors of some kind or another. They were all working very hard and the roof space of the gym was filled with a vast susurration of sighing and panting exercisers.

The staff were also mixed male and female. Their bodies stood out, they were so beautiful. The women had high firm breasts, not small, but full and rounded. Their waists were neat and small and their hips firm, and their legs long and strong looking. The men were like my guide, not all quite as stunningly muscled, but they didn't have an ounce of flab between them.

For the first time I seriously considered enrolling. I

would love to get close to all this manflesh.

I felt a hand resting lightly on my waist. I stiffened slightly and stood up.

A second hand came on me so that my waist was lightly clasped.

'You have a very good shape,' my guide said to the back of my head. His hands ran gently down to my hips. He gripped a little tighter. 'I'd have to see you without clothes on to check, but I'd think you would find our regimes easy. You have a very harmonious body already.'

I turned in his arms and found myself face to face with a powerful golden naked male all of three or four inches away from me. 'Perhaps you should check,' I said. 'I would need to know what my money was buying.'

'Here?' he said.

I looked along the gallery. It was quite open. 'Perhaps I'm shy,' I said. 'Have you somewhere more private? After all, if I had a high opinion of my body I wouldn't be here, would I?' I looked at him from under my lashes and tried to blush.

I was sorry to stop watching the gym. It was a lovely sight and I felt roused and alert. But I couldn't resist being 'checked' by this lovely specimen of manhood.

He took me, naked as he was, to a small room off the gallery. He shut the door and turned the handle to lock it. 'Feel better?' he asked.

'Mmm,' I said. 'I suppose you think it very feeble of me to be shy about showing my body.'

'I wouldn't have such harsh thoughts, but certainly you wouldn't feel shy after one of our courses. We all have bodies. You would be justly proud of yours.'

I unwound my little fur. 'I've forgotten your name,' I said.

'Peter.'

'My name is Harriet,' I said at random.

'How lovely,' said Peter moving in. 'Let me.'

He undressed me. He undid the buttons on my jacket and slid it off. He unzipped my skirt and let it fall to the floor so I could step out of it. He unbuttoned my shirt and slid it off. He removed my slip and then knelt to release each stocking and unroll it down my leg. He removed my garter belt standing very close to me with his arms round me. He did the same with my bra. Then he removed my panties.

'Lie on the couch,' he said.

I lay down.

He began a light dry massage, exploring the depth of the flesh on my bones with probing expert fingers. He kneaded my breasts and then he turned me over and worked down my back, exploring in particular my plumper areas.

It left me breathless.

'Off the couch, now,' he ordered gently.

I stood up.

'I want you to run on the spot,' he said. 'Don't take any notice of what I do. It's just a quick check to see how out of tune you are.'

I began to run. He watched me critically and then he put a hand under one of my breasts and felt it as I bobbed up and down. He stood in front of me and took the other breast, standing apparently absorbed in thought as he hefted their weight and I jigged in front of him.

He let them go and went round behind me. Then I felt his hands lightly clasping my buttocks, not enough to impede me as I ran but enough to feel the wobble of them.

After this he held one of my wrists and took my pulse. Then he strapped a blood pressure pad on me and read the meter. After this he took a thermometer from a sealed sterile pack. He shook it thoughtfully.

By now I was red and hot. I could feel sweat beginning to trickle between my breasts and from under my arms. I found the cool impersonal attentions of Peter very rousing and I was sexually keyed up. I felt slightly foolish and I was panting.

Peter went round behind me. 'Keep running,' he said quietly. I felt him at my buttocks again. The next moment I squeaked.

'I have to take your temperature,' he said. 'It's the best way.'

He had slid the thermometer between my buttocks and into my arse, as though I were a dog and he a vet.

I gritted my teeth and ran on. I could feel the little tube inside me. Peter stayed behind me presumably watching. It must be a comical sight, bobbing about as I jogged on the spot.

Peter's voice was remote. 'In our literature it says we offer a sexual therapy too. We revive interest and ability. We remove fear. We instil confidence. A person in tune with their body needs to enjoy the sexual aspects of life. It is one of the harmonies.'

He deftly removed the thermometer and presumably read it. 'Lie down again, on your back,' he said.

I heaved my sweating tired body onto the couch and lay there gasping slightly. Peter felt me rapidly all over. His expression was quite detached as his hands went over my sticky body. He began to stretch me, pulling my arms and legs.

'How come,' I panted, watching his gently swinging cock, 'you don't get a hard-on doing all this to women? I mean, considering how in tune you must be.'

Peter stood back suddenly from me and I assumed I had transgressed. Sex might underplay the clinic's sales pitch but I shouldn't indicate the staff could get involved.

'It is a matter I have under control,' said Peter. 'You would have the same control too, if you underwent our therapy. See?'

He stood there smiling at me. As he did so, his cock

began to grow. Under my fascinated gaze he became fully erect in about ten seconds. He had a wonderful swelling capacity and the final golden rod that projected stiffly from his body was at least ten inches long.

Peter touched himself lightly so that his cock bounced. 'I do weight training,' he said. 'I lift little weights with it.'

'You can switch it on and off?' I gasped. I had never been so genuinely impressed.

'And off, yes,' said Peter. I watched dumbfounded as his cock settled back to half its size, resting against his balls. 'I have to be able to do this,' he added. 'The sight of so much beautiful womanhood would have me permanently up, otherwise.'

He looked meaningfully at my body stretched out naked before him.

'I'm so impressed,' I said sincerely. 'Your skills are fantastic. I have a sweet sad sorrow though . . .'

'You do?'

'For the old-fashioned way of turning the sexual urge off.'

He looked puzzled. 'What's that? Something mystic? Yoga, perhaps?'

'No, no.' I sighed. 'I mean fucking.'

There was a moment's silence. Peter licked his lips. His cock grew a little and flattened again.

'Right,' he said hoarsely. He tried to smile. His eyes ran up and down my body. 'I'd better show you the showers.'

What a waste of a man, I thought, as I showered off my sweat. Too much self-control is a bad thing. If he'd been less good at being good, we could both have had a lovely time through there with no one else the wiser and our two selves much happier.

But it wasn't to be. Peter showered and dressed and together we walked down to the lobby.

They wanted me to sign but I said I had come in on a whim and now had to go home and check my agenda over the next few weeks to find a clear patch in my appointments. I would get in touch. They were more urgent than that and wouldn't accept anything so vague. I gave them a false name and address and walked out looking as opulent as I possibly could.

I was revving the Porsche before I realised I'd forgotten to ask about ghosts.

I cursed myself as I drove through the Yorkshire countryside. I had been on the ball until we reached the gym. There, in the seat of my enquiry, all thoughts of Lane End Cottages and Roger's problem had gone clean out of my head. I had become obsessed with a pair of pretty male buttocks and a naked swinging cock. I had forgotten the point of my being there and pursued, unsuccessfully, a nice boy who was a prude rather than a gigolo. Really, it was shameful. I was supposed to be a professional investigator even if I was freelancing.

Annoyed with myself, strung-up and sexually aroused and unsatisfied, I pulled into a pub carpark to get something to eat. I used the Ladies to attend to my hair and make-up, and then I came through and ordered a glass of white wine and a seafood salad.

The pub was dark with varnished oak beams and lots of nooks and corners lit by little more than reflecting horse brasses. There was a fire to one end and I sat so that I could get the benefit of the glowing flames. It wasn't cold inside, but the day was raw enough to make a fire psychologically comforting. I could see through the tiny deep-set window by me into the carpark. The Porsche sat comforting within my view, lean and spare and magnificently powerful.

Damn men who said no.

As I watched and waited for my food, sipping my wine, I saw a Roller glide in and dispose itself next to my Porsche. A chauffeur climbed out of the driver's seat and came round and opened the door. A small elderly man got out and smoothed his hair. He looked at my car as though he might just approve of his own car's temporary playmate. Then he came into the bar.

He ordered a drink and some food in a subdued voice. Then he approached my corner rubbing his hands.

Piercing eyes from under bushy eyebrows looked me over. 'I hope you don't mind my joining you,' he said in a spare, precise sort of voice. 'The fire is most attractive.'

Great, I thought bitterly. This is my day for insults. Peter can do without me and this old bird wants the fire, not my luscious charms.

I nodded graciously and drank some more wine. The man hesitated a moment as I put my glass down. 'Perhaps I can refill that for you?' he asked.

I looked at him properly. Not a business man. An academic? I wasn't sure they earned enough these days to run a Rolls Royce, nor would it be politically correct even if they could afford it. Students would squat in it.

His frame was shrinking, but the suit had been a stunner in its day. The shirt looked like heavy silk. There was an air about him, though he was stooping a little.

I had it. The law. 'Thank you,' I said demurely. A QC, no doubt. With family money.

He returned with my drink and handed it to me. I thanked him and took a sip. Then I looked up in query.

The old buzzard was watching me. 'I had the landlord open a decent bottle,' he said gently. 'I always come here when I've been at York and I know he keeps a decent cellar. I thought you looked like a young lady who might appreciate it.'

I assumed the chauffeur had gone to the public, and was playing darts over his beer. I wondered if the lawyer beside me frequently picked up women in pubs. I had the feeling he knew the Porsche was mine. He struck me as the kind of man who would pick up on that sort of detail.

The landlord brought my salad, a brandy for my companion and a plate steaming with a suet pudding, greens and mashed potato. We began to eat.

The food disappeared rapidly and neatly into him. He made no conversation, concentrating on eating. The landlord brought a jam rolypoly and custard to follow. My companion demolished all the nursery food with evident enjoyment and then sat back. He sipped his brandy and asked my permission to light his cigar.

'Please do,' I said. I had long since finished my meal. The wine was very good.

We had hardly spoken. His small rather hard eyes looked at me thoughtfully. 'You're a lawyer,' I said.

'A judge,' he corrected gently.

'You've been trying cases this morning.'

'I gave judgement on a particularly nasty case of sexual assault.'

'Aggravated?' I asked sweetly.

'What do you mean?' He knocked the ash off his cigar with a caressing tenderness.

'Did she flaunt it? Was she pretty? Was her skirt short? Did she dare to walk alone?' I leaned forward. 'Did she tempt him?'

The judge looked at me expressionlessly. 'She met him through a dating service. She thought she liked him and then changed her mind. He didn't like that and went ahead anyway. I gave him fifteen years. Does that answer your question, young lady?'

I smiled and leaned back. 'Yes.'

'So when I invite you to come home with me for an hour or so, you know you can change your mind at any time. And Arthur will bring you back here to your car.'

I could hardly believe my ears. I was being propositioned by a man in his sixties in cold blood.

I could be cold too. 'You aren't young any more,' I said cruelly.

'I am not young, as you so bluntly observe. But I am

able. You look like a young lady who has had a difficult morning. Perhaps a business deal has gone wrong. Perhaps your husband has admitted adultery. You are cross and out of sorts. I have a nasty taste in my mouth from the case I have just tried. We might be useful to one another since our paths have crossed. But no matter if I disgust you. I assure you I would not have let you down, if that was your fear.'

I was intrigued rather than repelled. I watched him as he sat there smoking. He was a very confident man, taking what he thought was my rejection in his stride.

'Perhaps I will let you down,' I said.

Now it was his turn to watch me for a long minute while he decided whether I was teasing or meant what I implied.

'It's a possibility,' he admitted. 'But I am a very good judge of character. I think the experience would be mutually pleasurable despite the gap in our ages. If you have not seen an elderly man naked before, I can assure you that the face ages faster than the body. I've never been sure whether this is an advantage or not.'

Again he made me gasp by his bluntness. I laughed suddenly. 'Why not?' I said, and picked up my bag.

The back of his car was a microcosm of luxury and comfort. He poured us both a brandy and sat back in his corner, several feet away from me, to observe me with greater ease. The windows were tinted and it was all one way glass, including what separated us from the impassive chauffeur driving in the front.

'You were right,' I said as soon as we were settled. 'I have had a very frustrating morning.'

'May I ask in what way?'

'I propositioned a lovely young man in conditions of considerable intimacy and he rejected my advances. It made me cross.'

'I find that hard to believe. You have a certain air, my

dear, that makes it inherently improbable that any male fortunate enough to catch your eye would pass up on the opportunity.'

'That's kind of you but I assure you it's true.'

'May I ascribe my good fortune to that young man's foolishness?'

It took me a moment to unravel what he meant. 'No,' I said. 'Not at all. You intrigue me. I want this. Had I had sex already this morning, it would have made no difference.'

He absorbed the compliment. 'What I want to do,' he said carefully, 'is to kiss you between your legs.'

The car glided quietly. It smelled of leather and very faintly, of cigars. I was in a moving gentleman's club. We were secret from the world we passed through. No one could see in.

I wriggled and slipped my panties off. I lay back on the wide seat and hitched my skirt up. I opened my knees.

The judge stared down and looked into my sex. He lifted one ankle and laid the leg over his lap. He ran the other hand up my leg and felt where my stocking top was a dark mark against my white thigh. Then he slipped off his jacket.

He had broad shoulders, lacking muscle indeed but not scrawny. He loosened his tie slightly and smoothed his hair again as I had seen him do in the carpark. Then he opened a case on the floor beside him and drew out his wig. He settled the wig on my chest. Then he bent down and put his head between my legs.

I felt his warm breath first. My pussy expanded and opened like a flower. I felt my juices begin to run. Then something touched me, just a bare caress. He had nudged me gently with his nose.

He nuzzled on into me, separating my flesh and giving himself access to my tender underparts. I lay still gazing at the roof of the car in a happy daze. I opened my legs wider and felt my flesh unleave. The judge tongued me slightly and I could not help but sigh with pleasure.

His tongue came snaking out. He probed delicately. I shut my eyes, I was so happy, and surrendered my entire cunt up to the elderly tongue intent on investigating its charms.

He licked up and down with his tonguetip stiff. He found my clitoris and ran round and round it. He nibbled it slightly. Then he pushed his face in harder. I moaned slightly and could not help pushing into the judge's face. I felt his teeth. I was sure they were false teeth. No one had ever bitten my sex with false teeth before. I had hardly had this thought when I felt the judge's mouth close over my cunthole. I thrust at his face. He sucked and then his tongue went into me. He began to suck and lick me properly. He kissed my lips, he kissed and sucked my little bottom, he bit my clitoris and he sucked and stabbed into my hole. My whole vulva shuddered with delight. I felt all my juices running sweetly. Under the wig my chest heaved and my stomach fluttered. The judge caught my hair in his teeth and pulled. I began to cry out. I was in orgasm. He clamped his mouth back over my quivering juicy sexual parts and sucked me into climax.

I lay back happily with a smile hovering on my lips after this. Then I came to my senses slightly and began to sit up.

The judge was wiping his face with a silk handkerchief. He smoothed his hair and removed the wig from my chest.

I pulled my skirt down and sat up. 'Thank you,' I said gravely. 'That was a delightful experience.'

The judge looked at me. His face was lizard still in the gloomy interior of the car.

'What might I do to please you?' I asked softly.

'There is no need. Arthur can take you back to your car. I have enjoyed myself extremely.'

Dry old buzzard! 'I could return the compliment if that would please you,' I said softly. I was determined to get a look at the judge's sexual equipment.

He looked at me consideringly. 'We are almost at my house,' he said. 'Would you like to come in?'

'Yes, if I can be of use to you,' I said boldly. I wanted sex, not being shown the extent of his pad.

Five minutes later we turned in between gates with stone eagles on top of them. We drove up a long track and stopped in front of a large country house. Arthur opened the door of the Rolls and I climbed out.

The judge was with me in an instant. We climbed the steps together and went in.

It was warm, old-fashioned and gloomy. I saw no sign of a wife. I was taken to a high-ceilinged square room panelled in dark brown wood. Books lined the walls and there was a large heavy antique-style desk with green leather on its top. I remember the green leather had a kind of gilt edging to it, punched into the leather.

Worth a bomb, I thought. The old guy's loaded.

There was a hearth with a real fire lit. The carpet was subdued crimson with a pattern of birds and plants on it. The curtains at the full-length windows were heavy dull crimson velvet. It wasn't my style of home furnishing, but it definitely had its points.

Set in the panelling was a cupboard I hadn't noticed. The judge opened this and I saw almost a little room beyond, the cupboard was so large. There was a bright red glow from the dark interior and I realised the judge had his robes hanging there. He must have had some at the court as well. Whether he kept his robes at court or whether he took them backwards and forwards with him I didn't know. Or care. Now he took robes from the cupboard and began to put them on.

Many men would have looked foolish. The judge didn't. The red robes went over his dark suit and obscured it. He arranged a sort of stole thing about his neck. The inside of the cupboard door had a full-length mirror. The judge placed a wig on his head and arranged it to his satisfaction. Then he took a small square black hat and arranged that so that it perched on the top of his wig.

He walked over to his desk and sat down. He reached over to his right and arranged within comfortable distance of his hand a tape recorder. He then placed his hands down on the desk in front of him.

I saw he was nervous or excited at last, not because his basic impassivity was stirred, but because he was sweating lightly and marking the leather top to his desk. I found his excitement infectious. He was setting the scene. What did he want me to do? Parade naked? Be beaten?

'You offered to do me a like service to the one I performed for you,' he said in his dry precise way.

'That's right,' I watched him alertly.

'Perhaps you would be so good as to do that now, while I sit here, if you would not be too cramped.'

The desk had a generous kneehole. I rather thought I could get into it without trouble. I nodded my head in acquiescence.

'You will not mind a soundtrack?'

'Not at all,' I said cordially. I dropped to the floor and crawled under the desk. The old buzzard opened his legs. I felt for the fastening of his trousers and opened them. I reached in, grinning to myself. It's nice to grope a man. I like feeling in to the slightly damp hot jungly atmosphere of a man's groin. I like feeling the soft slug of flesh stir and swell under my probing fingers. I like tickling his hair. I like getting my palm under his lovely balls and cupping them and feeling them hard inside their soft bagginess of flesh.

It was claustrophobic under the desk. The long red robes flowered out either side of the judge's legs so that even if Arthur or some household servant had come in, I would have been invisible. I crouched between the judge's legs as though I was in a tent. The robes were very clean and smelt faintly as if they had just come back from the cleaners.

I found his cock in his cotton underwear and began to work it free of his layers of clothing. It felt small and soft, like a tender young creature new-born, too small to be out on its own.

I grinned at the thought. I believed the judge when he said he wouldn't let me down. I had the feeling I was in for a pleasant surprise.

I began to stroke the little limp thing and tickle it. I played with his balls and ran my fingertips lightly up and down the stem of his sex. Above me, out of my fabric cave, I heard talking begin.

Had the judge called people into the room? Was that how he got his jollies, being sucked while he talked to people? I was about to object when I realised I was listening to the tape recorder.

I ignored it. My job was down here. I teased the growing penis out and began seriously to make it grow. It responded readily. I couldn't see too well but it seemed to me the judge had grey and straggly pubic hair. If he did, it was his only sign of ageing down here. His cock was growing splendidly and firming under my eager fingers. The delicate foreskin was drawing back over the swelling head. I leaned forward and kissed it.

I felt his body shudder. I kissed the elderly penis in front of me again. It didn't seem desiccated. It was full and rotund. He was a juicy old judge, then.

I put my lips around the swollen head and ran my tongue over the enflamed surface. I sucked slightly, enjoying the taste of man in my mouth. My fingers played with his balls. I also tickled the root of his cock. I sucked the head deeper into my mouth and then simply sucked on the cock itself.

He must have turned the tape recorder up. I could hear it now despite having my head muffled between his thighs.

'Edward Anthony Baker,' said a high harsh voice. 'You are sentenced to hang by the neck . . .'

For a moment I froze. Now I knew what gave the judge his thrills. He wanted to be taken at the moment someone was sentenced to death. He orgasmed as he pronounced death. He couldn't do it in court so he simulated the situation here at home when he had a willing partner to hand. Me, on this occasion. He couldn't sentence people to death any more but plainly he was missing the fun he used to have.

Now, on the tape, he was able to listen to judgements being passed that had sent people to the condemned cell and from there to their deaths. Meanwhile his cock was big and urgent in my mouth.

I continued mechanically with my work. I liked the end of his cock and tasted the preliminary dribble of spunk. I teased the swelling balls and grasped the stem of the cock with my hands, drawing back the skin to expose the heated tip further. I pressed my lips around the ring where the skin attaches to the cock. I let him feel my teeth. Then I closed my mouth round as much of the organ as I could and began to suck him with deep regular sucks.

I heard the poor saps getting theirs on the tape recorder. I took it I was hearing the real thing, recorded in situ. No naughty suck-offs for the condemned men, but then I suppose that if I'd known what any of them had done, I would have found my quality of mercy pretty strained. Not that I liked hanging, but I got angry enough sometimes to think we didn't do enough to punish people, these days.

Then again I would read about prison conditions and feel we did too much to punish people. We degraded and brutalised people who might have re-entered society . . .

What the hell. Here was I getting deep into ethical issues when what I wanted to do was give this man a really good suck-off. I twined my tongue wickedly round the fat tube of manflesh I had in my mouth and played exquisite music with my fingers deep in his balls.

I felt his body begin to quiver and tremble. The recorded voices sentencing people to death got so loud the sound began to distort, which seemed appropriate, somehow. I sucked cunningly and I bit gently and I fingered cunningly. The judge called out and began to shake in my mouth. I tasted him then as he started to come. This was what he wanted under the bench, in court, surrounded by the police, the prisoner, the defending and prosecuting counsels, solicitors, ushers, court officials, the public – he wanted this, what I did, while he pronounced sentence of death.

He was speaking, uttering inarticulate words as his cock spasmed and he shot spunk into my mouth. I sucked and swallowed and sucked again. His hips jerked, I felt his balls move and then he was done, leaning back exhausted, the tape recorder switched off.

I kissed the soft sweet thing his iron-hard sex had reduced to. I licked it a little in fond memory. Then I tucked it back where it belonged, fastened the clothing that protected it and crawled out from under the desk.

I fetched my bag and fixed my hair and lipstick. I thought of the lipstick that would be smeared over the judge's pants and wondered who did his washing for him. The judge had stood up without saying a word and gone to remove his robes.

When I looked up, he was holding a balloon glass of brandy out for me. I accepted it and sipped the fine alcohol. It was very good, my palate told me so though I haven't educated it in any way. It was the soft strong mellow way the spirit sat on my tongue that told me it was good.

The judge smiled, a thin-lipped dry smile. 'The afternoon has certainly improved upon the morning,' he said in his precise way.

I agreed with him. We stood quietly together in front of

the fire, drinking our brandy in peace. I sighed. 'I must go now,' I said. I had a long drive back to London in front of me, though the Porsche ate up the miles.

'It's been a great pleasure, my dear.'

'On both sides, I assure you.'

He called Arthur and told him to drive me back to my car. Then he shook hands with me and I left.

I should make quite clear that I do not include all these intimate details to titillate the reader seeking a vicarious sexual thrill. Though names and places are changed, and details are changed where they might give a definite clue to a real person or situation, all that is described in these files is absolutely true. If the *burning desire* phenomenon is to be understood, then this record should be as full as possible. I don't understand it, neither do any of the principals in this record. The information is included so that the reader may judge for his or her self. The police won't believe us. The press won't touch it. Only as if it was fiction can we get the details published. But if anyone out there recognises that the things we describe are happening to them, then they may draw their own conclusions and act accordingly. We can warn against disaster but we can't prevent it happening.

No one believes us. They will, of course, one day, if this record doesn't get lost. Meanwhile we have included every scrap of evidence that might be relevant, in case someone, *someone* understands what it is that is going on. We also include all this detail so that readers can identify the difference between normal carnal practice and the *burning desire* phenomenon.

Really, by this stage, I had all the information I needed within my grasp. I was persistently, almost wilfully misunderstanding. I was treating it like a game.

It wasn't a game. It was deadly serious. And time was running out.

FILE SEVENTEEN

The Theatre of Dreams

Joel Bannerman had four women to make love with him. They were desperate to make love with him. When he wouldn't make love with one of them, they loved and kissed and had sex with each other. His prowess had never been greater but he was acting a part. He was possessed. He felt the women to be possessed. They acted like great lovers but who was pulling the strings? Who made their bodies dance endlessly to the same tune?

He felt tongues wrap like hot wet flannels, evening after evening about his giant sex. It had grown with use, he could swear it was bigger.

Mouths caressed his balls and sucked them. Tongues entered his most private and personal places. Breasts crushed him. Vulvas pressed upon his face. He lapped orgasming women and they sucked his cock till it burst into fountains of spunk. His cock sank into Solomon's mines of jewelled and dazzling sexual bliss. Caverns of rippling female flesh clasped his endlessly huge cock and caressed and sucked and drew from it galaxies of desire and universes of fulfilment.

He lay spread-eagled on a bed of live female flesh. If he moved he was kissed. His nipples were sucked. His arse was explored. His cock was a toy that never palled. He felt he was drowning in sex but he couldn't stop, he had to go on, his belly ached with an unquenchable fire of lust and only endless coition could calm him.

He wasn't calm. He was doped. The sex was narcotic. His feverishness became a stupor, his jerking hips automatic, his ejaculations mere repetitions . . .

Still they continued, the five of them, evening after dazed and crazy evening until sleep took them and released them from the puppetmaster.

At night, alone in the flat he rented, Joel slept the uneasy sleep of the exhausted. Even here he was not at peace. In his dreams they came to him, the winged Valkyries, to hover over his corpse-like repose and point the way to other female things, deadlier things that descended on the vulnerable man to suck, not his blood, but his spunk.

Succubi. His body was stolen as he slept. In dreams they took him sexually and stole his health and his vigour in the sick sex-making of their kind.

And he was helpless.

FILE EIGHTEEN

Testimony of Roger Greaves

I kept phoning Red Marsden to tell her to come over. She was never in. I left messages on her answerphone but she didn't respond.

Maybe she was working. I wondered what she did. I suppose she found missing persons, lost dogs, stuff like that. Maybe she sat in her car and spied on separated wives, to see if they had a man round, a man their divorcing husband could claim ought to support them.

Funny how marriage debases sex to a matter of payment. Maybe Red had the rights of it, staying single. No one would suggest her boyfriends ought to pay her way, but it would be different if Janie and I ever split up. I would have to pay.

I was sorry I had switched Red onto this nonsense in the house. I felt an urge to undo the mischief I had caused. I needed to reach her, though, and she was out all the time. When I went round to her place, I saw her car where she kept it. That was really strange. She was away from home without her car.

I guessed she had a man. She was the hottest female I had ever known and no doubt she was at some provincial hotel or seaside hang-out, shacked up with some chance-met man.

Just looking at Red made you lick your lips. You didn't care how many other men she went with. If anything, it made her more attractive. She was a dynamo. She gave out plenty. She got better with time, too.

I always had strange fantasies about Red. I liked to imagine myself sprawled naked, arms and legs relaxed and thrown out. My eyes would be shut. Maybe I was lying on a blanket in the sun. My skin was all caressed and soaked with the sun.

There would be shadow at one point. Red would be sitting by me, her shadow a cool splash on my body. Her hand would reach over my nakedness, dry and warm. She would clasp my cock.

That was it. That was the fantasy. Myself naked. The sun. Red's hand on me, touching my cock, moving slightly.

I didn't need to carry the fantasy forward. It was a mental tickle, not a sex-replacement. I had a lot of sex in my life. It was just an idle fancy to stimulate my mind mildly, in the way watching actors simulating sex did on TV. I liked to see their bodies pressed together, the woman's breasts crushed against the man's chest. But what I was liking was not the characters portrayed having sex together. No, what I liked was the thought of the paid actor and actress, forced into propinquity, ordered by an impersonal script to writhe together naked or almost naked in a bed while the sound technician and cameraman and director hovered over their squirming bodies, the director saying, more of this, less of that.

That's what tickled my fancy. That's what made my cock slightly swell. It wasn't what they acted. It was the fact that they were acting. There have to be times when they don't even like each other, as they press sexually together on command.

I got through to Red in the end. She sounded tired when she answered the phone. I chuckled to myself. Some man somewhere would be feeling even more tired, if I knew anything about Red.

'How are you?' I asked.

'So so. How're things at your place?'

'Marvellous. Red, we need to talk.'

'Sure. Though I hardly know what to say. Tomorrow, sometime?'

'Come over, sweetheart.'

'Is Janie away? I guess she must be, for you to phone.'

'She's here. She's in the bath just now. Don't worry about that side of things.' I laughed to myself. I was enjoying teasing Red.

'I'm too tired to get straight what it is you're saying, Roger.'

'It's simple enough. Come over. I need to apologise for the wild goose chase I sent you on.'

'You do? What wild goose chase?'

'This nonsense about our bedroom.'

Red was quiet for a while. 'Nonsense?' she repeated faintly.

'Nonsense. There's nothing wrong with the house. I've taken it off the market. Janie's mother has gone home. We've moved back into the bedroom. I don't know what came over me, Red.'

Again she took a moment to reply. 'I'm struggling with this, Roger. There was definitely something odd about your house.'

'No.' I was firm. 'We were crazy to think so. Janie was being gorgeous. You were gorgeous, you always are. And I responded like any normal man.'

'I don't agree.' Her voice was remote.

'Come over and sort it out. It's OK about Janie. You'll see.'

'Are you serious?' She sounded bewildered.

'I am. Come tomorrow.'

'I guess so. If you are sure.'

'I'm sure.' I laughed. 'Come about midnight.'

FILE NINETEEN

Red Marsden – a meeting between old friends

Roger's phone call left me distressed because it seemed peculiar. I slept late the next day and then showered and dressed and went down the street to the deli where I bought some breakfast. I picked up papers on the way home and settled in my flat to eat and read.

I felt drained and dull. I turned the pages listlessly. The headline news was as distressing as usual. A small news item caught my attention – 'Phoenix in flames'.

Somehow, lately, I had read or talked about or thought about too much burning. Flames had popped up everywhere. The headline stood out and my eyes drifted down the item.

The Phoenix was a theatre in a provincial town. It had burned down. What made the item newsworthy was that the theatre had burned down some twenty years previously and had only just been rebuilt. It had not even mounted its first production, which was in rehearsal at the time of the conflagration.

The cause of the fire was not yet known. Two bodies had been found in the ruins. Their identities were not yet known either.

I sat on the floor with a mug of coffee by me staring at the news item. Something about it tantalised me. I wrinkled my brow in thought. The name of the theatre. The name of the provincial town. The fact that the theatre was new, or rather newly rebuilt. All of these apparently random facts fitted neatly into my mind, almost as if they were things I had known before and forgotten, things of no significance.

Then I had it. It came back softly to me, satisfyingly as the memory fitted properly into place and I understood.

Joel Bannerman. That was why I had heard of the Phoenix. Joel was an old flame (I was getting to dislike that term, I don't know why) and we had parted company on amicable terms some two years ago. Joel was heavily into theatre and so moved about quite a lot in the course of his developing career. We kept in touch in a desultory way. Sometimes, when he found himself in London and he was alone, he would ring me up and we'd get together for old time's sake.

I liked Joel. He was good at what he did. When what he did was me, I remembered it. The man had style.

When Joel had been appointed director for the season by the Phoenix management, he had phoned me up so I could congratulate him. I had done so and promptly forgotten all about it.

This was his theatre that had burned down. He would be out of a job. Poor Joel, what a rotten break.

I lifted the phone. Ten minutes' hard work beginning with Directory Enquiries gave me a number I could reach the theatre management on. Eventually someone was found who could speak to me.

'I read about your theatre in the paper today,' I said. 'I'm an old friend of Joel Bannerman. Can you tell me if he was harmed in the fire?'

They told me no. I asked for a number where I could reach Joel. Instead, the girl at the other end took my number and promised to hand it over with the message that Red Marsden was trying to get in touch.

Joel had my number, of course, in his little book, along with numerous other old girlfriends, I had no doubt. But it would be good to hear his voice and be assured he was OK. He might need cheering up, too. For some peculiar reason, I felt I needed cheering up myself. A feeling of doom hung over me that was quite out of character.

Joel got back to me the same day. I hung around in my flat all day bored and tired and too idle to go out. I didn't like the thought of the coming evening, either. Roger had been odd on the phone. I didn't want to go to his house that evening and had almost decided not to.

'I'm sorry about your theatre,' I said to Joel. 'It's good to hear you are OK yourself.'

'It's horrible,' he said. 'I don't know what to say, what to do. That damned management, they wouldn't pay for a nightwatchman. All this might have been averted if the theatre had been properly guarded and protected at night.'

'Were they close friends, those who died? You must be feeling terrible.'

'I am feeling terrible. But none of the company was hurt. It's awful to say, Red, but I'm so relieved. The police haven't identified the two corpses but we think they must have been vagrants. Tramps, coming in out of the weather for the night. It's been bloody cold up here, and wet. There was a cupboard window left open at the back, it seems, and it looks as if they got in there, poor souls.'

'Was the fire their fault, then? I mean, were they on meths or something, and dropped a match?'

'I don't know. I don't know anything except I'm out of a job.'

'It happened before, twenty years ago.'

'And before that, they tell me. This is the third time. It burned down after the war sometime, in the fifties, I think. I can't see them rebuilding it, Red. It's too unlucky.'

I had that feeling again I had had when I read the news article. I had come across these facts before. I had noted them at the time and subsequently forgotten them. Something that had seemed unimportant at the time was gaining a significance I had previously missed.

'What are you going to do?' I asked slowly. I was thinking.

'Christ knows.'

'I mean immediately. Can you come to town? Can we meet?'

'I'd love to. I'd better stay here, though. There is an enquiry about the fire and the company all have to be sacked and sent home. It's a dismal business, Red. I wish you could come here and cheer me up.'

'If you mean that, I could. You're only two hours up the motorway.'

We fixed it up. I packed rapidly. I was following an intuition as much as succouring an old friend.

I forgot all about Roger. I fetched my own car, an old heap, and got it to start. It was very different from the Porsche I had been driving. But it went and it would take me to where I was going.

Joel was as handsome as I remembered him. He had gone grey very young and it suited him. The man would be pompous as he got older but he was fine just now. Too many actresses made it easy for him and over time he would stop bothering to be nice to the women he wanted to bed.

He looked haggard. He didn't want to go out and I was tired from the drive so we had some food sent round and Joel opened wine.

It got very late. He couldn't relax. He was twitchy. The phone rang once or twice and he jumped when it did, really startled.

Finally I asked him what was wrong.

He stood still and looked at me. He had been padding round the room touching things as he told me about the play they had been going to perform.

'I need to tell someone,' he said and stopped.

'About the fire?'

'No. But something was going on. It doesn't matter. It's not important, but it was odd.'

I sighed. 'Everything's odd these days. It's because the millenium is getting close. Tell me if you want to.'

He sat down on the edge of the couch and looked at me. I was lounging on the floor in front of the gas fire. The weather blustered against the window, cold and black.

'You're pretty broad-minded,' he said.

I lifted heavy-lidded eyes and smiled from under my lashes at him. 'Joel,' I scolded softly.

'I'm not boasting,' he added.

I didn't believe him. 'Go on,' I said. I stretched like a cat and lay on my back.

'Take off your clothes,' he said.

'I thought you wanted to talk.'

'I do. I want to talk to you naked. You naked, I mean.'

I began to undo my blouse. 'This isn't what you think,' said Joel. He seemed crazy to me but I had no objection to revealing my body for him. I stripped slowly, taking each garment off with deliberation. I would be angry if I failed to rouse him, though. It always makes me angry when a man rejects my advances.

I lay naked in the firelight. I had a cushion under my head. The fluffy hearthrug was comfortable under me. I closed my eyes and smiled to myself. If the man got dull I could at least go to sleep.

I felt a movement. Joel sat on the floor by me and looked at my long white thighs. His eyes lingered over my flat belly. My large full breasts were flattened and drooped each to one side of me, the nipples long and dark in the uncertain light of the fire. Each of my ribs showed as the firelight put a sheen on it. My mass of red hair flowered all around my head, spilling over the cushion and onto the floor. The red hair of my sex looked coppery-dark. I let my long legs sprawl open, with one knee slightly raised. I watched Joel.

He put his hand over my sexual mound and let my

crisp curls fill his palm. Keeping his hand there he looked into my face.

'I call them the C2s,' he said.

'What?'

'The second-rate luvvies who come on at the director. You know? The girlies who aren't going to make it without the director's cock stiffening between their legs.'

He stroked my fleece.

'You don't like it?'

'I love it,' he confessed. 'I'm a director, remember. I don't want these bimbos to fall for me. I like knowing it's the job they have up there between their legs.' He put a finger into my cunt quite suddenly, so that I jumped with surprise. 'You wouldn't believe what they'll do to get a part, Red. They don't just let me put it there.' He wriggled his finger in my pussy. 'They let me put it there.' He put the juice-soaked finger into my mouth so that I tasted myself and my own arousal. 'And even there,' he added. He knelt and moved over me swiftly. A moment later the same finger was in my rear. I squealed and clenched sharply.

Joel laughed a little bitterly and sat back. 'It's not unlike ordering people around on stage,' he said. 'Can you see what I mean? I'm the voice that tells them what to do, though they generally get a say in the business if they are any good. They do it because the script says so, because that's what pays the rent. I like that in my sex-life, too. They don't screw me because of me, Joel Bannerman. They screw me for the job. Because they think it's in the script.'

'Does it make any difference?' I asked.

'Other things being equal, yes. I mean, if I have two actresses equally right for the part and one will go to bed with me and the other shows no interest, the bed fodder will get it. But I'm not fool enough to fill my own productions with rubbish just for the sake of a quick lay.

Talent on the boards first. The sex comes second.'

I grinned. 'You bastard.'

He shrugged. 'It's how the world goes, Red. You know that.' He licked a fingertip and drew a circle round my nipple with it. He licked the finger again and touched the little soldier. I shivered pleasantly. It was very late, deep in the night, and the room was very dim.

'It's early in the season here,' he went on quietly. 'We were set to open in December. Those of the company who were suitable would know they might get months of work if this first production went OK and I liked them. I wasn't surprised when little Sandy made a play for me.'

'A successful play?' I liked this. I liked Joel talking about his other women while he worked himself up to having me.

'Yes. I mean I wasn't surprised that one of my actresses should present herself to me as bed fodder but it being Sandy surprised me. I've directed her before and she hadn't seemed to be that sort of a girl.'

I laughed to myself. When we fancy a man we're all that sort of a girl.

'She came on really hard. She made an appointment for me in the theatre, she didn't want to come here, she didn't want wining and dining, she didn't want to show off that she had access to the director's cock. She just wanted to do it and she wanted it in the theatre.'

'So you had it in the theatre.'

'On the stage. Using the set. She went crazy. I went crazy. She actually, get this, Red, she actually masturbated herself on the bedpost in front of me. I'd never seen anything like it.'

He used his fingers to open my sex. He prised apart the leaves of flesh. After touching my vulva he sniffed and licked his own fingers.

I felt cold.

'The next night Carol made the same suggestion.'

'Two,' I said lightly. 'Very good.'

'Carol is gorgeous. Tall and slim and elegant. She's into pain. She left me gasping. I left her asleep.'

'Here?'

'In the theatre. Using the set. Then Carol caught me and Sandy.'

'Oh dear. Fireworks?'

'No,' said Joel deliberately. 'She joined in.'

I was silent. My intuition was paying off. I was hearing something very important and I knew it.'

'Carol, Sandy and I met again. It was always at the same time, about six in the evening, in the theatre, on stage. I could never run a rehearsal late because the three of us got twitchy as the time approached. The management were pleased because I wasn't using expensive overtime but we weren't making the progress we should have been with the production. Believe it, that's what counts with me, Red. Sex is fine. The girls are lovely. But it's the production I care about. That's what lives on.'

Joel opened my legs wide and stared into my sex. 'I saw those girls do amazing things together. When they weren't at me, they were at each other. I've never seen anything like it.' He bent over and kissed me on my clitoris. I felt tight inside. I was very aroused, sexually and mentally. Both would need relieving.

'Then Robina joined us.'

'Oh no,' I said weakly.

'Evening after evening. With three women. For an hour, an hour and half we did everything the human body can do in the act of sex. I penetrated them everywhere. I didn't know which woman I was in half the time. Sometimes I would start in Robina's cunt and end up in Sandy's rear. Carol would kiss my arse. She liked to put lipstick on it and kiss it. I had fingers pushed into me. I would suck one girl while another sat astride my sex and took me. I've had two girls kissing my sex at the same time. I've watched them kissing and sucking each other to climax.

I could pull out of one girl and put my wet cock into another without either complaining.'

He stopped. I knew exactly what he meant. 'No one caught you?' I said. 'There was no trouble?'

'Emma caught us. She joined in too.'

'Joel!'

'It's the truth. I swear it.' He bent over me and began to kiss my pussy. I felt wet on my thighs and realised to my astonishment he was crying.

He sat up. 'It was like a private harem,' he said huskily. 'I came to my four lovely girls night after night. They pleasured me and serviced me like something out of the Arabian Nights They turned me inside out with sex. They didn't say anything, we had no words. It was dream-like, except that it was also frenzied. Do you know what I mean? Can you understand? Can anyone?'

'I understand,' I said but he didn't hear me.

'Every evening I staggered home afterwards. I slept but I had terrible dreams, dreams of vampire-like women descending on my helpless body and sucking all the life-juices out of me. But I couldn't stop it. As it got nearer to six every evening, I became more and more worked up. I was possessed.'

He nuzzled my sex again. He wasn't ashamed of his tears. In his world everyone showed their emotions. No one held back.

I drew his head onto my breast. 'What do you want of me?' I asked.

'Something normal,' he whispered. He kissed me so I could taste my sex on his lips.

'You're afraid.'

'Of course I'm afraid.'

'And now, since the fire?'

'The spell is broken. But I can't bear to be at the ruins of the theatre. The firemen and police just think it's excessive sensibility but it isn't. I keep feeling that Sandra and Emma, or Carol or Robina are dead. They aren't. It was two tramps. But I feel as though it was the girls.'

'You've spoken to them since?'

'I've had to. They are awkward with me, as if they were ashamed. I'll be glad when they've gone and I think they will too.'

There was a great deal to consider. My thoughts were undergoing a revolution. I could feel everything shifting inside my head. I was seeing things from new perspectives, or I would be when I gave myself a chance.

'Have you had any normal sex since you started all this business with the four women?'

'Normal?' Joel whispered. 'What's normal? You tell me, Red.'

'Have you had sex with anyone else?'

'No.'

I took his clothes off. He put me straight over onto my hands and knees and took me like a dog. His body was over mine and his hands were on mine where they rested on the floor. He covered me, my rump jammed into his belly and his cock deep inside my body. At one point he rolled over on his back holding me tightly round my waist so that I came round on my back on top of him. He continued to buck his hips and have me even in this odd position. As we got more excited I sat up on him and rode him hard.

He came fiercely and we lay side by side. Joel sat up and opened my legs. I knew his own sex juices would be visible in me.

'Here,' he said lazily.

'What?'

'Fix your lipstick.'

I reached for my bag and obliged. Joel took an instant camera and he made me purse my lips and pout them. He took several full face pictures of me using the flash.

Then he made me roll over and go on my hands and

knees again. He wouldn't let me wipe myself so I guessed he was getting a buzz from seeing my used sex. But it wasn't my pussy he was intent on. He made me reach round behind myself and open my buttocks. Then he very carefully applied lipstick to my little pouting arse.

'There now,' he said. I had my face on the floor as both my hands were busy helping him get at the area he was interested in. My bottom felt nice with the lipstick on. 'Hold still,' he added.

The camera flashed several times. I had trouble holding still as I was shaking with laughter. I shouldn't let him take such dirty photographs of me but my face wasn't in them, I was hardly identifiable.

'Squeeze it, Red. Make it move,' he ordered. Obligingly I squeezed my little rear and made it move as much as I could. I could pout it out and suck it in quite a lot when I really tried.

'Now hold still again,' he said. I jumped. He was inserting something in my bottom. It was small but long. He slid quite a way in.

'Hold still,' he said huskily, and again he took pictures of me.

'Now, you can let go and roll over.'

I did so. He had removed the thing he had penetrated me with. I saw it was a pencil.

'Fix your mouth again,' he said. I obeyed. I wondered what he was after. He put the pencil into my mouth so it projected out. He took two photos. The photos took a long time because each one had to come out of the camera and be developed.

He had laid all the photographs down on a coffee table in a line. When he was finished he put on a table lamp so that the pictures were illuminated.

'Come and see,' he said softly.

I went over and looked at myself and at my naked bottom. I saw my pursed lips and puckered arse. I saw the pencil sticking out of my bottom and sticking out of my mouth.

Joel picked up two photos. One was my face, one was my arse. Using scissors he cut round the lipsticked orifice. My sweet wet pussy was cut away. My nose disappeared. Only the reddened pursed lips remained.

They were indistinguishable, arse and mouth.

'It's my business,' said Joel. 'I manipulate appearances. Now let me kiss you.' He rolled me over and he kissed my arse passionately and sexily, as he had kissed my mouth on former occasions.

I enjoyed it.

Afterwards I said: 'Was it like that with the four girls?'

'No,' he said.

'Tell me,' I insisted.

He looked at me. 'I could fool with you. I could have fun. You responded to what I did and I responded to you. We could talk. It was exciting but we weren't frantic. With the others it was certainly exciting. But it was frantic. I was desperate. It wasn't sex so much as drugs. I couldn't stop. It was wonderful but it was out of control. I couldn't stop.'

I was too tired to discuss things then. Now I really did have all the answers even if my tired brain couldn't assemble them coherently. Moreover, I was grateful for a chance to delay, if only by one night. I knew I wasn't going to like my conclusions. I wasn't going to believe the only explanation of what had been happening in my life. The logic of the circumstances was inexorable, but I didn't want to know it.

When I woke up the next morning there was lipstick smeared on Joel's sex. I'm not going to say how it got there. I don't usually wear lipstick in bed but on this occasion I had worn it in more than one place.

Joel was a happier man.

FILE TWENTY

Conclusion: Burning Desire

In the early hours of the morning following their sexual congress, Red Marsden told Joel Bannerman something of her recent history.

She told him that the fierce greediness and sexual obsession he had experienced with the four female members of his company was something she understood, all too well. She described her experiences with Roger Greaves and his wife Janie, and what had happened to other people who had slept in that damned and terrifying room.

She described the punishment room at Planefields School with the rows of student bottoms uplifted to receive the swishing caress of the cane as administered by a young male master.

She described the ideas room of the author, Jason Wells, where he realised his sexual fantasies in reality and in print.

She described the nude gymnastics of the Health Clinic.

She recalled the testimony of Billy Toomer, and his account of the happy and sexually free Linda Campsey, remembered over fifty years.

Joel said: 'I don't understand.'

'Sex and fire,' said Red Marsden. 'I'm talking about sex and fire. Think of your theatre, Joel, your four wonderful women and the flames that burned.'

'No,' said Joel.

'I approached all these places through the list Sonja gave me.'

'Sonja?'

'Sonja. She works for a group who investigate self-igniting humans.'

'Stop it, Red. This is sick.'

'Think about it. Sexual heat. You've felt it, Joel. So have I.'

'Sex is everywhere, Red. You know that, you of all people.'

'Yes, me of all people. That's how I know. I've tried to sort out the difference, Joel. I've tried to be honest with myself. I adore men. I love your bodies, what you do with them, what you do to me. I've had a lot of sex since Roger started me on this business. But I can tell the difference. Last night with you, it was lovely. I made love with Sonja. Did I tell you that? I love women sucking me now. I love their mouths closed like velvet over my cunt. Joel, I want to be sucked by a man and by a woman in turn to feel the difference, your strong mouth and her soft one.'

'Stop this, Red.'

'I made love with Roger at my place and it was dynamite. He's the first man I slept with, you know that, Joel? He started me off. He got me going.'

'I'm not listening, you crazy bitch.'

'I've had men friends. You. Many others. I can't get enough men, I don't ever want to stop. It makes me feel alive, having a man between my legs, feeling his body press on mine, experiencing the dirty things he wants me to do. I love to suck cock, Joel, you know that.'

'Why are you saying all this?'

'I'm going to write it all down. I'm going to describe every sexual act I've taken part in since this thing started. So much of sex is normal, people do it all the time. But this is different.'

'What thing? I can't understand you.'

'This thing of sex and fire. I'm going to describe the various acts I've performed with men and with women and see where the difference lies.'

'What difference?'

'The one you're talking about. How it was with us last night, how it will be in a moment when I stop holding myself back from taking you into me, how it was with Sonja and all the others. That's one thing. That's normal. Then there's the other thing. With Roger in his bedroom. With his wife in the same room. With them both. With my friend Nick in the same place. Then there's you, here, in the theatre, with those four females. It's a place thing, Joel. Can't you see what I'm getting at? It isn't us, it's the place.'

'The place?'

'Where somehow we move from being normal and sexy into overdrive. The place where we become furies. Where we become possessed. Where we fuck ourselves into oblivion. The place that catches fire. No, the place where we catch fire.'

'You've gone mad.'

'No. I'm coming to my senses. I'm beginning to understand. It's the place that matters. There are fires in special places. Humans ignite. At the school where they smack naked bottoms. At the gym where they run around nude. In Roger's house where respectable people indulge in orgies. In your theatre . . .'

'All acting companies tend to be a little loose in their morals. I don't mean all actors and actresses, because some of them are terrific prudes. But all companies of adults working closely together and away from home tend to go in for a little adultery. You've exaggerated this, Red.'

'In your theatre which keeps burning down.'

'No.'

'Think about it, Joel.'

'Think about what? Lightning bolts striking my theatre because one or two members of the company are a little naughty? Grow up, Red. You sound like a tin-pot evangelist trying to throw a scare.'

'No. It's the people who burn. The building usually escapes, only I guess a theatre is particularly inflammable. The people can't help the sex, however prudish they naturally are. It's a compulsion, you know that yourself. You've been there, Joel. The sex doesn't come from the people, it comes from the place. From the building. No, from the place, because your theatre burned down and was rebuilt and it happened again.'

'You don't know there was sex here before. Well, of course there was sex. I mean, you don't know there was extraordinary sex.'

'But I do. There was at Lane End Cottages.'

'Where?'

'Roger's place. I'll have to get back. I can't remember the details. Before Linda Campsey there was a woman who caused a scandal and then caught fire. And one before her. Jenny somebody. I'll have to check.'

'How do you know all this?'

'We had a local historian investigate the deaths relating to the cottages. We thought the place was haunted.'

'Now I've heard everything. Ghosts. Ghosts who set fire to the place.'

'To the people. Look, we can check my idea. You must be able to get hold of a history of the Phoenix, or whatever it was called before.'

'The Tivoli.'

'Right. Find out when it burned down before. Then we have to find people who remember it. They'll know if there was a scandal at the time. And we need to know how this fire started. The seat of it ought to be those two squatters, poor souls. The effect must have been ready to occur but instead of you and your harem igniting, it was them.'

'You can't be serious.'

'I'm going back to the school and to that health farm. I need to find out if there were any naughty goings on when the tragedies occurred. The author's house, too. A fireman died there. I need to find out if the neighbours knew of anything going on. Any extraordinary sex, I mean. That would really tie things up.'

'Sex and fire?'

'Yes, Joel. It might sound incredible but these buildings, these places I've been talking about have some power. The power manifests itself as a frenetic sexual possession followed by flames.'

'You are trying to tell me that a school birching a few pubescent bottoms and nudism on a health farm equates to what I did with those four women, or what you say you did with this Roger character?'

'No. You're right, of course. I'm not there yet. I'll find the link, I know I will. I must investigate the history of these other places, Joel, including your theatre. Then I might understand properly what the hell is going on.'

The difference between normal and abnormal sex is clear to anyone who has experienced both. It's hard to describe the difference to a third party but that was what Red felt she had to do. She felt she had to be scrupulously honest in her descriptions of sex so that another investigator could rely on her testimony. She knew she could be so far into the thing that she had gone beyond understanding it. But if she wrote it all down, someone else might be able to disentangle truth from self-delusion.

At this point Red believed there was an objective phenomenon with which she had become involved via Roger Greaves. It existed at Lane End Cottages independently of the people who lived there, or more importantly, slept there. Anyone could experience it. Red also felt it existed in the Phoenix Theatre. She felt there was a case for it at the Jason Wells home, the private school and the health farm. She knew she needed to know more about these places, and why its expression was muted in these places and so virulent in the others.

It existed in various potencies, for want of a better word. She simply didn't know enough to get the whole picture clear.

Before leaving Joel she extracted a promise from him that he find out more about the previous history of the Phoenix. Then she set off for the school.

Planefields revisited

No more front door stuff. I knew what I had to do. I didn't bother with false personas. There was a simple way to check up if my burning desire hypothesis had any validity.

I haven't said much about my job. Maybe it sounds as if I am hopelessly underqualified for real work and so I pretend to do a little of this and that to keep the money coming in.

This is not so. I am very qualified for my line of work, but they aren't the sort of skills it is wise to advertise.

For instance, I can pick locks. I can disconnect most domestic burglar alarm systems. I am very good at effecting illegal entry.

I can't prove these skills. Having entered a place and achieved whatever it is I have set out to accomplish, I usually leave it looking undisturbed. That's the measure of my success, that no one realises what I have done. But I have my list of satisfied customers who know enough not to ask stupid questions.

So I'm good at listening to what shouldn't be overheard, seeing what is intended to be secret and I can record either, on equipment that won't be detected.

Enough of this. It is sufficient to say that I entered the Planefields School with little difficulty and found that I was able to roam the long empty corridors at will, once night had fallen.

They weren't my object, though. I went down through the kitchens and out to the back parts of the house. I found the flagstoned room with the whitewashed walls and the two sinister punishment rails.

I set up my equipment and retreated.

And was caught.

He must have been coming anyway. He couldn't have heard me. I walked noiselessly in rubber-soled shoes. I was dressed from head to toe in black, close-fitting black. I even wore black silk mask to hide the pale blur of my face and fine black leather gloves to hide my hands.

I heard his footsteps and froze, becoming one with the shadows. He passed me by and leaving the door of the punishment room open, he put on the light.

Even then all would have been well but he came back out of the room.

I didn't dare to move even though some of the light spilled over me. If he was intent enough on his own purposes, he would miss me though I was there to be seen. Movement would give it all away.

It didn't work. He saw me. He gave an angry shout and reached out.

I know a little judo, too. I let him take my arm and I pulled it to tighten his grip. I caught hold of him with my free hand and twisted my body hard, hooking with one foot.

He fell with a startled grunt. He slid along the floor tiles and ended up on his back in the doorway of the punishment room.

It was Mr Findhorn. He lay on the floor looking dazed. I knelt over him in case he was concussed. I had forgotten the stone floors to this part of the building. I hadn't meant to hurt the man.

He had guts, did that schoolmaster. He grabbed at me while I was off-balance. Actually I was thinking again what an incredibly sexy man he was, with that dramatic Byronic style of looks.

This inattention to my own safety was disastrous. I was grabbed as I have said, and I fell across his body.

We tussled. 'You're a woman,' he suddenly said. He had me pinned now, using his superior strength. He reached for my mask.

'No,' I said.

He was on top now, in every sense. 'Why not?' he asked, holding me down.

'Let me keep the secret of who I am,' I pleaded huskily. 'But punish me for my wrongful entry.'

I felt him go still. 'Punish you?' he asked.

'Like the girls. Punish me like you punish the girls. Only more so. Go further. Do what you want.'

I wasn't acting. This wasn't part of the plan. This was lust. I meant every word that I said.

He released me warily. I continued to lay on the floor. My hands went to the belt of my black jeans. I undid them.

Mr Findhorn moved back a little further to give me more room. I sat up slowly and slipped off my black rubber and canvas shoes. Then I wriggled out of my jeans.

'Punish me,' I whispered. 'Beat the panties from my bottom. Do what you want. I'm a woman, a woman in the wrong. I'm not a girl. There's no one else here. You are free to do what you want.'

I stood up and walked over to the punishment rails. Then I bent over.

I heard him get to his feet and approach. I shut my eyes. My blood thundered. I hardly knew what I was doing. I was flooded by a dazzling feeling of ecstasy. I straddled my legs wider and waited.

I flexed the muscles of my pussy. I squeezed my little arse and pouted it. I was almost in orgasm with anticipation. The reality was going to be something tremendous.

He said nothing. I saw from between my own legs that

he had unbuttoned his shirt and pulled it out from the waistband of his trousers. His tie hung free from the collar, loosened but not removed. He rolled up his sleeves.

My pussy was weeping at the thought of what was to come.

Mr Findhorn took the switch and smacked his palm a couple of times. Then he hit my cheeks.

He kept doing it. I heard the rod whistle through the air again and again. My panties shredded and scraps of lace fell from them. He beat me frenziedly and I cried out with the pain. Orgasm bubbled hot in me. My flesh writhed. Moments later his huge cool cock was deep in my furnace and he was taking his ease in my tortured person.

I sobbed as he took himself to climax. He had unfastened his trousers to penetrate me and gradually they slid down his legs to crumple round his ankles. He hit my bottom hard with his body as he poked me and I cried out at every stinging blow. I couldn't tell apart the flexings of my pussy and arse from the stinging pain of my chastised bottom.

He stopped and hung over me, panting. Then he pulled out and without fixing his clothes, he pulled me upright.

Even that hurt.

'Now me,' he said. 'You do me.'

He hobbled over to the rack of birch rods. He replaced the fine thin flexible switch he had used on me. Instead he took a thicker one with far less flex. He handed this to me and hobbled back to the rail, impeded by his dropped trousers. His cock hung low. He bent over the punishment rail with a small sob and gripped the lower one. He waited.

His arse was white with a fluffy covering of coarse curly black hair. For a moment I stroked it. His buttocks clenched so that they felt hard and unyielding. I put my hand between his thighs and pressed each thigh in turn. He understood and opened his legs further.

Now I could feel his wet dangling cock, his spongy balls. I felt them from between his legs for a moment or two. Then I stood back. I felt the rod I was holding. I hit my own palm lightly. Then I smacked his bottom.

He jolted. I hadn't hit him hard. There was no mark.

I tapped his bottom a couple of times and then hit really hard. He gripped the lower rail so that his knuckles were white. I saw the thin red line across the white buttock.

I hit him again. The rod whistled and struck. His flesh jumped. I had deliberately crossed the former mark and now his right cheek was marked with an X.

Now I decorated the left buttock with a similar pattern. I broke off from my work to put my hand between his thighs again.

He felt wonderful. His cock was long and firm. His balls were swollen and hard. I felt his cheeks, they glowed faintly where I had struck them. I smacked him again.

'That's not how to do it,' said a voice.

I turned in horror. I was naked myself below the waist.

At the entrance to the room a girl stood. She wore a blazer, navy blue with red and gold piping sewn on around its edge. She wore a red and gold striped tie. Otherwise she wore nothing. I could see her breasts. I could see her delicate patch of pussy fur. I could see her long slender legs, her youthful thighs.

She must have been eighteen at least, one of the most senior girls. It wasn't hard to work out why she was here and why she was dressed as she was.

Now I knew why Mr Findhorn had come. I had interrupted an assignation.

Silently I held up the rod. She came towards me, smiling. The smoky fluff in her groin was a soft mouse grey that invited the hand, it looked so sweet.

She took the instrument with amusement. She was familiar with this, then. I was surrendering an old flame.

Flame. Not a word I liked.

All this time Mr Findhorn had said nothing. He had stood himself upright at the girl's entrance and he watched her as she took the rod. He did nothing to cover his nakedness though he stared at hers.

She tapped the palm of her hand with the rod. 'Bend over, sir,' she said.

She had hazel eyes. They slitted with amusement as she looked at me. 'Like this,' she said.

She began to smack his bottom with the rod. She began with light feathery strokes, very rapid, that alternated on each cheek. After a while she varied the rhythm and every so often put in a real stinger, full-strength, so the man she chastised winced and cried out.

I felt hot and excited despite having been poked. I went round to where I could see his sex. It was painfully stiff, rigid, in front of him.

I ducked under the rail. I knelt at his body. He had to lift up his upper half so I could get in.

I took the iron-hard sexual organ into my mouth. The girl beat his bottom. His cock was in my mouth. It shivered and quivered as if it had a mind of its own. I sucked.

Mr Findhorn began to cry out. The girl beat him now hard, now softly. His rear must hurt terribly. She played it as if it was drumskins and she made music of his pain.

I shut my eyes and savoured the cock in my mouth. I sucked to the tune of the girl. Mr Findhorn shook and jerked and quivered and finally he gave a great sob and his cock burst open in my mouth and I tasted his liquid manhood, hot and strong.

The girl had stopped beating. She placed one cool young palm across his burning bottom. With her other hand she grasped the swinging balls between his furred thighs. I sucked the diminishing cock. Between us Mr Findhorn shook in the aftermath of his dual release from pain.

I moved away and got to my feet. I found my trousers

and put them on. I slipped on my canvas shoes.

I looked at the other two players in our strange little game. The girl was on her knees with her mouth up against Mr Findhorn's rear. She kept laying her cheek against his flaming posterior. Then she would part the stinging cheeks and kiss between them. She bent low and kissed the backs of his balls and his damp cock. She licked and kissed the whole area.

I saw the girl's breasts pouting out from between the open flaps of her blazer. Her tie hung crookedly between her breasts. Her sweet bottom was in my view as she bent to service the master. I knew a passionate longing to take her in my arms and kiss her. I wanted to kiss her little bottom and run my tongue along the length of her wriggling young vulva. It was a burning desire.

I took myself from the room. Once in the cool dark cavern of the kitchens I was able to feel some relief. I found the exit I wanted and removed myself from school premises.

My cameras were strategically placed. I had opted for time lapse photography, still pictures taken at five minute intervals. That meant that the time covered before the film ran out was as long as I could get without constant film-changing. I would only come back once.

I hardly needed to do anything other than retrieve my expensive equipment. My experience had given me all the information I needed on one particular topic.

It was necessarily a subjective assessment, but I felt the room had power, sexual power. It was muted when compared to the frenzy of Roger's bedroom, but it was real, nonetheless.

All I needed now was to know whether the former owner of those living in the house had been involved in extra-special sexual activity at the time of the fire twenty-odd years ago, and whether there were any more strange occurrences coming from before that time.

Not my work. It needed someone skilled in researching local history. I had a pal who enjoyed rootling about in old newspaper files. He was a retired journalist and to look at him you'd think he last enjoyed sex about the time of the Boer War. Not so. He was a versatile and kinky lover.

He would help me, I was sure.

Meanwhile there was Jason Wells.

Sin in Suburbia

It was no problem. I didn't go to Jason direct. If I had done that I would have to reassume my Charity Fulsome character and no doubt I would be subjected to the strange and painful sexual practices, and the humiliations I had experienced before. I had been made to dance on the man's cock. I had jigged with pain, my vagina contracting about his cock till he had been brought to orgasm.

I wasn't planning to let myself in for that again.

I don't even think it would have helped me. Jason didn't know anything about the past history of his house. It was his neighbours that I wanted.

I became Australian again. The dead fireman was a distant relative of mine. I was over in the country of the Poms trying to find someone who knew him, who could tell me about him.

I tried several houses before I struck gold. She was in her seventies, she had all her marbles and she was bored. She welcomed me in, gave me coffee and biscuits and told me the entire history of the neighbourhood from the year dot.

She had been born several streets away and moved to the house she currently occupied when she married, though her husband was long gone. I learned a lot about her life and how the London district had developed, none of which was relevant to the enquiry I was conducting.

I also learned about Jason Wells' house.

'It was no. 13, dear,' said Mrs Melbury. 'It was always an unlucky house. None of us children liked it. We thought a bad man lived there and we all avoided it.'

'Did a bad man live there?' I asked innocently. Getting dates for this jumble of events would be difficult. Mrs Melbury hopped about with chronological insouciance.

'It was what our nannies said. I think they just wanted to keep us away. The house was notorious but for quite different reasons.'

I started to tremble like a bloodhound on the scent. 'And those reasons were?' I asked delicately.

'Sex, my dear. Ladies of ill-repute. They lived there in quite shameless splendour. I can picture them now with their short skirts and shingled hair. So racy. So popular with the gentlemen.'

'So why did they tell you a bad man lived there?' I asked. 'Surely they must have realised you could tell the difference between two prostitutes and a gentleman.'

'Because a man died there. He was burned in his bed. That is, in her bed, if you see what I mean. He must have been a client, I suppose.' Mrs Melbury gave a titter. 'He was a greengrocer, very comfortably off. He was well known in local golfing circles, quite an important man in local business eyes, a civic notability, you might say.'

'Do you remember the year that this happened?' I asked.

'Now let me see. In the twenties, anyway. The police took the girls away and the house was empty for a while, that I do remember, because we all thought it was haunted and used to dare each other to play in the garden. I remember!' Mrs Melbury smiled at me in triumph. 'It was a scholarly gentleman, someone associated with the British Museum, I think, who came next.'

She frowned slightly. 'Now I remember, there was something of a scandal about him, too. His maids, I think. A little kitchenmaid complained. There was a terrible scandal, very quickly hushed up. We all thought the child hysterical, she would only be sixteen or so, but he left the house soon after.'

'What sort of accusations were they?' I asked.

'Oh, that he expected his servants to provide certain services, of course. The girl had objected. She was frightened. She said he caught fire one night and certainly, I do vaguely remember him being all bandaged. Perhaps I'm getting muddled and he was the bad man.'

'Can you tell me when this was?' I asked. 'You see, my cousin died from fire. I'm wondering if the same sort of accident keeps occurring.'

Mrs Melbury considered. In the end the best she could come up with was some time in the twenties for the dead greengrocer, probably the earlier part of the twenties. Her information had come more from her older sister than from what she had gathered herself, because she was very young at the time. And thrilled.

The professor was after the war, she was sure of that. The house suffered bomb damage in the war but had been repaired.

I had to go carefully now. 'This cousin of mine, he was a second cousin really,' I said. 'Can you tell me anything about him?'

Mrs Melbury primmed her lips.

'My auntie would never tell me anything,' I said cunningly. 'She said he was no better than he should be.'

'Well, in that case,' said Mrs Melbury, and told me what I wanted to know.

It had begun with curtains drawn in the daytime. Being a fireman he was on shiftwork. Then his wife had fled the marital home, for reasons, it was whispered, connected with unnatural practices in bed. He had begun to bring women home, women of a certain kind. Shrieks and laughter had been heard, even in the daytime. He was often drunk and had been threatened with dismissal. Then he had burned in his bed, no doubt in a drunken stupor.

Much of this was based on gossip, innuendo and surmise. But I had my connection.

Sex and fire.

Revisiting. Planefields School had been fun. Mrs Melbury's reminiscences left a bad taste in my mouth. Now I had to go back to the Health Farm.

The Sexual Therapist

Peter, the golden muscle-man at the clinic had told me about their sexual therapy programme. When I read a newspaper report of the inquest on Helen Bellman, the woman who had died three years previously in the gym at the clinic, it came as no surprise to learn that she had been a specialist in the field.

The inquest was coy but it was plain that suicide as a verdict was seriously considered. There had been complaints about Helen, it appeared. Some clients had not liked their therapy. Helen's behaviour became odd, her colleagues testified.

I considered it. Reading between the lines, I felt I had what I was after. To confirm it I needed to be on good terms with a member of the staff. Helen's death was so recent they would be aware of it. It would still have consequences. Whatever Helen had done, the clinic would still be actively guarding itself against a repetition.

Peter had resisted having sex with me. I didn't think it was because I wasn't his type. He didn't want to lose his job, that was it. Helen had gone too far and the rest of them now exercised iron control. That was the way I read the situation.

I needed to flesh out this idea a little. Maybe Peter preferred boys and I had misread his rejection of my advances. There was only one way to find out.

I hired the Porsche again, they are marvellous aphrodisiacs and I was intent on a seduction. I trailed him leaving the clinic. He appeared to live on the campus, for want of a better word, but he came away to visit a local pub. When I saw him disappear inside, I followed.

He was drinking something clear and fizzy with a slice of lemon in it. He had a paper open at the racing page and he was bent over the bar quietly studying it.

I ordered a gin and tonic and waited for him to recognise me. If I had failed to switch him on, he would find me forgettable. If it had been an effort to reject me, he should still know me, even in different clothes and in a different location.

He looked up. He looked more closely. 'Harriet,' he said.

'Hi, Peter. Can I get you a drink?'

He folded the paper slowly. He looked as fit and able as he had looked before.

He had a gin and tonic. Good. Now I knew he didn't carry this fitness thing beyond the realms of common sense.

'You are back in the area,' he said politely. He raised his glass. 'Do you live round here?'

'No.'

'Are you signing on for a course? I hope you are.' He gave me a sunny smile to tell me how interested he was in making my body harmonious.

'No.'

'Did we fail to interest you? I'm very sorry about that. I think you'd enjoy it.'

'I don't think I would,' I said with deliberation. 'There are things I can bear to do without and food is one of them. I'm not much struck with exercise but I can bear that. What I can't bear is being denied and being tempted at one and the same time. I'm too used to indulgence. I'm not signing up for that.'

'I don't understand.' He looked genuinely puzzled. Not one of the brightest, our Peter.

I looked him in the eye and smiled lazily. My voice was

very soft when I spoke. 'I couldn't stand to have wonderful men like you around me quite naked, and me not being able to do one damn thing about it. I like to exploit facilities, Peter, and you have very fine equipment. As a client, I wouldn't be allowed to use it, would I?'

He blushed. He actually blushed. 'We can't,' he stammered. 'There was a scandal. A woman therapist did. We really can't.'

I sighed inside myself. That was my proof. 'I'm not a client,' I pointed out.

'I'm not with you.' The poor dear looked bewildered and frightened.

'I haven't signed up so I'm not out of bounds,' I said patiently. 'You have the equipment. I have the desire. You tell me, Peter, whether I can avail myself of the opportunities you might offer. This is personal, you understand. This is between you and me.'

The Porsche was outside. It takes ingenuity, but that's a quality I have in plenty. We took it deep into the countryside and there in the gloaming Peter spread-eagled himself over the beautiful snout of the car and I climbed aboard. Then, quite naked, I spread myself breast down on the same slinky bonnet and Peter took me from behind. After this we climbed into the car. I made him sit and I sat across his lap, facing him.

His cock tickled my sexual parts. Because I was virtually kneeling astride him, I was wide open underneath. Peter sucked my nipples while his cock took a breather.

'I couldn't bear you to teach me about sex and not have it off with you,' I whispered in my Aussie twang.

He groaned. 'It's very difficult. But Helen went mad. She had her whole class tied up in knots. The clients were all screwing each other. Helen gingered them up. They did terrible things to each other. Finally someone complained.'

'What did they do?' I whispered. His cock rose and fluttered against my pussy.

'They made wheels of love. She had them kneel in a circle. Then ones got between and lay on their back.'

Peter was whispering too. His cock kept growing. Now it was pushing into my willing wet hole.

'You see, a man would put his face between the legs of the person lying in front of him. He'd suck or kiss her sex. She would suck the hanging cock of the man kneeling over her face. In his turn he would suck the sex of the next lady lying on her back in the chain. And so on, around the ring.'

I moved up and down on the firm column within me. His head was right back. I could bite his exposed throat.

'Tell me,' I said.

'Helen went round them. She would encourage them to suck harder. She taught them how to help their partners to orgasm. She would slip things into the men's arses, pretending to measure their sexual activity or something. She was crazy, crazy.'

'You took my temperature that way.'

'I know.' His voice was husky. 'It's practical. In the mouth it can be bitten or it can fall out. But I loved doing it. I loved sliding it between your cheeks.'

I rose up on him and let him fall out of me. I worked my way round in the cramped space of the car. Then I lowered myself sitting on his lap with my back to him.

He whimpered slightly. He held my cheeks apart. I wanted to feel him in me, big and hard. As his thick cock began to push into the restricted space of my rear, I felt this was the culmination of desire. This was the apex of greed. It was a nonsense in biological terms but so was almost all human sexual activity, since we did it for pleasure not for procreation. My pleasure was to be greedy. I wanted this badly.

The young man filled me absolutely. I cried out with stifled pleasure. I wasn't being driven by a crazed compulsion. Nothing made me do this. I was a free agent doing what I wanted to do, however aberrant it was in some eyes, because I adored it.

I bent forward and he fucked hard into my illicit place. His fingers fumbled round and he tickled my clitoris as he did so. I felt the glory of his coming. My own orgasm rumbled like thunder. When I lifted with agonising slowness off his golden prick, I felt weak and happy.

He put his fingers into his own spunk and rubbed it round so that my vulva was tickled. Then he reached forward to where my breasts hung down. My forehead rested on the fascia in front of me. We were sitting in the passenger seat of the car.

He massaged my nipples with spunky fingers. I relaxed, pleased with myself. I had confirmed what I had suspected about Helen Bellman.

She was a victim of burning desire.

My journalist friend traced the clinic's history as well as that of the school. The clinic was difficult because twenty-eight years ago it had been razed by fire. Then it had been a farm cottage. The site had been abandoned after the fire. Later the land had been bought by property developers. The clinic had followed.

Fire. Colin, my friend, couldn't get a whiff of sexual scandal, though. He did better at Planefields. The wife of the former owner, a man who had died, had been suing for divorce at the time of his death because of his adulteries.

It wasn't much. Adultery occurs everywhere, at all times. But at least we knew he was sexually active, if nothing else.

I wrote it all down. It didn't look a great deal. So much of what I felt was subjective, due to the difference between perfectly lovely and innovative sex between active human beings, and the terrible compulsion that I had mentally labelled burning desire.

The compulsion was associated with places. It had a

history. In Roger's house it had surfaced several times. In 1843 Jenny Wilkes had indulged in 'lewd and licentious practices' and died. In 1893 Alison Makepeace was in the business of exposing her private parts and she had died engulfed in flames. In 1943 Linda Campsey had given the lads a good time and died herself, poor girl.

The clinic stood on the site of a cottage that had been burned down twenty-eight years before. We had no evidence of sexual scandal here. Then three years ago Helen Bellman, sexual therapist, had led her class a merry time until someone complained and she was stopped. She died in the gym on fire.

Planefields. My friend had unearthed a fire in the 1930s. He could find out little about it. But the fire in 1972, when it had been a private house, was a good example of a self-igniting human. The owner had died in a flagged passage. Colin had discovered he rather considered he had a free hand in matters sexual and was accused of bringing Carnaby Street to his house, in the shape of the mini-skirted dolly-birds that then abounded. His wife had begun divorce proceedings before the tragedy.

Jason Wells. I had found Mrs Melbury very helpful. The house had a history of scandal and fire. Roughly every thirty-three or thirty-four years a fresh incident occurred. There were the flappers back in the twenties. There was the professor in the mid-fifties. There was the fireman in 1988.

The theatre. It had been burned down in 1973. Now it had been burned in 1993. I knew about the sex associated with the second event, because Joel had given me a first-hand description.

I had visited all of these places except the theatre. I knew all of them were scorching, to use an appropriate metaphor. I had played games in Jason Wells' ideas room. I had been sexily punished at the school. I had seen abundant naked flesh at the health farm. I had gone crazy at Roger's house.

To tell the absolute truth, it was only at this point I fully realised the danger at Lane End Cottages.

The phenomenon had a period, as scientists say. It recurred. In each place it existed, it had a different period. The effect could be predicted. The period at Lane End Cottages was fifty years.

Every fifty years the phenomenon exploded. 1843. 1893. 1943. And now it was 1993.

There would be burning. It needn't be Roger. It needn't be Janie. But it would be some poor soul, present when the phenomenon reached its climax.

Vagrants had been unlucky at Joel's theatre. They had absorbed the deadly effect leaving the company untouched.

Thank goodness Roger no longer used the central part of his house. I must phone him immediately and tell him to keep everyone clear of it.

Then I remembered. A week ago Roger had phoned me to come over, everything was fine, they were using the house again.

I was to come at midnight.

My blood ran cold. That was the day I had read about Joel's theatre and gone racing up the motorway. I hadn't wanted to go to Roger's and I had put that strange invitation out of my mind.

I was back home after my delightful experience with Peter. I had been sorting through my notes, assembling my ideas. Now, with my heart racing, I dialled Roger.

There was no answer. I looked at my watch. He could be out for the evening with Janie. He could be away for work and Janie at her mother's or out with a friend. They could be just not answering the phone.

I would have to go there. I would have to stake the place out. I couldn't let Roger and his wife be at risk.

I didn't want to go down there alone. I found the whole thing really creepy now. I needed help and there were few people I could tell, few who would believe me.

Sonja would believe me, though. She researched this kind of thing. She and her group were the ideal ones to contact. That's what I would do the minute I had a chance, tell her group what I had discovered.

Meanwhile I needed a friend. I phoned Sonja and begged her to accompany me. I would explain on the way.

Burning Desire

'I have this lover,' I explained.

'Male or female?' Sonja was curled up in the passenger seat of my car. I could smell her, a faint peppery scent.

'Male. He's the director of a provincial theatre.' I named it. 'It's just burnt down.'

'He's OK?'

'He's a troubled man. But he taught me something recently.'

'Go on.' Her voice was amused.

'He made me put lipstick on my mouth and purse it. He took a photograph in close-up of it.'

'It?'

'My mouth. Then he put lipstick on my arse.'

'That sounds interesting.'

'He made me pout my arse and he took photographs of it. He used an instant camera. He took the developed pictures and cut round the two orifices. They looked the same.'

Sonja thought about this. 'I see,' she said eventually. 'I must try it.'

'The point is that things that are different can look the same.'

'Go on.'

'But maybe they are the same. Maybe we think of things as different because of the way we have named them, but in reality, as our eyes can see, they are the same.'

'Our mouths and our arseholes.'

'Absolutely. If we called that puckered skin round our anuses lips, then the similarity would stand out. We call our buttocks cheeks as it is. Reduce the fatness of our bottom cheeks, blow out our facial cheeks, purse our lips and the whole area bears striking resemblances. Do you like being kissed on the arse?'

'I do,' said Sonja throatily.

'Since Roger got me going on this, I've been having very similar sex,' I said.

'That's a pity.'

'Fire and ice. Restraint. Buggery. I'm insane to have it up my backside these days, you know that?'

'We'll have see what we can do.' Sonja's voice was still husky.

'It began in Roger's house. But I've carried it around with me though it's been expressed in a gentler, more controlled form. But most of the places I've been having sex in lately are associated with the burning phenomenon. Not your place, Sonja. Nor my own. Nor the place Joel rented. And I had it off in a car in a field. But when I was being beaten at the school and when I was in Jason's house, I was on site, as it were.'

'It's different on site and off? You're sure?'

'I'm sure. I've definitely done things I first did on site, off site later on. But they've been different. And the closer the phenomenon is to erupting, the stronger it is. So the theatre was very strong indeed for Joel and his ladies. And Roger's house . . .' I stopped.

'Is burning,' said Sonja quietly.

'I hope not. I hope we're not too late. It's due to erupt, the burning desire. That's why it was weak in effect at the health clinic, they've only recently had their self-igniting human. The situation was eased. But Roger's is primed to explode. We have to stop him, get him and Janie out.'

'Yes,' said Sonja. 'I understand.'

We were winding through black-dark lanes deep in rural Kent. I hated it. Rain slashed at the car windscreen every so often. The wind bawled through the trees and the tyres hissed as the potholes in the roads filled with water.

The cottage was dark when we arrived. I was glad to see it intact but it didn't really mean much. The buildings usually survived. It was the people who suffered.

There was no car in sight but the double garage could be hiding them. I went up to the front door and beat on it, ringing the bell. Then I went back to the car and pressed the horn for a long moment.

Sonja climbed out and stood shivering under the porch canopy with me.

I didn't hear anyone come to the door. I saw it begin to open. Relief flooded through me.

The door kept opening wider. I took Sonja's arm. My mind was racing to find a way of explaining that would edit out Rog's adulteries.

I couldn't see the figure in the doorway. I thought I heard 'come in'. The rain was so cold and at that moment it sloshed at us, malevolent and personal.

Warmth gusted out into the night. Sonja and I stepped over the threshold.

It was dark inside. The warmth lapped up at us and I opened my coat. 'Come through,' said the voice and laughed, a low cosy note.

Was it Janie? Why couldn't I tell? Why weren't the damned lights on?

Why had we been let in so easily? We could have been anyone?

I passed through the kitchen and into the central part of the house. I knew instantly I had made a terrible mistake. I turned to stop Sonja from following me but I was too late.

Rog's bedroom door was open. Compelled, Sonja and I walked in.

It hit us like a wall.

Rog said: 'You took your time.'

I mewed, tearing my clothes off. Beside me Sonja was doing the same thing. There were candles lit. I saw Janie was quite naked and she helped Sonja, touching her, stroking her, kissing her body as it was revealed.

I walked over and sat on Rog's cock. As it slid up into my body I closed my eyes and entered heaven.

I remember little of what happened next. All my consciousness was Roger's cock inside my sex, moving, and people kissing my breasts, my lips, my throat. Janie and Sonja, kissing me while Rog fucked me. I fell backwards in bliss and found a warm musky place. I wriggled my face in and kissed it. Flesh leapt into my mouth. The taste flooded me. Pulpy parts were sucked and tongued. Lips sucked where Rog's cock had been. My hands felt things, warm wet places, alive moving things.

We tangled in permanent coition without shape, without beginning, without end. We writhed between our various parts. Then Rog had us three women bent double, holding our ankles or steadying ourselves on the bed. He rammed his sex into one of us and jerked his hips. Then he slid it out and put it in another hot wet sucky slidy pussy. Moments later he was in a third. He played musical chairs with us, each woman an eager hole slidingly wet and welcoming.

I made him come in my backside where I now loved to be ravished. Janie put something up me there and placed her long delicate fingers inside my pussy to feel it. I kissed her mouth, I kissed Roger's, I put Roger's cock inside Sonja and I kissed his arse as he fucked her.

Time passed. Our bodies jerked and slowed. Sleep came.

I woke cold as ice in a warm bed of human flesh. The candles guttered, almost burnt out. I was feverishly frightened. We had to get out. I began to cry. These were my friends in mortal danger.

I bent over Janie and kissed the wide sensual mouth. She stirred and woke.

'It's Red. You're in danger. We have to get out.'

Her hand caressed my breast. I crawled over her and found Roger. I kissed his penis, crying into his pubic hair. I shook him awake.

'Darling,' he mumbled, his hand coming between my thighs.

Janie laughed.

'Sonja,' I cried. 'Wake up.'

I turned back to Roger. I lay across his body feeling it wake up underneath me. His wife stroked my bottom. 'You'll burn,' I whispered to Rog. 'One of us will burn. That's what it is, see. That's why the sex is different.'

'I like the sex being different,' said Rog. 'Kiss her pussy, Janie, and I'll kiss yours.'

'No,' I said urgently, feeling Janie's lips soft and tender waking my pussy-flesh, rousing me.

'The people burn,' said Sonja.

'I like your friend,' whispered Roger to me. 'I want her astride me.'

Janie kissed me and I whimpered at the sweetness of it. Sonja climbed astride Roger, her little body harsh on his big one, his huge upstanding cock sinking upwards into her cunt, the one I had loved and tortured.

I sobbed and kissed Sonja's breasts. 'We have to get out, get away,' I pleaded.

Sonja jigged up and down. Roger cried out and stabbed upwards. I licked her nipples. One of her hands clutched Janie's breasts for support. Janie nuzzled and sucked my aching aroused pussy.

Roger moved faster. I felt my orgasm roll through my belly spreading fire and release. Sonja was staring, her eyes gleaming pools in the filtered moonlight. The clouds must have cleared. She screamed as she approached climax.

I tore my weeping body running with lovejuice from Janie's sweet mouth. I caught her and held her, trying to protect her from something I didn't understand, couldn't control. Rog was grunting feverishly as he rose to climax, thundering up into Sonja.

She orgasmed speared on his wonderful cock, her mouth wide open, gasping her ecstasy of pleasure.

Flames shot from her mouth.

I screamed and clamped my hand over her mouth. I felt Rog shudder as his cock released. I dragged Sonja off his cock even as he jetted spunk. We lurched over to the window. I dropped Sonja and picked up a chair. I smashed the double glazing with demonic strength. I beat the broken glass away and picked up Sonja. I took her frail sobbing body and threw it into the rainsoaked moon-flooded freezing night.

I blundered back to Janie. 'Get out, get out,' I screamed. Roger scrambled off the bed and grabbed her. I pushed them to the window. As I did, I knocked over the candlestick on the dresser.

They tumbled into the night. I followed.

We stood shivering. I had my arm protectively round Sonja.

'The flames,' said Janie.

'We must stop them.' Rog sounded stunned.

The candle stubs had ignited the curtains torn in my frenzy to escape.

'No,' I whimpered. 'Let them burn.' I hugged Sonja more tightly. 'Let it all burn.'